Run Rabbit Run

Run Rabbit Run

Kate Johnson

First published 2012 by Choc Lit Limited
Penrose House, Crawley Drive, Camberley, Surrey GU15 2AB, UK
www.choclitpublishing.com

A CIP catalogue record for this book is available
from the British Library

ISBN-978-1-906931-73-5

MIX
Paper from
responsible sources
FSC
www.fsc.org   FSC® C014728

Printed and bound by CPI Group (UK) Ltd, Croydon, CR0 4YY

To everyone who's emailed, Tweeted and Facebooked
to ask what happened to Sophie next.

Prologue

Four in the morning and I was painting over the number plate of my boyfriend's car with black nail varnish while I hid in a camera blindspot in a car park in Dover for the early crossing to Calais. A 3 turned to an 8, a P turned to an R. Job done, I sprayed the whole thing with hairspray to fool the cameras, and got back into the car to wait, hat pulled down low over my face.

In the ladies' room on the ferry, I nabbed a shower cubicle and, wincing, cut off my long blonde ponytail. Masses of hair fell into the shower tray, clogging the drain. I poked it all down with my hands and rubbed some cheap brown dye into what was left hanging around my ears.

The result was not pretty.

The bar area of the ferry looked like a refugee camp, tired families and lone backpackers setting out their own little camps, marked with rucksacks and coats and unfeasibly large pushchairs. I glanced longingly at the bar, and had it not been for the long drive ahead of me I'd seriously have considered beer for breakfast.

Little cameras blinked everywhere. Trying not to be noticed, I found an ATM and withdrew everything in my bank account as Euros, then went out on deck, huddled into my coat, and mainlined black coffee.

An hour later I drove off the ferry and onto the wrong side of the road. French lorries beeping madly at me, I swung the Vectra back into the right-hand lane and followed signs towards Paris. I didn't want to go to Paris, but it was a start.

Twelve hours after that, having stopped once for coffee and refuelling, eyes blurry with exhaustion, I saw a sign for a campsite in a small seaside town on the Riviera and pulled in. I drove up to one of the bright courier tents belonging to those big luxury camping companies and asked if they had any pitches available. They did. I paid in cash, registered with a fake name, and hauled the car around to a small plot with a big tent on it.

I had a pillow and sleeping bag, a handful of personal possessions, clothes and toiletries. The lot of it was dumped on the floor next to the camp bed, onto which I fell, exhausted and near tears.

You would not believe the trouble I'm in.

Chapter One

Phone calls in the night are rarely a good thing.

When Luke Sharpe's phone rang in the invisible hours of the morning he knew it was one of two things. Either work, which meant some sort of crisis, or Sophie, which meant some sort of crisis.

He rolled over and glanced at the glowing screen. Work.

'Sharpe,' he yawned into the phone, feeling anything but.

'What the hell is going on with your girlfriend?' exploded a furious voice on the other end.

Luke blinked at the empty side of the bed. She hadn't come over last night, and he'd fallen asleep waiting to hear from her.

He wasn't concerned. Sophie was a walking magnet for trouble and she could generally take care of herself. 'What's she done now?' he asked.

'Shot an MI5 officer and disappeared, that's what,' said Sheila.

That got his attention. Sitting up in bed, Luke said, 'She's what?'

'Shot Sir Theodore Chesshyre dead,' said his boss. 'Where is she?'

'She–' Luke blinked and tried to put this together. Sophie didn't go around shooting people. Well, not often, anyway. And certainly not people she was trying to get a job from.

He pinched the bridge of his nose, but didn't wake up. Not a dream, then. Excellent. 'Why would she shoot Theodore Chesshyre?'

'Your guess is as good as mine, Sharpe.'

'She went to see him for a job interview.'

'To which she apparently took her gun. And explain to

me, Sharpe, why she still had the gun? I have it registered here as destroyed. Sunk in a Cornish harbour.'

Bugger. 'Why would she take her gun to a job interview?' he said vaguely. Truth was, Sophie owned two guns; the one Sheila was referring to and a little revolver Sophie had liberated from a dead enemy a few years ago. The thing hadn't been registered to anyone, so she'd just kept it quiet as a back-up. If Sophie was going to shoot anyone on the QT, she'd have used that.

'You tell me. While the gun is missing from the scene, ballistics have identified the bullet. It's a nine millimeter Parabellum and matches perfectly to bullets previously fired from a SIG-Sauer P-239 registered to one Sophie Green. We keep records of that sort of thing,' she added crisply, before he could say anything. 'Unless someone created two SIG-Sauer P-239s with identical rifling on the barrel, I'd say the evidence is pretty incriminating. So, Sharpe, where is she?'

'Not here,' Luke said, because that was the only honest answer he could give his boss.

Although, given that he'd just noticed a scrabbling sound coming from the kitchen, he wasn't entirely sure if that was true.

Quietly, he picked up his gun.

'I didn't ask if she was with you, I asked where she was.'

'I honestly have no idea,' Luke replied.

While his boss ranted on in his ear, he swung out of bed and padded into the living room, gun loose in his hand. Please God, don't let her be stupid enough to hide under the coffee table.

The living room was dark, but it was also entirely empty of Sophie. After a year together, he was pretty attuned to her presence. Besides, Sophie was about as subtle as a house fire.

The phone on the kitchen counter wasn't showing any new messages, but that wasn't what caught his attention.

What caught his attention was the cat travelling box on the floor beside it.

Unease churned in his gut. A small tabby paw shot out through the bars at the front of the box and a pitiful miaow escaped.

If she'd brought Tammy here it wasn't going to be good news.

'Look,' he said into his phone, 'this is the first I've heard of it. It's three a.m. for God's sake. Sophie's not here, I wasn't expecting to see her until tomorrow, I'm her boyfriend not her keeper, and I have as much idea about what's going on as you do. Okay?'

There was a short silence. 'If you're keeping anything from me –'

'I swear I'm not.'

Another silence. 'Keep me informed,' she said, and rang off.

Luke put his phone down, let Tammy out of her box and scooped her into his arms. Her tiny body vibrated with a huge purr as she snuggled against him.

'You okay, Tam? Been here long?'

She wriggled again, so he put her down and went in search of cat food. Since Tammy was Sophie's cat and lived with her, the best Luke had to offer was a tin of tuna.

This met with Tammy's approval.

'Pee on my floor and you're going to your granny's house,' he warned her, then went to start up his computer. While he waited, he switched on the TV and keyed in BBC News 24. The newsreader was running some story about the American president and Luke waited for the story to change. Politics. Earthquake. Entertainment. Royal family. American president.

So the news wasn't that big. Well, how could it be? 5 didn't go around broadcasting their business, did they?

On the other hand, if they thought a national news

campaign was the way to get information about Sophie, they'd blanket every network on TV.

It was a mistake. It had to be a mistake.

He checked online news agencies but turned up nothing. Ran a search on Sophie's name in conjunction with Sir Theodore's. Conspicuously nothing. Finally, he searched for Sophie alone, but apart from her Facebook account and a one-line profile from the bookshop where she worked, there was nothing.

He had a hack into police frequencies, but got nothing there, either.

MI5 clearly didn't want to broadcast this, at least not just yet. Perhaps they didn't consider Sophie to really be a suspect, or perhaps they assumed they could find her fast enough that a public appeal wasn't necessary.

He scanned his email for any relevant messages. Nothing from Sophie – she wouldn't be that stupid – and nothing from anyone she was likely to have confided in, either.

If this was all true, if she really was on the run, then Sophie would know MI5 would hit up her friends faster than she hit up a shoe sale.

Luke started making calls. Not to Sophie, because if she'd been daft enough to take her phone with her then the second it rang there'd be a trace on it. And if she hadn't taken it with her, there would be no point calling.

He called Maria, who berated him for waking her in the middle of the night, but sharpened up when he told her why. She wasn't with his department any more, but she was still Service and she was still Sophie's friend. 'I'll see what I can find out,' she promised, and ended the call.

Harvey answered, 'Why are you calling me at three a.m.?'

'Because you're in America so it's late evening, and because Sophie has gone off the deep end,' Luke replied.

His American friend laughed. 'Buddy, I hate to break it to

you, but she did that years ago.'

Luke's fist clenched. All right, so Harvey might be married to Sophie's best friend, and he might have helped Sophie out of some dire situations, and he might be an official liaison from the CIA, but ...

... but Harvey had kissed Sophie a couple of times, and in Luke's mind there ought to be a law against anyone else kissing Sophie.

'She's in trouble,' he said shortly. 'Accused of murder. 5 are after her. It's ...' he tried to think of the phrase Sophie used.

'A whole mess of crap?' Harvey guessed.

'That's the one. You heard anything?'

'Not my playground, but I'll see what I can find out.' Harvey paused. 'You okay?'

Luke snorted, and resorted to Sophie's trick of Buffy references to lighten the mood. 'Sophie's in trouble. Must be Tuesday.'

'It's Friday for you, buddy.'

'She can be in trouble on Fridays, too,' Luke said, with feeling.

I slept right through until morning, woke up and staggered to the shower block to wash away the terror-sweat that had accumulated in my pores all day yesterday. Unfortunately, I also washed away some of the cheap dye. My wet hair looked dreadful: hacked and uneven, the colour of diarrhoea. I looked like I'd just fallen down a French toilet.

I sternly reminded myself that the goal of this exercise was not to look attractive. Rather it was the opposite. I wanted no one to notice me.

Dressing and popping in my coloured contact lenses, I made my way into town. There are people who wouldn't consider coloured contact lenses to be the sort of emergency item one might pick up from one's flat in a dash to pick up supplies when one is in terrible trouble. Those people wouldn't include me.

In the bar next to the camp shop the TV was playing the news, in English. It was only a matter of time before the story broke.

I made one quick stop in town at the first phone shop I came to. Pay-as-you-go, no contract, the biggest hurdle being my inability to understand the French instructions. But I understood that it had GPS, which was pretty much all I needed right now.

Eventually I found what I needed: a slightly faded looking shop front with pictures of eighties' hairstyles in the front. The peeling legend over the door simply read Sandrine Le Bon.

Deep breath, Sophie. You've done the hard part already.

Ever notice how it's the bits after the hard part that make you want to cry?

I pushed open the door and half-a-dozen women looked me over. The radio was playing French pop. The air was thick with hairspray and perm solution. A woman with sky-high hair greeted me, '*Bonjour, cherie.*'

'*Parlez-vous Anglais?*' I asked, and she nodded.

''Ow can I 'elp you?'

I took off my baseball cap and Sandrine (for I assumed it was she) gasped. '*Cherie!*'

The other women, customers and staff, all turned to look at me and made Gallic noises of disgust.

'I know,' I said. 'I need something different. And can you dye it? I want dark hair.'

Sandrine did not like the idea of me with dark hair, and to be truthful neither did I, especially as I'd spent so much money on lightening it. Naturally, my hair is a sort of nondescript dark blonde but it's sort of, shall we say, *assisted* by my local hairdresser every now and then.

But I was firm. It's all right for Gwen Stefani to want a platinum-blonde life, but I didn't need the attention. Sandrine dyed my hair dark brown and cut it into a Meg Ryan crop that looked okay when it had been blow-dried, but I knew would look a cow as soon as I walked out.

I paid her in cash and left, my once-long blonde hair short and brown, my blue eyes hidden behind brown contact lenses, my tall posture stooped. Just another tourist.

He called various colleagues, half of whom told him this was MI5's problem, not 6's, and half of whom seemed to have developed amnesia when it came to his girlfriend. Being that Sophie was 5'10" in her bare feet, tended to wear ludicrously high heels and a lot of bright pink, wore a DD cup and had a mane of hair that would make a lion envious, coupled with her inability to keep her mouth shut for five consecutive minutes, he doubted anyone had really forgotten her.

He called the police, who stonewalled him. He called airline contacts to see if Sophie had been stupid enough to get herself on a passenger manifest. She hadn't, but he hit gold with a cross-Channel ferry.

She'd gone to France in the very early hours of the morning. He didn't bother asking why: it was the quickest and easiest way to leave the country without anyone asking questions, and from there she could drive anywhere. The description on the ferry booking matched his car but the registration number didn't. He wondered how professionally she'd managed to alter it.

Luke glanced at the clock, and was surprised to see it was mid-morning. She could be anywhere by now.

He was just about to log off the computer and attempt some sleep when something caught his eye. *BUFFY NEWS: Joss Whedon to direct Stephanie Plum movie.*

All right, so he'd hold his hand up to being a *Buffy* fan, but it was Sophie who was always going on about Stephanie Plum and – Sophie was always going on about Stephanie Plum and –

– Sophie was a *Buffy* fan and –

He opened the email as fast as he could and swore when his computer took its time.

'*Buffy* creator Joss Whedon has signed up to direct every movie in the Stephanie Plum series. It's a huge coup ...'

The piece was nonsense, especially as Sophie had jabbered on excitedly about the movie already being made. Joss Whedon could barely buy a cup of coffee without Sophie hearing about it. She'd have told him if this was true.

Which meant ...

He scanned the email for clues, and when he found one, he smiled.

'If you do not wish to receive further emails, please call this number.'

A French mobile number. Halle-bleeding-lujah.

He memorised the number, deleted the email, and crossed to the front window. His car was indeed missing, but Sophie's great lummox of a Defender was parked there instead.

'Cheers, Soph,' he muttered.

Across the road was a plain silver Ford. Inside it sat two people. Nothing about them spoke of anything unusual, which in itself was a great screaming clue that they were there to watch him.

He looked at the phone in his hand, then at the Ford. There was only one person left to call and he really, really didn't want to call him.

Tammy wandered over and started twining around his ankles, purring hopefully.

'I hate this guy,' Luke told her. Tammy didn't seem to care.

Wincing, he dialled.

'You know where she is?' Docherty asked without preamble.

'No idea. You?'

'Went to France. Haven't tracked the car yet.' Docherty paused. 'You want company?'

Luke hesitated. His flat would be bugged the second he stepped outside, or possibly while he was sleeping. There was probably a tap on his phone line already, although he expected Docherty would have nullified it from his end. Nonetheless ...

'I'll put the kettle on,' Luke said, and Docherty disconnected.

'I don't suppose your mummy told you where she was going, did she?' Luke asked Tammy.

The cat gave him a look of contempt.

'No,' he sighed, 'I suppose not.'

The TV in the camp bar was still showing the news in English, and I bought a beer while I stood and watched, heart in mouth, baseball cap pulled low over my face. But there was nothing about me or Sir Theodore. Not even one line about a man being found dead in his office, police are investigating. Which probably meant that the police weren't investigating. Sir Theodore had been MI5. Clearly, they'd leapt on the story before it reached the ears of the public. I wasn't sure if this was a good thing – after all, I didn't want my face all over the news – or bad. The quicker MI5 picked up on my involvement, the quicker they'd trace me.

I really ought to move on from here.

It wasn't really warm enough to sunbathe, being only April, but I am British and therefore if there's sand and sea I have to at least take my shoes and socks off and paddle. I lounged around on a towel for a while, feeling rather chilly, reading one of the paperbacks I'd picked up on the ferry.

It was rubbish, so I put my headphones on and listened to Skunk Anansie for strength.

I bought an overpriced sandwich and a Coke from the beach café and read another book. The sun started to go down and I wondered what the hell was taking him so long. Was my phone broken? Out of signal? Had I got the number wrong? Misunderstood the French instructions? Or had he not understood the message? Deleted it as spam or just ignored it? Maybe he hadn't even checked his emails today. Hell, if he went missing I think I'd have better things to do.

But he's a trained spy. He's good at what he does. He'd check every angle. And he'd know that email was fake as soon as he saw it.

I just hoped to hell no one else would.

Just as I was gathering up my things to go back to the tent for the night, the phone rang. Number unknown. I took a breath, and answered.

'Sophie?'

Luke. I nearly broke down at the sound of his voice.

'Luke,' I said, and heard the catch in my own voice. I wanted to run into his arms like Melly and Ashley in *Gone With The Wind*. There ought to have been music swelling.

'What the hell is going on? Where are you? Do you have my car?'

I smiled. 'Yes, I have your car. Have you ... heard?'

'Have I–?' He made a sound of disbelief. 'I got woken in the middle of the night with the news.'

Middle of the night. I hoped he was exaggerating, otherwise I had less of a lead time than I thought.

No. If that was the case they'd have found me already.

'Who called you? Is it on the news?'

'My boss called me, and no, it's not. 5 seem to have jumped on it pretty fast. But inside the community, it's all over. Either they're pumping me for details or they're pretending they don't know me. Sophie, you've been accused of *murder*.'

He sounded tense and worried. Good. If he'd been calm I'd have been heartbroken. Luke's a damn good spy but he's not as cool as he thinks he is. When I met Luke he seemed about as emotional as your average coffee machine, but I fear I've unlocked a door that can't be shut again. He'd like you to think he doesn't have any emotions, but lately it seems to me he's been letting his heart dictate to his head, which is a dangerous thing in a spy. As I well know.

'I didn't kill him,' I said in quiet tones. 'I found him dead but I didn't kill him. Luke, where are you calling from?'

'Docherty's phone.'

'He's there?' I was surprised. Ever since I had a very brief liaison with Docherty, months ago now, when Luke and I were not together, Luke has hissed and spat at the mere mention of his name. They used to be friends well, acquaintances, really, but I didn't think Docherty had even been in the country since that night. He's a pretty shadowy character, and to be honest he scares the living daylights out of me.

But I was touched that Luke had turned to him.

'He's been trying to find you all day.'

'Any luck?'

'You got on a ferry, or at least your passport did. How far are you from Calais?'

I hesitated. Luke would never tell anyone where I was, but even so ... 'Quite a long way.'

'You're not going to tell me, are you?' His voice was flat.

'I can't.'

Luke sighed, a long deep sigh. 'Why did you run?'

Sheer blind panic.

'Because he was shot with a bullet from my gun and my

13

fingerprints are all over his office and I was seen going back in there late at night.'

'Why did you go back in?'

'He offered to lock my valuables in his desk while we had dinner. I was going back to fetch my bag.'

'Why did you take your SIG?'

'I didn't,' I said wretchedly. 'I thought I'd get into trouble – you know, with scanners and everything –'

'Especially since you're not supposed to have it any more,' Luke supplied helpfully.

'I don't know how it got there. My revolver was still in the gun safe when I got back to my flat and there were no signs of a break in. But someone must have stolen my SIG and used it to frame me. Someone who knew where I was going to be.'

Luke sighed, and I sensed monumental restraint in him not pointing out that the strongest security feature my home boasts is an irascible tabby cat.

A thought occurred to me. Dammit, why didn't I think of it before?

Well, you try being framed for murder and tell me how clearly you think.

'There wasn't any CCTV in his office, was there?'

'Disabled. Sophie, you shouldn't have run, especially not with the gun. It doesn't look good.'

'Yeah?' I snapped, my voice rising, 'What would you have done? Hung around to be arrested?'

'You didn't do anything.'

'Yeah, because they so often believe that line in court.'

There was a bit of a silence, and then for the first time since I'd seen Theodore Chesshyre's body, I felt hot tears bleed out from my eyes.

'Sophie, where are you?' Luke asked, and he sounded tired. Desperate.

'I can't tell you. I'm going to move on soon anyway.'

'And then what? Keep on running?'

'I don't know,' I wailed, dabbing at my eyes with my towel, filling my lids with sand and therefore crying harder.

'Okay,' he sighed. 'Look, just – just keep in touch, okay? This is a safe number?'

'Brand new today. My old phone is still at home. I knew they'd trace it.'

'Good girl,' Luke said. 'Listen, they'll be checking all ports for your passport. Probably checking for my car, too. If you want to move around I suggest you get a new passport.'

Yeah, like they sell them at the *supermarché*. The whole reason I'd picked a campsite and not a hotel was the reduced likelihood of them looking at my passport when I checked in. 'From?'

'I'll sort it out.'

I gave him my fake name and told him to call me when he had it sorted. I didn't yet have anywhere for him to send it, but I figured I'd cross that bridge later.

Then there was a pause, while I tried to figure out a reason to keep him on the line a bit longer. I thought of Tammy, my poor sweet baby tabby cat, locked up in her travel box on Luke's living-room floor.

'Are you looking after Tammy?'

'Yeah, she's fine. I tell you, Sophie, I am not looking forward to explaining this to your parents.'

Oh, Christ. My parents don't even know I used to be a spy. Yes, don't laugh too hard.

'Tell them an alien entity has taken over my body.'

'Ha ha.'

'They watch too much *Star Trek* anyway.'

Another pause.

'I miss you,' I said quietly.

There was a pause. *I love you.* Say it, Luke.

'Keep safe, Sophie.'

I sighed. He does love me, I'm pretty sure he does, it's just – well, Luke's about as comfortable having emotions as most people are with having stomach flu.

'Don't do anything stupid,' he added, and there was a note of pleading in his voice that made me smile.

'What, like leave the country?'

'Or leave bloody fingerprints everywhere. Okay. Docherty needs his phone back. I'm going to try and find another number I can call you on. I'll let you know about the passport.'

'Bye,' I sniffed, and ended the call before we got into an endless round of 'No, *you* hang up,' and I started bawling. I really didn't want to draw attention to myself.

At the camp shop I got some bread and cheese for tea. And some wine. I was feeling sorry for myself, not least because I was really hungry and there wasn't much I could cook on a two-ring hob. I don't eat meat, which should make a stay in France quite interesting.

Having eaten, I read a bit more of my book, got into my pyjamas and slid my SIG under my pillow.

Then I put it under the bed, because I didn't want to accidentally blow my brains out.

Then I moved it from there, because it looked slightly obvious. Where could I put it?

Eventually I settled with it in one of the deep canvas pockets that lined the wall of the tent bedroom, and drank some more wine to calm my nerves. I brushed my teeth with bottled water and lay back on the bed, eyes open, brain swirling.

Chapter Two

I have been woken in many different ways in the last year or so, some of them very pleasant, some quite nasty, some too dirty to repeat, but I don't recall ever having been woken by someone pressing a warm gun to my head and saying, 'Be very quiet or I'll blow your fucking brains out. Savvy?'

Wow, someone's been watching too much *Pirates of the Caribbean*, I thought, but I opened my eyes and looked up at my assailant. I couldn't see a lot in the dark, but I could see that he had longish, darkish hair, concealing his face. English accent, no particular region.

Oh, and a silencer on his gun.

'What do you want?' I asked as quietly as I could.

'Unzip that sleeping bag.'

'What?'

'I'm not going to do anything. Just unzip it. I need to hide out.'

I considered the alternatives. I could yell, and then he'd shoot me. I could go for my gun, and then he'd shoot me. I could let him get into my sleeping bag, and then he'd shoot me. Maybe.

Maybe getting shot was a better alternative than *definitely* getting shot, so I unzipped it a little way, and he gestured with the gun.

'All the way.'

'I'm not that kind of girl.'

He didn't seem to think this was funny. 'Open it all the way.'

I unzipped the bag all the way down and he reached out with one hand to pull it out from under me, making a blanket of it. Then he lay down on the camp bed with

17

me, under the sleeping bag blanket, and wrapped his arms around me. He had my back to his chest so I couldn't look at his face, and the gun pressed against my stomach.

Silence, then I asked, 'Who are you hiding from?'

'Everyone.'

'Who are you?'

'Shut up.' The gun nudged my ribs.

'How long –'

But I didn't get to ask any more, because voices came from outside.

'*Ouvrir! Attention, ouvrir!*'

I guess it's hard to knock on canvas.

I hesitated, then I moved to get up.

'Stay right where you are,' said the man with the gun, pressing it tighter into my belly. For possibly the first time in my life, I was glad of my substantial build. Maybe all that fat I never got around to getting rid of might slow down a bullet.

Allow me my delusions, all right?

'They want me to open up. It could be the police.'

'You think? Don't move.' He climbed over me, wriggling down under the sleeping bag, his head against my breasts.

'Hey!'

'Stay here or I'll shoot,' he threatened, head under the covers. I heard the front zip opening, footsteps on the ground sheet. Low French voices.

I needed to do something.

'Oh,' I gasped, quickly shoving the sleeping bag aside and yanking down my pyjama top, 'oh, don't stop …'

It was hard to see in the dark, but I could *feel* his incredulity.

'Oh yes!'

Hesitation, then the zip on the bedroom compartment came open one inch. Perverts.

Speaking of which, my assailant was getting in on the action. One hand cupped my breast while the other, the one with the gun, burrowed down inside my pyjama bottoms.

I began to get distinctly nervous. 'No! No, er, don't stop! Oh, er, Joe, that's so good!'

A face looked in through the gap at the top of the door. I screamed and yanked the sleeping bag over us both. The face looked shocked, then a flurry of French apologies ensued, the zip was closed, the tent emptied.

A dark head appeared from under the sleeping bag blanket. 'Very convincing.'

'Well, you weren't doing anything.' I shoved at his hand and he removed it and the gun from the region of my crotch. 'I mean, you weren't – I had to – look, who are you?'

He pushed my pyjamas back into place and his lips brushed my shoulder. 'Joe, apparently.'

I scowled.

'I'm someone you never saw. Savvy?'

And then he was gone.

I woke in the morning to a mobile phone chirping out the Marseillaise and wondered who the hell was insensitive enough to have their phone turned up so loudly.

Then I realised it was mine.

Swearing, I reached out of my deliciously warm sleeping bag into the chill of the morning air, picked it up and checked the display. I didn't recognise the number, but then, why would I?

I pressed the Answer button and tried a Gallic, '*Âllo?*'

'Sophie? Docherty.'

I felt a shiver run through me. I hadn't seen or spoken to Docherty since our night together – must be seven, eight months ago now. He was gone when I woke up, leaving only his scent on the pillow to assure me I hadn't imagined it all.

'Hi,' I said. 'What time is it?'

'Eight, where I am. Nine, where you are. Did I wake you?'

He sounded amused. I made a face. 'I'm sorry I slept late,' I said with as much sarcasm as I could at such short notice, 'but I've been having a slightly traumatic few days and – how do you know where I am?'

He laughed, a deep sound. 'I know you got on a boat to France and I know you haven't left the country.'

'You can't know that.' Pretty much every country bordering France was in the Schengen zone – that is, a borderless state. Passports not required to pass from one country to the next. No records.

'Plus, you answered your phone in French.'

I made another face. Docherty was probably triangulating my location as we spoke. Probably he could do it in his sleep.

I wondered if Luke had tried using my phone to find me. He could do it easily through official channels, but then why would MI6 let him? I was hardly an official concern to them. I was 5's problem. I doubted anyone in Luke's department gave a damn about me, except probably as a way of knocking Luke off his golden-boy perch.

'How do you know I got on the ferry?'

'I know everything.'

'Do you know who killed Sir Theodore?'

A pause. 'How grateful would you be if I found out?'

I swallowed. Docherty's idea of gratitude was probably pretty similar to his idea of an apology. 'Grateful enough not to tell my boyfriend you're still propositioning me.'

He gave a low laugh. 'Do you know all the security tapes got mysteriously wiped? Somehow the system failed to record anything.'

'Didn't anyone see it?'

'Security guard. AWOL.'

'Why doesn't that surprise me?'

'The man on the door says he saw you go back in an hour after Sir Theodore.'

'Half-an-hour,' I corrected, then kicked myself. A normal, sane person wouldn't get as far as the Tube entrance barrier before she realised she'd left her handbag elsewhere. 'I thought he'd gone AWOL?'

'No, just the man in the monitor room. Why did you go back in?'

'I left some stuff there.'

'Did you see Chesshyre?'

I closed my eyes and remembered. I'd been remembering it a lot lately.

'I saw him.'

'Alive?'

'Quite the opposite.'

'But you didn't call for help?'

'He was a little bit beyond help by then.'

'But going off and leaving him does look a bit suspicious,' Docherty said.

'What was I supposed to do? Hang around and explain that although my fingerprints were everywhere and he was killed with my gun, I wasn't the one who did it?'

'By running away all you did was confirm your guilt.'

'*I am not guilty!*'

Docherty paused and I could picture him holding the phone away from his ear.

'Do you still want that passport?' he asked.

'Yes,' I said. 'Please.'

'Have you changed your appearance ...?'

'I have short brown hair,' I said, running my hands through it. Ulk, it stopped so suddenly. I haven't had hair this short since ... well, since I've had hair. 'And brown eyes.'

'How short?' Docherty wanted to know. 'For the photo.'

'Meg Ryan. *Addicted To Love.*'

Another pause. 'That's a film?'

'No, Docherty, it's how I feel about you.'

A pause. I winced.

'Just Google it.'

'That I will. Are you keeping your scars covered up?'

I frowned. How did he know about them? He hadn't seen me naked since I'd got them.

That is, unless he had some surveillance I really didn't want to think about.

'I am,' I said. 'It's hardly hot enough to display them.'

'That depends which ones you mean,' Docherty said. 'I'll call you back with an address soon.'

'An address?'

'To get your passport from. Speak to you later,' and he was gone.

Great. I could see myself having to knock on the door of a seedy little back street in Paris, asking for Monsieur Manky and handing over all my Euros for a bad forgery.

I got dressed and ran errands, fetching food and a newspaper – thankfully the camp shop catered for British tourists – and scuttled back to my tent. Every man I saw looked like last night's gunman; that is, since I had no idea what the bastard looked like at all, he could be anyone. He had dark hair and an English accent. It wasn't much to go on. The only people I knew for sure were English were the campsite couriers, whom I regarded with deep suspicion. The guy who'd checked me in had dark hair and he had been eyeing me with interest. As far as I knew a gun wasn't standard issue for a holiday rep, but then times were a-changin'.

Nobody knew that better than me.

'She's not happy,' said Evelyn, the moment Luke stepped into the office.

22

'No shit. Are 5 talking yet?'

'Not a word. Haven't even requested a liaison, which means –'

'– they're watching our every move on the sly.' He slugged the rest of his coffee. Black, with an extra shot, the way Sophie took it.

'They're watching *your* every move,' Evelyn corrected. She frowned, her perfect pale brow creasing. 'Luke, they're probably at your place right now, bugging everything in sight.'

He drained the last caffeine-saturated drop and threw the cardboard cup at the bin. 'I know.'

'You're being remarkably sanguine about it.'

'Sanguine,' Luke said, leaving her behind as he strode to Sheila's door. 'Also means bloody.'

He knocked and entered. Sheila sat at her desk, immaculate in Armani, ice-blue eyes on the huge iMac screen on her antique desk. Her hair was peppered with grey, her make-up soft and subtle, and her posture would make a sergeant major weep with delight.

'Look what the cat dragged in,' she said crisply.

'You look wonderful, too,' Luke said, dropping into a chair.

Her cold blue gaze snapped to him. 'Heard anything yet?'

Luke was an Eton boy. He'd joined the RAF straight out of school, been recruited by the SAS and then the security services had come calling. He'd never willingly displayed any emotion in his life and he'd been lying since the day he opened his eyes.

'Nothing,' he said. 'Wherever she is, she's gone to ground. Have 5 got anything?'

'Nothing they'll share,' Sheila said.

'Which means they have something?'

'I expect so. Any fool can trace her whereabouts. If the

damn French would let us use their surveillance we could track the car easy as anything. Why she thought taking your car would slow us down I don't know.'

'Because a silver Vectra is a lot more invisible than a bile-green Defender,' Luke said.

He didn't bother to ask whether they'd searched Sophie's car. He'd had a cursory glance around inside it, but there was a conspicuous lack of confessional notes or handy bullet casings. In fact, there was a conspicuous lack of anything. The CDs were all neatly stacked in the door bucket, the hairs from her parents' dog had been brushed from the back seat – probably taken in evidence, hah! He hoped they enjoyed trying to incriminate a daft canine in a murder enquiry.

Even her flat looked suspiciously clean. He supposed it was possible her mother had been round to tidy up – a habit which Sophie had complained about at length – but he had a pretty strong idea that the only dusting going on in that place had been for fingerprints.

Sheila drummed her fingers on the desk.

'This isn't our jurisdiction, Sharpe. It's 5's case. She killed their man, she's a threat to their security. They're not co-operating with us on this, they don't want us on it.'

'Do we answer to 5 now?'

'No. But you answer to me. I'm going to give you a clear instruction, Luke, and it is not one of those instructions you can feel free to creatively interpret. Is that clear?' He nodded. 'You do not investigate this case. You do not use our resources or contacts to discover the whereabouts or motivations of your girlfriend. Do not let your personal life interfere with your professional life. Understood?'

'Understood,' Luke said, standing.

'I need you on the Kyrgyzstan case. Evelyn has a potential new agent I need you to vet.'

Luke nodded crisply. 'Understood,' he repeated.

Which wasn't the same as agreeing.

I passed the rest of the day reading, listening to music, taking walks into the town for bits of food and essential things I might need, kidding myself that everything was okay. But it wasn't okay. I was wanted for murder. MI5 had me on their shit list. My parents would be going insane. Poor Tammy would be orphaned. My car, my lovely strong Ted, would be left to rust because Luke hated driving him.

Luke would go off shagging other women who weren't wanted criminals. Not my lovely Luke!

At this point, let me gift you with a word or two about the man I love.

Whereas I consider myself to be reasonably attractive, probably the phrase that describes me best is 'scrubs up well'. Good enough for men who fancied Jessica Rabbit when they were teenagers. But I'm not an absolute stunner, and I don't delude myself that I can stop traffic. Whereas Luke can, and often does.

He can't help it. He just sort of *glows*. Golden blond, cheekbones like the Matterhorn, blue eyes you could drown in. Broad of shoulder, slim of hip. Pointlessly good-looking. If you siphoned off a tenth of his sex appeal, it could power a dozen other men.

He's what you'd picture as a secret agent. Smooth, smart, at home in any situation. He looks just as fantastic in sweatpants as he does in a suit. He can shoot a moving target from what appears to be any distance. He speaks several languages. He was expensively educated. He can fly any plane or helicopter you care to name.

He likes Saturday morning cartoons and *Buffy* re-runs. He bought Tammy a wind-up mouse for Christmas. He gets on with my parents. He laughs at silly place names.

He's arrogant and charming, emotionally illiterate and burning with passion. When he missed my birthday because he was on assignment in Saudi Arabia, he presented me with an antique emerald-and-diamond ring on his return.

'If you mention the M word,' he said as I slipped it onto my right hand, 'I will never have sex with you again.'

I didn't mention the M word. Luke's not the marrying kind.

And needless to say, sex with him is not to be missed.

I closed my eyes, and tried not to think of him.

I failed.

As the sky started to darken I got up to switch on the electric light (all mod cons in these tents, look you) and then decided I might as well go to bed. Who knew what tomorrow might bring? I needed to get as much sleep as I could, especially since Docherty had woken me up so early. I locked my valuables in the boot of the car, out of sight, and zipped myself in for the night.

Although in view of last night, I took my back-up pistol out of the car and brought it into the bedroom with me.

My sleeping bag looked inviting, although I found a couple of dark hairs on it that disconcerted me. Who was that guy? Why had he come to my tent in the middle of the night? And why were the gendarmes after an English guy – one with a gun? No petty thief, him.

I made sure the safety catches were firmly on and tucked my guns into thigh holsters. So what if it was slightly uncomfortable? This time, I'd be ready.

And ready I was, when I heard someone unzipping the tent flap about an hour after I'd gone to bed. I lay still for a while, eyes closed, wishing it was a figment of my imagination because I was so damn tired. But then I heard the crackle of the groundsheet as someone walked over it, and I pushed back the sleeping bag and rolled off the bed as silently as I could.

This was not very silent.

'Alice?' came a whisper from outside the bedroom compartment. That was the name I'd checked in under. I ripped open the zip with one hand, the other on my SIG-Sauer.

The dark-haired campsite courier stood frozen in the middle of the canvas room. *I knew it!*

'What are you doing in my tent?'

He ran his eyes over me. I think it was too dark for him to have seen the guns. I *hoped* it was too dark for him to have seen the guns.

'Came to see if you wanted a drink.'

'No. Thank you.'

'But ...' his eyes darted nervously, 'you weren't answering so I thought I'd come and check you were okay ...'

'I'm fine,' I said, and I thought I saw his eyes lingering around my thighs. I really hoped he was just perving. Not looking at the guns. Damn.

Hell. I'd have to leave. And I didn't even have my passport yet. How far away could I get without using it?

'Please don't take this personally,' I said, and he looked terrified as I reached for my SIG to smack the side of his head with it.

'Indeed,' came another, newly familiar voice, and before I'd had time to react, someone else's shooter had bashed the courier unconscious.

I whirled around but he caught me from behind, a hand over my mouth. What the *hell*? Last night's gunman. Complete with big nasty pistol, currently aimed at my temple.

'Be quiet,' he said, 'or I'll shoot you. Savvy?'

I fully believed him.

I'm not scared, I told myself as his hand left my mouth

27

and trailed down my neck to my breast, then over my arm to the SIG still holstered under my hand. He took it from me, the barrel of his own gun still against my temple, and I said in a low voice, 'I need that.'

'Not any more,' he replied, his breath hot against my neck, and I shivered as his hand moved across my waist, caressed my hip and my thigh, and then took the revolver from its holster.

I squeezed my eyes shut. Damn, fuck and bugger, in that order. I needed that, too.

'Now what,' he said in my ear, 'is a nice girl like Alice M. Robinson doing on her own in a campsite in France with two guns?'

'Can't be too careful these days,' I said, as he took my hands and held them behind my back.

'You don't need a SIG-Sauer to be careful.'

'You know your guns.'

'I know yours, too.'

'I'm really going to need them back,' I said.

'Tough.'

'Who are you?'

'Right back at you.'

'I'm Alice Robinson,' I said. 'You told me that.'

'You're registered as Alice. That doesn't mean you're her. Hello,' he added, his fingers caressing mine. He'd found the ring. The ring a smarter person would have kept out of sight. 'This looks nice.'

'Don't touch that,' I said, panicking.

'Why? Triggered to a grenade?' He ran the gun barrel down my neck, my chest, right down my front. 'Don't think there's anything hiding under there.'

'Stop feeling me up,' I said through gritted teeth. I may be stacked, but that's not my fault.

'Not enjoying it?'

'Guns aren't my thing.'

'Could have fooled me.' I heard a clinking sound and then something closed around my left wrist. A handcuff. *No.* I tugged my right wrist away, but he was ahead of me and clicked the bracelet home as he pressed the pistol into my belly.

'Now,' he said, 'please don't take this personally,' and a second after he stepped away, there was a sharp pain in my head and everything went black.

Chapter Three

I had no idea how long I'd been out, but later I realised that it could only have been a few minutes. Any longer, and I was pretty sure the gunman would have returned. I was alone, no sight of either the courier or the gunman, and my hands had been cuffed behind my back to one of the upright poles of the tent. And I was bloody frozen.

It didn't take me long to lift up the pole and slip the chain underneath. The tent wobbled alarmingly, but held, and I wriggled through that legs-through-arms-manoeuvre to get my arms in front of me. I quickly decided that the best course of action was to haul ass out of there and consequently threw all my belongings, bits of food, clothes, toiletries, the lot, into my sleeping bag, retrieved the keys from the zipped pocket under the bed, and locked myself in the car. I was missing both my guns and –

Oh bollocks. Oh *no*.

He'd taken my ring.

Right, now I was pissed off.

It was tough driving with handcuffed wrists – changing gear was certainly interesting – but I squealed out of the campsite, annoying several residents as I went, and was just on my way past the couriers' tent when I saw the gunman dumping an unconscious courier outside. He turned and saw me, his mouth dropped open, and his gun came up.

I floored it, and missed being shot in the head by a good few feet. The bullet hit the back of the car somewhere and I winced. Luke was not going to be pleased.

I saw him running after me – why? I was hardly in an F1 car but seriously, *running*? and took every turning I came across to lose him, ending somehow up by the sea, then cutting back through the town, ricocheting around corners in the darkness, twisting out of the Vectra the sort of performance I never knew it was capable of. Eventually I found a road out of town and rammed pedal to metal. The roads were quiet, I found a motorway, and aimed the car towards Grenoble.

The sky was light when I pulled in at a picnic stop to get something to eat and empty my bladder. It's a sign of how desperate I was that I used the French toilet, as opposed to just peeing in a bush or in my seat. Either might be preferable. I grabbed a sweater from the back of the car and draped it loosely over my hands and wrists. This, I hasten to add, did not make it easy to use a toilet which is essentially a hole in the ground.

I got back in the car, still shuddering, and plugged my phone into the hands-free kit, then reached back to try and sort out the mess in my sleeping bag. I knew I had some food in there somewhere.

But as I turned around in my seat I caught sight of the word POLICE emblazoned across the side of a car nearby. In it were a couple of gendarmes eating croissants.

I was out of there in seconds.

Probably they'd just stopped off for breakfast. The French equivalent of coffee and doughnuts. But I wasn't taking any chances. I accelerated back onto the A6, and headed towards Lyon.

Docherty called after an hour, while I was stuck in traffic and worrying about petrol consumption.

'Please tell me you have a passport for me. I hate this country.'

He laughed. 'Where are you?'

'In the car. In a traffic jam. On the A6. I think,' I added, peering around a lorry at a road sign 'Maybe the E15. I'm not sure. Could be both.'

'How far are you from Avallon?'

'That would depend on where Avallon is.'

'On the A6 between Dijon and Auxerre. Ish.'

'Ish?'

'I'm Irish. I don't do directions.'

I scrutinised the map and eventually came up with the town. 'Burgundy?'

'Yes. Maria's aunt has a vineyard. Call me when you get closer,' and he was gone.

Great. I put Crowded House on the stereo for comfort and rode out – or rather, sat out – the traffic jam. At least the gendarmes weren't following me, and unless someone walked by and peered at my hands in my lap, no one could see my handcuffs

At Lyon I followed signs for Dijon and then for Auxerre and when I saw a sign for Avallon, I pulled over. This road was smaller and quieter, winding through beautiful valleys. I always feel so much calmer when I'm in deep countryside.

I called Docherty for further directions. The way he read them out to me, I was pretty sure they'd come direct from Maria.

'Don't tell Luke where I'm going,' I said.

'Wouldn't dream of it.'

'And don't let Maria tell him either.'

He laughed, a deep dark sound. 'I think she can probably be trusted to keep a secret.'

Maria is a former colleague of mine. Like Luke, she's ex-military, and like Luke, she's confident and beautiful and very good at what she does. When our little operation, SO17, was disbanded, she had no trouble finding another position in the secret service.

In fact, everyone but me found it easy to get another job.

I set off, and reached the vineyard just as it was getting dark. I was exhausted. Luke's car was not the most comfortable of rides for a long journey and it was bloody hard driving with my wrists four inches apart. I'd tried to keep a finger on the wheel while I changed gear but that made the car swerve horribly as my wrists pulled each other around. Consequently I'd been thrashing the car in the wrong gear for most of the journey, until I could find a bit of road straight enough to take my hands off the wheel to change up or down.

The roads were degenerating into tracks that were less and less passable and by the time I got to the house I was pretty much driving over grass between neatly placed vines. I wondered what kind of wine Maria's aunt made. And if I'd be allowed to drink any.

Or all of it.

The knock came as Luke was checking his kitchen for bugs. He'd already found two in the living room and one in the bedroom – in the bedside lamp, how stupid did they think he was? – and now he was considering the problem of whether he could get a new computer without anyone noticing. He was absolutely certain his existing machine would have been compromised.

He'd picked up a new mobile from the supermarket. Computers were less easy to come by.

He glanced at the door. Please God, it wasn't Sophie's parents come to commiserate or cry or rant or whatever it was emotional people did when their daughters got accused of murder.

A glance through the peephole revealed Docherty, standing there in the twilight looking like a vampire with a five-o'clock shadow.

Docherty had been in the army, and he'd been in private security. Luke wasn't entirely sure if he might have also been in the IRA. He was shady as the night, he had access to people and technology and cars Luke could only dream of, and he wasn't above putting a bullet in someone's head just to keep them quiet.

And he seemed to have taken a shine to Sophie.

Luke opened the door, put his finger to his lips and mimed, 'Bugged.'

Docherty nodded. Luke wouldn't put it past him to have disabled the bugs with a radioflash and shot the surveillance team. The guy had more secrets than Batman.

He held out a DVD case.

'*Busty Babes Go Wild*,' Luke said, regarding it. 'How well you know me.'

'Thought you might get lonely,' Docherty said. 'What with your girlfriend missing and all. Reckon she's a real ride.'

Luke narrowed his eyes. 'You'd better not be speaking from experience.'

Docherty grinned. It made him look like a piranha. 'A bit of busty company, since you'll be missing your busty girlfriend,' he said. With a flicker in his eyes, he added, 'Take a look inside. There are more pictures.'

Luke opened the case. Inside was a DVD and a little red booklet. A British passport. Casually, keeping it between his face and the case, he flipped it open. The information page was at the back, as in an older passport, which was good. No biometric details. A picture that couldn't be used by facial recognition software. Taped to the back of it was a matching driving licence.

He memorised the details, filing away the passport number in his mind, not that it was any real use to him. He could only trace it through official channels and that would be by way of a colossal giveaway to whoever was watching him. Alice Maud Robinson. Made her sound like a pensioner. Her place of birth was given as Harlow, which would drive her mad since she hated being considered an Essex girl. Docherty had kept the right year for her birth, but changed the date.

'There's no way in hell she's a Scorpio,' Luke muttered.

'What's that?' Docherty asked, warning in his tone.

'I said hell, these girls are scorching,' Luke said. He studied the picture of Sophie Docherty had manipulated. 'Whoa, look at that one!'

It didn't look a lot like her. Eyes dark and hooded, complexion heightened, hair a dull mousy brown and hacked brutally short. His Sophie was all lush curves and long, soft hair, her skin pink and white, her eyes a warm blue. The woman in this picture looked dull somehow, her cheeks gaunt, her mouth unsmiling.

'I know how you like blondes,' Docherty said.

'Maybe I could get a taste for brunettes,' Luke said.

'Don't keep it too long,' Docherty said. 'When you're done with it, I've another friend to send it to.'

'Oh? Anyone I know?'

Docherty's dark gaze was steady. 'Maybe. But it might take me a while to find the address.'

'Maybe I could help you with that.'

Docherty was still a long moment. He could have discovered Sophie's whereabouts already, Luke knew. And he could be keeping them to himself. Trying to work out why would drive him mad.

'I don't think so,' Docherty said.

Luke closed the case with a snap. 'Thanks, mate,' he said, handing it back, 'but I'm not in the mood for skin flicks. Besides, I'm not sure I could enjoy it properly with an audience.'

Across the road, a shadow moved inside the car.

'Thanks for showing me though,' he added as Docherty tucked the DVD case inside his jacket. 'Cheered me right up.'

As Docherty left, Luke gave the unmarked car a wave.

The farmhouse was a big crumbling affair with vines crawling all over it. A woman stood in the doorway, watching me rumble up the drive.

She came to the door as I parked, and when I sat there trying to will myself to move out of the car, she came over. An attractive woman in the Faye Dunaway mould, with soft-styled hair and quite a bit of eyeliner, she looked me over warily through the open window.

'*Madame Bouchard?*' I asked, giving the name Docherty had told me.

'*Oui?*'

'*Je suis Alice. Une copine de Maria. Elle – elle vous dit j'arrive?*'

She took pity on my terrible French. '*Anglaise?*'

'*Oui.*'

Cécile Bouchard looked me over – my flat, ugly hair, my un-made-up face, my pyjamas. And my handcuffs.

'What is zees?'

'Oh.' I looked down at them. 'I don't suppose you'd have a hacksaw?'

She smiled. Then she laughed, a hacking smoker's laugh. Jesus. That was a sixty-a-day laugh.

'Come wiz me,' she said, and I got out of the car, locked it clumsily, and followed her around to the back of the house where there was a woodpile and an axe.

'Put your 'ands there.' She gestured to the block with the axe, and my eyes widened.

'Um, are you sure?'

'I have the good, eh, *quel est le mot*? Wiz zis *hache*.'

I really hoped that meant she was a good aim.

I spread my wrists as wide apart as I could, like Leonardo DiCaprio in *Titanic*, and closed my eyes. There was a great whoosh, a sudden thud, and then I opened my eyes to find my wrists separated from each other, and mercifully still attached to my arms.

I waved them around and grinned at Cécile, who plonked the axe back down and grinned back at me.

'Are you 'ungry?'

'God, yes.'

'*Excellente*. I 'ave lots of chicken.'

'Er, I don't eat meat.'

She stopped and stared at me. So handcuffs didn't faze her, but vegetarianism did?

France. Different planet.

'Do you drink?' she asked suspiciously.

I sized her up. Old wellies and a pretty red dress, hair in her eyes, the scent of Chanel and cigarettes.

'Yes,' I said, and she looked relieved.

'I 'ave lots of wine. Last year's vintage.'

This might have been an impressive thing, perhaps to someone like Luke who knew all about fine wines and vintages. But to someone like me, whose favourite kind of wine was whatever had a Buy One Get One Free sticker on it, it meant zip.

'What kind of wine do you make?' I asked politely, and Cécile laughed.

'*Bourgogne.*'

Of course.

She found some kind of vegetable stew in the huge pantry of her cavernous old kitchen (stone sink, bare floors, crumbling staircase winding up to a studded oak door, the lot) and poured me out a lot of red burgundy. Then she lit up a cigarette and proceeded to regale me with stories told in Franglais of when she was a little girl during the war, and her mother had been in the Resistance, and used to lead all the German soldiers on, and there was a lot of controversy over who her father was but Cécile didn't care. She had inherited this vast decrepit house and the vineyard and made pots and pots of money selling bad wine to tourists. She kept the good stuff and sold it in the village. She was an eccentric, and as a Brit, shouldn't I understand eccentricity?

I was so tired and hungry the wine went straight to my head. I nearly fell asleep with my face in my stew. Cécile was rambling to herself about a man called Pierre (at least, I think that's what it was, only about every third word was in English now), the table was fogged with smoke and there were empty bottles all over the place, candles guttering in the draft from under the wobbly door, when my phone shrilled and woke me up.

It was Luke. He'd got himself a new phone, assured me the line was secure – he'd probably scrambled it using a hairpin, a gold earring and a spider web – and talked to me about nothing for ten minutes.

'So did you have any particular reason for calling me?' I asked during a lull after several minutes spent discussing what Tammy would and wouldn't eat.

'Maybe I just like talking to you,' Luke said, and I went all gooey inside.

We spoke a while longer, or rather Luke spoke and I yawned, and eventually he told me to get some sleep, and he'd get back to investigating who killed Sir Theodore tomorrow.

I hung up and tried blearily to remember my schoolgirl French. 'Cécile,' I said, then louder, 'Cécile?'

She woke with a snort and looked up at me blearily. '*Cherie?*'

'Is there somewhere I can sleep?' Right now I'd take the fireplace, so long as it was warm. 'Er, *ou est … je … dormir?*' I pantomimed it.

'*Oui.*' She creaked to her feet and stubbed her fag out on

the bare table. '*Allons-y.*'

She stumbled up the crumbly stairs and pushed open the studded oak door. There was a hallway, slightly smarter, with a rug and furniture, and a proper staircase with oak rails that might have looked quite grand had it not been so dusty. Cécile led me up it for one flight, turned down a corridor, opened another door, went up a stone flight ... and then I lost track. Eventually she pushed open a door and I looked into a room with a bed.

'*Ici,*' she said. '*Couchez-vous ici.*'

That was pretty much all I comprehended before I fell into a deep, deep sleep.

I'd hardly slept the night before, having been awoken by the man with the gun who stole my weapons and my ring.

He woke me again when the sun had dropped low in the sky, almost a day after I had arrived at Cécile's, gun pressed to my head.

'Cécile,' he yelled.

I opened my eyes, aching with tiredness and hangover, and groaned.

'Not you again.'

'Me again,' he said. 'Cécile!'

She answered in distant French, and he yelled something back in the same tongue that I think was along the lines of *Get your arse up here.*

'What are you doing – hey, that's my gun!' I yelped.

'Shut up.'

'Did you follow me?'

He nudged the safety off with his thumb. I shut up.

There were footsteps outside and Cécile pushed the door open, fag drooping from her lips. 'Jacques,' she said, '*que faites-tu?*'

'*Elle est une criminelle dangereuse,*' he replied, gun still pressed to my temple.

'What? No, I'm not,' I said.

'Shut up.'

'Hey, if you're going to go around telling people I'm a dangerous criminal, I think I should be allowed to defend myself.' He gave me an incredulous look. 'Oh, come on, like that bit was hard to translate.'

'*Oui*,' Cécile said. 'Take away ze *pistolet*, Jacques.'

Jacques? He didn't look like a Jacques. He looked like a – well, I don't know. A headache in a suitcase. Dark hair hung in long strands around his face, dark eyes that were narrowed at me, a shadowed jaw, broad shoulders. Oh yes, and my gun, which wasn't moving.

'Jacques,' Cécile persisted, and he lowered it, but still kept it ready.

'That's mine,' I said. 'He stole it from me.'

'I commandeered it,' he told Cécile.

'You stole it! And you knocked me out and handcuffed me to the tent pole – which, by the way, was a really stupid – hey!'

He'd delved under the duvet and grabbed my hands. The cuff bracelets with their little clinking chains were still there.

'You broke them!'

'Well, duh.'

'How?'

'*C'était moi*,' Cécile said proudly, her voice still husky and slightly slurred, more than her accent should have allowed for. Cécile was an old soak. 'Wiz the ... *quel est le mot, l'hache ...*'

'Axe,' I supplied helpfully, and she beamed at me.

Jacques turned angrily on her. 'What the hell for?'

'Because she was chained,' Cécile waved her hands. 'Jacques, what 'ave you been doing wiz her?'

'She,' Jacques waved the gun furiously at me, 'framed me.'

My mouth dropped open. 'I did bloody not. I don't even know who you are!'

'So why are you on the run in a foreign country under a fake name? Sophie Green,' he said accusingly.

Damn. Damn and buggery. I sat up in bed under the watchful gaze of my own gun and looked down at myself. I was still wearing the pyjamas I'd had on when Jacques knocked me out and handcuffed me, having been both unable and disinclined to change since. My short ugly hair was greasy and messy and my face must have looked appalling.

'What makes you think I'm Sophie Green?' I asked as calmly as I could.

'Well, let me see. Under that terrible haircut you still look like her, you have her driving licence in your wallet –' too late I looked round and saw it open on the table by the bed – 'and you have her SIG-Sauer P-239. Or should I say, had. And,' he pulled down the front of my top, prompting another cry of outrage from me, 'you even have her scars.'

All three of us looked down at the marks on my chest, two long pink scars made by someone who had tried to stab me with a carving knife at Christmas. Jacques tilted up my face, the better to make out the old cut there, and then my arms where I'd been slashed on one forearm, one elbow.

We glared at each other for a bit. Actually, he was quite cute. Not the first cute maniac I've come across, though, and probably not the last.

'Why are you here?' he asked.

'None of your business.'

'It damn well is.' The gun was raised again. He'd taken off the silencer and I hoped it wasn't lost. That had been a present from Luke.

Which reminded me …

'I want my ring back,' I said.

'Tough shit.'

'I want it back,' I said as threateningly as I could despite the tears that had sprung up from nowhere at the prospect of it being lost forever. 'Give it to me.'

'Jacques,' Cécile said, and asked him something in rapid French. He replied, their conversation got more heated, and then Cécile repeated firmly, '*Donne-le moi, Jacques. Donne-le moi.*'

Jacques looked very sullen, but he eventually dug in his jeans pocket and handed something over. My heart swelled.

'My ring!'

Cécile inspected it, squinted at the hallmark, then looked up at me. 'Yours?'

I nodded eagerly.

'She ees very precious.'

'It is to me.'

Jacques shot me a look of pure disgust. I lobbed it right back.

'She has the gold most excellent, eighteen of the carats, *oui*?' I nodded. 'And ze *émeraude*, she has per'aps one of the carats?'

I squirmed happily. Luke said he'd bought it off some Arab sheikh's wife. I'd thought he was exaggerating, but he must have spent some money on it.

Because, in addition to being gorgeous, clever and funny, Luke is also loaded. I figure there must be a dozen ugly, stupid, boring, poor men who are pretty annoyed that he got their shares.

Cécile handed it over and I slipped it back on my finger where it nestled happily. Jacques looked mightily pissed off.

"Oo gives you ze ring?" Cécile asked. 'Ze man who telephoned yesterday?'

'Ask Jacques,' I said, 'I'm sure he'll know. He seems to

know everything else about me, even the made-up bits.'

Jacques glowered at me. 'It's Jack, not Jacques,' he spat, 'and I'll bet any money you swindled the ring from your MI6 boyfriend.'

So he knew about Luke. Wonderful.

''Ee is a man most in love,' Cécile told Jack. ''Ee telephone her last night for many of the hours.'

Well, about twenty minutes actually, but I wasn't going to correct her.

'Does he know where you are?' Jack asked.

'No. How do *you* know?'

'I stuck a tracer on your phone.'

I went cold.

'You see, that first night it was just happenstance I ended up in your tent. I was looking for somewhere to hide out. Somewhere people don't ask questions or check ID. But there was something about you, Miss Alice M. Robinson, that was disturbingly familiar. Wasn't till I started hacking into some government files that the name Sophie Green came up. An APB on you. Complete with picture. You're wanted for murder, Sophie Green.'

There wasn't much I could say to that.

'Why doesn't your boyfriend know where you are?'

'Is that any of your business?'

'Boy,' he snorted, 'you must really love him.'

I glowered at him but, mindful of the gun, said nothing.

'Aleece is a guest –' Cécile began, and Jack laughed loudly.

'Her name is not Alice. Her name is Sophie and she's wanted for murder. Wanted by the police and MI5 and by me,' he snarled, his face close to mine, 'because she killed Irene Shepherd and pinned it on me.'

'I didn't kill anyone,' I croaked, and then honesty forced me to add, 'well, not this year.'

Jack gnashed his teeth and stormed out of the room.

Great, just what I needed. A delusional psychopath – why did he think I'd killed this Shepherd woman? – with a gun. Oh, and some mysterious access to confidential files. Annoyingly, that might come in handy. If only he didn't hate me.

I looked up helplessly at Cécile.

'Your name is Sophie?' she asked.

I nodded.

'But your friend send the passport for Aleece.'

'You have it?'

She nodded.

'Can I have it?'

'It is true? You keel zem?'

I shook my head vigorously. 'No. The police think I did but I didn't, I just found him, and as for that woman … I've never heard of her. Please,' I tried to make myself as appealing as possible, 'would Maria send a murderer to you?'

Cécile looked thoughtful.

'Why does Jacques sink you have killed zat woman?'

I ran my hands over my face. 'I don't know,' I said wearily, as the man himself stomped back into the room, looking like thunder.

'Get up,' he said, waving my gun at me.

'Only if you ask nicely.'

He narrowed his eyes. 'I've got a .45 here that's asking very nicely.'

'It's a nine mil,' I said smugly.

'It'll still kill you.'

Belligerently, I pushed back the covers and got out of bed, holding my hands high so he could see them. Jack had a coil of rope around his shoulder and he let it slide down to his hand in one fluid movement, like Fred Astaire with a top hat.

'Hands out,' he said, and Cécile protested in French.

'You have a thing about bondage?' I asked, and Jack said nothing, grabbing my wrists instead and twisting them behind my back before wrapping the rope about them tightly, roughly. 'Careful! I have scar tissue there,' I grumbled, and he pulled the rope tighter. 'Bastard.'

He poked the gun in my back and said, 'Downstairs. Slowly.'

'Or what? You're going to shoot me with my own gun?'

'Why not? You shot Irene with mine.'

I frowned as I half-tripped down the stone stairs to the main landing. This was beginning to sound familiar.

'Had you been to see her that day?' I asked. 'Had people seen you together?'

'You would know. You framed me for it.'

'Do I look smart enough to frame anyone for anything?' I snapped, and Jack hesitated.

'I wouldn't put it past you,' he said.

'What's that supposed to mean? And can I get a sweater or something? I am bloody frozen.'

'So I see,' Jack said, looking at my chest as he reached past me to open the door.

'Pervert.'

He nudged me with the gun and I went down the main stairs before he pushed me and I tripped and broke my neck and was dead, dead all over the floor. Melodramatic, me? Never.

In the kitchen, he pushed me down onto a chair and tied my ankles to the legs, wrapping another piece of rope around my waist to hold me there firmly. It was a far cry from the hospitality I'd received last night.

Cécile, arguing with Jack all the time in French, fussed around lighting candles – I wondered if she even had electricity – and pouring wine and getting bread and cheese out of the pantry. She offered me some ham, and I shook my head politely.

'*Bien sûr*,' she said, and whirled back to the table to get me some cheese.

'I'm not hungry,' I lied, because I was starving, but how could I eat with my hands tied behind my back and my arms pinned to the chair?

'Jacques?'

He was leaning against the table, in black jeans and boots and a faded t-shirt. He looked menacing and brooding and quite like he'd practised the pose in front of a mirror.

'No,' he snapped. 'Thanks.'

Polite, to her at least.

'I can't believe I'm tied to a bloody chair,' I rattled it. 'Couldn't you at least let me get dressed?'

'No. Why did you kill Irene Shepherd?'

'I didn't. I don't even know who she is.'

'You're lying.' He hefted my SIG.

'Don't you call me a liar.'

Cécile babbled something in French that I think was along the same lines. I'm not sure why I was being so belligerent. I think it's just part of my nature. Besides, Jack revealing those scars reminded me of the last time someone had threatened me with death. And last Christmas, when someone else had had a go.

Then there were the high-school kids who tried to kill me in New York. The crazy Czech who thought I was dead right up until the minute I shot him. The duo of former colleagues who tried to bring me down by any methods possible.

Do I have 'kill me' taped to my back? Is it like some sort of beacon that only crazy people can see?

'You've killed before.'

I knew this'd come up.

'Yes, but both of them were crazy people who'd spent

quite a lot of time trying to kill me. It was self-defence.'

'Kill or be killed?'

'Exactly.'

'So what did Irene do to make you want to kill her?'

'Nothing! I –'

'So you just killed her for the hell of it?'

'No! I didn't kill anybody!'

'You just said you did.'

I could see now why he'd tied me down. I could have killed him, then.

'Listen,' I said. 'One of them had pillaged his way across Europe murdering academics because he was looking for an ancient artefact. He blew up the house I was staying in and nearly killed both of the people who lived there. And the other one sabotaged a plane full of people so that it crashed into a primary school. Seventy-eight children died. And all the passengers – a hundred-and forty-three people in total. Not including my boss and another colleague who are both dead because of him. I didn't murder him. I shot him because he was trying to shoot me.'

'Ah. I see,' Jack said. 'You both reached for the gun, right?'

I narrowed my eyes. 'I reached for my gun as he was aiming his. You can check my record, since you seem to know so much about me.' I cocked my head. 'How do you know so much about me?'

'None of your business.'

I wondered if he was related to Docherty.

'Then if you do know so much, you'll know I didn't bloody kill him!'

'Who?'

'Theodore Chesshyre.' I looked up at Jack. 'You do know about Theodore Chesshyre?'

'I know you shot him then left the country.'

47

'Right. So if I was in the business of framing people, don't you think it might be slightly likely that maybe I might have thought about *framing someone for this one?*'

Jack stared at me. Cécile, when she'd caught up, laughed and said something to Jack in French. He scowled at her and said, '*Non.*'

'What did she say?' I asked.

'I say 'e should untie you. Jacques, you are being ze pig.'

Jack muttered something uncomplimentary under his breath.

'I'm going out,' he said, standing up and making no effort to untie me. He picked up a packet of Cécile's cigarettes from the table and stalked out of the kitchen into the evening darkness.

'*Il est un cochon,*' I muttered.

'*Oui.*' Cécile came over and started pulling at the knots that tied me to the chair. 'But he is in trouble.'

'What, you mean the murder thing? Someone killed this Irene woman and made it look like Jack did it, right?'

'Yes. There is a person who steal his *pistolet,*' she made a gun gesture at me, just in case I'd missed that one, 'and they find his, uh ...' she waggled her fingers at me.

'Fingerprints?'

'*Oui.* Everywhere. He has visited her.'

'Who was she?'

Cécile frowned. '*Un juge.*' When I looked confused, she explained, 'She decide who go to the prison, *oui?*'

'Oh, a judge. And why did he visit her?'

'I do not know. He says she was alive when he visits. But the videos, they do not show this.'

'Videos?'

'The cameras, in the house.'

I presumed this meant the judge had CCTV, and I also presumed it had been wiped. 'Yeah, but did he do it? Shoot her, I mean.'

Cécile sent me a piercing look. 'If he has killed her, then you have killed this Theodore.'

'Thanks for clearing that up.'

My bonds released, I stood up and stretched. 'So how long has he been on the run?'

'*Alors*. What day is it?'

I counted up inside my head and realised in shock that it was five days since I'd found Sir Theodore. 'Tuesday. Uh, *mardi*.'

'Zen it is eight days. The Tuesday *dernier, oui*?'

I nodded. 'Right. Okay. I really need to go and get some proper clothes on and maybe take a shower? Uh, *une douche*?' I gave her a hopeful look, and she nodded and smiled.

'Zere is a bathroom –'ere, I show you.'

She led me back upstairs and opened a door with a latch on it.

'Tonight you must sleep in anozzer room,' she said, and gave me a sly look, 'unless want to share wiz Jacques?'

I got the impression she'd have been perfectly happy with this arrangement.

'No,' I said, 'but why does he get that room?'

She shrugged. 'It always is his room.'

'He stays here often?'

'He ees my nephew,' she said, and left.

Chapter Four

That damn car was still outside.

Luke drummed his fingers on the table and wondered how long it would take to construct a hologram to project normality onto the outside of the building. He'd searched and searched for bugs every time he returned to the flat, but they always sneaked in and replaced the ones he'd disabled.

Time for a new strategy. Looping footage was old-hat, but he'd been taken in by it before. The trick was to be smart about it. Anything with a clock in it was out, and he'd have to make sure Tammy wasn't in the room. Watching a cat walk the same path every hour was going to raise a few suspicions.

He checked the angle of one of the cameras in the bedroom. It was aimed right at his bed.

'Perverts,' he said, and resisted the urge to wave at the camera as he got into bed. A few hours footage of him sleeping ought to be enough to loop, and it'd allow him to get on with helping Sophie while they weren't looking.

He recorded himself watching TV with a beer, careful to accidentally knock the camera out of position so the screen couldn't be seen. He'd had the radio on permanently to annoy the audio bugs, and he kept it that way even while the TV was on. Yes, they could isolate one sound from another, but he'd bet they'd give up when all they got was Radio 1 and a football match.

He stood for a while, staring at the alarm pad by the door. Doubtless by now they knew his codes. He could see no signs that they'd been breaking in.

'Oh, sod it,' he said, and disabled the system.

Now. Every time they saw him leave the house, they broke in. So what if they never saw him leave?

His flat was on the first floor, in the loft of an old barn. Very little of his living quarters was visible from the road. This was a purposeful arrangement.

So ... if they never saw him leave, they'd have no idea if he was in the flat or not.

There was only one way in or out, and as it was an outside staircase directly from the yard it was also impossible to hide. How else could he get out?

Luke leaned against the kitchen counter for a while, thinking. His flat was above a roofer's yard, with men and vans coming and going all day. If he could get down there, he could shove on some old clothes and a hat and jump in one of the vans. No one would see him leave at all.

His gaze went to the cupboard by his front door. It held winter coats and sporting equipment, and this time of year he didn't go in there much. But if he'd worked it out right, the cupboard was above the far corner of the lumber store below.

Luke fetched a saw and some ropes, and got to work.

Next morning I was feeling a lot better, more prepared and a hell of a lot cleaner. I had to be nice to Jack, and that was my main priority, because I needed three things from him. One, the return of my guns. Two, everything he knew about Irene Shepherd, how she'd died and who might have killed her. Three, his help in finding that person.

Because I was increasingly beginning to suspect it was the same person who'd killed Sir Theodore. The MO was so similar.

But when I went down to the kitchen, I found it empty. There were no other exits than the stone stairs and the back door, so I went outside. The yard contained the Vectra, and nothing more.

Upstairs on the ground floor, as I guess it would be with the house being built into a hill, there were several rooms that opened off the hallway. I'd guessed a lot of the house must be out of use, and from the look of it I was right. This place was damn huge. All the rooms were full of beautiful but rather neglected furniture, and they were all freezing cold. They were also empty of either Cécile or Jack.

I made my way up to the first floor and started knocking on doors. Several bedrooms, including one that had crumpled bedclothes and bits of women's clothing strewn around that I guessed were Cécile's. Then the pretty (pretty cold) room I'd slept in, huddled in my sleeping bag, blankets and jumpers. Bathrooms. Cupboards full of spiders, which I hastily closed up again. I knocked on the door to Jack's room and when there was no answer, crept up the stairs.

Empty, but at least there were signs of it having been slept in. Last night, after Jack left, Cécile quizzed me about Luke until even I got bored of telling her how wonderful he was, and went to bed. The only useful information I'd got out of her was that Jack was Maria's little brother. I'd wondered if that was how he'd found me here, if Maria had known and let it slip, but in reality it seemed far more likely that Cécile had been the one to be indiscreet. This didn't fill me with an overabundance of confidence.

I went back down to the kitchen and sat down at the table to take the back off my phone. I removed the battery and sim card, but underneath them the circuitboard looked perfectly ordinary to me. That is, baffling. I'd no idea if there was a tracer in there or not.

But how else had Jack found me here? He couldn't have followed me. Had he just called his aunt for a chat and she'd let it slip I was here? The coincidence was a bit too unreasonable.

I was just going in search of some coffee when I heard

voices outside. Cécile and a man with a purple nose came into the room, jabbering so fast I couldn't even make out the odd word, and eventually seemed to notice me.

'Jean-Paul,' she tugged him towards me, '*voici Aleece, elle est la petite amie de Jacques.*'

Even my schoolgirl French could translate that.

'Alice,' Cécile said to me, 'this ees Jean-Paul, 'e works in the vineyard for me. 'E arrives for *le petit dejeuner* – breakfast. You weel eat wiz us?'

I nodded gratefully and stuck out my hand to Jean-Paul, who wiped his palm on his trousers and crushed my metacarpals. Wincing, I turned away to help Cécile, and said under my breath, 'I'm his girlfriend now?'

She shrugged. 'Jean-Paul weel say nothing. 'E doesn't speak no Eenglish and 'e does not speak much anyway.'

This I found to be blatantly false, as he grunted in French to Cécile all the way through the meal and totally ignored me. Not that I minded. My head was full of other things. First, call Maria to check Jack out. Then either find Jack or call Luke, whichever presented itself as easier.

As Jean-Paul lumbered away back to his grapes and I inhaled another pint of coffee, I asked Cécile, 'Where is Jack this morning?'

'Eh?' She looked up from her croissant. 'Oh. I sink 'e goes to the village for …' She waved her hand, apparently having mislaid her translation skills after talking to Jean-Paul. 'To use ze telephone.'

'What's wrong with yours?'

'I don't 'ave one.'

Great.

I went back up to my room and looked at my phone for a bit. I was nearly out of pre-paid vouchers for it and would need to buy more, although to be honest it was bloody confusing trying to top up with the instructions all in French.

Right. I'd call Docherty. He'd been in contact with Maria.
He answered on the first ring. 'Did you find it all right?'
'I've been here since Monday night.'
'How lost did you get?'
Totally. 'I was fine,' I said. 'Traffic was bad all the way.'
Docherty said nothing.
'I got the passport,' I said, holding the envelope Cécile
had given me the day before. The picture in it was horrific.
'And the driving licence – thanks.'
'You're welcome,' he said silkily.
'But, uh. What did you send with them?'
Docherty gave a low chuckle, which in itself is rare for
him. I stared at the box that had been inside the envelope,
which appeared to contain some kind of miniature condoms.
'Fake fingertips,' he said. 'Should you need them. They
scan that kind of thing in America, should you need to go
there.'
'Oh,' I said, feeling rather foolish.
'There are contact lenses, too,' he said.
'I already have contact lenses.'
'Ah, but these are patterned. They should fool an iris scan.'
Sometimes, the knowledge contained in the people I
considered to be my friends really scared me. 'Why would I
need to go to America?'
'I have no idea,' Docherty said, 'your thought processes
baffle me.'
'I need to speak to Maria,' I said. 'Do you know where
she is?'
'Probably at work and being monitored for her connection
to you.'
Dammit. 'Do you know anything about her brother?'
Then, remembering Maria had an endless supply of relatives,
clarified, 'Younger brother, Jack.'
I heard computer keys clacking. 'Lives in America. He's a

bail enforcement agent.'

'A bounty hunter?'

'If you like. Got into trouble a few times in his youth for computer hacking. Sealed file.' Keys clicked a bit more. 'Ah. He was looking at government files. Conspiracy theorist, looks like. Why're you interested?'

'No reason. Cécile said something, that's all.'

'I shall tell Luke you've been enquiring after other men,' Docherty said smoothly.

'You will tell Luke nothing,' I said, more sharply than I'd intended. I could imagine his reaction to being told I'd been threatened not once but twice by Jack, who had also had his hands inside my pyjamas.

Docherty just gave a low laugh.

'Thanks for the info,' I said, and hung up, massaging my temples.

'And who is Luke?' came a voice from the doorway, and I nearly had a heart attack.

'Jesus, Jack, you scared me. You shouldn't be eavesdropping.'

'Maybe it's my business to eavesdrop. Who's Luke?'

'My MI6 boyfriend. Which you knew, so stop pretending you don't.'

He picked up the wallet that was by my bed and opened it to Luke's picture. 'He the guy in here?'

I nodded.

Jack studied the picture for a moment, his face inscrutable. 'You know him?' I asked.

He shrugged. 'Maria's mentioned him. I think she has a thing for him.'

'I really don't think he's her type,' I said, smiling.

It had come as a bit of a shock to me to discover Maria was gay. But not, she said, as much of a shock as it came to her. Jack raised his eyebrows. 'Jealous?'

'Of Maria?' I wondered if he knew. 'I don't see her as a threat.'

He shook his head. 'You don't see my sister as a threat. You must be damn sure of this guy, then.'

I nodded. 'I am.'

'Been together long?'

What was this, twenty questions? Since when did he get so nice?

'A year,' I said. 'Well – we broke up for four months last year and then got back together at Christmas. And then he was working abroad for three months so ...'

'Really it's only been five months.'

'But since last April. Which makes a year.'

'Why'd you break up?'

Because I was an idiot. 'Why'd you want to know?'

He shrugged. 'Curious. You're all immovable now, but you can't have been that sure before Christmas.'

I sighed. 'Lots of things. Work ...'

'And?'

I scowled. 'It's none of your business.'

'Fine, okay.'

'Do you have a girlfriend?'

'Me? Nah.'

'Why not?' Cruel, I know, but I was single for bloody years before Luke and I've had my share of Bridget Jones inquisitions.

'No time.'

Right. I guess bounty hunters don't get a lot of time.

'Where did you go this morning?'

'Village. Made a phone call.'

'To?'

'Aren't you a curious bunny?'

'Curious, yes. Bunny ... Do you see a tail?'

'No,' Jack said, but in tones that told me he'd been

56

looking.

I wondered how he'd got to the village. There'd been no car out in the yard except for mine. I hadn't seen anything that might belong to Cécile. The only village I'd passed on my way in was at least five miles away.

'So how do you –' I began, but Jack was already halfway out of the door.

'See you at lunch?'

I blinked suspiciously. 'Er, yes …'

He nodded, and was gone.

What a strange man.

I plugged my phone into its charger, realised I was short on credit, and went downstairs, car keys in hand.

'I'm going to the village,' I said, waving my phone, 'to get some credit?'

Cécile blinked at me.

'For my mobile? *Uh, les petites cartes, avec l'argent, pour le téléphone?*'

'Ah, *oui*,' she nodded, 'go to ze *supermarché*, *le bureau de tabac* 'as none.'

Rightiho.

He knew something was wrong as soon as he walked in. Not a single person made eye contact with him, not even the ones who ought to have been better actors.

He made straight for Sheila's office, intercepted briefly by Evelyn. Her lovely face was marred with concern.

'She wants to –'

'– see me,' Luke interrupted. 'I guessed.'

Evelyn chewed her lip. It was pink and plump, Luke noticed dispassionately, and probably kissably soft, but he had absolutely zero desire to go anywhere near it.

Very occasionally, he wondered if Sophie had done some sort of hypnotism on him. Or a spell of some kind. For a man who had stopped counting lovers a long time ago, monogamy was something of a shock.

'Is it anything in particular I've done?'

She winced. 'Begins with "Sophie". Ends with "Green".'

'I haven't done her in a week,' he said, just to see if that would shock her. Evelyn's beautiful eyes went wide, but she didn't say anything. Luke pushed open the door to his boss's office and folded his arms.

She looked up, apparently not surprised he'd barged in, and said, 'Close the door.'

Luke left it open. 'What do you want?'

Sheila regarded the open door for a moment, then said, 'Well, if you're going to be childish, Sharpe, that actually makes this easier. I'm standing you down.'

He stared at her. Part of him had expected this, but the rest of him was outraged she was being so petty.

'What have I done?'

A merciless smile flashed over her features. 'Sophie, although I do hear it's been a while.'

'She's in another country,' Luke said evenly.

'Which one?' Sheila asked almost pleasantly.

Fury ballooned inside him, making him lightheaded. 'Don't know, but she's always wanted to go to Iraq. And I hear Afghanistan is nice this time of year. Perhaps you should go look for her there.'

'That's not where you've been looking for her.'

She held up a tiny device, and his stomach flipped over. He thought he'd been careful, dammit.

He almost laughed at his own stupidity. Sheila had been in the Service since he'd been learning how to talk.

'You've been spying on me.'

'I rather think espionage is my job, Sharpe.'

'On your own officers?'

Her eyes hardened. 'You've been using our equipment to

investigate your girlfriend's guilt.'

'She's not guilty,' Luke fired back.

'No, I'm sure it was an accident. Or that she was framed.'

Her eyes glittered. Damn her, she bloody *knew*. Had she overheard his conversations? Were 5 passing her their intel? Had she bugged his phone? Dammit, how was he supposed to hide from a veteran spy?

'You've been hacking into French surveillance to trace her face or car. You've been calling Interpol. And you've been doing it on my time.'

Luke said nothing. All he had to track Sophie was a passport number, which she hadn't even used yet.

'You've made only cursory contact with our agent in Kyrgyzstan. He has high-level access to the security services. His information suggests that they may soon become a political power in their own right. You don't think this is information we need?'

He stayed silent.

'And you haven't even found her,' Sheila added, a faint trace of scorn in her voice.

He glared at a spot above her left shoulder.

Her gaze was cool. 'Take some time off, Sharpe. That's an order. Full pay,' she added.

'Great. I'll make a start on my Christmas shopping.'

'It's April.'

'What the hell else is there to do?'

They eyeballed each other for a long moment, then Luke said, 'Anything else?'

Sheila turned back to her paperwork. 'Yes. I wouldn't buy much for Sophie. You probably won't see much of her come Christmas.'

Years of training and a lifetime of self-discipline meant that Sheila avoided being beaten to a bloody pulp right then, but Luke considered later that she had no idea how close she'd come.

He stormed out of the office. No one asked for his security pass – well, hell, they'd just disable it anyway – which was almost a shame, because he longed to throw it at someone.

Outside, the spring day was irritatingly mild and pleasant. Luke stormed down to the riverfront and threw himself at the bench under the rotunda, glaring at the sparkle of sunshine on the Thames.

Ten minutes up the road was Thames House. Were it not for the trees on the far bank he'd be able to see it across the water. He could barge in there and demand to know what they had on Sophie, but he didn't expect it'd get him much more than a swift kick in the kidneys.

'Goddammit,' he said out loud. 'God bloody damn it.'

He was effectively cut off from all his official contacts. He had no access to security systems, to databases, to surveillance. Rubbing his eyes with the heels of his hands, he considered his assets. A phone-line to Sophie, which he daren't use somewhere so obvious. A passport number he was unable to track. A flat he had an escape hatch from. A small tabby cat.

Oh yeah. James Bond had nothing on this.

On the road behind the SIS Building was a convenience store with a small coffee concession. Luke ordered a double espresso and a large chocolate muffin and tried not to look at the cigarettes on sale behind the counter. He'd beaten that beast years ago, and when he'd relapsed at Christmas it had been Sophie's disapproval that had him flushing half a pack of Golden Virginia down the toilet.

The coffee and muffin were surprisingly expensive. Luke paid with a twenty and got hardly any change. Frowning, he wandered back to his bench, set the coffee down and stared in amazement at the packet of Dunhill Internationals in his other hand.

'Okay,' he said. 'Okay.'

'Didn't know you smoked,' came a voice from behind him.

'I don't,' he replied, not looking round. The box glowed red and gold in the sunlight.

'So they're a good luck charm, are they? Something to match your lighter?'

Evelyn sat down beside him. Of all the support staff, she was one of the more intelligent, perceptive and friendly. She was also impossibly beautiful. She was, in fact, exactly the sort of woman Luke would have had in bed within twenty-four hours of meeting, if not for Sophie.

He'd been frightened that committing to a relationship with Sophie would mean he wasn't allowed to sleep with other women. What was even more terrifying was the realisation that he didn't want to.

'Lighter's a practical thing to carry,' he said, taking his from a pocket and flicking the lid open and shut a few times.

'Of course, but most people carry disposable Bics. Not –' she held her hand out, and Luke passed it to her – 'not eighteen-carat gold Dunhill Rollagas lighters worth more than my first car.'

'What was your first car?' Luke asked, because Evelyn was obviously not the sort of girl who bought a clapped-out Nova for a few hundred quid and drove it until the gearbox fell out.

'A Mini,' she said, and Luke snorted.

'Cooper?' She nodded. 'Worth considerably more than my lighter.'

'Why do you assume it was a brand new Mini?'

Luke just looked at her.

'All right, but it's a considerably better investment than a ten-grand lighter.'

Luke took back the lighter and stared at it. It had a nice

heft to it, the flick of the Rollagas catch was satisfying and the flame it produced was clean and strong. But it was just a lighter. He could smoke his head off just as well with the help of a packet of Swan Vestas.

'It was a gift,' he said distantly.

'From who?'

'My grandmother.' He looked at her sideways. 'And you had to stop yourself from saying "whom" there, didn't you?'

Evelyn's perfect brow furrowed. 'It's not my fault I had a privileged background,' she said.

'Nope,' said Luke, who rarely mentioned his own if he could help it.

'I mean, what the bloody hell is it good for? An Oxbridge degree and then a useless job as a PR girl for a publisher. A complete inability to relate to anyone not called Bunty or Camilla. The emotional ability of a fruit fly.'

'Yeah, and all that money gets really boring,' Luke said.

Evelyn flashed him a look, apparently trying to work out if he was joking.

'Plus, you're not a useless PR for a publisher,' he added, flicking the lighter open and closed, open and closed.

'No. Well, the Service was the only way I could think of to … to have some sort of life. To break out. To not be like everyone I grew up with.'

'You don't have to be rich to feel like that,' Luke said, because she'd just echoed what Sophie said when he had recruited her to SO17. And Sophie's idea of posh was Tesco Finest.

'And it solves the problem of being unable to have a proper relationship with anybody,' Evelyn went on. 'Intelligence officers don't get to have relationships.'

Luke snapped the lighter shut. 'Yeah, well I do,' he said.

'Luke,' Evelyn began, then faltered. 'Look, when you first came here, you had a bit of a … reputation.'

He slouched back against the bench, arms folded. 'This should be good.'

'All those years with your little agency –'

'Though she be but little, she is fierce,' Luke growled, because he was damn proud of SO17 and the work they'd done.

'Well – yes,' said Evelyn uncertainly. Clearly not a Shakespeare fan. Mind, neither was he: Sophie was the one forever quoting. 'You were known as a bit of a ... er ...'

Luke waited politely.

'Well, if this was the nineteenth century, I'd have said "rake",' she said.

Luke blew out a sigh. 'A rake is indiscriminate, a wastrel, a womaniser.'

This time it was Evelyn who waited politely.

'Oh, for God's sake, do you think I was a monk? I had affairs, Evelyn, with women who knew what they were getting into. I never tricked anyone into thinking we were going to have a relationship when it was patently impossible.'

And he hadn't. He'd truly believed so at the time. He'd had discreet affairs with elegant, sophisticated women who weren't looking for a wedding ring, or even someone to wake up with in the morning. It suited him just fine. No emotional attachments, just mutual pleasure, no one got hurt. Life had taught him perfectly well to keep his emotions in check.

Maria had once said to him that the only thing he had an emotional attachment to was his SIG-Sauer. Luke figured it was a sign of his emotional maturity at the time that he thought this was a good thing.

Then Hurricane Sophie had blown into his life, the levees had cracked, and a lifetime of emotion had unleashed itself. He'd always known it wasn't a good idea to let himself care about anyone, and then Sophie had chipped away until he couldn't help it, until he not only liked her and respected her but loved her, and now the strength of his feelings terrified him.

'You think it's better to behave like that, do you?' he asked Evelyn. 'To never form attachments to anything or anyone, to get so detached from humanity that you can't even empathise with anyone?'

'You're a spy, Luke,' Evelyn said quietly. 'You don't need to empathise with anyone.'

Luke stared at the river for a long time. Then he stood up, and silently walked away.

The next two days passed without much incidence. I read more French newspapers, my grasp of the language slightly improving. I ate lots of Cécile's rather erratic but very generous vegetarian meals. I had sporadic, short conversations with Jack, who at least didn't seem to be trying to kill me any more, but hardly appeared interested in my life either. He wasn't around much, taking long walks or helping out in the vineyard. I occasionally caught him looking at me oddly, but he always glanced away when he saw me watching. I'd tried talking to him about Irene Shepherd, but he'd started to get a murderous look in his eye. I figured I'd let him get to see what a sweet, kind, non-murderous person I was before I probed any further.

At least I figured out how he was getting to the village. There was an old motorbike parked up next to the Vectra one morning, and as I watched, Jack started it up and revved noisily away.

I'd look good on that bike.

I spoke to Luke every day and it got easier in some ways, harder in others. Putting the phone down was torture. He was my only link to the real world and I missed him like hell. I missed looking at him – my wallet photo was getting a little ragged – touching his skin, breathing in his scent.

I missed his arms around me when I slept, his kiss when I awoke. And yes, I missed the sex, too. We tried phone sex but I got the giggles and spoiled the mood somewhat. Luke told me I'd better get my arse in gear and track down the real killer, because he wanted to get laid.

He can be so sweet sometimes.

'I went to see your parents today.'

'Why?'

'Because I like them. To see how they're doing.'

'Why – what's wrong?'

'Er, you're wanted for murder? They're worried about you, Soph.' He paused. 'I told them I'd spoken to you.'

I closed my eyes. If I thought about my parents too much I'd start crying. 'And?'

'And … they're glad you're okay. Want to talk to you.'

'You didn't give them my number?' If anyone was looking for me they'd have taps on the phone lines of everyone I knew. My parents would have been their first port of call. The only reason I wasn't worried about Luke was that he knew the system inside and out – and how to circumnavigate it. He was an MI6 officer. He had connections.

'No. I told them it was dangerous.'

'Did you use that word?' I asked, knowing it would scare them to hear the word 'danger' and their only daughter included in the same phrase.

At least, I damn well hoped so.

'No. I used words like "extreme caution" and stuff.'

'Stuff, huh?'

'Yeah. Your mum wants me to tell you she loves you.'

I closed my eyes, tears starting. 'Tell her I love her, too.'

'I already did.'

'Thanks.'

I sniffed as quietly as I could.

'Sophie?'

65

'Mmm?'

'Are you crying?'

Another sniff. Damn. I hadn't meant that one.

'No. Why would you think I'm crying?'

'Because your voice has gone all wobbly and you're sniffing and I know you always miss your mum when you're away from home.'

God, my mum. It was one thing to want Luke there to hold me and joke with me and kiss me and make love to me, but ... I just wanted the security of having my mum there. Someone in charge. Someone to hug and make it better. Luke's parents died when he was quite small and he's never really understood how close I am to my family. They live in the same village and I see them all the time. And even when I don't, they're just there and if I need them they always want me around.

I sniffed again and this time my voice broke. 'I wish I was home.'

'I wish you were, too,' Luke said gently. 'Sophie, I'm doing what I can. We'll get this sorted out and then you can come home. We can watch *Buffy* for hours and hours.'

I watch *Buffy* as a kind of therapy. That's something Luke does understand about me.

'Soph, please don't cry,' he pleaded.

'I can't help it,' I sobbed. 'I'm stuck in the middle of Frogland because someone framed me for a murder I had no reason to commit but everyone thinks I did. The police are after me, Luke. I'm wanted by *MI5*. And I'm bloody miles and miles from you and I miss you. I really miss you,' I cried.

'I miss you, too. Do you have that passport yet?'

'Yes, and I look hideous in it. I hate being Alice Maud. It's a stupid sodding name.'

'You chose it,' Luke said with a touch of amusement. 'Look, if you have the passport, can't you leave the country?'

'And go where?'

'Here?' Luke asked quietly.

I closed my eyes. 'I'd be seen, Luke. You don't think they'll be watching your flat and mine, and my parents' house and Maria and Angel and everyone?'

He sighed. 'Yeah. I know. There's been a car outside since Saturday morning. Jesus, this is a mess.'

By the time I hung up I'd managed to stop crying, although my nose was stuffy and my throat was raw. I got up to find some Sinutabs to clear out my sinuses, but as I passed the part-open bedroom door I saw Jack leaning against the wall outside.

Clearly, he'd heard every word.

'Do you always listen in on people's private conversations?' I asked, wiping my eyes.

'Only when they're of use to me.'

'And how was that of use to you?' I sniffed, trying not to sound bitter and failing somewhat.

Jack didn't answer me. He looked at me for a while, his face impassive, then he said, 'Cécile's made you a casserole. She told me to come and get you.'

I nodded and took in a deep breath to try and get my nose unblocked. 'I'll be down in a minute,' I said, but he didn't move and watched me cross to my toiletry bag and rummage for the tablets. My toiletry bag is the size of some people's suitcases, and carries roughly the same stock as a small pharmacy. I had a bit of a health scare last year. Well, not so much a health scare as septicaemia. And then I sort of nearly drowned just before Christmas.

I'm a little cautious with myself these days. At least, when I'm not on the run.

Jack watched, fascinated, as I popped various pills. 'Hypochondriac much?'

I ignored him.

'What made those scars on your chest?'

'A gentleman wouldn't have noticed,' I said tartly, then relented. 'Someone tried to stab me at Christmas.'

'Whatever happened to peace and goodwill?'

'It's a terrible world,' I agreed.

After dinner I declined Cécile's offer of drinking until I passed out, and went back up to my room. Jack had shoved back his chair and walked away the minute he'd finished eating. I wondered if he was this miserable with everyone, or just people he suspected of framing him for murder.

It was when I closed the curtains that I heard a sudden bang. I might have dismissed it, had I not also seen a tiny flare of light that I recognised as muzzle flash from a pistol shot. For a second I wavered, then I grabbed my fleece, shoved my feet into trainers, and ran down the stairs. Cécile was snoring, her head on the kitchen table, pre-war music warbling from the scratchy gramophone in the corner. She didn't see me grab a big, sharp knife and dash out into the night.

The house was surrounded by what had probably been a garden at some point, but what was now, through sheer neglect, no more than a lumpy meadow with bushes creeping in from the edges. I ran over it, tripping once and nearly cutting my own arm off, to the woods at the end. I hadn't been down here before, but from my bedroom window I'd seen that the trees went back quite a way, then parted at a stream or small river. It was in this gap that I'd seen the light flash.

Panting, not used to such exercise and definitely not wearing the right bra, I crossed my arms over my chest and ran into the trees. It's all right for girls in films to rush around all over the place without knocking themselves out, but I believe that if God had intended for me to be a runner, He wouldn't have given me a double D.

Reaching the river, I scanned left and right and then saw,

a hundred feet away on the far bank, two figures huddled by the edge of the water. One of them was holding the other one under and without thinking, I yelled, 'Hey!'

The drowner looked up, saw me, and shoved the drownee under the water. In the darkness it was impossible to tell who it was – I couldn't even see if it was male or female. Whoever it was pushed the body further into the water and ran off into the darkness.

'Hey,' I yelled again, outraged that they were leaving without giving me their full name, address, daytime telephone number and date of birth. 'Come back!'

But of course, 'Come back!' is probably the most completely pointless thing to say to someone running away. What did I expect to happen? The drowner would stop, put his or her hands up and say, 'It's a fair cop,' when I eventually caught up?

No, the figure just disappeared into the dark woods, and was lost to me in seconds.

I looked for a way to cross the water and saw a rather precarious-looking bridge made of a few felled logs, not far from the body. Now, I'm not good with heights and my balance is less catlike than … lemming-like, but I nevertheless skidded and slipped my way over the slimy wood, losing my balance and falling painfully on my face as I reached the other side.

The body was floating gently, face down, anchored by some weeds that had wrapped around the ankle. From the size I could tell it was a man, and I knew without seeing any more of him that it was Jack.

I waded in, gasping at the utter coldness of the water, hoping desperately that the things slapping at my ankles were just more weeds, and grabbed at Jack's body. I flipped him over and dragged him by the ankles out of the water, back onto the dark, muddy bank, and tried to remember what Luke had told me on my one, extremely brief, first aid training session with SO17. Unfortunately, since it was Luke training me, the mouth-to-mouth info got a bit ... well, shall we say intimate, and leave it at that.

This left me desperately trying to remember back nearly twenty years to my frigging Brownies First Aid badge.

I checked his breathing. No breathing. Hell. I checked his pulse and felt nothing ... nothing until I shifted grip, desperately, and felt something thud very gently under my fingers. Thank God for that. He might not be the world's nicest guy, but he could help me clear my name, and I needed him alive.

Luke said when they pulled me from the water in December I wasn't breathing, and I'd been in there a hell of a lot longer than Jack. He was still alive, I just needed to get him breathing again.

I stuck two fingers in his mouth and pulled out some river gunk, then I started breathing into his mouth, trying not to think about the gunk, pinching his nose and remembering how hard it had been in that Brownie class to get the dummy's chest to inflate. Apparently real people were even harder, because I was huffing into Jack's mouth for bloody ages and very nearly gave up when his chest suddenly rose, he spluttered and heaved and I sprang away just in time to avoid a mouthful of regurgitated river water.

I rolled him on his side and leaned back against the rough bark of a tree, cold and wet and exhausted, watching Jack sick up more water and lie still for a while, his chest rising and falling reassuringly.

Eventually he moved his head and looked up, and I gave a little finger wave.

'What the hell –?' he croaked.

'You're welcome.'

'Where'd she go?'

'Who? The person who had your head under the water? Ran away.' I made a running motion with my first two fingers. 'I did think about pursuing but somebody confiscated my gun,' I added pointedly.

He rolled onto his back and lay there with his arms wide. 'She hit me,' he said. 'I lost balance and the next thing I knew I was underwater.'

I was impressed. It had taken me almost a week to remember how I'd ended up in the water. Also, he'd said 'she'.

'Did you recognise her?' I asked.

Jack shook his head. 'Didn't see her face. Definitely a woman, though.' He coughed some more, then said suspiciously, 'What are you doing here?'

I sighed. 'Performing one of my trademark reversals. You know, drowning you then bringing you back to life?'

Jack scowled at me.

'I was saving your ungrateful behind.'

'How –?'

'I heard a shot.'

'Oh. That was me. Guess I missed.'

'You guess?'

He rubbed his head. 'I'm not thinking too clearly.'

I supposed I could cut him some slack. 'Yeah, well, maybe you lost a bit of time. When I nearly drowned –'

'Wait, you got stabbed, *and* nearly drowned?'

'I had a busy winter.' I wrinkled my nose. 'Spying is a dangerous job.'

'Yeah, but you're like a lightning rod. I looked at your file. More people tried to kill you than Castro.'

'S'not my fault.'

'Wanna bet?'

'Hey, someone just tried to kill *you*.'

He shrugged and sat up. 'Occupational hazard.'

'Oh, you think being a bounty hunter is more dangerous than being a spy?'

Jack gestured wordlessly at his sodden clothes. Guess he had a point.

'Any idea as to who it might have been?' I asked.

'Possibly the person who killed Irene Shepherd?'

'I thought I killed Irene Shepherd.'

Jack narrowed his eyes at me. 'Don't you start.' He tried to get to his feet but swayed and fell like timber. I stayed where I was and said, 'That'll be the near drowning.'

'Shut up.'

'We have to get back across this river, you know.'

'I can make it. Just ... give me a minute.'

It took longer than a minute for him to get strong enough to walk back across the bridge, holding reluctantly onto me. All the time I was worrying more: who was this woman, why was she trying to kill Jack and how did she know where he was?

'Jack?' I asked as we walked across the meadow.

'Yeah?'

'How did she know where you were? Or was she just a random person trying to kill you?'

'I think she is involved with this whole thing.'

'You haven't told anyone you're here, have you? Used a mobile or anything?'

'No. Just the village payphone.'

'It could be bugged.'

'Why would anyone bug it, unless they knew we were here?' Jack asked suspiciously.

I raised my palms. The only person who knew I was here was Docherty, and he wouldn't ...

No, he wouldn't.

Would he?

'Anyway, it wasn't. I checked.'

'Did you bug my phone?' I asked.

'Shouldn't a government officer like you be able to tell?'

Dammit. There was no way I could answer that without looking like a bigger idiot than I did already.

Jack smirked. It was a very loud smirk.

'Shut up,' I said. 'How did this woman find you?'

'Maybe she saw you,' he said.

'I hardly think so. I changed my hair and everything.'

Jack gave me a dead look.

'We probably need to leave.'

He looked at me. 'We?'

'Yeah. If she knows I'm here, too … Jack, didn't it occur to you that maybe this might involve the both of us? That we might have got framed by the same person?'

He said nothing.

'We could work on it together …'

'Work on it? This isn't the bloody Famous Five, Sophie, it's not a case for you to work on.'

'So how do you propose we clear our names? Or is your solution just to hide out here forever? Because I for one would like to go home to my boyfriend and my parents at some point. I have a flat and friends and a life –' okay, so that was pushing it a bit – 'and I am not about to give them up because someone stole my gun!'

Jack was silent for a bit. He stumbled on a rough bit of earth and I caught him, his clothes sodden and cold, his skin like ice. He pulled away from me, angrily, and stalked off ahead.

Fine. Stupid men. See if I cared.

I went straight past the sleeping Cécile and up to my room, changed into clean clothes and packed all my things back into my case. I put my new passport in my pocket, along with my car keys and wallet, which was rapidly emptying. My stash of Euros wasn't going to last me forever.

I lugged everything out to the car, then went back to the kitchen and started collecting food. The rest of the casserole, in the equivalent of a Tupperware box, bread, cheese, fruit, a bottle or two of wine ... hey, it could get boring out on my own. I put that in the car and went back in to leave a note for Cécile.

Jack was standing in the kitchen, keys in hand, a bag over his shoulder. He glowered at me. His clothes were clean, but his hair was still wet, his skin pale.

'My bike is faster,' he said, 'but your car can carry more.'

'So it can,' I said. 'Where are you going?'

'Away. With you.'

I raised my eyebrows. 'Says who?'

'Me.' He sighed. 'You said it yourself, we can do more together.'

'Once more, with feeling.'

'And someone knows we're here.'

'They could still be watching.'

'They could have sabotaged your car.'

'Or your bike.'

We met eyes.

'It's Cécile's bike.'

'It's Luke's car.'

We nodded at each other and I said, 'Okay, but you have to do one thing for me.' I held out my wrists, where those damn handcuff bracelets still jangled. 'Unlock these?'

Jack gave the ghost of a smile and did as I asked.

I went to the chalkboard by the door, scrawled, '*Merci et au revoir*, Jacques & Alice,' and we went out to the car.

'Number plate,' he said, frowning at it.

'What about it? I altered it.'

'No good. Cameras these days have auto-recognition

for number plates. Won't take five minutes for someone to connect this car with the one that got off the ferry in Calais. You're lucky you got away with it so far. Wait here.'

He disappeared around the side of the house, and a few minutes later came back with a pair of French number plates. Minutes I spent mentally flagellating myself for not thinking about number-plate recognition. Hey, I had a lot on my plate.

'Did you just nick those off Cécile's 2CV?' I said.

'No. Jean-Paul's.' He had a screwdriver in his other hand and set about changing the plates.

'Should we respray it, too?' I asked sourly, annoyed that I hadn't thought of doing this myself.

Jack ignored me.

'It could use an Opal badge,' I said. 'French cars don't have Vauxhall insignias.'

'Well, it'll have to do.' He moved to the back of the car and fixed the plate there while I resigned myself to re-packing the car with both our luggage by myself.

When he was done with the number plates, Jack went to the driver's side and I shook my head.

'Oh, no. You do not get to drive.'

'I could not be as bad a driver as you.'

'When have you even seen me drive?'

'When I shot at your bumper.'

We both looked at said bumper. There was indeed a dent in it.

I narrowed my eyes and gave Jack my scary look. It has floored lesser men. 'Do you want to annoy me?'

Apparently Jack was one of these lesser men. He got in the passenger side, looking sulky. It was a look that suited him unfairly well.

'Oh,' I said as I started up the engine, 'and I want my gun back.'

'Which one? The one you stole, or the one that's unlicensed?'

'Hey, I'm gonna renew it.' Maybe. Sort of. Or get Luke to modify the file that says I'm not supposed to have my gun any more.

'Yeah, sure, they'll renew a licence for someone wanted for murder.'

'I told you, we'll figure that out.' The car bounced down the drive on suspension that was not designed for French country lanes.

'What are you, Miss Marple?'

'Don't you Miss Marple me.'

'You know, this car could be prickling with explosives.'

'Did I ever tell you about the time I got an Aston Martin blown up? Jack? Jack?'

Chapter Five

She stood on the doorstep in the morning sun, pink-cheeked and adorable in a knitted beret and baby-doll coat. Angel looked exactly like her namesake, which made it all the more confusing when she got her claws out. It was like being savaged by a fluffy toy.

'You look terrible,' she told Luke.

'And you look wonderful. What's your point?'

'That you need to get out. Have you done anything since she disappeared apart from obsessively check up on her?'

'Yes,' he said, irritated. 'I've been working. You know, my job.'

Angel cocked her head. 'They've kept you on your current case?'

His face betrayed nothing. Luke was almost sure of that. 'I'm between cases.'

Unfortunately, in addition to being sharper than she looked, Angel was also very, very good with people. 'If you're doing that reading-me-like-a-book thing,' he said, 'I don't think it's going to be one of those ones with the pink shiny covers you and Sophie love so much.'

'No, I think we're looking more at Kurt Wallander,' Angel said. 'Can I come in?'

'People will talk,' Luke said, but he stood back to allow her entry.

'I won't insult your intelligence by asking if you know about the spooks outside,' she said, unfastening her coat. 'Are they on your side?'

'They're MI5.'

'Question still stands,' Angel sighed.

'I'm considering taking them a cup of coffee,' Luke said. 'Surveillance is boring as hell.'

She smiled. 'And are they listening in as well?'

He smiled back at her, his first real smile since the news had broken. 'They think they're listening to me watching *The Thick Of It*. I'm enjoying thinking up new ripostes to Malcolm Tucker.'

Angel put her hands primly on her belly. 'Well, please don't demonstrate. If the baby can hear classical music I'm sure it can also hear swearing.'

Luke rolled his eyes but said nothing, pausing the recording and giving Angel a significant look. She nodded. Big Brother would think it was weird if they didn't hear a conversation going on.

'Was there something I could help you with?' he asked Angel.

She draped her coat over the kitchen counter and leaned against it. Her baby-blue eyes were calm and bright.

'Yes,' she said. 'I need you to come shopping with me.'

Luke blinked. 'I'm sorry, I thought you just said shopping.'

'I did.'

'Yes, but you're pregnant, so I'm going to assume some crazy hormone has made you forget that my girlfriend, who also happens to be your best friend, is on the run from a murder charge and if I don't clear her name soon, it'll never get cleared.'

Her face remained calm. 'And I'm going to assume you're under a lot of stress right now, so I'm going to disregard that hormones comment.'

Luke ran his hands through his hair in frustration. 'I can't go out now,' he said.

'Why? You've clearly been investigating this for Sophie – I won't ask what your boss thinks of it – and I doubt any more information is going to come to light in the next few hours. Besides, you've got an iPhone, haven't you? You can keep Googling while I try on maternity dresses.'

Luke stared at her, trying to work out how to ask if she'd gone crazy without getting slapped.

Angel wandered round the counter into the kitchen and opened the fridge.

'You want something to eat?' Luke asked doubtfully. 'Drink?'

'No, I'm fine, thank you.' She stared at the contents of the fridge.

'What?' Luke said.

Angel shook her head. 'Beer, cold pizza, more beer, remains of a Chinese takeaway, and some vodka.'

'There's Coke in there, too,' he said defensively.

'This is not food,' she said, turning back to him.

'You try grocery shopping when MI5 are watching your house!' Every time he went out he had to resweep for bugs. It was getting insulting now, like they thought he was too stupid to notice.

Angel ignored this. 'When was the last time you had a shave?'

Luke ran his hand over his jaw and tried to remember. 'It's not high on my list of priorities.'

She put her hands on her petite hips. 'Luke Sharpe, as the Official Best Friend of your girlfriend, I'm staging an intervention.'

'That's not funny.'

'It's not meant to be. Precisely how much use do you think you are to Sophie in this state? You said you were between cases. I'm going to read between the lines here and –'

'Don't,' Luke said, suddenly weary beyond belief.

Her gaze softened. 'You need to get out,' she said. 'Get some fresh air, and think about something else. My dad always said when he was having trouble with something, he needed to stop thinking about it and the answer would quite often come to him all by itself.'

He ran his hands over his face. That packet of Dunhill's was calling to him from the kitchen cupboard where he'd hidden it.

'Is this trouble of the song-writing variety, or of the spying kind?' he asked, because Angel's late father had taken time out of his busy career writing chart-topping hits to do a little bit of light espionage on the side. As one does.

'I always assumed it was music, but knowing what I do now it could be either,' she said crisply.

Luke stared longingly at the cigarette cupboard.

'Besides,' Angel delivered her killer blow, 'you're under surveillance. Wouldn't you like to waste their time all day?'

I stopped for petrol outside Grenoble and bought some very strong coffee to keep me awake. Jack, who'd flaked out almost as soon as we hit the motorway, woke up and asked if I wanted him to take the wheel for a bit. I wanted to say no, it was my car (well, more mine than his) and he'd be all weak from the drowning, but I found myself handing over the coffee and switching seats.

The next thing I knew, it was daylight and we were in Italy. I woke up and saw road signs for Turin and Milan and, rather stupidly, asked where we were.

'Germany,' Jack said, straight-faced.

'Ha ha. When did we cross the border?'

'Couple of hours ago. You really can sleep through anything, huh?'

'What's that supposed to mean?'

'That I had to get your passport out of your pocket and you never noticed.'

I scowled at him, until I remembered the borderless state effect. 'Pervert,' I said.

Jack grinned at me.

'Especially since I happen to know there's no passport check between France and Italy, so if you really have been digging in my pockets, I'm going to want a better explanation.'

His smile faded. I let him think about that for a few minutes, then said, 'All right, I have my alias. Does your passport say Jack de Valera or do you have something better?'

'If anyone asks, I'm Jacques Dubois, I'm French, and you're my English girlfriend, Alice. We're visiting my cousin.'

'Who lives where?'

'Just outside Milan. Little town called Maniago.'

'Boy, you thought about this a lot.'

He shrugged. 'An alibi is a useful thing.'

'Don't I know it. What's her name?'

'Valentina. Vallie.'

'Her address?'

'Piazza della Repubblica 12a.'

'You really need to get out more.'

He gave me a sideways look. 'That's her actual address.'

'You mean there really is a Vallie?'

'Yep. We're a couple of hours away.'

'Does she know we're coming?'

Jack gave me a sideways look. I guessed not.

This was confirmed when we turned up at Vallie's flat, a tiny couple of rooms off a pretty market square, and a tiny, model-gorgeous girl threw her arms around Jack and gabbled and scolded in that terribly demonstrative Italian style of talking where they look like they're having a major fight, but are probably talking about the weather.

Then he said, '*La mia ragazza*, Alice,' and yanked me into a threeway hug, whereupon Vallie kissed both my cheeks and babbled a bit more.

I really hoped he'd just introduced me as his girlfriend,

and not as some kind of swinger who wanted a fling with his pretty cousin.

Eventually Vallie wafted off towards the bedroom, leaving us alone.

The apartment consisted of a cramped living room, even more cramped kitchenette, a tiny bathroom, and the bedroom into which Vallie had disappeared. From the glimpse I'd caught before the door slammed, it was too small to contain her possessions. But then, given the sheer quantity of shoes, clothes, expensive lingerie and cosmetics nearly bursting from the room, I doubted even the grandest palazzo could have held it all.

'She says we're early,' Jack said into the sudden silence.

'I thought she didn't know we were coming.'

'No, I mean early in the morning.'

I looked at my watch. It was nearly ten.

'Late night?'

'Looks like it. And,' he listened, 'not a solo one, either.'

I could hear a male voice coming from the bedroom, rumbling low between Vallie's giggles and the slamming of wardrobe doors.

Jack flicked on the kettle. 'You been to Italy before?'

I nodded. 'To Venice with my school, and then to Rome about a year ago.' My first assignment with SO17. Seriously, was that a whole year ago? 'What does Vallie do?'

He shrugged, opening cupboards and closing them again. There was little sign of any actual food. 'Something in fashion.'

Probably modelling. She was exquisite.

'So ... We're staying here?'

'Yep. She's going out this afternoon so we get the place to ourselves. Including her laptop.'

'Great. I've been meaning to check my *Buffy the Vampire Slayer* message boards,' I said sarcastically.

'To look up news articles. See if we can get into MI5 files.'

Am I the only person in the world who thinks that getting into highly confidential, madly protected, government files might be hard? Jack and Luke and Docherty all seemed to think it was a piece of cake.

Eventually Vallie wafted out, towing a handsome stubbled man who was about twice her size and looked me over before purring, '*Ciao, bella.*'

God, if he thought I was *bella* when he'd spent the night with Vallie, he really needed an eye test. Or maybe she was secretly covered in scales or something.

'Jack, Giovanni,' Vallie waved her hand between the two men and babbled a bit more. She gestured to me. 'Alice.'

The way she said it made the name sound very sexy. Maybe being an Alice wouldn't be so bad.

Giovanni took my hand and kissed it, murmuring things that I'm sure were quite inappropriate for someone whose girlfriend was standing right beside him.

Jack grabbed my hand and pulled it away, glaring at Giovanni. Oh yeah. I was supposed to be Jack's girlfriend.

'Nice to meet you,' I said primly, which Vallie and Giovanni seemed to think was hilarious.

Vallie said something to Jack that I think was along the lines of *We're off, ta ta*, and he responded in kind.

'*Ciao*, Alice,' she called, and Giovanni echoed it as the door shut behind them and Jack and I were left alone.

'Wow, he liked you,' Jack said, sounding surprised.

'You know, I used to be quite hot before all this.'

'Yeah,' he unearthed a laptop from under some debris on the table, 'sure.'

I flipped him the finger behind his back.

'Saw that,' he said.

'I was thinking a watch,' Angel chattered, as Luke carried

her bags through the busy shopping centre. 'Something classic. Something that will last. Something he can pass on to his son.'

'You're having a boy?'

'I have no idea. But there's always next time,' she sparkled.

Luke shook his head. 'Doesn't Harvey already have a watch?'

'Oh, yes, one of those boring practical ones. Shoots grapple hooks or emits toxic gas or something. I meant a proper watch.' She grabbed his wrist. 'What's yours?'

'Tag Heuer.' Another present from a dutiful relative. Luke was surprised they hadn't monogrammed it so he'd be stuck with the damn thing forever; but on second thoughts, they'd probably forgotten his initials.

'Beautiful. Do you think Harvey would like something like this?'

'I doubt it,' Luke said. 'Tag Heuers are for people of class and breeding.'

She bashed his arm. 'That's my husband you're talking about.'

'I know.' He grinned. Winding Angel and Sophie up about Harvey was always fun. The guy was just too good to be true. Nobody had the right to be handsome and smart and brave and nice all at the same time.

Luke would hold his hand up to the first three, but he'd never considered himself nice in any way.

'I'm just going to pop to the loo for a minute, okay?'

Luke nodded, and turned to idly gaze at the watches on display in the jewellery shop window. That one was too flashy. That one too dull. That one was too … *English* for Harvey. And that one was right next to the engagement rings.

When Angel reappeared, Luke was still staring at the shop window.

'Pretty rings,' Angel said, standing beside him.

He made a non-committal sound.

'I'm a diamond solitaire girl myself, but I think something more colourful would be Sophie's style. Sapphire or emerald. Perhaps a cluster.'

He stared determinedly at the display.

'White-gold would suit her. Her complexion's too cool for gold.'

'We need to look at watches,' Luke said, a shade coldly, and Angel, bless her heart, agreed with him instantly.

She bought Harvey his ludicrously overpriced watch – Luke seriously had no idea how much had been spent on his own but he honestly couldn't see the point of it – and dragged him round Mothercare before she finally admitted defeat. Luke smiled and chatted and explained to every single person they met that he was just a friend, and Angel didn't mention Sophie again.

But she was there, with them, all the time. She was there when Angel saw a pendant with a cat on it that Sophie would love. She was there when Luke saw a *Buffy* poster in the window of HMV. She was there when they passed the shoe department of John Lewis, from which Sophie had needed to be escorted many times before she spent her annual salary on frivolities she'd never wear.

She was there, heaped upon his heart, weighing down every smile he summoned up.

He drove home and packed Angel's bags into her Mini, helped her behind the wheel and stood waiting for her to close the door.

She bit her lip and looked up at him. 'Are you going to marry her?'

Luke stared at the car door and saw Sophie in white.

She was a lunatic. She had no prospects, even when she wasn't on the run. His family hated her. She was fast-mouthed and sharp-tongued and soft-hearted, and she'd turn his home into a lost-cat sanctuary given half a chance. She was young, irresponsible, bright, mad, and everything he'd spent his life ordering himself to believe he'd never wanted.

He nodded. 'Think I am.'

She smiled, not the girlish smile she'd been giving all day but an honest, tired, slightly watery smile.

'These hormones will make me cry,' she muttered. Louder, she said, 'Keep in touch, yes?'

Luke nodded again, and Angel drove away.

He let himself in, made two cups of coffee and took them down to the Ford parked outside.

'Here,' he said when the spooks inside wound down the window. 'Surveillance is boring as hell.'

Then he went back to his flat and stared at the wall until the white dress and the diamond ring faded from his vision.

I called Luke but his phone went straight to voicemail. Hoping this meant he'd turned it off for security reasons, and not that he'd lost it or the phone had been compromised, I left him a message about Jack and Irene Shepherd.

'We're safe for now,' I added. 'We ... we had to move on, but we're safe. I'm safe.' I paused. 'I love you.'

If I concentrated hard, I could almost hear him saying it back to me.

Jack stood at the stove, cooking something that smelled delicious. This was a new sensation for me. I sometimes cooked for myself, and sometimes for Luke too, but he always maintained he was terribly institutionalised and that his idea of cooking involved the defrost setting on the microwave. I suspected this was a lie, and he just did it to annoy me, but the fact remained that the only time I ever saw men cooking was on TV.

'So did you get anything?' I asked, gesturing to the laptop as we started eating.

'Got your detailed work history. Reads like a movie plot.'

'Thanks.'

'A bad movie. Have you ever met anyone you haven't ended up shooting?'

'You,' I said chasing a bit of pasta around the bowl, 'but the day is still young.'

He ignored this. 'What did you tell lover-boy?'

'You mean Luke? I told him our exact location. He's sending a task force out here to catch you.' I looked at my watch. 'Should be here in five.'

'That's not funny.'

'Who said I was joking?' I sighed. 'You done with that laptop?'

'You cannot check your horoscope.'

'I want to look up some news sites.'

He gestured to me to use it, and I flexed my hacking fingers.

Unfortunately, while I am perfectly willing to work alongside computers, they hate me with a passion. Even Italian ones. I had to stumble through the language options and switch settings to English before I could make sense of anything, and even when I'd done that I could find out nothing useful. I ran a search for Irene Shepherd, but all I got was that she'd been found dead two weeks ago in her home in Connecticut, shot in the head by a gun that was found at the crime scene and registered to one Jack de Valera, a British-born bounty hunter whose beat was miles away in Ohio.

A thought occurred to me, and I reached for the little care package Docherty had sent me. Fingertip and iris scans in America. A crime scene in America.

Slowly, I typed in a few search terms. I'd need 72 hours'

notice to get an ESTA visa waiver to get into America, but once I'd got it, it was valid for two years.

Please God, I wouldn't still be in need of it by then.

Quietly, without quite knowing why, I applied for authorisation.

To cover my silence, I asked Jack, 'What were you even doing in Connecticut?'

'I wasn't. I was in Ohio.'

'But you said you went to see Irene. And she was found dead in Connecticut. And I might be a little shaky on American geography, but I'm really pretty sure they're quite far apart.'

Jack blinked and slowly set down his coffee. 'I went to see her, and then I left and got on a plane, and when I landed I found out my gun had never got on the plane with me.'

I shook my head, my airport training taking over automatically. 'That's impossible. You handed your gun in at check-in, yes? Then the police –'

' – were obviously intercepted by someone who got a hold of it and took it back to Irene's house and shot her with it.'

'While you were on the plane?' I asked. 'That's what we call an "alibi".'

'Yeah – it's funny, but records for that flight seem to have vanished in some kind of computer glitch. That's what we call a "set-up". I got on another plane and left the country.'

I whistled. Whoever had done this was good. Scarily good. 'You didn't stay and try to figure out what had happened?'

'Neither did you.'

'Yes, but I knew MI5 was involved.'

'Irene Shepherd was a Supreme Court Judge. And you must have seen the cop movies,' Jack picked up his coffee again, 'these guys forget which order they're supposed to put the shooting and the asking of questions in.'

I made a face and went back to my search. And, I don't

know, maybe Google doesn't like me, because I found nothing.

Luke, on the other hand, had been luckier.

'So who's this guy you've been spending all your time with?' was his greeting when I answered my phone.

'What, Jack? Oh, just some good-looking young bounty hunter I picked up in France.' I leaned back and sipped my coffee. 'Very good in bed. You'd like him.'

'You're not half as funny as you think you are.' There was real bitterness in his voice. I took pity on him.

'I couldn't be. Look, he's Maria's little brother, all right? We're in the same boat, we might as well, um, paddle it together.'

'I don't like him,' said Luke stubbornly.

'This time yesterday you'd no idea he existed.'

'Still don't like him.'

'Jealous,' I scoffed, with no small measure of delight.

'Damn right. Should be me spending every hour, every minute with you, Soph. Not some bloody lunatic bounty hunter on the run.'

'It's fine, Luke. Really. He's just helping me out. Don't you trust me?'

A pause, then he sighed and said, 'Of course I trust you. I love you. I'm just a bit stressed here, all right?'

I let that one slide, in light of the L-word and all. 'Did you find out anything about Jack and this Judge Shepherd?'

'Yes, and I want you to appreciate that it wasn't easy. The FBI have leapt on this just like 5 have over here.'

'You have friends in the FBI?' I asked.

'No, I hacked in,' he said distractedly.

'Yeah, 'cos that's not hard,' I mocked.

'Not for me. Okay, here we go. I have to tell you, Soph, it doesn't look good.' I heard paper rustling. 'Basically, there's evidence of him all over. Fingerprints, saliva on a coffee cup, a couple of hairs on the carpet. The external camera has him arriving and leaving a few hours later. Internal cameras have been, of course, wiped.'

'When was she killed?'

'Not a hundred percent sure, she wasn't found until the next morning, but it was likely while your friend was there.'

'But Luke, come on. This is ridiculous. The gun was still there, for God's sake. They might as well have scrawled, *It was me, I dunnit* all over the walls in blood and signed it at the bottom.'

Luke was silent a few seconds, digesting this. 'I don't know where your mind has been the last week,' he said. 'And besides, are we talking about you or Jack here?'

I looked around to make sure Jack was still in the shower and hadn't crept up behind me.

'Both. Luke, it's all so fake.'

'MI5 don't seem to think so.'

'Great.' I slumped in my chair. 'Okay, look. What do you have on Irene Shepherd?'

He sighed and I could hear him flicking through papers. 'Irene Shepherd. Aged 63, never married, no children. Lived alone in a great big McMansion in Hartford, Connecticut. Found by her daily maid who came as usual at eight in the morning. Appointed seven years ago after ten years' legal practice in New York and five in England ... Harvard educated, fourteen honorary doctorates ... when not on duty at the Bar, lectured at Harvard. Great respect, good reputation, excellent lawyer and judge ... yada yada yada ...'

Fourteen doctorates. I have five A levels and I think that makes me smart. Okay, so half of them are essentially all from the same drama course, but I thought it was pretty clever of me to figure out the loophole that let me do that.

'So no enemies?'

'None that anyone can come up with. And believe me,

these guys have everything. They have the addresses of all her friends, ex-boyfriends, employers and employees. Half of them have been pulled in for interviews and some are even being tailed.'

I sighed. 'But ... I mean, if she was a judge, she must have passed sentence a few times, right?'

'You'd think so.'

'So, I don't know, there must be a few ex-cons who don't like her?' I drummed my fingers. 'How long does a Supreme Court Judge serve for? Is it a lifetime position?'

'Ten years,' Jack said, coming silently out of the bathroom and making me jump. I hadn't even heard the shower stop. I looked up and he was wearing a white towel – just a towel – that made his skin look very dark. And wet. And ...

I have a boyfriend. I love Luke. Very much. And I really need to stop looking at Jack's abs.

'Listen,' I said to Luke in a slightly shaky voice, 'I'm going to go and look some of this up online.'

'You think you can get better out of Google than I did from the Bureau?'

'Talk to Harvey. See what he can find out. Access Ohio records or something.'

'Ten-Four, kemosabe.'

'What does that even mean?' I asked, smiling.

'If I told you, I'd have to kill you. I'll speak to you later, okay?'

'Okay. Bye,' I said, and ended the call before I got all mushy in front of Jack.

'Ohio?' Jack asked, still standing there looking hot in his towel.

'I'm checking you out,' I said, and immediately wished I'd said something else. 'Your record. Irene Shepherd.'

'You won't find anything,' Jack said, looking through his bag for clothes.

'Already have,' I replied smugly.

'On me?'

'No, her.'

'You won't get anything on me.'

'That's not the same as having nothing to get, is it, Jack?'

Jack said nothing.

Chapter Six

Are you going to marry her?

He'd never before considered that he might ever marry anyone. In his entire life, Luke had never had anything that might be termed a relationship with anyone. He had affairs with women that were purely about sex, and he had professional acquaintances, but he didn't have friends and the less said about his family the better.

A few months ago the thought of marrying anyone, even Sophie, would have been laughable. But then she'd left him and the ache he'd felt for her was unbearable. She'd said she wanted to focus on her career, and Luke couldn't find a good enough argument against that. After all, wasn't that what he'd spent his own life focusing on?

But he'd missed her. Missed her terribly. And when she'd confessed to him how ill she'd been after those bloody kids tried to OD her, his heart had stopped beating for a moment. *She was hurt and I wasn't there. She could have died and I wasn't there.*

He stared at the ceiling, sleep utterly evading him. *Are you going to marry her?*

She wore his ring already. Wore it every day, and apparently had no idea he'd bought it as an engagement ring. In the rush of terrifying emotion that followed 'I love Sophie,' he'd got so caught up in ridiculous fantasies that when he saw the ring and knew it would be perfect for her, he'd bought it and got as far as planning his proposal before he realised what he was doing.

Three months' absence had him doing foolish things. And now a week's absence had him going down the same path. He couldn't ask Sophie to marry him. Not really. Much as he hated to admit it, Evelyn was right, and he couldn't have a personal life. Neither could Sophie, if she was going to stay in the same game as him.

Except it wasn't that. Not really.

'You,' Sophie had said to him once, 'have all the interpersonal skills of a speeding bullet.' And he'd been angry at the time, but she was right. He'd spent his life ruthlessly repressing every emotion that came his way, and thanks to his family, the one he'd been most successful with was love. And now Sophie had prised that out of him, and he didn't know how to control it.

He'd already jeopardised his career in the name of love. Pretty soon the rest of his life would career out of control. Rashly falling to one knee might seem like the right thing to do now, but it would be like making decisions while drunk. He couldn't trust his own judgement.

Luke lay awake, staring at the ceiling, waiting for his feelings to go away.

I hugged myself under the thin duvet, imagining Luke's arms around me as I slept, his body warming me, his breath on my neck. I felt complete when he held me. Revoltingly, sappily, disgustingly complete. I imagined his long, clever fingers stroking my arms, his warm lips brushing my neck, and I turned in his embrace, feeling the heat of his body against mine. He held me close and lifted his mouth from my neck and kissed me, and then I knew.

I knew I wasn't dreaming it, and I knew it wasn't Luke.

I yanked my head back so quickly I almost got whiplash. Eyes suddenly wide open, I stared at Jack.

'You're not Luke,' I said, and the sleepy look on his face vanished.

'No, I'm really not.'

'I thought you were Luke,' I stammered, lifting a hand to

wipe his taste from my mouth and yelping when I realised where said hand had just been. And then I noticed that Jack's hands were in even more inappropriate places, and I shoved him away, doing my best to leap out of Vallie's sofa bed in an affronted manner and managing to scramble around, getting tangled up in my pyjamas, before hitting the TV in the corner and ricocheting onto the tiny square of floor space not covered by furniture.

Jack glared at me.

'You thought I was him.'

'Well, duh.' I pushed my hair out of my eyes and fought to get upright. 'Why else would I have been kissing you?'

'You hardly kissed me,' Jack said, and I nodded violently.

'No. Right. I didn't. No kissing went on. I want that in writing.'

'Kissing sort of went on,' Jack mumbled, flopping on his back and glowering at the ceiling.

'You started it.'

'I started it? You were the one getting all snuggly and, and touchy,' he accused.

'I'm sorry.' I even had my hands on my hips at this point. 'I'm not used to sleeping with men who aren't Luke. I woke up with you and just sort of assumed –'

'Oh, you *assumed*? Well, you can *assume* this. There's a chair. Looks comfy, don't it. Savvy?'

And with that he spread himself in the middle of the bed and closed his eyes determinedly.

Bastard.

I looked at the chair, which hadn't even been comfortable to sit in. It was way too minuscule to actually sleep in.

I crawled into it and tried to make myself comfortable. Fat chance. It was like sleeping in a hamster-sized hammock.

Now that I was looking at the bed with only one person

in it, it looked ridiculously big. Surely we could both sleep in it and not touch?

But hadn't that been the plan last night? Even in my sleep, I was managing to get into trouble.

I sighed loudly, stretched my legs out on the sofa bed, kicking Jack as I did, and closed my eyes. It was a long time until morning.

He woke alone after about an hour's sleep, and continued to stare at the ceiling.

The loft apartment had exposed beams and high apexes. Luke had painted the walls magnolia and exposed plain oak floorboards. His bedlinen was high quality and very plain, as was every other bit of furniture in the place. His clothes were hidden in bespoke wardrobes and drawers. His books, films and music were ordered and shelved in the living room. His open-plan kitchen was a symphony of oak and marble and steel.

It was calm, ordered, simple.

A few weeks ago he'd caught Sophie staring at the exposed beams with a calculating look in her eye. 'I'd paint them,' she said. 'Did you know, the Tudors used to paint every available surface? All those stylised designs. You could have a frieze of roses or ivy all along there,' she pointed to the beam above the bed, 'or even real ivy – silk stuff anyway – and tiny little lights. And a tapestry on the wall. And a patchwork quilt on the bed.'

Luke had simply stared at her until a pink flush crept over her cheeks.

'Well, that's what I'd do, anyway.'

Her own bedroom was a riot of pink and purple, swags of fabric and trails of glittering fairy lights. Scented candles and half-used pots of moisturiser cluttered every surface. She'd painted a mural of giant mad daisies on the wall of her living room, and piled mounds of cushions everywhere. The kitchen was a 1970s' nightmare of melamine and linoleum, the cupboards disorganised and half-full of food well past its sell-by date. Her bathroom was a demilitarised zone of towels and bottles and make-up, scattered everywhere, spilling over onto each other, barely a square inch of floor or shelf space visible.

Luke had carefully designed his apartment to be clean, calm and sleek. Sophie's flat was what madness looked like.

He stared at the ceiling, and it was boring as hell.

It was Sunday morning, but that didn't really make much difference to Luke any more. He didn't have any hobbies and he didn't go to church. He'd had his fill of shopping with Angel.

He'd spent the rest of Saturday researching Irene Shepherd, and trying to work out whether he was worried by Sophie telling him, 'We're safe.' *We.* Sophie and Jack were not a 'we'. Sophie and Luke weren't even a 'we'. Sophie hated 'we'. She thought it was smug and annoying.

He swung out of bed with a sigh. He hadn't spoken to Sophie since yesterday and he'd exhausted all avenues of investigation last night. The only connection he'd found between Sir Theodore and Irene Shepherd was that they'd once worked at the same law firm, but it was highly tenuous and he didn't really believe Sophie's idea that the two murders were connected.

He didn't believe she could trust Jack. Hell, look at the messes she'd made before, trusting the wrong men. She'd nearly been drugged and raped a year ago, all because she fancied some Norwegian tosser, and the less said about the fiasco concerning Docherty the better. The fact that she'd shot both of them didn't make him feel any better.

Luke wasn't entirely convinced that her judgement had improved when it came to himself.

He wandered into his living room and glanced out of the window. The silver Ford was gone. He looked up and down the street and registered every vehicle there.

Two hours later, they were all gone. Nothing parked outside his house for the rest of the day that shouldn't be there.

He ought to have felt elated, but it was despair that overtook him.

He dialled Evelyn's number. 'Who have 5 got on Sophie's case?' he asked without preamble.

'I'll just look into that for you,' she said in a smooth voice. He heard computer keys tapping and Sheila's voice in the background. 'Is it all right if I call you back with the information?'

She ended the call, and five minutes later his phone rang again.

'She was right behind me,' Evelyn said. 'Are you all right?'

'Bloody marvellous,' Luke said flatly. He didn't bother to ask why Evelyn was in the office on a Sunday. Terrorists didn't work office hours – which was just damn rude of them – which meant the security services often didn't, either. 'Who do 5 have on the case?'

Her voice dropped. 'I'm not even supposed to know this,' she said, 'but a friend of mine is support staff there and –'

'*Evelyn.*'

'Harrington,' she said.

His stomach dropped. 'Robert Harrington?'

'You know him?'

Luke punched the wall. The plaster cracked, his knuckles bled, but he didn't feel pain in his hand. He felt it in sharp, icy spears through his heart and his gut.

He felt fear, barbed and spiky, eating him from the inside.

Robert Harrington, MI5's pit-bull. He'd hunt Sophie down and then he'd snap her in his jaws and shake her until she stopped screaming. He was a patriot, the kind who viewed any threat as a personal insult. He was so horrifyingly loyal to the Service that he truly didn't understand the meaning of leniency.

He'd taken the surveillance away from Luke's house. He thought Sophie was never coming back.

'Luke?'

'I know him,' he said, surprised his voice came out so normal. Then, because even if Evelyn was hiding somewhere, somebody would still probably be listening in, he added, 'He's very good at what he does.'

He ended the call and his phone bounced on the floor.

Harrington.

Shit.

I don't know what I did all night, except that it wasn't sleep. I counted sheep and ran through times tables in my head (getting stuck at about seven; I blame the school system for allowing us calculators). I tried to get all of England's monarchs in chronological order, with dates too, and sometimes even spouses (can anyone remember which one was Catherine Parr and which one was Catherine Howard? And how lazy was old Henners for marrying three women with the same damn name?). And then some time after the sky got light, I drifted away.

It seemed like about ten seconds before I felt someone touch my face, and I sleepily still thought it was Luke, smiling and snuggling up to his hand before I remembered, and opened my eyes, and saw Jack peering at me, looking stony.

'Vallie's up,' he said. 'I heard her go in the bathroom.'

'So?'

'So, next she'll come in here, and if she sees you in that chair, she'll know something's up.'

Sighing, I remembered that there was a pretence to be kept up here. I crawled back into the bed and turned my back on Jack, facing the wall, as far away as I could be without falling off the edge.

'Why is she even up so early, anyway?'

'Sunday. Church.'

'You don't go?'

'Not unless someone's died.'

The sofa bed wasn't the most comfortable mattress in the world, but after the chair it was heaven. It was warm and soft, and I was drifting away as Vallie opened the door, looked in and smiled at us. She waved and whispered, '*Ciao*,' and then the front door clicked shut.

I closed my eyes and slept.

When I woke again the sun had changed its angle and the air was scented with coffee. I groggily checked my watch. It was mid-afternoon.

Rolling over, I found Jack sitting up in bed, fully dressed, laptop on his knees.

'Morning,' he said, not looking at me.

'Afternoon,' I corrected.

'Whatever.' He frowned at the screen.

I sat up. 'Good read?'

'Very. Irene Shepherd worked at an English law firm for five years before she went back to America.'

'I know,' I yawned. 'Luke told me.'

'Did he tell you the firm she worked for was Barton, Barton, Chesshyre and Holt?'

I blinked at him. 'When you say Chesshyre you're not spelling it like the county, are you?'

'Nope. Your Sir Theodore was a partner, before he jacked it in to do something shadowy for the Home Office. He gave her glowing references. Apparently they were good friends.'

'That's nice. They can share a table in heaven. I don't

get this connection. Why should two people who worked together ten years ago be killed now? Have they seen each other since?'

'I don't know.' He looked at me. 'We'd have to find out.'

I didn't like that look. That look said something bad was following.

'And how are we going to find out?' I asked.

'Firstly we check airline records.' I relaxed. I could do that standing on my head. 'Then we go and ask the people at Barton, Barton and Holt. I'm guessing they'll have taken the Chesshyre out by now.'

I started to feel a little ill. 'And where are their offices?'

'In the grand old city of London.'

Figured.

'Um, I don't know how you feel about this,' I said, 'but I sort of left the country for a reason. Like, people are after me. People in London.'

'People who think you're in France,' Jack said. 'Unless your boyfriend has told anyone your alias?'

'No,' I said firmly. Luke would never do that.

Although Docherty knew it, too …

'Look, London is the most surveillanced city in the world,' I said. 'They have facial recog software everywhere. Don't you watch *Spooks*?'

Jack gave me an incredulous look.

'I'm just saying, there's a huge amount of surveillance there. The odds of the two of us – both wanted for murders which I'm pretty sure MI5 will have worked out by now are connected – just wandering around without being found? Come on, Jack.'

'Wear a hoodie,' was his advice.

'I never wear hoodies,' I began, 'they make me look so chavvy –'

Then I paused. I never wore hoodies for the same reason I

never wore hoop earrings or scraped my hair back. You can take the girl out of Essex but you can't take the Essex out of the girl.

'I don't like that look,' Jack said. 'That's a calculating look.'

'Do you think Vallie would mind if I borrowed a bit of make-up?' I asked distantly.

'Don't reckon it'd suit you. She's Italian and you look like you're made out of milk.'

'Yes,' I said, 'exactly.' My gaze snapped back to him. 'How long would it take you to grow a beard?'

He raised his eyebrows. 'Does this mean we're going to London?'

I chewed my lip. Part of me just wanted to see if I could get away with it. Part of me knew it was the only logical place to go. The rest of me screamed that it was a really bad idea.

'Right,' Jack said, taking my hesitation as agreement. 'We can get a flight out of Milan in a couple of hours –'

'Wait, what about the car?'

'The car will have to stay here.'

'What about the guns?'

Jack paused. 'Shit,' he said, and I smiled a little triumphantly. Not too triumphantly, however – I didn't want to leave my guns behind. We couldn't just chuck them in our luggage – that was what scanners were for. Nor could we check them in as licensed firearms. I had one gun registered as destroyed, and one not registered at all. I didn't know what Jack's arrangements were, but I had a feeling they were along the same lines.

'Then we drive,' he said. 'Get a ferry. It'll take longer.'

'You think?'

'But they hardly ever check private cargo. You have a British passport and mine is French. We'll be fine.'

Yeah, right.

Vallie and Giovanni were out at some party in the afternoon, so the flat was empty as Jack put our things in the car and I did a little light pilfering of Vallie's cosmetics. Jack was right, and none of her make-up suited me, but after I'd given myself a tide-mark around the jaw from her foundation, put on too much blusher and so much mascara my eyelids started to ache, I was on my way to looking like a different person.

I added the biggest hoop earrings I could find from Vallie's extensive collection and slicked back my hair into a very short ponytail. Chav central.

'You look like crap,' Jack said.

'Aha,' I replied, 'but do I usually look like crap?'

He opened his mouth, then thought better of his reply and just shrugged.

'Wise answer,' I said, and went into the kitchenette to assemble what food I could. It had taken nearly a whole day for me to drive the length of France last week, and that was without the journey over the Alps that we had to take now. In my estimate, it would take at least a day and a half, maybe more.

I stepped out of the kitchen to find Jack going through his cousin's handbag. He extracted a cash card and continued looking for something else.

'What are you doing?'

'PIN number.'

'What? She's not going to have –' I broke off as he pulled out a bit of paper with numbers written all over it.

'Vallie's as sweet as she is pretty,' he said, 'but she's not the brightest crayon in the box.'

'Are you going to steal her money?'

'No. I'm just going to borrow it.'

'Won't she miss it?'

Jack looked at me as if I was simple. 'She's a PR and

part-time model. She exists on freebies. She won't even look for her purse for days. It's fine.' I frowned, but picked up the pen resting by the whiteboard in Vallie's little kitchen. '*Ciao e grazie*,' I wrote, 'J&A x.'

Then we got in the car, and drove.

I woke, for the second time, in Jack's arms. At least we weren't kissing this time, though. I don't know, maybe there's some sort of natural instinct that makes you cuddle up to someone else in your sleep. It felt nice to be held, even if I did wish that the holder was someone else.

Jack was solid and warm, but he didn't feel like Luke. He smelled nice, or at least as nice as you can after a day-and-a-half of driving, but he didn't smell like Luke.

We were at a motorway services motel, about thirty miles south of London. Luke lived thirty miles north of the city. Every now and then he made vague, non-committal noises about moving somewhere closer to the SIS building, noises which I usually responded to by telling him he'd see a lot less of me if he did. I could be there in a couple of hours, be there in his arms, kissing him, touching him …

I gave my head a mental shake. This wasn't good. I couldn't just go back to Luke's, that was insane. Someone would see. There'd be people watching his flat.

I moved to get out of bed, but Jack held me tighter. It was nice, but not right.

'Jack,' I said quietly, then louder, 'Jack. Let me go. I need to get up.'

His eyes fluttered open. 'No kissing this morning?' he asked, his voice soft and sleepy.

'No. No kissing. Can I get up?'

He released me and I scrambled out of bed, trying not to flash my underwear and failing somewhat. Jack was watching me, smiling.

'What?'

'You were never a natural blonde, then?'

I scowled at him and locked myself in the bathroom. The shower water was hot and I stood under it for hours, brushing away any guilt at the thought of depriving Jack of hot water with the memory of him perving at me. A gentleman wouldn't look, and he certainly wouldn't comment.

Luke would, but then he is a bit of a bastard.

Hair washed, legs and underarms and then bikini line, too, shaved, I wrapped one big white towel around my head and the other around my body. Jack would just have to whistle for a towel.

He wasn't there when I came out, and I gratefully pulled on clean clothes in privacy, put on my chav make-up, and dragged my wet hair back into its Croydon facelift style.

Jack wandered back in as I stood poking out my tongue at my ugly reflection.

'If the wind changes,' he began.

'The wind already has,' I said glumly. I glanced at the papers he'd thrown on the bed. 'What's occurring in the real world?'

'Footballer scandals, trouble in the Middle East, politicians lying through their teeth,' Jack said.

'*Plus ça change*,' I said. 'There's nothing about Sir Theodore?'

'Nope. You can check if you want.'

'No, ta.'

My stomach let out a loud growl, and I recalled that all I'd really consumed in the last twenty-four hours was a bit of service-station food and a lot of coffee. Jack raised his eyebrows at me.

'Well, seeing as you've slept with me twice,' I said, 'I think it's only decent of you to buy me breakfast.'

He gave me a glimmer of a smile. 'I don't have any sterling.'

'Me, neither.'

'There's a bureau de change on the concourse.'

'Excellent. You can change some of Vallie's money.'

But when we came out of the café where we had breakfast and crossed back to the motel, an interesting thing happened.

Luke's car exploded.

It really just blew up. Flames and everything. The car next to it erupted, but thankfully we'd parked at the end of the row, next to a grass bank, so nothing else caught fire. Just Luke's Vectra, and an Audi with a whooping, bleeping alarm.

Jack and I stood and stared.

'That was our car,' he said.

'That was Luke's car,' I said.

'This is not good.'

'He's going to kill me.'

'It was only a Vectra.'

'He's going to *murder* me.' Then a more pressing concern nudged through the fog inside my head. 'Jack, someone followed us!'

Jack glanced at me. 'You have your gun?'

I nodded. I was wearing a seldom-used brace under my fleece. Highly illegal, but not high on my list of worries.

'We need to go and get our stuff from the room and get out of here.'

'We need stuff?' I asked, thinking of the old advice they used to give about not stopping to collect your belongings in an emergency.

'Passport, money? Stuff like that?'

'Oh. Yeah. Right.' Thank God I'd been too tired to be sensible last night and had neglected to lock it in the car.

Jack shook his head at me and walked across the car park, ignoring all the people pouring out of the motel and service station, staring at the two burning cars. Someone raced past us, screaming, 'My car! What happened to my car?'

'That is one unhappy Audi driver,' I observed.

'Ex-Audi driver,' Jack corrected, as we went inside and turned down the corridor to our room. I wondered if he was going to go all American cop show on me and hold his gun ready before bursting into the room, yelling 'Freeze!', but all he did was put the key card in the door with one hand and reach under his jacket with the other, ready to bring out his gun.

He nodded at me, and I nervously reached for my SIG. My gun still scared me. Mostly because I'd seen what it could do.

Jack pushed the door open, keeping well out of range of anything that could come from within.

Nothing came.

He pointed to my handbag and gestured for me to hold it out in front of the door. I did, wincing in advance, but again nothing happened.

Jack stepped into the room and I heard him moving around. Then he said, 'It's clear,' and I began breathing again. I went in and looked around. Everything was the same.

'Anything missing?' he asked.

I shook my head, looking through my case. 'Anything extra?' I asked, and Jack started scanning under the bed, the desk, the sink in the bathroom.

'I don't think so. We need to get out of here anyway,' he said, and I nodded and tipped my few remaining belongings back into my case. Seems wherever I go, I'm taking less with me. I'd brought all my essentials in with me, now that I was staying in a secure, locked-up place. In safe old England.

Outside, fire engines had arrived and were tackling the blaze. We went past, me silently apologising to Luke, and slipped onto the concourse where Jack called for a taxi to take us to the nearest train station.

In the back of the car, he took my phone from me and examined it from the inside out.

'What are you looking for?'

He glanced at the driver, who was listening to Bhangra music at earsplitting levels. 'Bug.'

'You think someone was tracing us?'

'Could be.' He frowned at the phone. 'I don't know.'

'Bottom line is, we need to lose these.' He got out his own. 'Fast.'

Without another word, he opened the back window and chucked both mobiles out onto the hard shoulder, where they smashed into lots of little pieces.

'Are you mad?' I twisted round in my seat and stared at the rapidly disappearing wreckage. The blast of a car horn behind us roused the cabbie long enough to glance back at the bits of plastic littering the road.

'There was a spider on it,' I said impatiently, and rounded on Jack. 'How am I supposed to –'

'Talk to your boyfriend? You'll have to do without,' Jack said, and I sulked. It made sense – someone had found us in France, and then again this morning. They could have been tracking the car, but even so ...

'Do you think someone was watching us?' Jack said.

'No,' I said, more to reassure myself than him. 'How could they know where we were? It must have been set ... before ...' I trailed off as I tried to work out where and when. Shit, it was more likely someone *had* been following us. 'Must have been on a timer,' I said firmly. 'If we hadn't got up so late we could be dead by now.'

'Thought you were used to near-death experiences.'

'You never get used to near-death experiences.'

Jack gave me a little smile, and it occurred to me that it had been only four days since he nearly drowned, and since then we'd driven practically non-stop, hardly eaten properly, little chance to rest. When I nearly drowned I hardly got out of bed for three days.

'Are you okay?' I asked. 'You know, since Friday night and all.'

He shrugged. 'I'm okay.'

Macho.

'How do you stop a man from drowning?' I asked, and Jack frowned.

'Get him out of the water and do mouth-to-mouth?'

'Take your foot off his head.'

He stared at me for a minute, then he looked away. But I could tell he was smiling.

The shock of crowds and noise that was London hit me hard. So many people, so many cars, the constant rattle and prattle wearing on my nerves. Every accidental touch made me jump, every unexpected noise. The Underground train, all those hundreds of people pretending there was no one else there, seemed like an oasis of peace and quiet despite the shriek of the train on its tracks.

We left South Kensington station and followed the directions Jack had found to BBC&H. I watched him trot up the well-kept steps and hung back, staring appalled at the shiny brass, the discreet door plaque, the heavy velvet drapes I could see inside.

'Aren't you coming?' Jack said.

'Have you seen me lately?' I said, peering at my reflection in a window. Suddenly my chav plan didn't seem like such a good idea.

'Yeah, you're being a chav.'

'Exactly. Do you think this place looks like it deals with chavs?'

He came back down. 'Well, it was *your* idea.'

I looked at Jack, who hadn't shaved in days and looked

in desperate need of a haircut. I looked down at myself in jeans and trainers.

'How far is Oxford Street?' I asked.

An hour later, courtesy of the cosmetics counter in Selfridges, I was de-chavved and looking more groomed than I ever have in my life. I know I'm old enough to have realised this by now, but it's amazing what make-up can do for you. There was a stand selling reading glasses, and I bought a pair with the lowest prescription: any sort of furniture to make my face look different. I bought a trilby to cover my flat hair and vowed to find a new way of styling it soon. Then I let myself loose in the clothes department.

Luke was right: I was far more dangerous armed with money than with a gun. It was a damn good job Vallie didn't pay close attention to her bank account. And, hey, at least I was putting the money back into the fashion industry whence it came, yes?

Outside, only a few minutes late, I looked for Jack. I'd told him to make himself look respectable, so I wasn't sure I'd recognise him and –

Whoa.

I was beginning to wonder if Jack really was a threat. He might not have designs on my life, but he sure seemed bent on becoming the good-looking man in my life.

He wore glasses too, and a three-piece suit that might have been made for him. His hair had been slicked back and although he hadn't shaved, he looked so glossy in every other respect that his stubble looked utterly designer. Every woman, and quite a few men, ogled him.

I tapped him on the shoulder and he turned with a look of surprise on that very pretty face of his.

'You look ...' His eyes travelled over me, and I raised an eyebrow, waiting for his comment on my sharply tailored suit and vertiginously beautiful heels. 'Different. Come on.'

Annoyed that he hadn't been more complimentary, I told him to make himself useful and flag down a taxi. Good-looking man, indeed. I wasn't feeling even slightly warm towards him now.

He did, and when we got out at BBC&H, I told the driver to wait for us with our luggage.

'Are you crazy?' Jack said. 'That'll cost a fortune –'

'We won't be in there long,' I said, smoothing down my skirt and trying not to think about how much it had cost. 'Trust me, we won't.'

He frowned, but followed me in. The lobby was very expensive and tasteful, and I straightened my back and pretended my suit was Gucci and my shoes were Prada. My hair was by Michaeljohn and my make-up Chanel. I was rich and important.

'May I help you?' asked the rather immaculate receptionist, and I had no doubt that her designer stuff wasn't imaginary.

I am wearing Prada, I am wearing Prada, I am wearing Prada …

'Hi,' I smiled, channelling Julia Roberts. 'I need to talk to one of your partners.' She opened her mouth to tell me they were all very busy, and I added, 'About Sir Theodore Chesshyre and Irene Shepherd.'

That shut her up.

'Mr Barton is currently out of the country,' she said, looking apologetic and even a little afraid, 'and Mr Holt is in a client meeting in Chelsea …'

'I believe there are two Bartons here?'

'Ms Barton is in court for the rest of today,' the receptionist said, looking at a huge computer screen, annoyingly angled away from us. 'But she is available tomorrow at … ten a.m.?'

I looked at Jack as if to say, What do you think? He frowned.

'Ten will make it a bit tight,' he said. 'Eleven?'

'Ten-thirty?'

'Ten-thirty will do fine.' I smiled, and turned to leave.

'Excuse me, miss?' the receptionist called, and she was nearly smirking. 'Your name?'

I gave a cool smile. 'Julia –' dammit, nearly said Roberts there – 'Julia Gere.'

'Oh,' the receptionist said, 'of course. Miss Gere.'

'Ms,' I snapped. 'Ten-thirty.'

And I clicked out of the place on my sale-price shoes and got into my waiting taxi.

'What,' Jack asked, getting in after me, 'was that?'

I smiled as elegantly as I could, which is to say a manic cheesy grin, 'cos I was damn pleased with myself. 'I didn't take A level Drama for nothing.'

'Do you do this often?'

'I'm a little bit out of practice.'

'I'm impressed.'

I beamed.

'Where now?' the driver asked in a bored tone.

I looked at Jack. 'We could do with somewhere to stay tonight.' Again, the thought flashed into my mind that I was no more than an hour away from Luke. I shook myself and asked the driver to take us to the nearest chain hotel. He did, we checked in, and I kicked off my heels and flopped onto the bed.

'Did Luke's car really get blown up this morning?' I asked.

Jack nodded, unzipping his bag and taking something large and bulky out. Vallie's laptop.

'Did you nick that?' I asked in amazement.

'Borrowed it.'

'With her permission?'

'Ah, she won't mind. She's family.'

I tried to imagine my brother's reaction if I 'borrowed'

his computer and took it out of the country without asking. Not pretty.

My stomach growled. It was getting late, and all that acting had made me hungry.

'Did I see a McDonalds on the way in?' I wondered out loud.

'I don't know. Did you?'

I nodded thoughtfully. 'You want anything?'

Jack shrugged. 'Cheeseburger and Coke.'

'Chips?'

He looked at me blankly.

'Fries. How long did you spend in Yankland?'

He ignored that. 'Cheeseburger, fries and a Coke. Do they supersize meals here?' I nodded. 'Supersize me.'

So many innuendoes, so little time.

I put my shoes back on and went out into the afternoon. There was a queue at McDonalds, made even longer by me having to wait for my veggie burger. On my way back, I spotted a phone shop and dashed in, bought a couple of phones, and made my way back to the hotel a happy little camper.

'Food,' I tossed Jack his meal, 'and phone.' I chucked him the box. 'Don't throw this one out of a window.'

He looked it over but said nothing, tearing into his food instead. Men.

I looked at him, sprawled on the bed in smart clothes, his tie loose around his neck, the white of the shirt making his skin look very dark. He looked gorgeous. He looked available. He looked like if I took the burger from his hands and kissed him, he wouldn't ask me to stop.

I finished my meal silently, thinking hard, and when I was done I washed my hands, took the two identical phones out of their boxes and programmed their numbers into each other.

'Jack,' I said, and he didn't reply. 'Jack?'

He was spread out across the bed, eyes closed, his lashes longer than mine. He was asleep.

I left his phone by the bed, removed the food wrappers and changed silently into my jeans and fleece. I tucked my gun into its hidden holster, my phone and my wallet into my bag, and left.

Chapter Seven

'You got anything new for me?'

Docherty paused. 'No.'

'I don't like that hesitation, Docherty.'

'I don't like that refrigerator you drive, Sharpe, but I don't complain about it.'

Luke ground his teeth. Outside, the streetlights flashed past, garish in the darkness. Currently he was driving a rental car, all the harder to trace. Sophie's car was too damn visible, not to mention torturously slow, and it almost certainly had been fitted with a tracker. He'd taken public transport to the airport, carefully ignored the check-in desks where he'd first met Sophie, and hired a Mondeo for twenty-four hours.

After that, he'd change it for a different car, with a different firm. Paranoia died hard.

'Have you heard from her?'

'Not lately.'

The really annoying thing about Docherty was that it was impossible to know if he was lying.

'She's probably not in France any more,' Docherty offered.

'Yeah, no kidding. What the hell is there for her in France?'

He drummed his fingers on the steering wheel. Chesshyre had been shot in London. He lived and worked in London. The sensible place for Sophie to be, if she was trying to get to the bottom of the case, was London. Hell, it was where Luke was.

He'd come begging to 5 for information, but Harrington wouldn't even see him.

He'd gone to BBC&H, the law firm that had employed both Shepherd and Chesshyre, but they'd remained tightlipped about the entire affair. Seemed someone else had already been enquiring there. On his way out of the law firm's office, he'd noticed a couple of men who hadn't been there when he went in, lounging around, looking as if they were poised to run.

Spooks.

Luke had got straight back in his car and turned himself homewards, seething.

London was a big enough place to swallow Sophie. Okay, so it was the most surveillanced city in the world, and not just by CCTV. On every street there were spies from every corner of the globe, watching and monitoring.

She might be able to go to ground here. But would she know how? Would she dare?

'She should be here,' he muttered, and Docherty, to his surprise, made a sound of sympathy.

'You miss her?'

'Of course I bloody miss her. She's my girlfriend. It'd be a pretty poor show if I hadn't noticed she'd gone.'

'She can take care of herself.'

'Can she?'

'Speaking as someone who's been rendered unconscious by her, yes, she can.' Docherty paused. 'You got anything from 5 yet?'

'Yes. Our friend Harrington is on the case.'

'Shit.'

'My sentiments exactly.'

'I'll see what I can do. Maybe spread some misinformation.'

'What, like that Sophie's back in the country?'

Docherty said nothing.

'Fuck me, Docherty, tell me she's not back in the country?'

'I couldn't tell you where she is,' Docherty said smoothly.

'That's not the same as not knowing, is it?'

'Not at all.'

The other really annoying thing about Docherty was that he knew more about Luke's girlfriend than Luke did. He knew where she was. He knew her alias and passport number. He had contacts Luke could only dream of.

You know the scent of her skin and the taste of her lips, he reminded himself, and saw red for a moment as he recalled that Docherty bloody knew those things, too.

'Call me if you get anything,' he said dispassionately, and dropped the phone onto the passenger seat.

He knew the scent of Sophie's skin and the taste of her lips. He knew that in unguarded moments she referred to herself as Tammy's mummy. He knew that she couldn't bear milk in coffee and that her hands ached when she was sad. He knew that she was beautiful, intelligent and funny, but that she only believed these things on rare occasions. He knew she was wildly jealous of her brother's ability to play the guitar and that she loved the smell of cold weather. He knew what she was proud of, and what made her ashamed.

He knew all these things about her, all the things that made her who she was.

But he still had no bloody clue what country she was in.

The flat was in darkness. I looked around carefully before I even turned the corner, but could see no car watching the place. No vehicles outside that didn't belong to either me or the roofer's yard below.

A pang of conscience poked at me as I thought about the fate of Luke's Vectra, but I pushed it aside. Tonight wasn't about cars.

I crept up the stairs, keeping to the shadows, and was about to punch in the code to disable the alarm when I realised it was offline.

Hell. Did this mean he'd been compromised?

With one hand I took my keys from my bag, and with the

other I reached for my SIG. The door swung open silently into darkness.

I could only see by the light from the open doorway and the window. I scanned what I could see of the room before I blocked the light from the door with my shadow. I could see no shapes there that weren't pieces of furniture.

Cautiously, heart pounding, I eased inside and closed the door as silently as I could. Silence enfolded me, thick and deafening –

– a tiny sound split it –

– and I pressed my hand to my heart in sheer relief.

'Tammy!'

She came trotting out of Luke's bedroom, eyes glowing in the dim light from the window. My gun clattered on the kitchen counter as I swung her up into my arms and hugged her close. My precious baby wriggled, squirmed, and then licked my nose.

'I missed you too, baby,' I said, hot tears burning my eyes.

Tammy swiped at my neck with her claws. I think that's the cat version of, 'I love you, Mummy.'

I let her down and switched on the light. Luke's flat looked exactly the same as always: neat, classy, devoid of personality. It was a beautiful space, but rather like Luke when I first met him. Desperately in need of someone to create some chaos.

I pinched the bridge of my nose and wondered if I should sweep for bugs. This posed several problems, not least of which was that I had no idea what a bug might actually look like.

Surely Luke would already have done this? Or, given that the alarm was disabled, maybe someone had come back and replanted them. I didn't know.

I turned a slow circle in the middle of the room. Nothing leapt out at me. I'd been here a good five minutes, and nobody had turned up outside. From here I could see into the bedroom and it, too, looked completely unchanged.

I waved at all four corners of the room. 'Anybody there?' I said out loud. 'Dudes, if you've been watching me this long and you haven't come bursting in with all guns blazing, then you're not the security service I thought you were.'

No response. Suddenly feeling horribly weary, I picked up my bag and gun and traipsed into Luke's bedroom.

His furniture in here was as expensive, classic and bland as in the living room, but here I could feel his presence. The slightly rumpled bedclothes. The jacket slung on a chair. By the bed was a paperback of essays on *Buffy the Vampire Slayer*.

I smiled. There was some teasing to be done about that.

The bed smelled of him. Luke wasn't really one for cologne, but when I laid my head on his pillow I could smell his shampoo and the spicy shower gel he used. I could smell him, the scent of his skin.

I closed my eyes, and breathed him in.

There was a light on in the flat. Luke's blood ran cold as he saw the warmth spilling out from the window.

Tammy could have stood on the floor switch for the standard lamp, but it wasn't likely. She barely weighed enough to trigger it.

He parked the car and waited for five cold, agonising minutes. Then he got out, gun in hand, and slipped quickly up the stairs, glancing about as he did. No unfamiliar vehicles. No one lurking in the shadows.

His heart pounded. He ignored it.

He put his key in the lock. Why the hell hadn't he reset the alarm? The door swung open and light glared out at him. Not the standard lamp. Kitchen lights. The bedroom door was closed and he knew he'd left it open.

Fear turned to a kind of sharp, vicious glee. How careless to leave the light on. He'd got them now. Harrington had sent someone to break in, which might be within his jurisdiction but sure as hell wasn't something Luke was going to let slide.

Quietly, very quietly, he closed the door behind him, then slid open a kitchen drawer and took out a set of plastic ties. He had handcuffs, but they were in the bedroom. These would do for now.

He padded to the bedroom door, took a breath and let half of it out.

Then he shouldered open the door and aimed his gun at the bed.

'Game's up,' he said. The light from the kitchen illuminated a figure lying on the bed, wrapped in a bulky fleece, head turned away from him. It flinched, but didn't move.

'Did Harrington send you?' he demanded.

'Don't shoot me,' she said, and Luke froze, every muscle in his body paralysed with shock.

She rolled over, hands up in a motion of surrender. 'Love of God, Luke, don't let me get this far and then shoot me yourself.'

He stared. The gun clattered on the floor unheeded. His voice came out on a wheeze. 'Sophie?'

'Yeah.' She looked up at him, eyes big and face pale, hair short and unfamiliar. Greedily, he took in every detail he could. Her hair was different, her eyes were darker, and she looked tired, but she was still the same. Still his Sophie.

His heart pounded. She was here. Sophie was here.

It was over.

Sophie stared at him hungrily, and he realised he probably wore the same expression as she did. That of a starving man faced with a big juicy steak. He could barely believe she was real.

'What are you doing here?'

'Passing through.'

His heart constricted. 'I thought you were in France.'

'Change of plan.'

It was hell being this close and not touching her. His fingers twitched with the need to memorise her skin. He ached for her. Questions could bloody wait.

He moved towards the bed and she met him halfway, arms flying around him, lips meeting his. Her soft body pressed against him and he held her tight, keeping her safe from harm. He kissed her, over and over, that amazing kiss which set him on fire, every time.

He came up for air but she kissed him again, which made him smile against her lips. His hands slid under her fleece and caressed her body through her t-shirt. She was hot, and soft, her curves wonderfully familiar.

'God, I've missed you,' he breathed when she let him go.

'Missed you more. Who's Harrington?'

He sighed, loosened his hold on her a little bit. 'The guy who's after you. MI5. Looks like a puppy dog but he's more like a pit-bull.'

'He's not watching this place, is he? I checked for surveillance but I wouldn't know a bug if it came up and bit me.'

He'd spent months trying to teach her. 'No. I hacked the bugs, they're showing looped footage when I'm not here. And I'm driving a rental car so it's harder to track.'

Sophie bit her lip. Her plump, luscious lip.

'What?' Luke asked guardedly.

'Erm, about your car …'

'You didn't leave it in France, did you? How did you get here?'

'Train.'

'Because …?'

'Your car kind of got slightly blown up this morning.'

Luke blinked. She offered him a contrite, I'll-make-it-up-to-you smile.

'Slightly?'

'Well, totally. Took out another car with it.'

Luke sat down on the bed, hard. 'You got my car blown up?'

She bit her lip again. 'Well, Jack might have got it blown up ...'

'Jack?' Another reason to hate the bastard. 'Where is he?'

'London.'

'You came here alone?'

She nodded, looking down at him anxiously.

Luke ran his hands through his hair and asked the question he'd been dreading. 'Why?'

Sophie sat down beside him and leaned her body against his. She stroked his cheek with one finger. 'To see you.'

Not because it's over. God bloody dammit.

Luke put his arms around her and held her very close. 'You know you shouldn't have?'

'I know.'

He sighed and kissed her neck, just below the ear. 'How long can you stay?'

Sophie closed her eyes. 'Long enough.'

I left him sleeping, looking twice as beautiful as Jack ever would, got dressed out in the living room where he wouldn't hear me, and left, kissing Tammy a tearful goodbye. Luke had explained that he'd made an emergency exit in the cupboard, and I dropped down into the roofer's warehouse.

'Blimey, love,' said one of them as I hit the ground and stepped on a bunch of pallets to replace the cover. 'Something wrong with the front door?'

'Just keeping a low profile,' I said. I hesitated, glancing up at the trapdoor, which was barely visible in its dark corner.

'You won't tell anyone it's there, will you?'

I widened my eyes appealingly. He grinned back at me.

'Not a soul.'

I started towards the exit, then paused. 'Uh, you haven't seen a strange car outside, have you? Or anyone loitering around?'

He shrugged. 'Oi, Baz,' he yelled, and a man carrying a dozen lengths of 2×4 as if they were matchsticks looked up. 'Seen anyone watching the place?'

'That Focus has been gone since the weekend.' His eyes rested on me. 'You hiding from someone?'

I bit my lip. 'Ex-boyfriend,' I said. 'He's been following me around. It's starting to get creepy.'

Both men looked outraged. 'Right,' Baz said. 'Come on, Tel.'

He and Tel marched outside. I hovered around the entrance of the building, watching them as they glared around the yard and then started out into the street.

Crap. There was a car parked there, a Mazda with a couple of shadowy figures inside. I hastily ducked back inside.

I heard someone hammering on glass, and then raised voices.

'… call the bloody police, mate –'

'We're just parked here!'

'Yeah? Got a car full of food and drink, 'ave you? To just park there?'

'Oi, Tel, he's brought a mate along with him.'

'Whatcha gonna do then, kidnap her? Is that it?'

'I told you, I have no idea what you're talking about …'

I smiled and sidled out to hide behind one of the vans. It wasn't long before one of the lads approached with a set of keys in his hand, looking surprised to see me.

'Hi,' I said. 'I need to get out of this yard without those

guys in the car over there seeing me. Ex-boyfriend,' I added. 'Baz and Tel are giving him what-for.'

The roofer glanced over and nodded. 'Baz's wife got stalked last year by her ex,' he said. 'You want a lift somewhere?'

I got him to drive me to the station, where I bought a ticket for the first train to London.

But as I stood on the chilly platform, surrounded by yawning commuters, the adrenaline rush of my escape wore off.

I huddled into my fleece, eyes leaking tears, wishing with everything I had that I could stay. Luke had begged me to. 'I'll hide you in the wardrobe when anyone comes round,' he said, an uncharacteristic desperation in his eyes. 'Smuggle food in. No one will know.'

I held him close and kissed his hair. 'You know I can't.'

'I don't want you to go again.'

'I'll be fine.'

'I want you here.'

And God, how I wanted to be there, too. Leaving was so damn hard. Luke looks so beautiful when he sleeps, so warm, so easy to touch. Sometimes I can't believe I'm allowed to touch him. He's a thousand times more sexy than I'll ever be. And he loves me. He told me so last night and I nearly stayed.

But there are other things I have to do. If I gave in to temptation I'd never leave and someone would find me and I'd go off to jail without a single chance to prove my innocence. And I know I'm innocent, I know it. I just have to make sure MI5, and whoever the hell else is chasing me, know it too.

I leaned my head against the window of the train as it pulled away. Around me, people read their papers and clattered on their laptops and started making important calls. I closed my eyes against it all, and saw –

– the bright blue of his eyes, the sheen of sweat on golden skin, the fine lines bracketing his mouth when he laughed, the curve of muscle. Fingers curved reflexively with the sense-memory of his firm flesh against my palm. The heat of his skin. The fine crisp hairs against my fingertips. The scent of him. The taste –

I should never have gone back.

London was cold and busy. I shivered in the cool air as I went back into the little hotel and knocked on the door of the room I'd left Jack in last night.

It opened in seconds, and Jack yanked me into the room, gun in hand.

'Where the hell did you go?'

'I had to see somebody.'

'You didn't answer your phone –'

'You threw it out the window.'

'Your new phone! Jesus, Sophie, I had no sodding idea where you were.'

He looked frightened. He actually looked scared.

'I ran out of notepaper, okay, or I'd have left you a note,' I said, pushing past and locking myself in the bathroom. I showered quickly, washing the gunk out of my hair, trying to make myself look presentable. But I just looked sad.

My phone rang just as I came out of the bathroom, and Jack snatched it up before I could get there.

'Hey!'

'No one else should have this number,' he snarled. 'Who the hell are you?' he snapped at the phone, and I winced, waiting.

Jack's nostrils flared as he listened.

'I'm the one she abandoned yesterday to go see you. Oh, she told you all about me? Did she tell you I didn't have a fucking clue where she was, if she'd been caught or killed or gone to the fucking cops about me? ... Yeah, well, I didn't know that. Hope she was bloody worth it, mate.'

He held the phone out to me and I took it, murmuring, 'So kind. Luke?'

'Young Jack seems like a pleasant fellow.'

'He's just annoyed because I didn't tell him I was leaving.'

Jack scowled at me and stormed into the bathroom, slamming the door as he went.

'You're making a habit of this. Sophie, tell me why I woke up this morning with just a phone number to remember you by?'

The remembrance hit me again, of Luke's hands on my body, his lips caressing my skin, the heat of him, the sound of my name on his lips. It smacked into me like a train on a track, leaving me breathless.

I gulped in air. 'I had to leave.'

'So early?'

'Got an appointment this morning.'

'An appointment? Please tell me it's for hair extensions.'

A shaky breath that was the closest I'd get to a laugh that morning escaped my lips. 'Could you be any more shallow? "Oh God, help, my girlfriend isn't a bimbo any more."'

'Did I ever call you a bimbo?'

'Oh, everyone calls me a bimbo.'

There was silence for a while. Neither of us were making a very decent attempt at levity here.

'What happened to your old phone?'

'Threw it out the window.'

'Why?' Luke asked patiently.

'Thought someone might have bugged it. They managed to find us to blow the car up.'

'Oh, my poor car.'

'Luke, it was a boring car. Don't mourn for it. Tell the insurance people your fugitive girlfriend stole it and trashed it. You'll get a new one.'

'You're not a fugitive.'

'Define that for me. I'm on the run from the law. In fact, I'm in the city where the crime was perpetrated. I really shouldn't be here.'

'You should be here,' Luke said, as Jack came out of the bathroom.

'Luke –'

'I'm serious. Come home, turn yourself in and get them to do the legwork.'

'While I sit in prison awaiting a trial that I'll never get? No, Luke, no. What, are you working for this Harrington guy?'

Jack's head swung in my direction.

'Harrington?'

I waved a hand for him to shut up.

'Look, I just want you safe,' Luke said. 'I don't like you running around with that psycho.'

'"Running around"? I'm not a bloody headless chicken. I can take care of myself.'

'As your kid-glove treatment of my car and your interesting collection of scars so amply show.'

'Oh, sod off,' I snarled, and cancelled the call, throwing the phone on the bed.

'He seems nice,' Jack said. 'Really.'

'Sod off,' I said, fighting an acutely sudden and painful urge to cry.

'Yeah,' Jack said, as someone knocked on the door. He answered it and took an iron from the woman in hotel uniform who was waiting there. Shutting her out, he spread out yesterday's shirt on the desk and plugged in the iron. 'Harrington?'

'Some guy MI5 sent after me.' I rubbed my temples wearily. 'Sounds like a bit of an arsehole.'

'He is.'

'You know him?'

'Ran into him once or twice. He won't stop until he has you.'

'Excellent.'

'They must be worried about you if they sent him after you.'

'Nice to know I concern them so.' I closed my eyes. Everything seemed so far away. Maybe if I just went to sleep I'd wake up and it would all be over …

'Sophie? Sophie, wake up. We have to be going.'

I blinked, and looked up at Luke.

Except it wasn't Luke. Another man was waking me up, another man was looking concernedly into my eyes.

'I wasn't asleep.'

'Sure you weren't.' Jack buttoned his shirt. 'We have to go or we'll be late.'

I stood up and looked around for my clothes. Skirt, jacket, check. Tights, check, have a spare pair in my bag. Shoes, check. Shirt?

'Dammit,' I said, looking at my creased shirt. 'Is there time to iron it?'

'Nope. Especially as I just took the iron back.'

I scrunched up my face. 'Okay, just give me twenty seconds.'

Jack looked sceptical, especially when he saw me extract nothing more than a bra from my case, but he said nothing as I went into the bathroom, put on the tights and the heels and the skirt and the bra, hoiked my breasts into a bigger, brighter cleavage, and fastened the jacket over the top. Yeah, that looked okay. Slutty, but professional.

'Very nice,' Jack said as I came out and sorted my essentials – guns, wallet, passport and make-up – into my bag. 'Like a high-class hooker.'

I flinched. Hot skin and the clench of muscle, his heartbeat against mine, the taste of him –

'Not today,' I said, my voice brittle. 'I really don't need that from you today.'

Jack said nothing.

'Are you taking the laptop?' I asked, trying to be businesslike.

'Erm –'

'Looks more official.'

'Boy, you play dress-up a lot, huh?'

'Just doing my job.'

'Doing your job so well you forgot about these.' He reached out and traced the criss-crossed red lines on my chest.

Dammit.

'It's okay,' I said, 'it'll be okay. Get us a cab and I'll sort it out.'

Jack looked dubious, but he hailed a taxi outside and when we got in, I took out my make-up and a mirror, and started to cover up the scars. Last month, when Angel got married, I was her maid of honour and my dress had a low, on-the-shoulder neckline. I nearly made the make-up girl weep with frustration, but she covered my scars reasonably well, dashing over after the ceremony, before the photos, and in the middle of the wedding breakfast to touch me up. The men of the bridal party had enjoyed it immensely.

'So was it worth it?' Jack asked as I put my make-up away, having tried my best to recreate the glossy look the Selfridges girl had given me yesterday.

'Was what worth it?'

'Scaring the hell out of me to go see your boyfriend.'

'You were scared?'

'You could have gone to Harrington. I don't know, you still could have. Just 'cos you got him to call you up –'

'You really are paranoid, aren't you?'

'With good reason.'

'It was worth it,' I said, and Jack looked out the window.

'Just because you don't have time for a girlfriend.'

Silence.

'Or is it that you'd rather have a boyfriend?' Jack gave me a dead look.

'Just thought I'd ask. You never know, maybe it runs in the family.'

A longer look this time. 'What's that supposed to mean?'

'Nothing. Just me messing around. I don't really think you're gay.' If he was, there was no God.

'Are you saying Maria is? What, she's a dyke 'cos she used to be in the Navy?'

'No, I'm saying she's gay because she's gay.'

Jack stared at me.

'That's not funny.'

'It's true.' I peered at him. 'I've met her girlfriend. Did you really not know?'

Jack looked furious. 'My sister is not gay.'

'Uh, can you spell denial?'

He snatched up his phone and started stabbing a number in. While I was impressed he knew it by heart – I don't know my brother's – I was also alarmed.

'You want them to trace your number?'

He lowered the phone, still glaring at me.

'You're making this up.'

'I swear I'm not.'

'Prove it.'

I rolled my eyes. 'How?'

Jack looked mutinous. Fine, if he didn't want to believe me that was his problem.

'This is it, mate,' the driver said, pulling up outside BBC&H,

and I started looking through my bag for my purse. And then Jack gripped my wrist, hard, and started shaking his head.

'No,' he said, 'don't stop. Just keep going.'

'But you wanted BBC&H –'

'Keep going,' Jack said, and the driver pulled back out into the traffic, scowling.

'What's that about?' I said, peering out the back window.

'You see the guy in the black suit? Grey hair?'

'Yeah.'

'Harrington.'

'Shit!' I ducked down in my seat. 'You're sure?'

'Yep. Someone must have tipped him off. Still think your boyfriend's trustworthy?'

I slapped him for that, but I was more frightened that he was right than angry that he was wrong.

There was a punchbag hanging from the rafters in Luke's flat. He'd bought it to keep in shape, but lately it had been functioning as a substitute for beating seven kinds of hell out of an actual person.

He didn't even bother to put his gloves on. The hard canvas grated against his knuckles with every blow, but he punched it harder and harder.

Like a thief in the night. He'd never known Sophie be so subtle before. Sure, she'd broken in – and out – of his flat a time or two, which pissed him off mightily, but never while he was actually there.

A quiet, expert escape. Didn't even stop for coffee. He'd fallen asleep in her arms last night, face tucked against her neck as she stroked his hair. That was new, too. Usually it was Sophie snuggling up to him. Usually she was the vulnerable one.

She'd been so ... different. Quieter. Withdrawn. Troubled.

All right, so a woman accused of murder, on the run from MI5 and some unknown pursuer – a person not above risking untold lives by blowing up a car in a public place – was allowed to be troubled. But through all the things Sophie had experienced since he met her, she'd never looked so haunted.

He'd watched her kill for the first time. He'd held her in his arms after someone threw a Molotov cocktail through her window. He'd seen her quite literally fight for her life. She'd been shot at, blown up, stabbed, injected with dirty needles, half-drowned, contracted blood poisoning and nearly faced the death of her cat, which traumatised her more than anything else. But she always came out fighting. He knew her. She was a swimmer, not a drowner.

Last night she'd pushed him down onto the mattress and kissed him with a dark intensity he'd never felt before. She'd taken off her clothes and pushed him, over and over, for more. She'd made love to him like a desperate woman. A woman who didn't expect to repeat the experience any time soon. Or at all.

She'd made love to him as if she was saying goodbye.

Luke slammed his fists into the punchbag, his heart breaking.

There were policemen outside the hotel, so we didn't stop there, either. This was turning out to be an expensive taxi ride, and I could see the driver getting curious. He looked at the policemen, then at us, and his hand strayed towards his radio.

'You do that,' Jack said, and I suddenly realised he had a gun on the driver, 'and you'll regret it. Savvy?'

The driver put his hand back on the wheel.

'Heathrow airport,' Jack said, and the driver nodded, clearly terrified now.

'Are you crazy?' I said. 'We can't afford to keep spending all this money on taxis –'

'You're assuming we're going to pay him, then?' Jack said calmly, and I shut up.

'Where are we going to go when we get to Heathrow?'

'Out of the country. You have your passport, right?'

I nodded. 'But all my stuff –'

'Unless you have anything back there that is vital to your health, then we leave it. You'll get it back.'

'The hell I will.' It was on the tip of my tongue to say that there were many things in my suitcase that were vital to my health, but I really didn't want to risk going back there for the sake of hair gel.

We got to Heathrow, and Jack told the driver to pull up in the covered car park. He directed him to a dark corner, and Jack got out and opened the driver's door.

Then he knocked him over the head with the back of his gun. The driver slumped forwards onto the wheel, and Jack fumbled for a moment with something I realised was the guy's cash belt.

'I can't believe you just did that,' I said, still sitting on the back seat, frozen with shock.

'Believe it,' Jack said, then swung his gun on me through the open door.

I stared, transfixed by the gaping black muzzle of the gun. Dark, shiny, deadly. Visions swam before me of my slumped white body in the back of the cab, bits of spattered brain dripping off the seats.

No! I made myself focus.

'What are you doing?' I asked Jack. All right, strictly speaking I was addressing the gun.

'Where were you last night?'

'I told you. I went to see my boyfriend.'

'Right. Your boyfriend who's MI6.'

'6 aren't after us,' I told the gun.

'No. But I bet they're pretty damn friendly with MI5, aren't they?'

'Actually there's a lot of interdepartmental rivalry,' I began, but Jack's eyes narrowed so I tried again. 'I didn't tell Luke where we were.'

'You did. I heard you. You told him we were in London.'

'London's a pretty big place!'

'Crawling with CCTV. He could have found you. Could have spotted us yesterday at BBC&H. Or,' the gun seemed to get closer, 'maybe you were the one who told Harrington where we were.'

'Why would I do that?' I yelped. 'Why would I bring the man who's chasing us – who's chasing *me* – down on us?'

'Well, maybe you're not who you say you are, Sophie Green,' Jack said. 'Maybe you're not an *ex*-spy after all.'

'Jack,' I said as steadily as I could, which considering the yawning barrel of the Beretta looming in front of me wasn't very damn steady at all, 'I am not working with MI5. Or 6. Or any government agency. I work in a bookshop. I'm *retired*.'

'You're a bit young for a pension,' he snapped.

'I can still be retired from my old job! I'm not a spy! I'm on your side! Jack, please.'

He regarded me unwaveringly for a long, terrible moment. Then he said, 'Get out of the car.'

'Why?'

'I'm the one with the gun, just do as I fucking say,' he said.

I raised my palms and got out.

'Get him out, too,' Jack said, gesturing to the driver. I glanced at him, a big man in his fifties.

'I'm not sure –'

'Do. It.'

I reached in and unfastened the driver's seatbelt. The front of the cab stank of cigarettes and halitosis. Where the driver was slumped forward I could see the blood on the back of his head, and I paused to check his pulse.

'What are you doing?'

'You could have killed him,' I said, but I was relieved to feel the blood thudding under his skin. I took the man's arm and tried to pull him out of the car, but he wouldn't move.

I glanced at Jack, an idea forming in my head. 'I can't do it by myself,' I said, even though I probably could. I'm hardly a weakling. 'You'll have to help me.'

Jack hesitated, then, swearing, he tucked the pistol into his jeans and came forward.

Whereupon I lamped him with my handbag, made heavy by all the essentials I'd piled in there.

Oh yes, and the weight of two guns.

Jack wavered, and I hit him again, frantic now. He crashed against the open cab door and went down.

'Oh God,' I gasped, looking at the two unconscious men in front of me. 'Oh God, oh God.'

I'd just knocked Jack unconscious. Hit him on the back of the head and knocked him out. All right, he'd done the same to me back in France, but this ...

... this felt very bad. I glanced around, terrified someone might have seen, but we were alone. I forced myself to calm down and think of my options.

I ought to put the driver's money back in the cab and walk away. I ought to sit and wait for Jack to come round.

Instead I looked around for CCTV and when I found the camera, fired my gun at it. The silencer muffled the sound, which was as well as it took me a couple of goes.

Then I took Jack's gun and the money belt, heaved him with some effort into the back of the cab and, as an afterthought, went through his pockets. Vallie's cash and cards were still there.

I put the lot into my bag, shut the cab doors, and walked away.

My legs were shaking as I emerged into the sunlight. My head was reeling. My face was hot and damp with perspiration. I made it inside the terminal, and forced myself to think logically.

Jack and the cabbie would be coming around soon. Depending on who woke up first, I'd either have a very angry ex-partner after me, or a cabbie reporting assault to the police. They'd be looking for me. They'd start here.

I nearly ran to the nearest cash machine and withdrew the daily maximum from all of Vallie's cards. The silly frivolous creature hadn't cancelled them yet. Then I made my way as quickly as possible, which wasn't very quickly at all in an airport roughly the size of China, to the coach terminal.

'Gatwick airport, please,' I said at the kiosk, and paid in cash.

I spent the journey planning what to do next. Getting out of the country seemed like a good idea, what with MI5 being after me, and after the cabbie incident, probably the police, too. I'd need to look different, because if there was the smallest suspicion that the people who'd robbed the cab driver were me and Jack, they'd start searching CCTV with facial recog software, and I'd be really screwed. Okay, so facial recog isn't a hundred percent reliable, but was fifty percent something I could gamble on? Sixty? Eighty?

Also, I needed to do something about the three – three! – guns I was currently carrying. I damn well wasn't going about unarmed, but how to get them on a flight?

It wouldn't be the first time I've travelled armed, but it's a very different situation if you're on legitimate business.

People don't really like the idea that they're on the same flight as a firearm, but it happens all the time. People take shotguns on shooting holidays quite often – you just turn up with the gun in one secure case, the ammunition in another, and your licence, and the police handle it. The cases are tagged and taken by the police directly to the aircraft, away from the public areas of the airport, and stowed in a secure part of the hold. At the other end the process is repeated. The guns go nowhere near the passenger cabin or the flight deck of the plane, and they're not allowed to be loaded with ammunition, either.

Yes. That is a speech I learned when I worked on check-in.

I took a breath and blew it out. I didn't have a licence for any of these guns. The only one I even used to be able to claim legitimate ownership of was my SIG and that was now officially at the bottom of a Cornish harbour. Even if I had the licence it'd be no good. Quite apart from the expiration date, the damn thing had my real name all over it.

If Luke was here he'd know what to do. Or Docherty.

Wait – Docherty.

Time to get myself further into debt.

Chapter Eight

'I didn't think it was possible,' said the cold voice in his ear, 'but she's in even more trouble.'

Luke glared out of the window at the car which had followed him back from London. Right now he wasn't sure if it was MI5 or 6. He wouldn't put it past Sheila to spy on him at home. Hell, she'd done it at the office.

'Enlighten me,' he said.

'Assault and theft. Kidnapped a taxi driver at gunpoint, robbed him and knocked him unconscious.'

He closed his eyes. 'How do you know it was her?'

'He was instructed to take two people to the offices of BBC&H, but they panicked on seeing someone outside and told him to go to Heathrow instead, where he was robbed. He gave a physical description that matches your Sophie and a young man also wanted for the murder of, coincidentally,' her voice dripped disdain, 'the murder of a former BBC&H partner. We do cross-reference these things. Which is why 5 had the office under surveillance. It seems she has a partner in crime. We're checking Heathrow's CCTV now.'

Fuck. *Fuck*. 'It wasn't her. Sophie wouldn't do that.'

'I'd lay odds she just has. Did you know she was in the country?'

Soft curves and damp skin, lips parted on a gasp, soft hair sliding between his fingers, wide blue eyes and the clutch of her hand on his shoulder –

'No,' Luke said as expressionlessly as he could. 'Why would she come back here? It's too dangerous.'

'She's stupid, and she's taking risks,' Sheila said bluntly.

Rage rose in Luke and he shoved it back down again. Sheila was right: it was a stupid thing to do. He himself had accused Sophie of monumental stupidity on more than one occasion. She was reckless and had a tendency to act before she thought. He knew that. He could say it to her.

Sheila couldn't.

'It could have been anybody,' Luke said. 'Someone's set her up for this, there's more to it than we know right now. And how detailed was this guy's description anyway? It could have been anyone.'

'A tall young man with dark hair, olive complexion, medium build –'

'Could be anybody,' Luke said dismissively, but the thought of this tall young man being comfortable enough with Sophie to answer her damn phone, spending all this time with her, God *damn* him, it was all too much. *She's mine. She was in my arms last night.*

He could only attribute what he said next to jealousy, lust, or anger. Some cocktail of the three.

'How'd he describe Sophie? Tall brunette with big boobs and a tendency to trip over her own feet?'

There was a pause, and Luke wondered what he'd done, specifically, to annoy her this time.

Then it hit him like a fist to the gut.

'How,' Sheila said, 'did you know she's a brunette?'

It turned out to be surprisingly simple to look like a different person. Some fake tan, those cheap reading specs, a scarf to cover my hair. I've been told ears are as distinctive as fingerprints, so I covered mine up. I used Vallie's money to book flights from and to several completely random destinations. Paris to Bombay. London to Amsterdam. Los Angeles to Sydney. I even checked in on a few of them. No one commented on my travelling without luggage on a long-haul flight. Trust me, when you've been up since three a.m. and have dealt with nervous flyers and lost passports, passengers with thirty kilos excess baggage who don't understand a word of English, and school parties where every single child wants to be reseated next to his friends but not near that loser from Mrs Smith's class, then you could check in a pantomime horse and barely notice.

I knew that eventually, if they discovered my pseudonym, I'd be tracked to a passenger manifest. But I was a step ahead. That was all I needed right now: to be one step ahead.

I tried not to let the thought hit me that Jack was half a step behind me.

I made it through Security without a single eyelid being batted, and in a wave of relief hit the shops. I desperately needed clothes and toiletries, although I confess I probably could have done without shopping in Chanel. What the hell. All the adrenaline was making me dizzy. I bought a smart new bag to stash all my new things in. When I passed Dixon's, I wandered in and found myself in possession of a shiny new smart phone. Hell, I had a long flight ahead of me. Learning how to use the damn thing might occupy a portion of it.

In the souvenir shop I bought a selection of baseball caps with Tower Bridge and Stonehenge on them. If I'd got this far, it meant no facial recog software was being used, but I didn't want to take any more chances.

I changed hats several times in the departures lounge, and coats and jackets, too. I'd already changed my outfit in the Ladies. Always trying to stay ahead of the cameras.

Shopping had helped erase some of my fears about getting on a flight with a fake passport. No one really checked. But then that's not what ground staff are there for. Their job is to check you have the correct document – that the passport isn't out of date or belonging to the wrong person, that it doesn't require a visa and that, basically, it's not going to result in the passenger being put on the next flight back, at the airline's expense.

The job of checking for fake or falsified documents falls to Immigration at your destination. And that was the part that bloody terrified me.

I ought to have spent the flight thinking about how to evade capture once I arrived, and what my next step would be regarding tracking down who'd really framed us. Framed me. I had no idea if I could trust Jack right now. But I was so tired. Guilty about all the shopping I'd done with stolen money. Frightened about the reality I was now living in. And angry. Angry with myself for being so damn weak and stupid as to go and see Luke, and angry for arguing with him, when who knew if I'd ever see him again? What if I was taken into custody when I landed, or chased down and killed, and the last words I ever exchanged with him were in anger?

I buried my face in my hands, and when the flight attendant asked if I was all right, I gave her a weak smile. 'Scared of flying,' I told her. 'Is it too early to get a vodka?'

I had to wait until we were fully airborne for my drink, but by then I'd calmed myself down a bit. *It will all be fine*, I told myself. *It will all be fine.*

I'm such a bad liar.

Lord of the Rings was on as part of the entertainment, so I watched that. Hours and hours of Viggo Mortensen and Orlando Bloom gave me very sweet dreams, and for a while I forgot that I was wanted for murder, theft, taxi hijacking (well, probably, by now), that my former partner-in-crime was out to get me, that I was armed with nothing scarier than a pair of heels, my boyfriend wasn't talking to me, and I was less than sure of the reception I'd get when I landed.

'Oh, Sophie,' Aragorn husked, drawing me into his arms as I brushed the blood and sweat from his face, 'I fought out there for you. You are the reason I want to save Middle

Earth. Come away with me to the Undying Lands, forget about that pointy-eared freak and –'

'Excuse me, miss? Can you fasten your seatbelt, please? We're beginning our descent.'

Right. Yes.

It was a relief to step out into the cold night air in Chicago. Waiting in the queue for Immigration, I started to get nervous. My ESTA had been approved and I'd kept a copy of the details with my passport, but hey, even when I'm travelling legitimately I get tense at Immigration.

The immigration officer asked for my fingerprints, and nervously, I put my index finger on the scanner.

In the bathroom on the plane, I'd already swapped my contacts and rolled on the fake fingertips. One of them kept coming off, which gave me panic attacks, but I stuck a sticking plaster over it, which seemed to work.

The woman never batted an eyelid – and neither did I, when the iris scanner accepted my patterned lenses. She read the address for my first night's accommodation, an address I'd utterly invented. She stamped my passport, wished me a nice day, and never once looked me in the eye.

I walked away without looking back, tickets for an onward journey in my pocket, tired and frightened and exhilarated all at the same time.

I'd got away with it.

'Tsow nee dzoo dzohng shih bah die,' he said to the phone.

Sheila paused. 'I wasn't aware you spoke Mandarin.'

He didn't. But Sophie had sat him down in front of the TV and demanded he watch every episode of *Firefly*, and he'd been physically unable to resist translating the Chinese insults. He wondered if Sheila knew what he'd just told her to do to eighteen generations of her ancestors, or if she was bluffing.

'There're a lot of things you're not aware of,' he said, and ended the call.

She'd ordered him down to London. He'd refused. She'd threatened to send someone to his flat to frogmarch him away. Luke reset all his alarms and checked his gun was loaded. She ordered him to tell her everything Sophie had said and done. Which was when he started insulting her in Chinese.

The really awful thing was that she was right. It had been really stupid of Sophie to come to his flat. It had been reckless. And no matter how much he desperately wanted to see her, how much he needed to touch her, he should have sent her away immediately.

He rolled his head back against the sofa and blew out a sigh. He should have warned her Harrington would trace her. He should –

Wait. How had Harrington known she'd be going to BBC&H? Why were they waiting for her there? He couldn't possibly have known that Sophie had been to see Luke, or he'd have been up here like a shot, rattling him for information. Sheila would have got wind of it.

Why were they waiting at BBC&H?

With a sick feeling, he realised the truth. They hadn't been waiting for Sophie. They must have been following him.

I slept overnight at JFK and took the first flight to Cincinnati, where I rented a car and drove eighty or so miles through the early morning to a small town called Waiting, which I imagined did a brisk trade in comedy postcards. It was the first time I'd ever driven in America, but after British traffic jams, French aggression and Italian lunacy, it was a breeze.

Wearily, I checked the directions from the sat-nav on my phone, and I was a few streets away from my destination when I saw a little girl walking along the pavement, long shiny dark hair draped over her backpack.

She looked a little alarmed to see the car stopping beside her, and when I wound down the window and said, 'Hi!' she nearly fainted.

'Oh my God! Sophie?'

'Hi, Rachel. How you been?'

She stared at me, her dark eyes huge. 'What are you doing here?'

'It's a long story.'

'Dad said you were on the lam.'

'Maybe it's a really short story.'

'Do you need a place to stay? I'm sure my grandparents won't mind if you crash at mine.'

I love this kid.

'Are you on your way to school?'

She nodded. 'The bus stop is just down there.' She cocked her head. 'Or you could give me a ride.'

'Hey, didn't your grandma ever tell you not to get into cars with strange people?'

'But I know you.'

'I'm still a very strange person.'

Rachel grinned. 'Only in the literal sense. Hey, I don't suppose you'd consider helping me cut, would you?'

'Cut school?'

I narrowed my eyes calculatingly.

'What do you have today?'

'Math. I hate math.'

'Very useful, though.'

Rachel looked sceptical. 'Like trig is useful.'

She was nine. *Nine*. How the hell did she even know what trigonometry was?

'And I have gym,' she added, trying to look sad.

'Okay, get in.'

I hated gym when I was a kid. Still do. That's why I'm not skinny.

Rachel directed me to the centre of town where there was an ice cream parlour, told me that their choc fudge sundaes were to die for, and I decided that of all the things I might potentially die for in the near future, an ice cream was probably one of the best.

'So,' Rachel said, digging into a sundae that was bigger than she was, 'spill. What did you do and why did you do it and why are you here and is anyone after you?'

I sighed. This was going to be a long session.

I was starting my second sundae and explaining to Rachel why driving in Italy is hell, when something started shrilling and beeping and I pawed through my bag for my new phone. But Rachel rolled her eyes at me and took a new iPhone out of her bag.

She checked the display, swiped casually at the screen and said, with a forty-something amount of ennui, 'Hi, Gram.'

I took a deep breath and let it out. Here's the thing. I came to Ohio because Rachel lives here, and she's one of only two people I know in America. The other lives in New York City, which is a much more obvious target for anyone looking for me. Who would expect I'd go to ground at the home of my friend's nine-year-old daughter?

I chewed my lip, the only flaw in my otherwise brilliant plan nagging at me. Namely, the particular friend whose daughter she was.

'I'm downtown. No, just – look, I can explain this – don't you dare! It's very – no, I can get a – okay, all right, I'll be there in ten.'

With a swish of her perfect, shiny black mane, she slid the phone back into her bag and sighed. 'That was my grandma. The school called her and told her I hadn't turned up. I'm only, like, half-an-hour late. Jeez. So now I have to go home or she'll call the cops and report me as missing. You wanna come?'

Yikes. Teresa Cortes had seemed perfectly nice on the one

brief occasion I'd met her, but I was suddenly afraid she'd turn out to be terrifying.

'Well ...' I said.

'You'll have to come,' Rachel said matter-of-factly. 'I need a ride or I'll be late. Come on.'

She trotted out of the ice cream parlour and I barely had time to throw down some money before I ran after her. Rachel is a bit like Luke that way: utterly certain that the world will follow her lead.

She leaned against the car, face turned up to the sun, the prettiest child I'd ever seen. In half-a-dozen years she was going to cause her father nightmares. He was probably already having them, just for practice.

I am so never having children.

256 Washington Drive was an ordinary, weatherboarded, all-American house with a big porch and a green lawn and a gigantic American Ford in the driveway.

As I pulled up and parked at the kerb, I checked my face in the visor mirror and recoiled. Not the best face to be greeting a matriarch with. But the only face I had.

'Ready?' Rachel asked me, and I wondered if my fear showed on my face.

'Ready.'

Teresa Cortes came out of the front door as we were getting out of the car. She was in her sixties, her skin supple and smooth, her black hair flecked with very small amounts of grey. She wore jeans and a white shirt and had baseball sneakers on her small feet. She'd emigrated from Mexico many years ago as a small child, and it was her colouring that Rachel had inherited.

'Rachel,' she began, sounding shocked, 'who on earth did you get a ride home with?'

Rachel grabbed my hand and towed me forward. 'Gram, you remember Sophie, don't you?'

Teresa stared at me. I extended a hand weakly.

'We met at the wedding? I was the maid of honour.'

'Remember, Gram? You said how pretty she was in her dress.'

Teresa blinked once or twice, then smiled and took my hand and said, 'Of course. I was so surprised to see you. You must come in and have a drink. How long have you been in town?'

She knows, I thought. She knows and she's going to call the cops as soon as we're out of sight.

'I just got in this morning,' I said. 'I'm not sure if maybe you might have spoken to Harvey recently?'

Oh, yes. Rachel is Harvey's daughter. You know, Harvey who's in the CIA. Before he met Angel he had a fling with a beautiful student, which resulted in Rachel. When Rachel was a baby her mother died in a plane crash, leaving her child to be raised by her parents.

That's the snag with this plan. Maybe I was a bit more sleep-deprived and terrified than I realised when I came up with it, but at the time it seemed like genius. Hiding in plain sight! No one will come looking for me!

I'd forgotten, however, quite how intimidating Rachel's grandmother could be.

Her eyes narrowed calculatingly. 'I have.'

'Then you'll know the position I'm in.'

A pause, then she nodded.

'I need your help. A place to stay. I promise you won't be in any danger – no one even knows I'm in the country,' I said, praying to all the gods I could think of that this was true.

'She didn't do it, Gram,' Rachel piped up.

'Rachel, go in the house. Go,' her grandmother said, and Rachel sulkily obeyed. 'You're wanted for murder.'

'Yes, ma'am, I am,' I said, 'but I swear to God I'm

innocent.' Backtrack, Sophie, don't blaspheme, you're in Middle America! 'Someone framed me and I need a place to stay while I figure out who and why.'

Teresa said nothing.

'Mrs Cortes,' I tried, 'Rachel is a really bright girl. Do you think she'd bring me back here if she thought I was guilty? Do you think Harvey would let me near her if he thought I was?'

She lifted her chin a little and looked at me. 'Harvey knows you're here?'

'No,' I admitted. 'No one knows I'm here. Please. I'm running out of places to go. If I get caught, they'll take me to jail and the trial will never, ever come up.' Overdramatic, but do you think I cared? 'I didn't kill anyone, but without evidence to prove that, I could go down forever.'

Another silence. I could tell she was thinking.

'All right,' Teresa said eventually, and I let out a big breath I didn't realise I'd been holding. 'But if there's any bit of trouble I'll call the police.'

'And you'll be within your perfect rights to do so,' I gushed gratefully. 'Wow – thank you so much. I really need this.'

'Come inside,' Teresa said, 'and we'll talk some more.'

Sheila's goons failed to turn up and drag Luke off to an oubliette, but the clawing sensation in his gut didn't go away.

They'd nearly found Sophie, and it might be his fault. Had he led them to BBC&H? Although if they already had the offices under surveillance, maybe not. What would have happened if Harrington had caught her? At very best, the evidence was so stacked against her that even a reasonably fair trial had a pretty good chance of convicting her. But the chances of even getting a fair trial with a pit-bull like Harrington were pretty small. He'd be more likely to fire accusations at her, lock her away in some interrogation cell and psychologically torture her into confessing. Or maybe actually torture her. The man was insane.

Or he might just shoot her on sight.

He lay in bed, staring at the ceiling but seeing Sophie, lying pale and unconscious on the deck of a scruffy fishing boat. She'd nearly drowned a few months ago and the memory of her limp, white body, heavy in his arms, cold and unmoving and bloodless, still haunted his dreams. He'd wake with a start, the memory of her icy flesh a physical sensation against his skin, only to find her warm and sleepy beside him, mumbling that he'd just kicked her in the shin.

'I had to fall in love with someone who gets nearly killed three times a year,' he muttered.

Maybe Sheila had a point. He needed to back off and let the evidence come to light. The more he interfered, the more MI5 became convinced she was guilty. Maybe he should just leave it. Sit at home like the Service's faithful Labrador and await news.

The inaction would drive him demented. But would it help? Was Sheila being cruel, or was she trying to help him?

He rolled over and thumped his pillow. Should have been up hours ago but wasn't sure what the point was. Sophie wasn't talking to him, Sheila was icily mad at him, and if he so much as looked at a picture of Sophie, Harrington would have him thrown in the Tower.

He shoved back the covers, stomped into the kitchen and defiantly grabbed the packet of Dunhill's. The gold lighter felt heavy in his hand. Slowly, he took out a cigarette, held it between his teeth, cupped his hand around it and flicked the lighter open.

The flame flickered abruptly into existence. Bright, blue and clean.

'The hell with it,' he said around the cigarette, and ducked to light it.

His phone buzzed.

Luke froze as if someone had just walked in and found him naked. His phone lay on the counter, within reading distance.

A text from Sophie's brother.

He put down the cigarette – he could go to hell later – and opened the text.

'Mum says have you heard anything yet?'

Sickness churned in his stomach. Sophie's mother. Her brother. Untold friends and cousins and colleagues. None of them knew Maria or Docherty – probably just as well in the latter case – and had no idea Harvey was CIA.

They had no one else to turn to for news of Sophie.

Sighing, he put down the lighter and texted back. 'I'll be there in ten.'

When he arrived, all their cars were in the drive. As he passed the front window, Sophie's mother leapt to her feet. She met him at the door, her face white.

'What is it? Is it bad news?'

'No.' He shook his head for emphasis. 'Last I heard she was fine. Listen, can I come in? I have an idea.'

It transpired, over milk and home-baked cookies, that Teresa had been a legal secretary in the days before her daughter died and left Rachel to be cared for.

'I don't know how the law works in England,' Teresa said, 'but I'm pretty sure leaving the scene of the crime is not a good thing.'

'What was I supposed to do?' I said. 'If someone had come in and seen me there, holding the gun that shot him, what would they have thought? I don't have a scrap of evidence in my favour so far. All I have to go on is my own knowledge that I didn't do it.'

'Which is not going to stand up in a court of law,' Rachel

said.

Her grandmother frowned at her, then said to me, 'Can you think that this man had many enemies?'

'He was a lawyer,' I said. 'Probably every case he lost created him an enemy. Plus he was involved with MI5 – there are bound to be loads and loads of people he pi – he upset.'

'Well, then,' she stood up, 'I suppose you need to find out which cases he worked on. Come on. You can use the computer in the den.'

I followed them into a little study where Teresa booted up a rather new and shiny-looking computer. 'You know how to use this?' I nodded. 'If you need any help, Rachel's your best bet.'

She left the room and I glanced at Rachel. 'So, kid,' I said. 'How're your Googling skills?'

'Pretty awesome,' she said modestly. Well, *of course* they were. Whereas I can never find anything on the Internet. Whatever I search for usually ends up bringing me porn.

There's probably a metaphor there somewhere.

'I need to get into the private files of a law firm called Barton, Barton, Chesshyre & Holt,' I said. Rachel tapped this in quickly and looked up at me, bright-eyed and inquisitive like a little bird.

I went still.

'How,' I asked, 'did you know how to spell Chesshyre?'

'My dad called,' she said. 'He told me you were in some trouble but he wouldn't say what. So I started looking around for news.'

My heart seized up. 'It's made the news?'

'No. Not yet. I mean, the whole murder-of-an-MI5-agent thing has come up on Twitter, but your name isn't linked to it. They just said stuff like "former service agent" and things like that. I mean anyone could figure out it was you.'

I began having palpitations, until I reminded myself that

Rachel was smarter than Doogie Howser. 'Anyone who knew the precise time and date where I'd last been seen, you mean.'

'Well, sure.'

'Your dad told you that?'

'Well, not told me exactly ...'

Her gaze shifted away.

'Rachel Harvard-Cortes, whose conversations have you been listening in on?'

'Only my dad's,' she protested. 'I put a bug on his cell ages ago.'

'Rachel, you are *nine*.'

'Yeah?' Her expression said, clear as if someone had written it there: What does that have to do with it?

'Your dad is a CIA agent.' Who probably had no idea what a devious little creature his beloved daughter was.

The same expression. 'Yeah?'

'You can't – you shouldn't – how did –' I gave up. 'All right. What else did you find out?'

Rachel calmly laid out pretty much the entire story. Harvey – and therefore the CIA, and therefore, unless their powers of deduction were worse than Tammy's, MI5 – had linked Judge Shepherd and Sir Theodore's murders. After yesterday's spectacular mess of crap, Jack and I had been linked together. However, as yet no one knew our current whereabouts. As yet.

I ran my hands over my face, horribly tired. My brain couldn't process any more.

'Okay, look. You're the genius here. Can you get BBC&H's records online?'

Rachel looked at me doubtfully. 'Will they be online?'

'There'll be a company intranet. Emails between partners. There's got to be a way of accessing it.'

Rachel frowned, but she said, 'Okay, I'll try. Beats gym

class any day.'

She began typing at the speed of light. Every bit of it looked like gibberish to me.

I started to feel really old.

After a while, clearly surplus to requirements, I wandered out onto the back porch and took out my phone, staring at it for a while as I tried to drum up the courage to call Luke.

I failed. I dialled Docherty's number and when he answered, asked how it was going with my guns. You see, I might not be as clever as Rachel, but I had worked out one solution for shipping my firearms abroad, and that solution was simple: get Docherty to do it.

'You really want me to send them to Harvey's kid?'

'Sure. Just don't tell –'

'Luke. Right. They're on their way. Should be with you tonight or tomorrow morning.'

I didn't ask how. For all I knew Docherty owned a teleporter. 'Excellent. Words cannot describe my gratitude.'

'If words can't ...'

I rolled my eyes. 'Actions can't either. We did this before, Docherty.'

'Sure, and it worked out fine then.' Yeah, so fine I hadn't even seen him since. 'I hear you got Luke's car blown up.'

Occasionally, I wondered what would happen if Docherty and Rachel ever met. It'd be like Lex Luthor teaming up with Hermione Granger. The world would have about five minutes to survive.

'Only by accident.'

A slight pause. 'Glad to hear it wasn't on purpose. That makes two now.'

'Yours wasn't on purpose either.'

'You going to apologise to him same way you did to me?'

I closed my eyes, but that didn't help because all I could

see was the night we'd spent together. It had been hot, intense, and wonderful in a terrifying sort of way, and it wasn't really something I was particularly proud of.

'Can we not talk about this?'

'You brought it up.'

'I did not.'

'Whatever. Why are you in Ohio?'

'Seemed like a good idea at the time. Well, listen. I have work to do. So ... thanks for the guns and stuff, and if you tell Luke where I am I'll castrate you.'

'You're welcome.'

I ended the call and sat there drumming my fingers for a while. Right, Sophie girl. Stop dwelling on the giant craphole that is your life right now, and think of something productive.

So what I needed to know was which cases Irene and Sir Theodore had worked on together. Then I needed to know if any of the people involved in those cases were likely to have a grudge against them, and if they did, were they free enough to act upon it.

In my head, I started working on a list of people who had grudges against me. It wasn't cheerful, but it needed to be done.

I counted eight enemies. Two were dead and the remaining six were in jail. All of them had been imprisoned in maximum security facilities. Several of them were still recovering from the injuries I'd dealt them while they tried to kill me.

I was still recovering from a few scars of my own.

I got up and was about to go back inside to see how Rachel was getting on, when my new phone chirruped and bleeped at me. I glanced at the display, and did a double take. It was a UK mobile number, and it wasn't Docherty's. My heart physically leapt.

'Luke?' I answered it cautiously.

'Yeah.'

'How did you get this number?'

'Why, trying to keep it from me? Docherty gave it to me.'

Bloody Docherty.

'Where are you? What did you do to your old phone?'

'Nothing. I just thought this one would be better.'

'He says it's registered to a Miss D Meanour,' he said, in exactly the same tone I use when I'm second-guessing one of my dad's terrible jokes. Half-speech, half-groan.

'What can I say, my creative powers are a little bit tapped by now.'

There was a long pause. I closed my eyes and pictured him beside me. If I tried hard enough I could almost imagine he was here with me. 'Listen, Luke, I'm sorry. About what I said before.'

'It's okay –'

'I mean, I'm under a lot of stress right now. I mean, a *lot*.'

'I know. So am I. It's –'

'It's really hard –'

'Really, really hard,' Luke said, exasperation in his voice, and I smiled.

'So, are we okay now?'

'We're always okay,' he said gently, and I felt a rush of love for him.

Before I started getting all soppy, I cleared my throat. 'Right, well, look. Could do with a little favour.'

'Such as?'

I explained my theory about the six people who might be gunning for me. Luke was silent.

'Well?'

'Soph … they're all in jail. I suppose they could have paid someone to do their dirty work, but it's all a bit soap opera, isn't it?'

'Well, check anyway,' I said, irritated. With him, and with

myself, and with Jack for planting the tiny seed of doubt in my head about Luke's intentions.

He's not working for Harrington. He loves me.

'How's young Jack?'

'Young Jack is less than ten years younger than you, Old Man,' I replied.

'He's an infant,' Luke said dismissively.

'He's not much younger than me.'

'Well, that's different. You're a competent adult.'

I stared, stunned, at the swing set in the garden.

'Soph?'

'I think that's the first time you've ever said that,' I said.

'Well. I mean, you're not really, I'm just trying to persuade myself of it before I go completely carrot top here. Suppose being with an infant bounty hunter is better than being alone,' he added, still sounding like he was trying to persuade himself of it.

'Ah,' I replied.

'What now?'

I bit my lip. Luke didn't even like Jack, so he ought to be happy with the news we weren't working together any more.

'Is this to do with that incident at Heathrow?'

'You know about that?' Of course he did. If Rachel knew about it, Luke had probably been called up by everyone he'd ever met.

'Young Jack threatened a cabby with a gun, knocked him out and robbed him. At least, I'm giving you the benefit of the doubt on who robbed him. The camera was on the wrong side of the cab to pick up enough detail about who it was, and the only witness was unconscious.'

'It was Jack,' I said, and the whole story came flooding out of me. 'He got paranoid after we ran into Harrington, especially after I'd been to see you. He thought I'd told 5 where we were going, or you'd passed it on. He turned on me with a gun, Luke, and I panicked.'

'What did you do?' he asked after the tiniest pause.

'Hit him over the head with my handbag,' I said. 'And put him in the cab. And shot out the camera. So he wouldn't be found.'

I heard the very faint rasp of Luke running his hand hard over his unshaven jaw.

'He was just a bit overwrought,' I said. 'I think I scared him by coming to see you. He thought I'd run off to tattle to Harrington.'

Luke took in a deep breath and let it out as a heavy sigh. 'Did he hurt you?'

'No. Has he … no, he can't have been found or you'd know about it, right? Maria would have got hold of me and called down some goddess of wrath on my head.'

'No. When the cabby woke up he was alone. But someone had fleeced him of all his takings.'

I kept silent. It's just money, I told myself. People have insurance for this sort of thing. It's not like I hurt anyone.

Except Jack, but that was for his own good.

'So you're on your own.'

'Yes.' I lifted my chin. 'It's better this way. You know, two targets are harder to find than one. Like that bit in *Butch Cassidy & the Sundance Kid* where they let one horse loose as a decoy.'

'That bit where the trackers aren't fooled and go after the horse they're both riding?'

I winced. 'Bad analogy. Look, I'm fine. I can manage by myself. Like you said, I'm a competent adult.'

'Oh God,' Luke said.

'And I can do this,' I said firmly. Maybe a bit too firmly. 'I'm *fine*. I can *manage*.'

'Are you okay?' Luke said doubtfully.

'*I'm fine.*'

'It's just, you sound a bit ...'

'Luke, do I have to remind you about MI5 and the murder charge and people trying to kill me? Again? Someone tried to drown Jack a week ago and someone blew up your car two days ago and Harrington found us yesterday –' God, had it really only been yesterday? 'So yeah, whatever you were going to say, I am a "bit".'

There was a pause.

'Sorry,' Luke said warily. 'Listen, I've got something that might cheer you up.'

'I'm not having phone sex with you.'

He laughed. 'Not that. Hang on a sec.'

I hesitated, ready to end the call if he was going to put Harrington on, but the voice that came next was not that of a hard-boiled MI5 agent. It was softer, female and older, a hint of a northern accent, vast acres of childhood memories flooding through the receiver just as she spoke my name.

Tears sprang to my eyes.

'Mum?'

'Sophie, love.' She sounded incredibly relieved. 'How are you? Are you all right?'

I sniffed, nails digging into my palm. 'I'm fine,' I managed. 'I'm good. How are you?'

'Oh,' I suppose it was a rather big question, 'relieved. Luke said he'd been in contact with you but I ... I just wanted to talk to you.'

I gripped the phone harder and closed my eyes, the last traces of mascara trickling down my cheeks.

'I'm sorry I didn't call,' I whispered, 'only –'

'It's all right, love. I understand. Luke's told us everything.'

Oh, God.

'Everything?'

'About you working for the government and all. Sophie,

why didn't you tell us?'

I opened my eyes and rolled them at the sky. 'Tell me in words of one syllable exactly what you think the Official Secrets Act is, Mum.'

She laughed. 'I suppose we might be in some trouble now, for knowing.'

'Hell, probably everyone knows now. It's on Twitter.' Though not, according to Rachel, my name – yet.

'Oh, well if it's on *Twitter*,' my mum said, and we both laughed weakly. I hesitated. How, exactly, does one ask one's mother if she knows one has been accused of murder, without panicking her into thinking one actually did it?

I suppose I'd better start by not talking about myself as if I'm the freaking Queen.

'Listen, Mum. You didn't – I mean, they've been saying – look, I didn't do it –'

'I know that,' my mother scoffed gently. 'We all know it.'

'We?'

'Your dad and Charlie, Angel and all your friends. I think I've spoken to them more these last two weeks than I ever have done before.'

I smiled at that. Probably my brother had been enjoying the chance to talk to all my friends, especially Angel, who he still fancies even though she's married and pregnant.

'Anyway,' Mum said, 'I'll hand you back over now. I just wanted to talk to you. See you're all right.'

'I'm all right.'

'And we'll sort this all out. Luke's been working round the clock to try and get a handle on it …'

'I know. So have I.'

'He says you're not alone? Some friend of yours …?'

'I'm fine,' I said, because she'd probably prefer to imagine I was with someone than that I was alone. Clearly Luke hadn't been letting her eavesdrop. 'And I'm eating properly and everything.' Another lie, but what the hell.

'I'm very proud of you, Sophie,' my mother said, and then there was a muffled sob, and she was gone.

He left Sophie's parents sitting on a log in the woods where they usually walked their dog, dissecting every nuance of what she'd said, and walked back to his car with Chalker. He'd never asked why Sophie's brother had that nickname – having been to school with boys known variously as Biffy, Tonto, Cleggers, The Berserker, Alice and Skidmark, he didn't really want to.

'You doing okay?' Chalker asked.

'Five by five.'

'That's what Sophie says.'

'It's a Buffy thing,' Luke said, getting out his keys.

Chalker rolled his eyes, looking uncannily like his sister when he did.

'This guy she's hanging out with ...?'

Luke waited politely, having decided not to divulge that Sophie was currently flying solo, at least until she did.

'Is he, you know, okay?'

'I haven't met him,' Luke said. 'But his sister is a friend of mine.'

'Sophie says –' Chalker began, then stopped, a flush on his cheeks.

'Sophie says a lot of things,' Luke agreed amiably. He could pretty well guess what Chalker had been about to say. *Sophie says you don't have any friends.*

'Maria is a work colleague of mine,' he said. 'I trust her implicitly. And she'll be doing whatever she can to clear her brother's name, so that's two of us on the case.'

Another lie. He didn't think it would be helpful for Sophie's family to know he'd been stood down and that Maria had barely managed to exchange half-a-dozen cryptic texts with her brother. She wasn't under lockdown just yet, but then Luke supposed he was serving as a cautionary tale these days.

'So he's all right? I mean ... it's just I don't want her to be ... you know, it must be horrible to have to do this sort of thing alone.'

Luke, who'd heard the aching loneliness in Sophie's voice, just nodded. 'I'm sure he's a great comfort to her,' he said as expressionlessly as he could, and opened the car door. 'See you.'

Chalker nodded and watched Luke drive away. He felt the younger man's gaze on him right down the lane, and the weight of it was still heavy on his shoulders as he turned onto the road.

He was tired, and he was worried. But he was also home, with an unexpected network of friends and family to support him. Sophie had nothing but a voice on the end of a telephone.

He parked in front of his own house and sat for a long moment in the gathering dusk, his forearms resting on the steering wheel. On the one hand, Sophie alone and friendless. On the other, the constant, day-and-night company of a good-looking young man. *Focus, Luke!* The company of a paranoid young man who thinks she's out to get him.

What if Jack gave too much away to Maria? What if he turned on Sophie?

What if Sophie just needed someone to cover her?

It must be horrible to have to do this sort of thing alone.

He got out his secure phone and dialled Maria's number.

I sat there holding the phone for what felt like ages before it rang again, and Luke's number flashed up.

'You okay?' He was gentle, cautious.

'Yeah,' I said, voice wobbly.

'Liar.'

'Like I'm even expected to tell the truth any more.'

'I think it meant a lot for her to know you're all right.'

I sniffed.

'Sophie?' Luke said, more gently.

'Mm-hm?'

'I'm proud of you, too.'

I closed my eyes again. A fat tear tickled my skin. 'Why, for getting away with murder?'

'Very funny. You've managed to evade me, and Harrington –'

'Only since yesterday,' I said.

Another sigh. I could picture him, leaning against the counter in his shiny kitchen, pinching the bridge of his nose and screwing up his eyes, the way he did when he was tired and exasperated with me.

It's probably not a good thing that this is an expression I'm familiar with.

'You don't think he blew the car up, do you?'

'I don't know, Luke. Look, I'm tired and hungry and I've been wearing the same clothes for two days solid, and since when did you decide you could tell my mother about SO17?'

'Since she wanted to know why her daughter was wanted for murder.'

I nodded to myself, and ended up like a dog in a car window. I couldn't stop.

'Okay,' I yawned, 'I really need to get some sleep.'

'Is it night time where you are?'

'No.' I smiled at his rather pathetic attempt at locating me. 'I've just been up all night.'

'I could trace your passport, you know.'

'I'd be gone by the time you found me.'

'Yeah,' he sighed, 'I guess you would. I'll get back to you on those six.'

I ended the call and sat there looking out at the low-fenced yard. Green grass and sandy paving, a set of swings in the corner, a bike flung haphazardly on the lawn. A safe, closeted, family garden.

I stood up and turned to go in and nearly fainted when I saw Rachel standing there, watching me.

'How long have you been there?'

'A while.'

'Were you listening?'

'You were right outside the window,' she said, 'I heard every word.'

I winced, recalling my comments about phone sex among other things. Rachel might be ludicrously smart, but she was still nine.

'My, what big ears you have,' I snapped.

'You want my help or not?'

I rolled my shoulders. 'Yes. Sorry. Did you find anything?'

'You know Docherty? Michael Docherty?'

I frowned. Was she asking, or just making a reference? 'Yes?'

'How … well do you know him?'

How long have you got?

'He's a … friend,' I said cautiously.

'You have a lot of "friends".'

'What can I say, I'm just Miss Popular.' I paused. 'You know him, too?' Maybe Angel had mentioned him.

'No.'

I relaxed.

'But Chesshyre and Shepherd did.'

Chapter Nine

The place was deserted, but Luke rather suspected that was the point. He had to give Jack points for thinking about the location: remote, empty both of people and anywhere surveillance could possibly be hidden, lacking in trees or bushes where an ambush could lurk.

Even if it was bloody freezing.

He huddled into his fleece, leaning against the car, squinting out across the dark sea. It wasn't the sort of beach where children played. It was the sort of beach where dead bodies got washed up. He wished like hell he'd brought Sophie's car to traverse it more easily. But his flat was back under surveillance, and even if he'd wanted MI5 listening in on his meeting with Jack, he was fairly sure the other man would shoot him dead on sight for bringing anyone else with him.

So he'd played cat-and-mouse with a succession of buses, taxis, the London Underground and his old favourite: pickpocketing car keys from someone leaving an underground car park, then aiming the remote at every vehicle until he got one that responded. It was risky, it was illegal, and it had made him smile for the first time since Sophie left his bed.

He'd return the BMW when he was done here. Probably. It was damn annoying being the good guy.

'Nice wheels,' came a voice behind him, and Luke cursed himself for thinking about his girlfriend instead of paying attention to his surroundings. Although what with the waves crashing on the sand and the cold wind blowing in his ears, a whole squadron of cavalry could have surrounded him and he probably wouldn't have heard them coming.

'Thanks,' he said, not turning, 'they came with the car.'

'You're Luke Sharpe?'

At that he turned, and faced Jack de Valera across the car roof.

'On my better days, yes. I'm Luke Sharpe. You're Maria's brother.'

'Jack.' Luke inclined his head in acknowledgement. 'What're you packing?'

'Ham sandwiches,' Luke said. It was a Sophie-like response, flippant and irrelevant, and he watched the younger man's eyes narrow as he took it in. 'And a SIG-Sauer P-229.'

'Show me.'

He took the gun from his waistband and held it by the barrel.

'Eject the magazine.'

Luke said nothing, but did as he was asked. He laid the cartridge down on the roof of the car, and Jack reached out for it. Luke kept his reaction private. He never let anyone touch his gun.

Desperate times, Luke.

'You can have this back when we're done,' Jack said, tucking the magazine into a pocket.

'And what are you carrying?'

A flash of rage crossed Jack's face. 'I'm not. Your girlfriend stole my gun.'

At that Luke laughed. 'Yeah, she does that. You know where she is?'

'No. You?'

'No.' He had a few ideas, but he didn't know. 'Why did you turn on her?'

'I'm asking the questions.'

Luke raised one eyebrow. He was maybe ten years older than this guy, but if, as Maria said Jack had been bounty hunting since his youth, then those extra ten years probably didn't account for much.

However, Luke did have one crucial advantage, namely a year of dealing with the stubborn, contrary, brilliant, corkscrew-brained entity known as Sophie Green. Jack, the poor sod, could never have developed the negotiating skills Luke had, although since he'd spent a week with Sophie he ought to have figured a few things out.

'I'm the MI6 officer here,' he said calmly. 'I'm going to ask the questions, and you're going to answer them. And if you don't, I'm going to have to do something I really don't want to.'

He saw Jack's dark gaze flicker uncertainly over him. The car hid most of his body, but it wouldn't be an unreasonable assumption that Luke might have more concealed weaponry about his person.

'I'm going to get in this car and drive away,' Luke said. 'Which would mean this whole trip would be wasted and I'll be no closer to finding out what you know about Sophie. I'm not going to hurt you,' he said. 'I'm not going to take you in. I'm not here on official business, which makes everything nicely untraceable. Quite frankly, I don't give a rat's arse what you've done and who you've done it to. Unless you've done it to Sophie.'

'I've done nothing to Sophie,' Jack said hurriedly.

'That's not the way she tells it.'

For a moment, something flickered in the other man's expression. Luke knew it well. Jack felt guilty about something – but what, exactly?

'Look,' Jack said, 'I want to trust her. I really do. But she runs off to see you – so she tells me – and then the next day, we're very nearly intercepted by MI5. And that's a bit too much of a coincidence for me. I want to know who told them we were going to be there. Because if it wasn't her, it was you.'

Luke cocked his head and considered this. Irritating as it was, the kid had a point. With his professional hat on, he could see how Jack had jumped to his conclusions. It wasn't even a very big jump.

'The man who is after you is called Robert Harrington,' he said eventually. 'He's a pit-bull. 5 love him because he gets results. Everyone else hates him. There's a strong possibility he's an utter psychopath. But he's on the side of the law and you're not. He will do anything to achieve his ends, do you understand? Anything.'

'How did he know where we were?'

'They had BBC&H under surveillance.'

He watched as Jack took this in. Saw the realisation come over his face of what that meant.

'When I went to the law firm to see what I could find they told me nothing. Someone else had already been sniffing around there. I thought it was probably 5 but now I realise it was probably you. Am I right?'

Jack hesitated, then nodded.

'Which probably put them on alert. Perhaps they recognised you. Perhaps 5 have a feed on their surveillance. Whatever it was, there were spooks outside when I left and they've been following me since.' Jack opened his mouth and Luke continued steadily, 'And yes, I shook them before I came here. I learned how to lose a tail while you were still in school.'

A low blow, but he had to take the kid down a peg or two. Simply the thought of this good-looking young guy spending so much time with Sophie irritated him like a thistle under his skin.

'How do I know you're telling the truth?' Jack said.

Luke shrugged. 'You don't. Just as you don't know whether I've got a dozen more guns secreted about my person. You didn't even pat me down. Wasn't smart to do this with the car between us.'

He saw the anger come over Jack's face, smiled and walked away. It was good to be in control again.

Truth be told, standing with the car between them wasn't such a mistake as it was a calculated risk. The vehicle could offer protection if he drew a hidden weapon. Not checking Luke for more than one gun, that was a mistake. But it was the only one the kid had made. His choice of location and his attitude were pretty good. In other circumstances, Luke might have thought about recruiting him.

He wasn't concerned about Jack firing on him. At least, not yet. The kid wanted something.

The patchy dunes gave way to a bit of straggly beach, and in the dullness of the early evening every lump of driftwood looked like a corpse. He walked for a little while, wondering if whoever was watching his flat had noticed him wearing hiking boots, and then he paused to look out over the sea. Somewhere out ahead of him was Holland. He seriously doubted Sophie had gone there. Shame: it would have been much more symbolic and poignant to stare out towards a shore where he knew she resided, but since she could be in bloody Africa for all he knew, he didn't see this as being very likely.

'Why'd you ask to meet me?' Jack said from behind him.

'I want to see who the woman I love is spending all her time with these days.'

Jack was silent. Luke wondered if Sophie had put it that strongly, if she'd described him as her boyfriend or her lover or the man she wanted to spend the rest of her life with. Presumably she had, at some point, at least mentioned him.

'Is everything okay between you two?' Jack asked eventually.

Why, what had Sophie said? Had she said she was having problems with him? Had she said she was leaving him?

Panic gripped him. The way she'd been with him that night. *As if she was saying goodbye.*

But Luke didn't betray his paranoia. Instead he said lightly, 'Peachy. There's just this little hiccup of her being on the run but as soon as that's sorted out, it'll be rainbows and butterflies all the way. You got a girlfriend?'

'No.'

'Boyfriend?'

'You sound like Sophie.'

'We spend a lot of time together. Usually.' Luke turned to face Jack, regarded him in the dying light. Handsome bastard, dark eyes and high cheekbones, which irritated Luke since Sophie had something of a weakness for cheekbones. She claimed to prefer blonds, but Luke figured this was something of a comforting lie since she'd spent the night with at least one dark-haired man that he knew of.

'I don't like her spending so much time with you,' he said abruptly. 'She's my girlfriend, I love her, and I'm jealous. That's the truth of it. She spent the night once with someone else and it nearly killed me to find out.'

'She cheated on you?' Jack looked surprised.

'No. We weren't together then. It was,' Luke paused to ungrit his teeth, 'a technicality. Doesn't mean I have to like it. But I also don't like the idea of her being alone. She's smart and she's strong, but she's inexperienced and – and fragile.'

'Sophie?' Jack snorted. 'Fragile?'

Luke knew his expression must have darkened from the look on Jack's face. 'Emotionally. I'm speaking here of emotions, young Jack, of which you may have heard. Women have them. They seem to find them important.'

'There's no need to get sarcastic.'

But there was every need, or else those emotions Sophie was so fond of would take over Luke's being and force him to sob uncontrollably.

'She's not a stupid, weak female,' he said. 'She's not the type to stand around and scream for help.'

'I've noticed,' Jack said with feeling, touching the side of his head, where Luke assumed Sophie had clocked him with her handbag. He hid a smile. Sometimes he wondered if Sophie thought she was a cartoon character. 'She's the type to make other people scream for help.'

This time Luke did smile. 'Yeah,' he said fondly. Hell of a woman, his Sophie.

He forced himself to focus. 'Look. I don't know where she is, she won't tell me for fear I'll follow her there, but she's still working on this case and she's making progress. But you know what she needs?'

'Strong medication?' Jack muttered.

'A partner,' Luke said, ignoring the thought that Jack was right. 'She needs someone to watch her back. You may not have noticed but she has very little idea what to do with that beloved gun of hers. Can't drive worth a damn. Doesn't speak any foreign languages beyond asking for a beer and a portion of chips. I assume you, like your sister, are bilingual?'

'Should the investigation take us back to France or Italy, I'm practically a native,' Jack said. 'If Judge Shepherd were found to have connections in the Middle East, however, I'd be less useful.'

'She's somewhere abroad,' Luke said. 'I don't know where. I hope to God it's not the Middle East, because she'd last five seconds before getting stoned to death.'

Jack regarded him, head on one side, for a moment. Then he said, 'You sound like you're trying to hook me up with her.'

Luke jammed his hands into his pockets. Partly because he was cold and partly because he didn't want Jack to see him balling up his fists.

'That's exactly what I'm doing.'

Jack went very still. Luke waited.

'I'm sorry, you're going to have to repeat that,' Jack said finally. 'You want me to hook up with your girlfriend?'

'In a platonic sense,' Luke said. 'Touch her and you'll be singing soprano for the rest of your life.'

Jack held up his hands in a gesture of surrender, but Luke noticed he didn't protest against the idea of fancying Sophie.

'You're a bounty hunter.' Jack nodded. 'How's your track record?'

'Never lost a skip yet.'

'Can you shoot?' Jack nodded again. 'Show me.'

'I would,' Jack said, 'but someone stole my shooter.'

Luke held out his own gun, and after a beat, Jack took it and slid the cartridge in.

'I could shoot you,' he said.

'For what possible purpose?'

'I might be a murderer. I might have killed Judge Shepherd. I might want to kill you so I can shag your girlfriend.'

'If you killed me, Sophie would kill you,' Luke said calmly. Sophie could be a berserker if someone she loved was threatened.

Jack considered this, and Luke saw agreement cross his face.

'Plus, if you were going to kill me, you'd have done it already,' Luke added. He pointed at a piece of driftwood about fifty yards away. 'Hit that.' Then, remembering Sophie's love of *Butch Cassidy & the Sundance Kid*, he added, 'And yes, you can move.'

'What?'

'Not a movie fan?'

Jack looked at him as if he was crazy. 'I can see why you and Sophie get on so well,' he said.

He aimed, fired, and the piece of driftwood jumped in the air.

'Nice,' Luke said. He cast about on the ground, and found a smaller piece. 'Now hit this.'

He threw it into the air and Jack, after a moment's surprise, aimed.

He missed.

'Again,' he said.

'Bullets don't grow on trees,' Luke said. 'It was close enough.'

'Look, what the hell is this all about?' Jack said, not handing the gun back. 'You want me to … what? Bodyguard her?'

'Something like that, yes. She can't do this alone. Well,' he amended, 'she could, I've come to believe Sophie can do anything she damn well chooses to, but she shouldn't have to do it alone. The two of you can work better together than alone.'

'If you think she shouldn't be alone, then why are you standing here talking to me instead of flying out to be with her?'

Luke shook his head. 'I can shake a tail for a few hours,' he said, 'but leaving the country? Sophie got out because they weren't watching for her. They'll have me before I can get past check-in. Who do you think issued my passport? All my aliases?'

'The guy who got Sophie a fake one –?'

'Doesn't want to sleep with me,' Luke said flatly.

Jack blinked at him.

'Sophie had a one-night stand with Docherty last year.' He forced his voice into dispassionate coolness. 'She also shot him a couple of times. They have a complex relationship, but the long and the short of it is that he wants her and he can't have her.'

Jack opened his mouth. He shut it again.

'I can trust him like a shark. You, on the other hand …'

'You don't even know me.'

'I know your sister. And I know Sophie decided to trust you, at least before you went batshit crazy on her and lost that trust.' He gave Jack a severe look. 'And I know that even if she'd never, ever admit it to herself, let alone anyone else, she needs someone to be with her right now. That's going to be you. And you're not going to tell her I sent you, either.'

'Why not?'

'She resents any implication that she can't take care of herself.'

Jack stared at the sea for a long moment.

'How am I supposed to know where she is?'

Luke took out his phone. 'I'll give you her number.'

'You're assuming she'll tell me her location? After I threatened her with a gun?'

'Well,' Luke said, pity staining his voice, 'you'll just have to be charming.'

Jack stared at the sea a while longer. 'Oh, Christ,' he said.

'What do you mean, they knew him?'

Rachel beckoned me back into the house and brought up a file on the computer. 'This is Theo's diary from ten years ago,' she said, scrolling to September and pointing to a name written in red. Michael Docherty. 'And this is Judge Shepherd's ...' The same name, on the same date.

'Can you tell what they wanted him for?'

'I don't know. There's just his name.' She looked up at me. 'You okay?'

'Will people stop asking me that? I'm fine!'

'It's just half of your eye make-up is under your eyes. And the other half is somewhere around your neck.'

I made a face at her. 'All right. I'm going to take a shower.' I paused in the doorway. 'Thank you, Rachel.'

She didn't look up. 'Like I said, it beats gym class.'

Teresa furnished me with towels and I stood under the hot water for what felt like hours. I think I was hoping it would wash away some of my guilt and uncertainty, but all it removed was travel dirt.

So on top of Jack and his paranoia, I was forced into doubts about Docherty. I wasn't sure which one worried me more. Jack knew a lot about the case we were investigating, but did I really think he'd do me harm?

And what about Docherty? He knew where I was. He knew my alias. Docherty, in point of fact, knew how I took my coffee and which shampoo I used and what I looked like when I slept. Docherty knew a lot more about me than I was comfortable with.

Okay, before we get any further: the thing with Docherty. Yes, it's true I got his car blown up. Yes, it's true I shot him. And yes, it's true I slept with him. These things are not unrelated. Basically, I thought he was a bad guy, so I shot him and stole his car. And then I felt bad about it, so I … um.

That sounds worse than it is. I shot him in the leg, just to incapacitate him, and took his car because, well, mine was out of action and his was an Aston Martin. And then someone tried to kill me by blowing up said Aston Martin. Truth be told, I felt worse about this than about shooting him, especially when he'd proved once and for all that he was on my side.

And the thing about the sex. I normally would steer damn clear of men as dangerous as Docherty, who is about as sane and safe as Batman, Loki and Doctor Horrible all rolled into one, but the thing is that Luke and I had just broken up, and Docherty was there, and … like I said, it's not something I'm proud of.

Rachel was already sitting at the table in the kitchen as

Teresa started ladling gravy over plates of delicious-smelling meat and greens.

'Um,' I began hesitantly, not wanting to offend her, but Rachel piped up before I got any further.

'I told her you don't eat meat,' she said. 'It's okay. Grampa doesn't either.'

'Bad for his heart,' Teresa said. 'It's a tofu fake-lamb thing.'

Lamb like Mother used to make.

Mother. Damn, I was doing fine with the homesickness until she called me up. I looked down at my plate and concentrated on eating.

'Have you found anything from the computer?' Teresa asked Rachel.

'Yeah,' she said. 'I have a name.'

'Who?' Teresa asked.

I sent Rachel frantic *No!* signals, which she calmly ignored and said, 'Michael Docherty.' Her eyes narrowed and she turned to me. 'Didn't you once –'

'Yes, but we're not going to talk about that right now.'

All eyes swivelled to me.

'About what?' Teresa asked pleasantly.

'It's not important.'

'It is if he's a suspect.'

'She –' Rachel began, and I glared at her extra hard. But she continued, oblivious, 'she once blew up his car.'

'Oh,' I relaxed, 'that.'

'There's something else?' Teresa asked, an edge of danger in her voice.

'I didn't blow it up,' I said. 'Someone else blew it up. It just happened to be in my custody.'

'Was it a nice car?'

'Aston Martin Vanquish.'

They both winced.

'Anyway, how do you know about that?' I asked Rachel.

'Angel told me. She calls me all the time.' Which was a very Angel thing to do. 'She tells me a lot of things about you and Luke and Docherty ... Like hey, she once kissed my dad,' Rachel told her grandmother.

'Before he met Angel,' I stressed.

'And then you kissed Angel, too.'

'There's a story behind that,' I said desperately.

'Do tell,' Teresa said.

'It's really not interesting,' I said, hurriedly standing up. 'Thanks for lunch. Really, it was delicious. Rachel, don't you have homework to do?'

Yes, it was ungracious. Next time you get accused of murder and find out that one of the three men you've ever slept with has possibly framed you and may be trying to kill you, tell me how polite you end up being.

And the kissing thing. I've explained this so often I have a spiel. I was passing on a message. From Harvey. It was nothing. Not that Luke, who took pictures, and Harvey, who wanted a video, would agree.

I spent the rest of the afternoon trying and failing to find anything on Docherty. Rachel didn't intervene. Guess I'd offended her. Wow, my track record was really improving.

Docherty had sent the passport to Cécile's house ... and then someone found us there. Or at least found Jack. But how had he known we were in England? Did he have a tracker on Luke's car? But why? And why wait so long to blow it up? Maybe he'd managed to trace my phone. Could he do that? Even when I kept changing numbers?

I supposed he could. But the thing is, it's just not Docherty's style. He's not ostentatious. He wouldn't play cat-and-mouse. Wouldn't grandstand. If he wanted rid of you, he'd just put a bullet in your head.

It was getting dark outside. I leaned over to switch on the

desk lamp, and as I did noticed some police reports in the printer tray.

Holy cow, Rachel was smart. I slapped my own face for being so rude to her, went online and emailed her links to all my favourite Buffy video clips, including the Pop-Up Video parody soundtracked by The Divinyls' *I Touch Myself* that Angel had forbidden me to tell her about on account of its adult subject matter, but which Rachel would almost certainly find hilarious.

Rachel emailed back from her iPhone in minutes. 'I guess you're forgiven. But what's Pop-Up Video?'

I reminded myself she was nine and had probably never even heard of VH-1, and settled down to read the report on Irene Shepherd's death.

Her body had been found in her office. She'd been wearing a bathrobe and nothing else – there was a bath full of cold water in the en suite. The bullet had hit her in the back of the head. She hadn't seen it coming. Gun found at scene of crime. Body discovered by maid. The house alarm hadn't gone off because Shepherd wasn't in the habit of switching it on until she went to bed.

I sat and drummed my fingers on the desk, then I typed in an Internet address and downloaded a new program we used to use at the airport. With this program, I started checking flights to Hartford, Connecticut, around the time of the murder. I ran a search on all airlines for Docherty, Michael. I'd travelled with him before and he'd used his real name then. But then he hadn't had any reason to hide.

It couldn't be Docherty. Surely I hadn't slept with a murderer?

There were no matches, but then that didn't prove anything. He obviously had no problem with fake passports.

I drummed my fingers a bit more, then, just for a laugh, typed in the names of the six people I'd sent to prison. Nothing there either.

Sighing, I went back to the BBC&H files and started cross-referencing Sir Theodore and Irene's cases again, saving all the names in a Word file, then searching for them on the flight database.

'Neat,' Rachel said from the doorway, making me jump. 'Where'd you find that?'

'What?'

'That program.'

'SO17. Used to use it a lot. Actually it's just a flight database we used to use at the airport.'

She nodded seriously. 'Anything useful?'

'No. I looked up Docherty, but he hasn't flown to the States in a while.'

'Maybe he used a fake name.'

'Maybe.'

Rachel chewed her lip. 'I'm sorry if I said too much about you and Docherty. Angel hardly tells me anything about him. Just tiny little bits that slip out.'

I looked back at her, standing in the light and warmth of the hallway, a little girl with skinny legs and a sweatshirt too big for her.

'It's okay,' I said. 'It's not a secret.'

She visibly relaxed. Sometimes I forget Rachel is just a child. 'Who is he? Docherty?'

I shrugged. He was a former colleague of Luke's, but in what capacity neither of them would tell me. I guessed SAS purely from his skill level. When I met him he was working in private security, which probably meant he knew where to hide bodies. He carried a matching pair of Heckler Koch .45s, and had a taste for theatrical cars. I'd only ever seen him wear black, apart from that one occasion I saw him wear nothing at all. He wasn't above blackmail to get what he wanted, and although he'd never threatened me physically, I didn't expect he'd think too hard about it if it would get him what he wanted. He made Luke look like the Good Angel.

He was a man of many talents, and just as many secrets. I had no idea what I actually meant to him, and if I ever thought about how much I ought to be able to trust him I frightened myself, because the answer was, against all my best instincts: not at all.

Rachel was still waiting for an answer. I told her as lightly as I could, 'He could be Batman for all I know.'

'Batman's lame,' Rachel said, standing on one foot and hanging onto the doorframe. 'Has to wear a special suit to do anything. Buffy could save the world in a cheerleading uniform.'

'Buffy sucked at cheerleading, remember?'

'Only because of a spell,' Rachel said dismissively.

I smiled at her, and she smiled back. Sweet kid.

Then she spoiled it all by asking, 'So how close are you to him?'

I raised my eyebrows and tried not to blush. 'What's that supposed to mean?'

'You think he'd tell you what he was doing at BBC&H?'

I rolled my eyes and tried to sound like a mature, competent adult. 'Rachel, if he really had framed me, do you think he'd tell me the truth about that? Anyway. There should be client notes or something in this system.'

'Not that I could find.'

Which probably meant they were unfindable. I've really got to stop surrounding myself with such superlative people. It makes me feel very inadequate.

Teresa appeared behind her granddaughter. 'I'm making dinner,' she said. Her eyes flickered over the data on the screen. 'It'll be about an hour.'

I nodded and thanked her, and she took Rachel away to help peel carrots.

I turned back to my notes, and started the long, slow process of searching for each name on my list within the flight database. It took ages, because it could only search for one at a time, and I was searching for all flights into and out of Hartford. Then out of London – all airports. Each search took forever.

It didn't help a lot that some of the appointments were just for J. Anderson or Mrs Beech or JB Finchley Esq. No first names. So many variables.

Gramps Cortes returned home from work, waved a vague hello and switched on the TV in the next room. I ate dinner with the family and made an attempt at polite conversation. Gave Rachel a hug goodnight and thanked Teresa once more for taking me in.

She regarded me with calm, dark eyes, and nodded. 'Anything for a friend of Rachel's,' she said, and she was so damn inscrutable I had no idea if she was being sincere or not.

I stifled a yawn and went back to the computer screen. No new matches found.

'Maybe we're going about this the wrong way,' I said to myself, pulling the keyboard toward me. 'Maybe it's not someone who came into contact with them together. Maybe it's just coincidence that they worked at BBC&H together.'

I closed my eyes, the enormity of it hitting me. Maybe it was someone who knew Sir Theodore through MI5, and Irene through an American connection. After all, she was a lawyer over here for ten years before she went to England, and she'd been a Supreme Court Judge for five years, too.

That made a hell of a lot of people to work through.

My back ached, my eyes were dry, my brain throbbed with overuse. I wanted to just give up. Let them take me. This was all too hard.

I allowed myself precisely five minutes to wallow, then pulled myself together and angled the keyboard closer.

'So then, Sophie girl. Where'd you want to start?'

It never failed to amaze Luke how Sophie could sleep through all sorts of noises in the middle of the night. Even when something woke her, she'd dismiss it as the house settling down, the ancient boiler, or Tammy.

Consequently, when he slept at her flat, he woke a dozen times a night. The place was noisy as hell. That damn boiler for one thing, creaking and groaning its way through the night like an old man complaining about his joints. He'd buy her a new one, if he didn't think she'd refuse out of some kind of middle-class pride.

Then there was Tammy, who made an astonishing amount of noise for such a small cat. Thumping onto the floor from some high perch, knocking over books or clattering stacks of CDs, bringing in live mice which she let loose, squeaking in terror, to run around the living room and once, memorably, the bed. Squalling with another cat outside.

So when he woke to hear her low growl he initially dismissed it. Just the Tamster picking on another cat twice her size outside the window.

Except she couldn't be outside the window, because he wasn't at Sophie's. He didn't have a cat flap. His flat was watertight.

Except for the trapdoor. And Tammy couldn't have opened that herself.

He came awake, alert, and opened his eyes very slowly.

The growl came from the doorway and he could make out the small shape of Tammy, back arched, fur bristled out, growling at something unseen in his living room.

Very slowly, very quietly, Luke reached for his gun. Beneath him a bedspring creaked and he held his breath, but there was no sound from the living room. No sounds at all, anywhere in the flat, apart from Tammy growling.

Achingly slowly, he gained his feet and crept to the door. It didn't creak. He could open it silently, although the change in light might alert whoever was in the living room.

Stop being ridiculous, Luke. She's probably just growling at a random shadow. She's a cat, not a guard dog.

But every beat of his heart told him something was wrong.

He inched the door open, leading with his gun, and something clattered in the kitchen.

Luke shoved out of his bedroom in time to see a figure bolting for the door. He squeezed off a round, but the figure – swathed in black, moving silently – threw itself into a roll, using the counter for cover. The bullet buried itself in a cupboard, and he heard glass shattering.

He leapt for the other side of the counter but the figure in black was already diving for the front door, whirling back on itself and raising an arm. Metal glinted in the moonlight and Luke hurled himself to the floor, but not before burning pain pierced his body and he fell, agony overwhelming him.

Chapter Ten

I was woken by my phone ringing. Luke.

But when I rolled over and peered groggily at the display, it wasn't his name. It wasn't anyone's name. A UK mobile number.

Cold fear flashed through me. Harrington.

I jabbed at the screen until it went silent, then chucked it under the bed and pulled the covers over my head.

'Ambulance,' said a voice.

Luke stirred. Something hurt. Something hurt a lot.

'Postcode: Charlie Mike Two Four ...'

Someone was reading out his address. Someone was also pressing hard on his shoulder, which hurt like buggery.

'Gunshot wound, upper chest, male, mid-thirties.'

'*Early* thirties,' Luke corrected, but his voice came out as a mumble.

'Sharpe? He's awake. Listen to me, can you breathe? Take in a deep breath?'

He tried. It hurt. Everything hurt. But he'd been in pain before. He took as deep a breath as he could manage, and let it out again. A woman knelt above him, unfamiliar, her face dark in the unlit room.

'Do it again.'

'F'koff,' Luke mumbled, but he took another deep breath. Checking for punctures of the lung. 'Breathing's fine,' he said, making an effort to be clear.

'No ... no, we can handle that.' She was talking into her phone again. All that breathing effort gone to waste. 'No ... I'm overriding you. Because I'm MI5. Just send that bloody ambulance, would you?'

She put the phone away. Luke stared up at her, thoroughly confused. Who the hell was she? Had she been the dark figure shooting at him?

Wait, Luke. Be logical. She just told you who she is. MI5 might sneak in and snoop around but they wouldn't shoot you in a panic.

Probably.

'Sharpe,' she said. 'I'm Sunita Sakib. I'm with MI5. You've been shot. Did you see the intruder?'

He attempted to sit up. Failed. Sunita Sakib pushed him back down again by means of pressing hard on his shoulder. His vision swam.

'I don't think it's fatal but there's no point aggravating it. Stay down and keep calm. My partner is searching for the intruder. We have more men on the way. Did you see the intruder?'

He shook his head. Nodded. 'Saw someone. In the kitchen.' He rolled his head in that direction but couldn't see over the counter. He saw Tammy, however, sitting on the work-surface looking down at him with an expression of polite curiosity.

'Male or female?'

Luke shook his head. 'Couldn't tell. Bent over the counter. Black hat, jacket.' He paused to think. The figure had been neither large nor small, and had moved too fast for him to discern a single feature. 'White.' But it had been dark. 'Maybe Asian.' Which narrowed the field massively.

She nodded, lifting her hand to check the bleeding. Shoulder wound. Could be messy. Likely broke, or at least chipped, the bone. Bullet could still be lodged there.

Facts. Recall facts. 'Knew how to handle a gun,' he told Sunita. 'How to dive. Forces. Maybe Service.'

'A professional.' Her lips thinned. 'Are you currently on anyone's hit list?'

'Dull day when I'm not.'

That earned a glimmer of a smile. Luke shivered, but then he didn't consider this surprising, since he was wearing boxers and the shredded remains of a t-shirt, which Sunita appeared to have ripped off him.

He heard a siren approach. Fabulous. Crappy ambulance beds, people poking at him, the stench of disinfectant. He hated hospitals.

'Sunita?' he said as the siren grew louder and he heard voices outside. Her men.

'Yes?'

'Could you get me some damn clothes?'

I slept late, woken eventually by the chiming of the front-door bell. It took me a while to figure out where I was, and by the time I'd worked it out, the bedroom door had been pushed open and Rachel bounded in, holding a package that was nearly as big as she was. It was covered in 'Fragile' stickers and express labels.

'Special delivery,' she said, placing it carefully on the bed next to me. I blinked at my name on the label, and then I smiled.

'Very, very special,' I said. 'Thank you for bringing it up. Now bugger off.'

'Aw come on, let me see!'

'It's not for childish eyes,' I said. 'Your grandmother would crucify me.'

Grumpily, she left, but I knew she would be loitering outside the door. I ripped open the package and, using the lid of the box to shield the contents, took out a carefully packaged gun and a full case of ammunition. My beloved SIG. Yeah, I know I'm scared of it, but Luke got me this gun. It's like his version of a diamond necklace. In an envelope attached to it was a licence for the SIG, in Alice Maud's name.

'Docherty, I think I love you,' I said, kissing the document.

'I heard that!' crowed Rachel from outside, and I went pink, even though no one could see me.

I went even pinker when I tucked the licence back inside the envelope and realised there was a note inside. In thick black handwriting, it read, 'Now you really owe me.'

Gulp.

Someone knocked on the door and it opened to reveal Teresa with a cup of coffee. She handed it to me and I gave her a look of adoration. Some people have alcohol addictions. Some people do drugs. I do coffee.

'Is that a gun?' Teresa asked, eyes widening.

'Yes – but don't worry, I'm not going to shoot anyone,' I reassured her.

'I don't usually let Harvey bring his gun in the house,' she said. 'I don't want them near Rachel.'

'How about I put it in the car?' I suggested. 'In the boot. The trunk. Locked.'

She looked troubled. 'It's not that I don't trust you –'

'It's okay,' I said. 'I understand.' I wouldn't want Rachel anywhere near a gun either.

Reluctantly, she nodded. I nodded in return, and closed the lid on the box, pushing it to the far side of the bed as Rachel sidled in.

She handed me a sheaf of paper. 'The computer found some more matches overnight,' she said. 'I don't know if these names mean anything to you?'

I looked them over. Sarah Wilde, JD Phelps, Robert King, Martin Colvin.

'Nope. What were they matched with?'

'The first three are people Theo had appointments with who've flown to America at the right time. Colvin was already over here, but he flew back just after. And Wilde

186

came over here the day before Irene was shot, then went back to London the day after.'

Our eyes met. 'You found anything else on her yet?'

'It's still searching.'

I thanked them both and Teresa shepherded Rachel out so I could get dressed, which I did in jeans and a t-shirt. Then I fastened on the shoulder brace Docherty had thoughtfully included, tucked my SIG into it, and fastened my hoodie over the top.

I considered myself from all angles in the mirror. The gun was a smaller, lightweight version of the piece Luke carried. For a semi-automatic, it was fairly unobtrusive. I couldn't detect the shape of it under my clothes.

I slipped my trainers on, took the gun case out to the car, ostentatiously waving it at Teresa as I passed her, and locked it in the boot.

Sorted.

Rachel was frowning at the computer screen when I went into the den.

'Seriously, don't you go to school?'

'I told them I was sick.'

'Rachel, you can't keep skiving off like this.'

She turned big brown eyes on me. 'Skiving? Is that, like, a British word, or, like, an old word?'

'British,' I said, stung by the 'old' comment. 'Teenagers say it. Got anything on Sarah Wilde?'

'Nope.'

'Well –'

'Nothing at all. It's like she doesn't exist.'

'But that doesn't mean anything. I can never find myself on the Internet and I'm pretty sure I exist.'

To demonstrate, I typed my name into the search box and waited.

Not a single thing came up. Not one thing. This was weird,

since I knew I had profiles on various social networking sites, fan pages and even on the bookshop's website.

I searched for myself on Facebook: nothing. I found my brother's profile, and Angel's, both of which were empty of any mentions of me.

I stared, shocked. MI5 had just erased me.

'You were saying?' Rachel raised an eyebrow.

'Yes, well, obviously before I became an international fugitive.'

You have to admit, that sounded kind of cool.

Rachel typed a few things and came up with the news stories about Sir Theodore. I wasn't named on any of them, but she pieced together tiny bits of info to produce a profile that sounded a heck of a lot like me.

'The ex-government operative, former airport worker ... formerly a video rental clerk ... used to work in a lab ... in a stationery shop ... How many jobs have you had?'

'A few, all right?'

'But you're ...' she cocked her head. 'Says on your passport you're twenty-eight.'

'Says on my passport my name is Alice.'

'How old are you?' Rachel asked, peering at me as if I was a museum piece. Exhibit: Sophie Green, 12thC, believed oldest in existence.

'Is it important?' I asked, frowning. Mentally, I was counting up past jobs. Before the airport there had been the lab, and before that the video place, and before that ...

All right, so there had been a lot of jobs. Temporary things while I worked out what to do next. Fillers, to tide me over. Keep money in the bank. The airport was the longest I'd ever stuck it out, and even that was only two years.

I didn't finish university. I just kind of ... assumed I'd work out what to do after a while. And all of a sudden, half-a-million temp jobs later, I'm not twenty-one any more.

All of a sudden, thirty isn't far away, and I still don't have a proper job. Or a proper flat. Being my mother's tenant doesn't count. The most adult thing I have to my name is an arrest warrant.

Well ... crap.

While I pondered this, my phone rang again.

'You're popular,' Rachel said. 'I heard it ringing in the middle of the night.'

'Yeah,' I said vaguely, scrabbling in my pocket for it. 'British time.'

But when I got the phone out it wasn't showing Luke's name, or Docherty's, or anyone's. Again. That UK mobile number.

I let it go onto voicemail. At least, this was the plan, but I hadn't damn well set up voicemail, so it just carried on ringing.

'Aren't you going to answer that?' Rachel asked.

If it just rang out, would anyone be able to trace me on it? Did I have to answer for that to work?

I hit the 'ignore' button and the bleeping mercifully ceased.

'Whatever,' Rachel said, and went back to the computer. I opened my mouth to tell her she really ought to be in school, but in my heart of hearts I knew no school in the world would teach her how to track down criminals. Besides, I also knew she was in a Gifted & Talented programme which basically boiled down to a More Homework plan. Let the kid have fun for a day.

I wandered outside into the sunshine and poked around on my phone, setting up voicemail. I let the machine do its own automated message – no way was I setting myself up for a fall. I called Luke about the names Rachel had found, but only got his message service. Being that I was calling his secret phone, the message had been tailored to me.

'Even the best of boyfriends has to sleep occasionally. Even the ones who are secret agents. Either that, or I've been shot or thrown into a woodchipper or something. I'll call you back as soon as I find all my fingers.'

I smiled and left a message, then sat listening to the birds, a car occasionally swooshing by on the road, the distant drone of a plane far above. Teresa talking quietly on the phone.

'... no sir, and I know this isn't your area, but I believe she's a dangerous criminal.'

Every muscle I had tightened.

'Yes, she has at least one handgun. No, sir, she hasn't threatened us, but –'

Fuck. I was on my feet, moving back through the house as quickly and quietly as possible. Ducked into the den, where Rachel was still studying data.

'Anything new?' I asked, trying to sound casual.

'No. I can't link any of these guys together.'

'Okay, well, let me have what you've got and I'll, er, I'll, er ... thanks,' I babbled, and backed away. Smooth, Sophie, smooth.

I made it up to my room, heart pounding, and leaned against the door.

She'd turned me in. The bitch had turned me in!

I began shoving things back into my bag. The folded printouts went in the side pocket. Damn it, she'd let Rachel help me out – to what end? Gathering information she could give to the police? Why allow me to stay in the first place? Why turn me in?

But I knew the answer to that, and I couldn't stay angry with her for it. Simply by being here I was endangering Teresa's family. She'd already lost a daughter, and now I was putting her beloved grandchild at risk.

I sat down on the bed. Rachel's genius help or not, I shouldn't have come.

I was beginning to run out of places to hide.

I got out my phone and found a flight booking app. Looked up flights out of Cincinnati. How far could I get without changing planes?

Then I shoved the rest of my belongings into my bag and made my way downstairs. Teresa passed by in the hall and I pushed my bag behind the turn of the stairs so she wouldn't see. Dammit. How to get it into the car without arousing her suspicions?

'Teresa,' I said, going down the rest of the way, 'is there a mall or something around here? A high street? I could use some new clothes, I can't just keep wearing these.'

'I can wash them for you,' she offered, face pleasantly unthreatening.

'No, that's fine. I could just use a couple more t-shirts, some more underwear, that kind of thing.'

She regarded me a moment. Then she said, 'There's one not far from here. When my husband gets home from work I'll take you there.'

'Well, why don't we go now?' I said, rapidly calculating how easy it would be to lose her in a busy mall.

'I can't leave Rachel home alone.'

The hell you can't, I thought. Rachel would make Kevin McCallister look like an amateur.

'She can come with us.'

'No, if she's seen I could get into trouble for letting her skip school. To help you,' she added, and I winced.

'Well, then, I'll go by myself. I don't want to trouble you,' I added, and Teresa's face stayed carefully immobile.

'Well, all right then,' she said, and gave me directions. I thanked her, smiled, went upstairs to retrieve my wallet, and scooped up the bag on the way. Went into my bedroom and closed the door noisily.

I waited a few seconds, then as quietly as I possibly could, tiptoed out of my room and into Rachel's. Her window overlooked the drive at the side of the house where my hire car was parked. Cautiously, I opened it, leaned out as far as I could, and let the bag drop down between the car and the house. I flinched as it hit the ground, but I reminded myself that as I'd already packed with the violence of an airport baggage belt in mind, a fifteen-foot drop would be nothing in comparison.

I sauntered down the stairs, poked my head into the den to tell Rachel I was going shopping, and tried not to let my goodbye show in my face.

'Laters,' she said, not looking up.

So much for goodbyes.

I walked out of the house, calling to Teresa, 'I won't be long!' and scuttled round to the driver's side of the car, which luckily was also where the bag was. Opened the door. Chucked the bag in. Then I scuttled back, because that was the damn passenger side.

'Drive on the right,' I told myself out loud, just in case Teresa had seen me, although she'd have had to be hiding behind the curtains to do so.

Then I got behind the wheel, slid out of the drive, and got the hell out of Dodge.

'Quite unbelievably lucky,' said the surgeon crisply. 'I hope you realise that.'

'Every damn day,' Luke said. 'Can I go home now?'

Her eyes narrowed. 'You most certainly can not. Do you know what the chances are of the bullet missing the scapular?'

'Low,' Luke said, smothering a yawn. He'd been there all day, in and out of consciousness, and now the pain meds were really beginning to kick in and he was starting to feel woozy.

'Didn't even nick the artery. No significant muscle damage ...' She actually sounded annoyed with him. 'Mr Sharpe, you must have a guardian angel, that's all I can say.'

Luke didn't dignify that with an answer.

'You're very, very lucky.' And she walked away. Luke watched her go, considering as he did that a year or so ago he'd probably have flirted with her a little more. An attractive woman, clearly skilled with her hands, who already knew what he looked like with his shirt off. He'd have done it automatically. A year ago.

He twisted to look at the heavy bandaging and hugely confining sling on his right arm.

'Yeah,' he said. 'I feel lucky.'

His head rested against the pillows propping him up. He'd been hurt before, of course he had, but never in his own home. The place was supposed to be a fortress. He had lasers on the windows and steel-reinforced doors. Yeah, so he also had a trapdoor exit, maybe he needed to secure that a bit better. But judging by the professionalism of the hit, the intruder probably had as much training in disabling locks and alarms as Luke himself had. God knew enough people had broken into his flat lately.

Who the hell had shot him? Who'd be breaking in like that? MI5 had no reason to shoot him. Hell, if it hadn't been for Sunita he'd have been in a much worse state. People died from injuries like this. Bullet goes half an inch one way or the other and the artery explodes. Death in minutes. Could have shattered the bone. Or there was the risk of lung injury. A shot to the body was a shot to kill.

Sophie still charmingly believed in the idea that sometimes a person might shoot to wound, not to kill. But Luke had taken firearms training from the best. He knew that if you were shooting at someone, you meant to kill them.

The person who'd shot him knew what they were doing.

The automatic, unpanicked, easy movements spoke of someone with years of training. That shot to the body would have killed him if he hadn't moved.

It wasn't 5. It wasn't 6. Probably. Who else? A foreign agent? That deal he'd been working on in Kyrgyzstan? Unlikely. A personal enemy? He'd never considered that he had any.

Wait. What about Jack?

Could he have followed Luke home? But why interrogate him? He'd been perfectly willing to co-operate with Jack earlier and he hadn't hidden the fact. Maybe Jack was a bit insane. In which case sending him off to help Sophie wasn't a smart thing to do.

No, it couldn't have been Jack. He had no reason to shoot Luke. Hell, if he'd wanted to he could have done it with Luke's own gun.

'It doesn't make any sense,' he muttered.

'People trying to shoot you?' came a voice from the doorway, and he looked over to see Evelyn standing there, immaculate as always.

'He didn't *try* to shoot me, he succeeded. He *tried* to kill me,' Luke corrected tiredly.

'He?'

'Or she. Couldn't tell.'

'Luke Sharpe, unable to tell a man from a woman.' She came forward into the room. 'Forensics have been checking your flat.'

'Is nowhere sacred?'

'Looks like two rounds, one that hit you and one in the floor that must have missed by a few inches. Low-calibre gun. Yours hit a cupboard. You'll need new glassware.'

'Well then, get me to John Lewis, there's not a moment to lose.' He covered his face with his good arm.

'On the counter ...' Evelyn hesitated.

Luke moved his arm and looked up at her. A tiny frown wrinkled her flawless forehead.

'On the counter …?'

'Coffee. Grains everywhere.'

He stared. 'My intruder was making coffee?'

'No. Your intruder was drugging your coffee. Barbiturates.' She hesitated again. 'I've seen the way you drink coffee. Strong and black, straight down. Doesn't even touch the sides. I'd hazard a guess it's the first thing you consume in the morning, too.'

He shrugged his left shoulder. 'Not an unusual habit, is it?'

'No, but … most people sip their coffee. You down yours so fast you'd have no idea there was anything wrong with it. This is someone who knows you, Luke.'

His head began to throb. Bit by bit, the truth invaded his foggy, medicated brain.

'Think about it. You wake up in the morning, first thing you do is make yourself some coffee. Half-an-hour later you're out cold. This person would even know when to come back and – well, do whatever they planned to do.'

Someone who knows you. 'What do you think they planned to do?' His voice sounded scratchy.

Evelyn shrugged. 'I don't know. Maybe they were after information. They thought you knew something, or had something they wanted? After all, you do have access to some pretty sensitive information.'

'No more than anyone else. I'm not even on a current case.'

Evelyn's neat white teeth bit into her plump lower lip. 'Well, you sort of are,' she said.

'No, you were there,' he began tiredly.

'Not an official case. Luke, what are you spending all your time doing?'

'None of your business.'

'You're looking for Sophie. You're trying to clear her

name. Don't you think it's possible the two things are connected? Your girlfriend goes on the run and someone tries to drug you?'

'Are you saying someone has it in for both of us?'

'Maybe. Or maybe they wanted to know what you know. Do you know where she is?'

'No.' No, dammit.

'You're gathering evidence for her, aren't you? Harrington would probably love to get his hands on what you know.'

'Harrington can fuck off.' He didn't for a minute think Harrington had been the one breaking in. He wouldn't do it like that, secret and underhand. He'd get a warrant and drag Luke in for questioning. He'd probably be doing that any day now.

He closed his eyes, overwhelmingly tired. 'Did Forensics find anything else?' His trapdoor? The illegally strong absinthe in the liquor cabinet? Photos he'd taken of Sophie naked?

'Haven't heard. I'll tell you if they do.' She took something from her pocket and laid it on the table by his bed. It was his phone. His official phone.

Then, her eyes steady on him, she took his unofficial phone from her other pocket and laid that down, too. She didn't say a word. She didn't have to. Luke was damn lucky she'd picked up both before 5 found them.

'You're being watched,' she said. 'Sheila has someone here, and I'd be amazed if Harrington doesn't, too. Possibly there's someone from CID loitering about.'

'I should sell tickets.' A thought occurred to him. 'What about Tammy?'

Evelyn looked blank.

'Tammy, the cat. Sophie's cat. I'm supposed to be looking after her. Tell me she hasn't been let out of the flat.'

Evelyn narrowed her eyes and held out her hand. Marring her expensive manicure were a collection of small, angry red

196

scratches.

'Charming creature,' she said.

'Someone needs to look after her.'

'It won't be me. I am not a cat person.' She said it with a delicate shudder, and Luke knew that if Sophie were here she'd be consigning Evelyn to a low circle of hell. Sophie claimed she could never get along with people who didn't like cats. She said it was a fundamental difference in life philosophies, like trying to get along with a racist or someone who enjoyed *The X Factor*.

Angel had overheard her and replied, 'That's a bit offensive to people who like *The X Factor*, Sophie.'

'*The X Factor* is offensive to me,' Sophie had replied. 'What's your point?'

'What are you smiling at?' Evelyn said now, sounding annoyed that he could find anything to be amused about.

'Nothing. Can you do me a favour?'

'Of course.' She smoothed down her jacket, which was perfect already.

'Can you pick up Tammy and take her to Sophie's parents? I'll give you the address.'

'I know where they live, everyone in the Service knows where they live,' Evelyn said irritably, 'but I am not picking that cat up.'

'Come on, Evelyn.' He tried to look weak and injured. 'I can't look after her, she'll be scared and hungry; she's only a small cat.'

'A small cat with claws.'

'If Sophie comes home and finds anything's happened to her cat, I'll tell her it's your fault,' Luke said, and enjoyed the brief expression of fear on her face.

'All right, I'll do it. But you owe me,' she warned. 'Is there a travelling case for it?'

It. Just because of that, Luke said, 'No, sorry. Try wrapping her up in a towel or something.' Besides, Tammy's travelling case was in the hall cupboard, right by his emergency trapdoor. Probably it wouldn't go unnoticed much longer, but he'd rather Evelyn didn't think he was a complete idiot just yet.

Evelyn let out an irritated breath. 'If I get tetanus from this, I'm blaming you.'

'Thank you, Evelyn. I'm in your debt, Evelyn. You're very kind, Evelyn.'

'I'm keeping score,' she said, and left.

I was waiting for my flight when my phone rang. I flinched automatically – was it Rachel? – before I remembered she didn't have this number. It was Docherty.

'Hey. Did your gun arrive okay?'

'Yes. Brilliant. Can't thank you enough.'

'I'm sure you could try,' Docherty said silkily. 'I can send the other two on if you want?'

My fingers tensed at the thought of what he might require in return for that. 'I'll get back to you on that,' I said. 'Hey, Docherty? Did you know Sir Theodore?'

'A little. Did some protection work at BBC&H a while back.'

'And Irene Shepherd?'

'Yeah, I think so.'

'Why did they need protecting?'

'The firm represented Thom Cooper.'

I winced in recollection. Thom Cooper had been accused of raping and murdering a teenage girl. He'd hanged himself before he was finally sentenced, due in no small part to the massive hate campaign conducted by the tabloids.

'Have you heard about the security guard?' Docherty asked.

I frowned. 'What security guard?'

'The one at the office block where Sir Theodore was killed. He'd vanished, yes?'

'Why does this leave me thinking he didn't turn up at home with the flu?'

'Because he turned up in the Thames. With a bullet in his head.'

'Oh.'

'One of your bullets.'

'Oh.'

'So that's two murders you're wanted for.'

'Oh.'

'As well as bashing that taxi feller in the head.'

'Um.'

'Sophie?'

'Mmm?'

'You okay?'

'Two.'

'Yeah.'

'Oh.' I shook myself. 'Any more news?'

'No, that's it. There are a lot of people crawling all over yer man's flat, but then there usually are whenever he's not there. 5 are back watching the place.'

'Fabulous,' I said, and signed off. I was about to put my phone away and pore over the map in my bag when it rang again.

'I am not shagging you in return for one gun,' I said.

There was a short silence. 'Never asked you to,' said Jack.

My face went crimson.

'How did you get my number?' I demanded, to cover my embarrassment.

There was a short pause. 'Ways and means,' he said eventually.

'Well, don't be cryptic or anything. Did you call me for a reason, or is this a social thing?'

'I wanted to apologise,' he said. 'I've been trying to get through to you since yesterday.'

'Apol – wow. Let me just call CNN and tell them to put this out as a special bulletin.'

'You're funny.'

'An apology and a compliment. I may swoon.'

'Look, Sophie. I'm sorry I suspected you of turning me in to MI5. I know you wouldn't do that. I was just … paranoid. You disappearing off to see your boyfriend and then Harrington turning up like that?'

'Luke has nothing to do with Harrington. For God's sake, he can barely leave his flat without Harrington's goons after him. He's not working for the guy.'

'I know,' Jack said. 'And I'm sorry.'

'Well … all right then,' I said, a trifle deflated.

'You accept my apology?' He sounded a little disbelieving.

'Yeah.' Sure, I was suspicious. I kind of wondered if he was planning something. 'And I'm sorry, too. For lamping you with my handbag and stealing all your money.'

'Yeah, thanks for that. I have a lump the size of an orange on my head and I had to steal some guy's wallet just to get around. Cops could have found me, you know. That cab driver's already reported us both.'

'I know. Probably best to lie low for a while.'

'That's what I've been doing.' He paused again. 'Listen, where are you?'

I laughed hollowly. 'Jack, I might have accepted your apology but that doesn't mean I'm an idiot.'

'You're at an airport. I can hear it.'

'World's full of airports.'

'Sure. How're you going to fly with your gun?'

'I have a licence for it. Matches my passport.'

I regretted that as soon as I'd said it. Then I wondered why. I was already risking a lot by flying when Jack knew my alias. He was resourceful enough to find Alice Maud Robinson on a passenger manifest.

'How in the hell did you get a fake gun licence?' Jack said.

'Ways and means,' I replied. 'Where are you?'

'Manchester. Getting a flight to New York.'

It was a good job he couldn't see me. My face evidently showed enough shock that people around me stared.

I was taking a flight to JFK. I figured that a hub airport of that size would be easy to lose myself in, and there were so many onward destinations nobody would be able to figure out where I was going.

'And what are you going to do once you get there?' I asked as steadily as I could.

'Make a connection to Hartford. There's not much we can do in London at the moment, they're crawling like flies all over BBC&H.'

I didn't need to ask who 'they' were. London wasn't safe for either me or Jack right now.

'So you're returning to the scene of your own crime?' I asked. 'Bit risky.'

'Not my crime,' Jack corrected. I could feel him reining in his own irritation at having to correct me. He was trying to be nice.

Bless.

'I left in a hurry before. No time to ask questions or investigate anything. At the very least I want to talk to Shepherd's maid.'

'Won't she recognise you?'

'She wasn't there when I visited. And I can disguise myself.'

'How?' I asked, because maybe he'd have some tips for me. I'd done the whole spectacles/fake tan/headscarf thing again and I looked like a deranged Amish. The guy who checked my passport had looked at me quite hard, making me sweat.

'I have coloured lenses,' Jack was saying, 'and glasses. Stopped short of a fake moustache, but I did pad out my cheeks. Like Brando in *The Godfather*.'

Now *that* was a good idea. I made a mental note to visit a pharmacy and get some cotton wool for the same purpose.

'Listen, Sophie, where are you? We should be working together.'

'Can't do it by yourself?'

'Two heads are better than one.'

I sat back and gazed around the departures lounge. Logically, I knew he was right. Hell, lately I'd been reduced to asking for help from a nine-year-old girl. No matter that said nine-year-old girl was smarter than Stephen Hawking. I needed someone to watch my back, to bounce ideas off. And, yes, I was terrified, trying to do this by myself.

But was it a good idea? Stubborn pride aside, was it wise to partner up with Jack again? He'd threatened me at gunpoint. Twice. Actually, three times. Volatile was not the word.

'I'll think about it,' I said coolly. 'Look, I have to go, they're calling my flight.'

'Call me,' Jack said. 'Or I'll call you. Whatever.'

'Yeah,' I said, and ended the call, frowning.

The flight to JFK wasn't long, and I spent most of it thinking. Going round and round the same argument in my head. By the time we landed I was no closer to a conclusion. Even meeting up with Jack could be dangerous. Was he really on my side? Why did he really want to meet up with me again?

Could I trust him?

Eventually I made a decision of sorts. I'd find out how much it would cost to get to Hartford, and if I had enough of Vallie's cash left, I'd go. If I didn't, then I'd get on a bus into Manhattan and go see Xander.

I had $380. The nice lady at the Continental desk said she could get me on a flight leaving in a couple of hours for $325.

Well. That was that.

I landed in Hartford as it was getting dark, and used up my remaining cash on getting into town. Stood around for a bit wondering what to do next. I needed a hotel room but I had no cash left and no cards that were of any use.

So I got out my phone – I bloody love this thing – and looked up local hotels. Found one within walking distance and lugged my bag there, contriving to think of the saddest things I could along the way. By the time I arrived I was suitably tearstained, and the woman on reception believed me when I said I'd been mugged at the airport and needed a room until the Embassy could send me a new passport and my bank could forward on a replacement credit card.

'You just pay when you leave, honey,' she said, and I felt bad for taking advantage of her. I mean, I fully intended to fleece Jack for money to pay, but I still felt dishonest.

In my small room, I freshened up a bit and changed into clean clothes. It was nearly half-past seven, and I was hungry.

An idea struck me. I used my phone to look up local restaurants. The receptionist might have told me, but then she'd probably wonder how I'd pay for my meal.

There was a small pizza place not far away and I texted the address to Jack, wondering if he'd landed yet.

'ETA 9pm,' he replied. 'See you there 9.30.'

I suppose I should have spent the intervening time getting some sleep, but I made the mistake of switching on my other phone. There were eight missed calls, three from Harvey and five from his daughter. I rubbed at my eyes, trying to remember when I'd given either of them my new number, but then I figured if Rachel could put a bug on her dad's phone and he still hadn't noticed it, then she could probably find my new number just by my phone being in her house. She'd probably written a new bit of software for it.

Tentatively, I listened to their messages. If Harvey thought I'd endangered Rachel he'd turn half of my body parts into detachable limbs.

Rachel began by asking where I was, then asking if I was okay, then getting a bit hysterical because I wasn't replying, then getting angry with me for walking out without saying goodbye, and finally sobbing and screaming that her grandmother was an idiot.

Harvey had left just one message, and it was icily calm. This in itself was frightening, since Harvey's usual demeanour is that of a friendly spaniel.

'I just had a call from my daughter. Seems you paid her a little visit. While you're on the run from the law and, I expect, from someone who's trying to kill you. While this may be an everyday occurrence in the exciting life of Sophie Green, and make for an interesting story to tell my nine-year-old daughter, *it is not something I want her involved in*. Rachel tells me Teresa called the cops on you and all I can say is, Sophie, I hope they fucking well catch you. I can't believe you'd endanger Rachel like that.'

Whereupon he hung up.

Wonderful.

I debated calling Rachel to reassure her I was okay, but for all I knew Teresa had turned her phone over to the CIA and they'd use it to track me. I considered calling Harvey, but to be honest I was too scared.

Instead I wimped out and called Luke, but I got no response. 'If I don't speak to you soon, it'll be because Harvey has had me eviscerated,' I said to his voicemail, then I switched my phone off and sat there in my hotel room, feeling very alone.

By the time nine-thirty rolled around I'd discovered the minibar and made good use of it. I needed a little Dutch courage to go ahead and meet Jack. Part of me said I should stay where I was and continue to work alone, but another part of me, a shamefully frightened part, said that I was well and truly alone now, with no help from my strangely silent boyfriend and a strong case of dislike from one of my most potentially useful allies.

'That's some nice going, Green,' I said to myself as I put on my boots and left the hotel, swaying just a tiny bit.

When I arrived at the restaurant, I spied Jack across the room, sitting with his back to the wall. He watched me approach, and I kept my eyes on him. If he did one shifty thing I was out of there.

I blame this eyes-on-the-target approach for walking into a table or two.

'Hey,' said Jack as I reached him.

'Hey.'

He looked up at me from under his dark fringe. 'Truce?'

'Depends. You gonna threaten me at gunpoint again?'

'You gonna run off to your boyfriend again?'

I narrowed my eyes at him. 'I could walk away right now,' I said.

Jack held up his hands. 'Okay. No more cracks about the boyfriend. Sit down.'

I hesitated.

'I'm not even armed,' he added.

I sat down. 'Just so you know, I could kill you with my fork,' I said.

'Wine?' Jack asked, and I smiled.

'Then again, maybe no killing will be necessary.'

So, all right, maybe I had a little too much to drink. By the time my plate was empty the walls were starting to move all by themselves and I have a slight feeling I was shouting.

'Can we have the bill please,' I slurred to the waitress, and Jack had to clarify, 'She means the check.'

'Right,' I said. 'Cheque. Even if you're paying in cash. I mean, bills. It's a stupid language. Stupid, stupid, stupid –'

'Okay,' Jack said, appearing at my side of the table in a second and hauling me to my feet, 'I think it's time to go.'

'Did you leave a tip?' I asked.

'Yeah, I left plenty.'

'You always have to tip in America. It's very important,' I told him.

'I know.'

'Twelve-and-a-half percent. No, double the tax. Like double the tax of Romania,' I joked, but either Jack hadn't seen as many *Friends* episodes as I had, or he'd lost his sense of humour somewhere around that second bottle of wine.

Or maybe it was the third. It was all a bit blurry.

'Bloody hell,' I stumbled over the restaurant doorstep and Jack yanked me upright, 'that's bloody steep. Shouldn't there be a notice or something? The land of health and safety rules. Like I could sue them. Like on *Ally McBeal*. D'you ever watch *Ally McBeal*?'

Jack shook his head. 'Don't have much time for TV,' he said.

'No time for TV!' I shook my head in pity. 'What a terrible life you have.'

I turned left, then swung back round to the right.

'What are you looking for?'

'Hotel. S'around here somewhere.'

Jack waited patiently. Then as I reeled off in what looked like the right direction, he followed me.

'Where're you going?' I asked.

'Not much point in partnering up with you if you're going to step off the kerb in front of a Mack truck,' he said, taking my arm as I stumbled. I didn't remember my boots having such terribly high heels when I put them on. Maybe they'd grown. Magic heels.

'Jack, am I really drunk?'

'Yep.'

'But I didn't drink so much,' I wailed. 'And I was eating, too ... Man, that was good pizza.'

'What's your hotel called?'

'Rio. No! Grande. Maybe. Not sure. It's down here,' I announced confidently, marching down a side street.

What seemed like hours later, we found the place, and Jack walked me in. I tripped and stumbled on the doormat, bringing him tumbling down on top of me, and for a long moment he lay there, looking down at me. And heaven help me, it felt nice. It had already been too long since a man had held me.

'So much for keeping a low profile,' Jack muttered, and hauled me to my feet.

We made it to the small elevator, and I leaned against the wall, lost my balance and slid down to the floor.

'I feel dizzy,' I moaned. 'Do lifts make you feel dizzy?'

'Not really.'

'They make me feel dizzy. See, it's all my brother's fault. When I was seven he ran me over with his bike and knocked me out.'

I looked up at Jack for sympathy, but got none.

'And I was off school for a week, I couldn't gerrout of bed, I was really ill,' I pressed. 'I had a haematoma and everything.'

'They can kill you, can't they?'

I nodded seriously and felt even dizzier. 'Yeah. I had head X-rays and everything. You know they damage tissue? I think they damage brain tissue.'

'No kidding,' Jack muttered.

Chapter Eleven

Evelyn drove him home, which was kind of her, Luke supposed. Especially since she was now sporting several more scratches and developing a nice bruise on her arm. He supposed she'd found Tammy's box, then. It was a source of entertainment to him every time Sophie tried to wrestle Tammy – who, he was led to believe, actually liked Sophie – into her box. The tiny tabby somehow managed to develop twice as many limbs and seven times as many claws than usual.

'Fight with a hedge-trimmer?' he asked.

Her lips thinned. 'That cat is a menace.'

'She's a sweet kitten really.'

'She bit me.' Evelyn indicated the bruise. 'Had I not been wearing a jacket she'd have drawn blood.'

Luke hid a smile. Tammy was a rescue cat, and she had a habit of lashing out when she was frightened. He didn't know if she'd been abused as a kitten or if she was just a bit psychotic, but he admired her spirit. And besides, it was good to see Evelyn's composure ruffled.

'Your Sophie must be insane to love an animal like that.'

'It's certainly one theory.'

The place was immaculate when he walked in. Cleaner than he'd left it, and he wasn't a messy person. The faintest of dark marks between the floorboards was the only evidence that anyone had been bleeding there.

That was the Security Service for you. Thorough. Precise. They'd have searched everywhere and put everything back exactly where they found it.

'More like it was before it was,' he murmured.

'Sorry?' Evelyn stood in the doorway, letting cold air in.

'They did slightly too good a job of pretending they

weren't here.' He wandered over to the bookshelves. No dust marks where the books had been pulled out. Luke couldn't remember the last time he'd dusted.

'I really must get searched by MI5 more often,' he said. 'They're excellent housekeepers.'

'Are you sure you're feeling all right?' Evelyn asked doubtfully.

'Yep. Look in the cupboard next to the hob, will you? The one with a hole in it.'

He didn't look round, but heard her footsteps on the kitchen tiles. He kept searching the shelves.

'It's empty,' she said.

'No broken glass?'

'All tidied away. Not a speck of it left.'

'And the bottom cupboard, last on the right?'

A moment, then, 'Saucepans. A turkey tray. A wok. Frying pans. What am I looking for?'

'Any cigarettes in there?'

'A packet of Dunhill's. I thought you'd given up?'

Thought the bastards might have requisitioned those. 'I have. Come over here.'

Obediently she came, standing a little too close to him. Luke pointed to his CDs, neatly lined up.

Evelyn stared for a moment, then said, 'I never pegged you as a Crowded House fan.'

'Saw them in Sydney. You're not looking properly, Evelyn. What's next to Crowded House?'

She peered. 'Led Zeppelin?'

'And next to that?'

'Daniel Barenboim, the Beethoven Sonatas. You have diverse taste, but –'

'Why would I put those three together? They're completely different kinds of music and they're not even in alphabetical order.'

Evelyn stood back and regarded the neat rows.

'They're …' she began doubtfully. 'In colour order?'

'Like a damn rainbow.' He regarded the shelves with disgust, the gradual fading of white to yellow, through green and blue and a small section of purple – he'd have to pretend that was Sophie's P!nk album – and on through red to brown and black.

'I don't understand.'

'Do you think I have so little of interest in my life that I'd sit around like a Nick Hornby character, reorganising my CDs by the colour of their spines?'

Evelyn said nothing.

'Hell, I'm surprised they didn't replace the cupboard door I shot.'

'I suppose it's kind of them,' she said uncertainly.

'No. It's not kind. They didn't have to do any of it. I bet when I go in the bathroom they'll have lined up all my toiletries in order of descending height and cleaned the hair out of the drain. Probably even put clean sheets on the bed. Bastards.'

He stomped into the bedroom and stood glaring at the bed. Utter, utter bastards. To come in here and invade every bit of his life was one thing, but to tell him about it? To place subtle little reminders everywhere that they'd poked into every little area of his life; that they'd exposed all his secrets.

The bed had been neatly made, even if the sheets weren't clean. Beside the bed the nightstand bore a tasteful display of condoms which had formerly been left inside their box in a drawer.

The bathroom was immaculate. Some MI5 officer was probably hugging himself with glee that he'd thought of scrubbing the hard-water marks off the shower screen.

But it was what lay on the pillow that filled him up with pure, unadulterated rage.

'I'm guessing you didn't leave this here,' Evelyn said,

looking a bit embarrassed.

Luke stared at the photo, a professional print. He'd persuaded Sophie to let him bring a camera into the bedroom one night and the results had been … well, pretty inspiring, if he was honest. But of all the images – which had probably been dug up from his hard drive and perved over – this was his favourite. Not graphic, but intimate.

Sophie lying asleep, her hand curled by her face, hair fanned out over the pillow. The curve of her pale shoulder, the sweep of her bare back, the delicious swell and dip of her buttock and thigh. The sweetest glimpse of her breast. The shadows of her lashes on her cheeks and the exquisite contours of her mouth.

He took this photo out sometimes and just looked at it. At the softness and beauty and warmth of the woman he loved. At the incredible intimacy and vulnerability she displayed, sleeping naked in his bed.

Sophie didn't know he'd taken that picture. It was just for him.

And now that intimacy was spoiled forever, shared and displayed among untold grubby strangers. His own private memory despoiled. Harrington could have picked an incredibly graphic picture of her from his hard drive, but he'd gone for this one. Known why it was important to him.

Bastard.

'You can go now,' he said quietly.

'Are you sure you're all right?'

He was seething with emotions he didn't have names for. His whole body ached. He needed to sleep so badly it made him want to cry.

'I'm fine,' said Luke, and it was the biggest lie he'd ever told.

My head felt hot and heavy even before I woke up. Christ,

how much had I had to drink? My mouth was dry and stale and my body ached. Blegh. Whoever invented the hangover wants shooting.

On second thoughts, maybe I'll just shoot myself. It's got to be kinder.

I felt at my wrist; I was still wearing my watch. Carefully, I peeled open an eyeball and peered at the time. Just before eight. I stumbled from the bed and made it to the bathroom to gulp down some water –

– and then I froze.

Stubble burn.

I had stubble burn.

I touched my jaw and neck, but it was unmistakeable. Luke's usually clean-shaven, but my first boyfriend had a weak chin and used to cover it up with what he thought was designer stubble. Took me a while to explain to him that it was the least pleasant thing in the world to have scrubbing all over your face while you were kissing.

And now it was back. Someone had been rubbing his stubble against my face.

Feeling sick, and not just from a hangover, I peeped back into the bedroom. The bed was rumpled on both sides.

Oh God. What had I done?

No, seriously, what had I done? I couldn't remember. I could have been having rampant sex with Jack all night and I didn't remember a thing. I remembered the feel of his body against mine, his hands on my skin – but was that from the time he'd manhandled me in France? Or was it a more recent memory?

He'd walked me to my room, and then ... did I invite him in for a nightcap? Had he stayed? Did we share a bed, as we'd shared one before?

Did I do more than just sleep with him last night? Did I, well, *sleep with him*?

Oh *God*. I cheated on Luke. I'm the lowest rat-bastard in the world.

I fell facedown on the bed, contemplating suicide. How could I even think of having sex with someone who wasn't Luke? Gorgeous, sexy, clever, kind Luke. Sometimes it amazed me that I was allowed to sleep with him at all. I half-expected some old school chum to turn up and pay Luke on a bet. Sleep with this tub of lard for a couple of months and you can have my Jag.

I'd blown up his car and cheated on him. He was going to hate me. Really, really hate me.

I sank lower into the depths of self-loathing and was somewhere around wishing I'd never been born at all when the door opened and Jack came in, carrying a backpack, looking clean, smelling nice, his eyes the right colour, not some horrible pink shade like mine.

'Morning,' he said pointedly.

'Murgh,' I moaned into the pillow.

'How are you feeling?'

'I wish I was dead.'

'You didn't drink that much.' He sat down on the bed and brushed the hair out of my face. 'You want some water?'

'Got any cyanide to go with it?'

Jack cracked a smile. 'Can't be that bad.'

Feeling horribly low, I turned my head and said in a small voice, 'Jack, why do I have stubble burn?'

The smile faded.

'You can't remember.'

'Um, no. Sorry,' I apologised immediately, 'I was really drunk. I'm sure it was, um, great ...'

Why am I *apologising*? To *him*? Stop being so bloody *British*, Sophie.

'So great you forgot. You know, I've made women pass out before, but they always remembered what I did to them first.'

Oh Christ.

'Maybe that's it.' I latched on to this idea, feeling nauseated by it but not wanting to hurt his feelings, especially not when we'd just declared a truce. Oh God, what if this was his idea of a partnership? 'Maybe it was so good you wiped my memory?'

'Maybe,' Jack agreed, his dark eyes getting darker. Uh-oh. He reached out and pushed me onto my back. 'Do you remember this?'

He kissed me softly, sweet and clean, his hands on my bare shoulders. I must have tasted disgusting, but he didn't seem to care. His hands roamed lower.

'Do you remember this?'

'Jack,' I said weakly, trying rather uselessly to push him away.

'And this?' His hands went under the covers and I shrieked and shoved them away. I was naked under there!

'Stop,' I begged. 'I – Luke – no, I – we didn't …'

Jack sat back and regarded me steadily.

'I have a boyfriend,' I said shakily, more to remind myself than anyone else. 'Oh God, I'm such a slut!'

Jack reached out to me and I recoiled.

'Sophie,' he said patiently, 'nothing happened.'

I stared. 'What?'

'Well,' he gave me a little smile, 'very little, anyway. You snuggle up to people in your sleep, did you know that?'

'But – but …'

'You passed out.' His gaze was steady. 'I didn't have my own room to go to so I stayed here. Thought I'd keep an eye on you. There's one bed. We both slept in it. And you cuddled up to me. That's about the extent of it. So before you commit *hara-kiri*, calm down.'

'So we didn't –?'

'Nope. I like my women conscious.' His eyes were

very dark. 'No need to send your boyfriend after me with a gun.'

'Oh God.' I flopped on my back, relief flooding me. 'Oh Jesus. I thought we'd –'

'We could if you want,' he said idly.

'No! No. I didn't even mean to – I was really drunk and I – I love Luke,' I said firmly. 'I really do. We love each other. I'd never cheat on him.'

'Sure?' Jack said.

'Sure. Really sure.'

'Right,' Jack said abruptly, and stood up. 'Come on, get dressed.'

'What? Where are we going?'

'First, to a new place. And then to Irene Shepherd's house.'

'New place? Why?'

'Because you made such a bloody exhibition of yourself yesterday and I don't want anyone to come looking here and remember you.'

My face coloured a little bit more. Right.

'Okay,' I said, 'but could you, like, look away, 'cos I'm not wearing anything.'

Jack shrugged, and then a thought occurred to me.

'Why am I not wearing anything?'

''Cos I took your underwear off.'

'But – even when I was unconscious?'

Jack gave a small smile.

My face went very hot. I remembered the first time I'd met him in that tent in France, the sleeping bag and the faked orgasm and him seeing my breasts before I'd even seen his face.

'You need to get yourself a girlfriend,' I said, and Jack eyed me for one long, inscrutable minute.

'It's on my to-do list,' he said eventually, and turned away.

I pulled myself into my clothes, washed last night's gunk

off my face and stumbled down to the lobby after Jack, who paid the bill in cash. The receptionist gave me an amused glance, but said nothing as we left the hotel, got into Jack's hire car, and set off across Hartford. It was a Friday, and traffic was busy. The endless stop-starting made my stomach heave and even behind my dark glasses my eyes smarted from the sun.

Jack checked us into the new hotel, another big, faceless chain, while I hung grimly onto the counter and tried not to throw up.

'Here.' Jack threw a little box at me when we were in the room, and after I'd picked it up from the floor (okay, so I can't catch. So what) I realised it was a hangover remedy. Paracetamol and Pepto-Bismol and lots of lovely, stomach-settling chemicals.

'You're a saint,' I croaked, tipping a load of it down my throat and locking myself in the bathroom to take a very long power shower and tell myself I wasn't going to die.

Being clean and moisturised made me feel a bit better – at least I didn't stink of Jack's cigarettes any more. I hung last night's clothes over some bathwater scented with shampoo and zipped myself into a dress, tights, shoes and coat. I made myself up and styled my hair as well as I could, and eventually emerged to meet Jack, who had long ago changed into a suit and was reading a newspaper, looking bored.

He ran his eyes over me, and seemed to be impressed. I struck a pose.

'Amazing what make-up can do,' he said, and I scowled.

'Are we going to Irene's house?'

'Yep.' He picked up my gun brace and fastened it over his shoulders.

'Hey!'

'What?'

'That's my gun. Give it here.'

'Nope. What happened to mine?'

'A friend is looking after it,' I said.

'Your boyfriend?'

'No. He's got plenty of his own. Give it back.'

Jack shook his head at me and said, 'Look, don't argue. Just come on.'

I sulked and looked out of the window on the way over to Irene Shepherd's expensive neighbourhood. The late judge's house was on a wide avenue with well-tended lawns and locked gates. Jack drove up to number 2455, wound down the window and pressed the button on the intercom.

'Fancy,' I said.

Jack ignored me. 'Hello,' he said pleasantly when a crackly voice answered. 'My name is Detective Laurence Danson. I'm here to talk to you about Judge Shepherd?'

American accent. Pretty flawless, too.

There was a pause, then we were buzzed through.

'Laurence Danson?' I asked, as we went through the electric gates.

'That's what it says on my badge.'

'What badge?'

Jack grinned. 'The one in my wallet.'

'And why do you have a police badge in your wallet?'

He raised an eyebrow, and I realised. 'You stole a cop's wallet?'

Jack looked smug.

'*You stole a cop's wallet?*'

'I didn't know he was a cop when I took it. He was in plainclothes.'

'Jesus.' I slumped in my seat. 'Oh Jesus.'

'He won't help you.'

'As if we weren't in enough trouble.'

'Ah, come on. He won't miss it. He'll get another one. I picked it up at JFK. Doubtful anyone around here will have a clue it's nicked. Do you have a badge or anything on you?'

'I still have my SO17 ID –'

'Perfect.'

'But it's out of date …'

'You're not going to be showing it her long enough for her to see the date.'

'Her?'

'The maid. Consuela Sanchez.'

We pulled up in front of the house and rang the doorbell. It was opened by a middle-aged woman in an apron. Her dark hair was pulled back in a bun and she looked suspicious.

'Yes?'

'Mrs Sanchez?' Jack's accent was back. 'Detective Danson, homicide.' He showed her the badge in his stolen wallet – his finger, I noticed, obscuring the photo – and she glanced at me.

'Alice Robinson.' I flashed my ID very quickly. 'Department of … Investigation.' Crap. Should have thought about that in advance. I hadn't realised until I opened my mouth that I was going to be affecting an American accent either. I really wasn't sure how convincing it was.

Sanchez opened the door wider and stepped back to let us in.

'I tell you what I tell all the others,' she said with a strong accent, as she led us down the hallway towards a large living room. 'I don't know who did it. The police say they have a suspect but I don't know why he kill her.'

'We need to know exactly how and where you found her,' Jack said.

'Didn't you look at the reports?'

'Yes, but I need to see for myself.'

Sanchez shrugged, and took us back out into the hallway and up the extravagant Twelve-Oaks-style staircase to a pink-carpeted landing. The walls were striped with pink and white and the drapes were pink and mauve. I pressed my hand to my forehead. This was not good on hungover eyeballs.

'I find her in here,' Consuela Sanchez said, gesturing to an office full of boxes. 'They come for all her paperwork, soon they say. But I have boxes and boxes of it to keep clean. Is not easy.'

'Where exactly was she?' Jack asked.

'Sitting in her chair with her head on the desk.'

'Shot from behind?' I asked, and Sanchez looked up. 'I haven't seen any reports yet,' I improvised, 'I've only just flown in. Could you excuse us? I need to talk to my colleague.'

Grumpily, she left the room, and I closed the door.

'Shot from behind at her desk,' I said. 'Pretty cut and dried.' I walked over to the desk and could see, under the boxes, a bloodstained blotter. 'Did you come up here when you came to see her?'

'Who cares about that?' Jack was staring at me. 'That's the worst accent I've ever heard.'

I scowled at him. 'I didn't want her to know I'm English.'

'You sound like you have special needs,' he said.

'Oh, like you're perfect,' I said, despite that his accent damn well was. 'And concentrate. Did you come up here when you visited?'

'Yes.'

'Why did you come to see her?' I asked, overwhelmed with curiosity.

'Tracing a skip.'

'All the way up here?'

'He came from here. She set bail on him.'

'Did you find him?'

Jack gave me a steady look. 'No, but then I was on the run.'

Fair enough.

'Consuela doesn't recognise you.'

'She wasn't here. Already left for the night, I guess.'

'How did the cameras have you going in and out?' I asked. 'I mean, aren't there timers on those things?'

'Yeah, but you can mess 'em around. I'd been here earlier, remember? Someone just probably messed with the loop,' he murmured, looking out of the window. 'Those front gates are electric,' he said.

'Yeah, and …?'

'I mean they'll shock you if you get too close.'

I joined him at the window and looked out over the pleasant back garden. There was spiky wire along the top of all the fences.

'The whole place is wired,' I said. 'Someone must have found a weak spot …'

'Or switched the power off. In the middle of the night, on her own, Shepherd wouldn't have noticed.'

'That the house was in darkness?'

'Probably a separate circuit.'

'But surely you must need to get in to switch the power off? And what about the security company? Aren't these things usually run remotely?'

Jack nodded. 'If it just went out for a short while they probably wouldn't have bothered. We'll check the garden,' he said.

The garden was huge and the electric fence ran all the way around the outside, occasionally hidden by hedges. It was all in good shape, and we tested it all the way around with a stick. No weak spots.

'They patched it up.' Consuela's voice came from behind us, and I jumped.

'Patched what up?'

'Where he got in. There was a dead dog on the fence to

hold it down.' She pointed to a shiny new bit of fencing. 'So he wouldn't electrocute himself when he climb over.'

Clever. Gross, but clever.

'Were the door locks tampered with?' I asked, remembering to try the accent again. Come on, Sophie, how much American TV do you watch? This shouldn't be hard! 'Had they been forced?'

She shook her head. 'He went in through the window. Climbed up the trellis.'

I turned to look at the house. The roses did look a little dishevelled. 'How did he know which window was her study?'

She shrugged. 'He had an appointment with her that afternoon,' she said, and I looked over at Jack. Of course.

'Why did he come to visit? Did you see him?'

'No, I already go home.'

'So he came here quite late?'

She shrugged in an affirmative sort of way.

'Do you know what he wanted?'

'Is that important?' Jack snapped, and I smiled at him.

'Of course. In my department we take time to investigate things like that,' I said sweetly, and Jack glowered. 'Did anyone else come visiting?' I asked. 'Anyone unusual?'

'People are always coming,' Sanchez said. 'Clients and colleagues, the governor was a friend ...'

'Anyone you didn't know,' I said.

'Well, there were a few. Charity collectors. Ms Shepherd always saw them. It was good for her image.'

Charity collectors. Well, I guess they could have been casing the joint. 'Which charities?' I asked.

'There was a cancer one and a blind one and a deformity one –'

'Deformity?'

'Yes. The woman had her own deformity. She keep her

221

gloves on but I could tell. She couldn't use her right hand properly.' Consuela shook her own for emphasis. 'And she didn't have all her fingers.'

A cold shock ran through me.

'Which fingers?'

Consuela frowned at me. 'Why do you need to –'

'*Which fingers?*'

The maid looked taken aback, but she pointed to the last two fingers of her hand.

'Would you excuse me a second?' I said, and stumbled away to another part of the garden, hauling out my phone as I did. I stabbed in Luke's number and waited. And waited. And got voicemail.

'You … Have … Reached … The … Voicemail … Service … For …'

Dear Christ, did it have to be so slow?

'Zero … Seven … Seven … Four …'

Stop any time you fancy, I thought, and when I eventually got to leave a message, gabbled, 'Luke. Alexa Martin. Are you sure she's still in jail? Not wandering around in America, shooting people?' I tried to calm down. 'I just need to know, okay? Call me back. And bloody start answering your phone, okay?'

Jack and Mrs Sanchez were heading back up to the house and I ran after them on unsuitable heels that kept sinking into the ground. I caught up as they went back into the house.

'One more thing,' Jack was saying. 'In the interests of interdepartmental co-operation,' what a mouthful, 'could you tell me who else you've spoken to about this matter?'

Sanchez looked blank.

'The other cops,' I explained, and she nodded.

'The local department,' she said. 'Detectives. And a man from the CIA …'

CIA? That was ... unusual. They didn't usually deal with domestic matters, and to be involved in what, on the surface at least, was a straightforward murder investigation, was odd. 'Do you have his name?' I asked.

'I have a card,' she volunteered, and trotted off to get it.

'Why are they involved?' Jack wondered out loud. He glanced at me, and I shrugged.

'You know anyone in the CIA?' I asked, and he shook his head.

'You?'

'Well, sort of,' I said, as Sanchez came back with a little card.

'Here you go,' she said, and Jack took it. He read it, shrugged, and handed it to me.

And then I nearly died.

The name on the card was James Harvard.

Harvey.

Oh, *fuck*.

His entire flat reeked of other people.

Angry beyond belief, Luke stormed around the place, swiping piles of CDs and books to the floor, tearing his clothes from the wardrobe, knocking all his toiletries into the bath. Destroying the neat, perfect order MI5 had created. They'd re-plastered and even repainted the wall where he'd punched it. Luke smashed his cricket bat at it to create a new dent, just to spite them.

But no matter how he tried to replace his belongings where they should be, nothing looked right.

His shoulder throbbed. His eyelids felt like lead. He shoved books back onto the shelves until he could barely stand. The surgeon hadn't wanted him to go home yet, but Luke had very little tolerance for hospitals.

That damn photo. He could barely look at the bed, at

the sheets he'd deliberately rumpled to destroy 5's order, but which now looked as if someone had just tumbled from bed, sleepy and naked, and was about to pad barefoot into his arms.

Sophie. Bloody Sophie. He knew she'd be trouble the first time he saw her. Smart, sexy Sophie, who genuinely had no idea how incredible she was. A brain that raced off in a million directions at once, zigzagging all over the place and always coming up with something mad but brilliant. Unable to see a sane solution to anything, some days barely even able to tell her left from her right. A lush, curvy body and a swing in her hips that made grown men drool. She didn't even seem to notice them staring. Bright, laughing eyes and that mouth – oh Jesus Christ, that mouth. Faster than a runaway train and twice as dangerous, pink and full and addictive. The first time he kissed her he'd seen fireworks.

'It's ridiculous,' he said out loud. 'She's ridiculous.'

There was simply no sense in it. She drove him round the bend, but he couldn't stop thinking about her, had never been able to stop thinking about her. She was everything he'd spent his life avoiding, and now he knew why.

Because of Sophie, he was under suspicion from MI5 and 6. Because of Sophie, he was damn close to losing his job. His family hated him even more than ever. His flat, his sacred personal space, had been violated. He'd been shot, for God's sake.

He'd known her a year, and his life was in tatters. If she kept this up he'd be dead by forty.

The picture of her on the coffee table mocked him. Sap, it said. Sucker. You've spent your life knowing it's a really bad idea to give your heart to anyone, and then what do you do? You let Sophie push and shove and bully you into falling for her. You let her wriggle and worm under your skin, get inside you, spread everywhere. Love is a cancer, and it'll kill you.

He wiped his hand over his face. The sensible thing to do would be to end it. Call her up and tell her it was over. No good for either of them. Hell, Sophie herself had said the same thing to him not six months ago. People like them didn't get to have personal relationships.

People like him didn't, at any rate. Sophie could career off into a brand new life without him, do anything, be anyone, and some poor other mad sap could spend the rest of his life being driven mad by her.

He should give up the idea of a life with her and concentrate on doing what he knew best, what he understood.

He knew that, and yet he'd been the one pushing to get back together with her.

'You really are a fucking idiot, Sharpe,' he said to himself, and stood up.

The packet of cigarettes was where he'd left it in the cupboard. His lighter – oh Jesus bloody Christ, they'd even refilled his lighter.

He stuck the cigarette between his teeth, flicked the lighter open with his left hand and lit up. The first breath of smoke swirled around his lungs and back out again. Glorious.

Now at least the flat smelled different, although in his heart of hearts he wasn't sure if it smelled any better.

He opened a kitchen drawer and took out the Yellow Pages. Flipped to Hotels. Called one at random and made a reservation. Called an airport hire-car firm and ordered a car.

Thought for a moment. He'd reorganised the cupboard by the front door this morning, and while he'd noted with fury that his secret trapdoor had been neatly sealed, that the dusty hiking boots at the back of the cupboard had been polished and that even his skis had been waxed and sharpened, he'd also seen that the nondescript, medium-weight black jacket he rarely wore still had its lining intact.

Luke held the jacket for a long moment.

Then he took a shower.

Dressed in plain black trousers and a blue shirt, he got in Sophie's car and drove to the supermarket.

Airports were easy. Full of CCTV. Anyone with any level of government access and half-an-ounce of intelligence could hack in and trace a person, especially if they had a human tail to pinpoint the quarry.

But a supermarket? No one would watch him in a supermarket. And by the time they figured out he wasn't just there to buy food, by the time they persuaded the supermarket security people to let them look at the CCTV, he'd be long gone.

He picked up a few t-shirts and jeans, clean underwear, some cheap trainers. He loitered around the toiletries section, staring with acknowledged irony at the condom selection, waiting for a member of staff to wheel one of those huge cages full of empty boxes by. Followed in their lee. Shoved his jacket in his shopping basket and jammed a baseball cap on his head, all of it done fast enough to seriously annoy his injured shoulder. Just enough time to take off the sling before the cage wheeled in another direction, and by the time the security cameras caught him again he was a man in dark trousers and a blue shirt – probably their cameras weren't in colour, but who would take the risk? – following another staffer through the employee-only doors.

By the time he exited the locker room and left the building through the staff entrance, he was a man wearing jeans and a plain t-shirt under a nondescript jacket, waiting for the bus opposite the petrol station. No one stopped him. If anyone saw him ripping out security tags they didn't seem to care. Dozens, hundreds of people went through those staff doors every day – and most of them, he guessed, weren't paid enough to care about a stranger wandering through.

By the time the bus dropped him off in town he'd taken

the tiny printed strips from the lining of his jacket and pressed them carefully into place in his passport and driving licence. Well. A spare copy of each, at any rate.

The first coach leaving town was for London. Luke got on, leaned against the window and closed his eyes for a second. Either he was getting too old for this, or it really was inadvisable to carry on these shenanigans two days after getting shot.

He opened his eyes, and called the Home Office.

'So let me get this straight,' Jack said with worrying calm. Outside the car, the traffic lights blared red for danger. 'You have been staying with the mother-in-law and daughter of a CIA officer who is investigating this case, who is quite possibly stalking me, and now he's mad at you?'

'That's about the size of it,' I said meekly. The lights changed and Jack rammed his foot down. The car shot forward, far too fast, just as it had at every junction since he'd hauled me, white-faced, from Irene Shepherd's house.

'And you didn't mention this to me because ...?'

'I didn't know he was on the case.'

'But you knew he'd speak to his daughter at some point! Didn't you think she might tip him off about what you were investigating and where you were going?' He was yelling now. Fair enough. I'd probably be yelling, too.

He'd seen my face when I read Harvey's name and dragged me out to the car, where he'd seemed genuinely concerned. I think he thought Harvey was like Harrington. A pitbull out to get us. 'No,' I said. 'He's my friend. But he's, um ...'

'He's um what?' Jack said.

'Well, sort of mad at me. Sort of really mad.'

At that, Jack's concern evaporated. Quickly. And now we were in the car, going way too fast, and he hadn't stopped yelling at me.

'I didn't tell her where I was going. I didn't tell anyone.'

'And you had to go and piss him off! Why did you go there? Why? What the hell's in Ohio?'

I said nothing. There wasn't much I could say.

He carried on in much the same vein all the way back to the hotel, snapping at me as he wrestled with the door card, 'It could have been him who found us in France –'

'Why would he try to drown you? And anyway, didn't you say it was a woman?'

'Fucking women,' Jack snapped, and stalked into the bathroom. He locked the door and I heard the shower drumming.

Great.

I sat down on the bed, shaking slightly. God. As a person I trusted Harvey implicitly: I absolutely adored him. But on a professional level I was never surprised to find he was keeping secrets from me. He'd been seconded to SO17 for a while, working in co-operation with us. The idea was we helped each other out, but more than once I found out he hadn't told me the whole story. Not that I ever told him anything, either, but it was still annoying.

And now he was really angry with me. He was chasing Jack professionally, and he was angry with me personally. I'd put his child in danger. Harvey the Labrador puppy had just turned into a Doberman.

I wiped my hands over my face, exhausted and frightened. I shouldn't have come here. I could just leave. Grab my things now while Jack was in the shower, and sneak out.

I slumped back on the bed. I had no money and no friends. Sneaking out would just be another stupid thing to do.

Wearily, I got out my phone and called Luke again. This time he answered.

'I was just about to ring you. Why are you so interested in

Alexa all of a sudden?'

'I shot her in the hand.'

'Yes. Good marksmanship. For once. But ...'

'Irene Shepherd's housekeeper said a woman came to the house the day before she was killed and she had a deformed hand.'

'So?'

'So, I ...' I realised that there must be millions of people with deformed hands. And that the one I was thinking of was in a maximum security prison five thousand miles away.

'She's not going anywhere,' Luke said. He sounded tired. 'She's really not. I can go up there and see, if you really want, but the Home Office are adamant that she's still locked up. It was just a coincidence, Sophie.'

I flopped back on the bed and ran my hand over my eyes. 'Luke, did you know Harvey is after Jack?'

There was a pause. 'No,' Luke said. 'Angel's Harvey? What – how do you know? Have you seen him?' He paused. 'Does this mean you've partnered up with Jack again?'

'Yeah. I know, I know, he threatened me with a gun and all, but, well, I need some help with this whole thing. Grieves me to admit it, but I can't do it alone.'

'Hmm,' was all Luke said. 'Have you seen Harvey?'

'No. He left a card with the maid. Who will probably go and call him now,' I said, so frustrated I felt like crying, 'and tell him we've been there ...'

'You're in Connecticut?'

I winced. 'For now,' I hedged.

'Find out anything interesting?'

'I'm being stalked by the man whose wedding I was maid of honour at.' And he currently hates me.

'Anything else?'

'Luke, you're not taking this very seriously.' Oh hell, maybe he already knew. Maybe he was going to tell Harvey.

229

'Does Harvey know I'm with Jack?'

'Shouldn't think so.'

'Does Angel know?'

'I haven't said anything.'

Yes, but did I believe him?

'Did you get anything on Sarah Wilde?' I asked.

'Yeah, I got that she has a fake passport.'

'How'd you figure?'

'According to my good friend Lucie at the Home Office –'

'How good a friend?' I asked, trying not to let my jealousy show, and failing.

I could hear the smile in Luke's voice as he replied. 'Oh, I've only seen her naked half-a-dozen times. Well, a dozen. Ish.'

Thing was, there was a distinct possibility he wasn't joking.

'You're really funny,' I told him anyway. 'And what did the naked Lucie have to tell you?'

'There are seventy-eight Sarah Wildes in the UK.'

Needle in a haystack. Crap. 'Really?'

'Lucie wouldn't lie to me. But listen, seven don't have passports, and fifteen are under eighteen. That leaves fifty-six, of which only thirty-three have used their passports in the last three years, and eighteen who've gone outside the EU.'

'And eighty-seven percent of statistics are made up. What does any of this *mean*, Luke?'

'None of them match the passport number of the Sarah Wilde who travelled to Hartford that week.'

I slumped. 'So ... what? She wasn't British?' Maybe I'd been jumping to conclusions. Sarah Wilde could be American, Australian –

'According to records the woman who got on that plane was travelling on a British passport. British citizen. Old-style passport, not biometric. Issued by the passport office in Liverpool. Ostensibly, at any rate.'

'So it's a fake? A good fake, if no one caught it.'

'Yes. Docherty probably fixed it,' Luke said sourly.

'Now who's jealous?'

Luke made a grumpy noise in the back of his throat. 'The point is,' he said, 'that someone was travelling with this passport who wasn't entitled to it. People don't do that for honest reasons.'

'Unless they've been accused of murder and are trying to clear their name.'

'Unless they've been accused of murder and are trying to clear their name,' Luke repeated dutifully.

'So whoever she is, she's probably our killer.'

'Well, she's probably Irene's killer. Sophie, shouldn't you be spending a bit more time trying to work out who framed you?'

'It's the same person.'

'How do you know?'

'I just know.'

'But –'

'I just do,' I said irritably, as the bathroom door opened and Jack came out, wearing a towel and a scowl. I closed my eyes and thought of Luke in the same get-up.

I'd seen him naked four days ago. It felt like four months. When I pictured Luke I was beginning to see Jack.

'Look, you can't just rest on your instincts, Soph, you need evidence. This is dangerous.'

There were times when I loved Luke utterly, and there were times when he was a patronising git. 'Oh really? I thought it was all for fun.'

'Sophie –'

'I have to go.'

'Soph –'

'Bye,' I said, and ended the call.

'Loverboy?' Jack asked, snatching at clothes from his bag.

'Sarah Wilde had a fake passport.'

'Natch.'

'It's an alias. Probably it was fake when she went to see BBC&H.'

'Who we can't go back to, because your best friend Harvey is now on our trail. He probably tipped off Harrington.'

'I don't think –'

'No, that's obvious,' Jack snapped, and stalked back into the bathroom to get dressed.

Harvey. Well, this day just got better and better. Why the hell were the CIA involved in this? Because Jack was a foreign national? Because Irene had once worked abroad? That didn't make sense.

Then a little voice reminded me what my old job had been, and I winced. Two connected murders, and the main suspects are a foreign national and a former British intelligence agent. Yeah. If I was the CIA I'd be all over that, too.

They'd probably assigned Harvey because they thought he'd have some special insights, having worked with me. It was a small measure of comfort that Harvey thought I was cheerfully insane, and hopefully wouldn't be able to predict a damn thing I did.

I kicked off my shoes and looked around the hotel room. It was as boring and featureless as every single other hotel we'd been in. Another big double bed. I should have complained about that but I was too hungover.

Jack came out of the bathroom in jeans and a charcoal sweater. He looked good in it. Stubbornly, I superimposed Luke's head over his. Yes. Luke would look better in it. If he wasn't a patronising git.

'You know we're gonna have to leave,' Jack/Luke said.

I blinked and shook my head. 'Why? We've only just arrived.'

'Yeah, and your friend Harvey could find us here.'

Well, at least he wasn't yelling at me any more. 'I have to get changed first.'

'Why?'

'I look too memorable in this dress.'

Jack, mercifully, didn't comment on that. I got back into jeans and a t-shirt and we walked out of the hotel without getting the bill. A year ago I'd never have done something like that. Now I found it hardly bothered me at all.

'So where are we going?' I asked when we were in the car.

'I'm tempted to leave the country again.'

'And go where?'

'I don't know.' Jack headed out of town. 'Who did you call when the maid told you about the woman with the deformed hand?'

'Luke. I wanted to check up on someone.'

'Who?'

'Her name is Alexa Martin. She was a colleague of mine at SO17 but she turned on us. I shot her in the hand.'

'Any particular reason?'

Yes. I was aiming for her head.

'She was irritating me,' I snapped. 'But she's still in jail. Max security. It couldn't have been her.'

'Any ideas who it might have been?'

'Well, it was a woman who attacked you in France,' I said, and enjoyed Jack's scowl at the thought of nearly being killed by a woman. 'And there's that Sarah Wilde person.'

'Who is going to be hard to track down because she doesn't exist.'

'We really need to talk to BBC&H.'

'Yeah. We really do.'

We both lapsed into silence, and pretty soon I became

aware that Jack was driving towards the airport.

'Not here,' I said.

'What?'

'The fewer connections the better. All that disguising stuff really takes it out of me,' I said, but that didn't seem to wash. 'Plus, well, don't you think Consuela Sanchez might mention something to Harvey about us? Hartford airport is the first place he'll check.'

Jack just stared straight ahead. 'Sure,' he said, and changed lanes.

He didn't seem mad. Maybe he'd just got past it now. Maybe he was in that oasis of calm that came before ripping my head off.

'Can you have a look at the map and see what other airports are nearby?'

All I could find were small, regional airports. We ended up driving the not inconsiderable distance to JFK, abandoning the car, stealing another wallet and catching the Red-eye to Heathrow. By now an old hand at transatlantic flights, I settled into my seat, ordered a vodka straight up and watched Sky News on my little TV screen.

After half-an-hour, I was asleep.

Chapter Twelve

Luke winced as another pothole jarred his spine and sent shooting pains radiating from his shoulder. Last night's cheap hotel bed wreaking its revenge on him for sitting up half the night, spilling whiskey all over it as he ranted and remonstrated with his absentee girlfriend.

Bloody Sophie. Because of her, he was practically on the run, too. Had to play these elaborate games of hide-and-seek just so he could make a phone-call without being watched or listened to or otherwise tracked. Just to get a car no one would recognise. And as soon as he decided to go home the games would start all over again.

The crunch of the gravel under the wheels of his rental car wasn't doing much to alleviate his hangover. Neither was the looming Gothic insanity of his grandmother's house.

Sophie's grandmother lived in a council flat in Sheffield. He'd never been there, but Sophie described the place as grey. 'Nothing else,' she said, 'just grey. Grey buildings, grey sky, grey faces. Grey, grey, grey.'

He considered Grandmother Sharpe's house as he lurched to a stop outside. It was pretty grey too, but not, he conceded, in quite the same way. It was grey in the way that steel was grey. In the way that Gothic castles were grey. In the way that a mixture of good and evil was grey.

He hadn't driven to the front door, but gone around to the back, where the house was less grand but more grey. In contrast to the grim splendour of the front of the building, the back had been added to over and over again, by people who expected no one of consequence would ever see it. An ugly patchwork of bricks and stone, windows in the wrong places, doors that were too big or too small, and drainpipes plastered on over the lot.

Maybe Sheffield council flats had something going for them, after all.

He opened the kitchen door, automatically shoving against it with his good shoulder. It had stuck when he was a child, and it still stuck now. The place was deserted but for an ancient Labrador dozing in an equally ancient basket by the fire, and a chicken carcass placed exactly in the centre of the table.

Luke glanced at the dog. He couldn't remember its name, but he remembered that, like all Labradors, its stomach was a bottomless pit. The chicken had been placed foursquare out of long habit so the dog couldn't steal it.

He nudged the chicken closer to the edge of the table, thought again how ancient the dog was, and put the meat right at the edge.

Then he wandered out, calling, 'Hello?'

Silence. Not surprising, really. This time of day the stable-yard might be frantic, but there would be no one in the house, except for maybe the housekeeper or his grandmother's secretary. The trainer had his own house next to the manège and the stablehands lived above the horses. They didn't come into the house unless summoned.

The kitchen smelled of mud, horses, dogs and chicken stock. Dust motes danced in the light from the window. Far away, a horse whinneyed.

If he closed his eyes, it was almost exactly like being eight years old again. He could be ten, on exeat from school. He could be fifteen, resenting another frigid family Christmas. He could be twenty-one, wondering why he'd expected his family to be proud of his latest promotion.

But the fact was he was always a child when he came back here. Always bewildered, angry, and grieving. He was a child when he was orphaned, and he'd always be that way to his family.

He made his way from the kitchen into the back hall, from where he could enter the larger of the utility rooms, the one that contained the deep freezer for the results of the winter hunting. When he was a kid he used to stand and watch the butcher carving the magnificent deer into hunks of red meat, right at this table.

From the large utility room, he turned into a series of hallways. Four of them, small and narrow and full of identical, unmarked doors. Open the wrong one and you'd find yourself in a cupboard full of rubber boots no one wore any more, or the old butler's pantry with its ancient bottles of poison, or, if you were spectacularly unlucky, in another small hallway, featureless except for another collection of anonymous doors.

Robbing this place would be like robbing a maze.

Normally, Luke would have considered the idea of hiding out with a relative to be really, really stupid. But quite apart from the fact that anyone looking for him would already have encountered his grandmother's freezing disdain for him, it would take an unsuspecting person about a week to search the place, and even then they'd never find the exit.

Luke navigated it on autopilot, hesitated over whether to enter the dining room or not and glanced at his watch. No, bugger, it was eleven in the morning. He retraced his steps through two doors and turned left. Next to the boot room was a large door, standing slightly ajar.

'Jenson, is that you?'

Luke rapped his knuckles lightly on the door and opened it. 'No,' he said.

His grandmother paused in her writing, but didn't turn from her desk. He saw her back stiffen, which Luke considered an interesting feat, since he was fairly sure her spine was a steel rod.

He waited for her to greet him or at least recognise him, and then he sighed and said, 'It's Luke.'

He waited. Oh, for fuck's sake. She knew who he was. He knew for a fact that she'd chosen this room for her office because it gave her a view of pretty much everybody coming and going.

'Your grandson? You may remember you once had a son, who for unknown reasons you decided to call Giles. He –'

'Got married, had a child, and then died,' said his grandmother. Her voice was like a ringing bell. 'I remember.'

She rose gracefully to her feet and turned. She didn't seem to have aged in the thirty-odd years Luke had known her. Forever elegant, white-haired, and softly lined.

When Sophie had watched Downton Abbey she'd asked Luke if his grandmother was like the Dowager Countess. Luke scoffed at the very idea. His grandmother made the Dowager look like an eager puppy.

'Is it acceptable now to visit one's relatives without announcement?' she asked.

'Well, I looked for a footman, but it must be his day off.'

She swept a disapproving glance over him. Luke let it slide away. He'd mastered that art by the age of ten.

'I hear nothing from you for years, and now this. Last time I saw you, you were off in the SAS, getting shot at.'

She made it sound like some kind of hobby.

Her sapphire gaze rested on his sling. 'What on Earth are you doing now?'

'Still getting shot at, I'm afraid,' Luke said. 'This isn't a social call.'

She eyed him shrewdly. 'It never is.'

Luke pinched the bridge of his nose. It had seemed like such a good idea last night with his friends Jack Daniels,

Jose Cuervo and Jim Beam egging him on. This morning the half-empty bottles had taunted him with his lack of resolve.

'You look terrible,' said his grandmother.

'Got shot three days ago and haven't slept in a fortnight,' he answered. 'You want to talk about the weather next?'

Her eyes were hard and bright. If they were revealed to be pure sapphire, Luke wouldn't have been surprised.

'You always throw affection back at whoever offers it,' she said, and Luke almost laughed.

'First, telling someone they look terrible is not affection,' he said, 'second, you've never shown the slightest thread of affection towards me my entire life, and third, I must ask you to appreciate the magnificent irony of what you just said. I'm here for my mother's engagement ring.'

There. He'd said it. For a moment his grandmother stood very, very still, then her right eyebrow shifted incrementally and she said, 'That dreadful girl —'

'You've never even met her,' Luke snapped.

'Your Great-Aunt Matilda told me all about her last year. A drug addict who started a screaming match at the garden party, and invited those terrible young people who nearly killed you.'

'Okay, first off —'

'I see she has made your habit of interrupting people worse.'

Luke ground his teeth. 'And your habit of not listening has hardly improved either.'

His grandmother stared at him stonily.

'Sophie is not a drug addict. Someone stuck her with a heroin needle in an attempt to force a lethal overdose. All she got was septicaemia. She nearly died, in case you're wondering. Those young people weren't invited by Sophie — I'll grant you the "terrible" though, since they were the ones who tried to kill both her and me. And before you level your next accusation,' he held up his hand to pre-empt her, 'yes, she did go running off to America while I lay bleeding to death. She thought I was already dead. She was trying to catch the killer. Any other accusations?'

'She's –' his grandmother stopped, caught his eye and went on more carefully, 'not our kind of people.'

Luke looked around at the beautifully proportioned office, where even the filing cabinets were things of beauty, and he looked out of the window, which had a triple aspect over the gardens, the parklands, and the stables. He looked at his elegantly cold grandmother, whose eyes were the same as his own, whose bone structure he shared, whose gene pool he'd been trying to climb out of for years. He looked at a shared history of chilly politeness and an utter lack of affection for an orphaned boy.

'You forget, Grandmother,' he said. 'I am not our kind of people, either.'

She stared icily at him for a long moment, then looked away, as if she was indescribably bored of the subject. 'I don't have your mother's engagement ring,' she said. 'It was buried with her. The rest of her jewellery is in the safe. I've been wondering whether to pass it back to her family.'

Luke felt his shoulders slump.

'There are other rings –' his grandmother began, a thread of uncertainty in her voice he'd never heard before.

'No. Forget it. Send it all back to my mother's family. I'm sure I have some cousins on that side who'll appreciate it.'

Another pause. 'It's quite valuable.'

'I'm sure it is. If you're asking if I want to sell it, then no, I don't. I don't need the money and it ought to go to someone who can get some sentimental benefit from it. Ought to have done it years ago, I just … I never thought of it.'

You never do think of family. She didn't say it, but he could see the thought in her eyes.

240

Well, they never thought of him either.

'I'll buy another ring. I just thought – I saw it in a photo and I thought it might be the sort of thing she'd like.'

The clock ticked.

'You're going to marry her,' said his grandmother quietly.

'I'm going to ask.'

'Where is she?'

Luke's head came up. Well, of course she knew, she knew everything. 'I honestly don't know,' he said. He sincerely doubted she'd still be in Connecticut now. Was she as tired as him? Were people watching her, tracking everything she did and everyone she spoke to? Were people shooting at her? Was she safe?

'It's difficult,' said his grandmother softly, 'losing someone you love.'

'I haven't lost her,' Luke snapped, 'I just don't know where she is.'

Something like a smile touched her lips. 'From what Matilda told me,' she began, and Luke shot her a warning look, 'she's a tenacious young woman. I'm not sure how terribly bright she is, but stubbornness can be a virtue.'

'God knows it is in this family,' Luke muttered.

'What I mean is, when offered a choice, some will sink and some will swim,' his grandmother said. 'Take you, for instance.' Those sapphires alit on his shoulder.

'Are you saying I'm a sinker, or a swimmer?' Luke said, confused. She'd never paid him anything even approaching a compliment before.

'I'm saying you'd never drown if you were pushed in,' said his grandmother. 'And nor, I expect, would Sophie. Now. I assume you'll be needing somewhere to stay?'

He stared at her. He'd expected to have to beg to stay here. He'd expected to have to sleep in the stables.

'I have twelve bedrooms, Luke, plus I think Jenson has a

spare room in the Trainer's House and since Tariq left there's space in the Head Lad's flat. We have stabling for forty-five horses, owners and jockeys coming and going at all hours of the day plus, of course, various estate workers. At the last count I had twenty-three permanent employees about the house and stables, five temps, five jockeys, horses belonging to seven different owners, plus four cars, seven trucks, three horse-boxes and two lorries registered here. Keeping a low profile shouldn't be hard. What's that face for?'

Luke realised he was gaping. 'It's just my face,' he replied stupidly.

For the first time in his memory, Luke's grandmother looked amused. 'I saw the hire car by the kitchen door. I can't imagine why you'd use one of those unless you were trying to hide from something.'

For a surreal moment, Luke considered calling Evelyn to see if his grandmother had ever been in the Service.

'You are my grandson, Luke,' she said. 'So you will stay here, and you will drive one of the estate vehicles, and nobody will even blink at the sight of you wearing a sling. This is a racing yard. Accidents happen. Now. It will shortly be lunchtime. Have you got over your aversion to pea-and-ham soup?'

Luke forced himself to nod, then cleared his throat and said, 'No one can know I'm here.'

'Trust me,' said his grandmother, sweeping towards the kitchen, and Luke winced as he recalled the fate of the chicken. 'It's the last place anybody would look.'

'So now where?' I said as we boarded the Gatwick Express. I was blinking with fatigue, and what with the jet-lag and all I really didn't know if I was coming or going.

'BBC&H would be the logical place,' Jack said.

'Yes, but isn't it a Saturday?'

Both of us paused to work this out. I had to look at the calendar on my phone to make sure.

'They're a big firm. They'll probably have someone in on a Saturday,' Jack said.

I frowned, not quite so sure. 'Well, in any case, we can't go straight to BBC&H looking like this.' BBC&H's clients were rich, discreet, élite. Someone like Luke would have fit right in. I wasn't Their Kind of People. If I was, I'd have stepped off the flight looking like a movie star, instead of a homeless person.

Grudgingly, Jack agreed, and we went to find another faceless little hotel to stay in. The address was different from the last one, but inside it was hard to tell it wasn't the same place. Same duvet, same pictures, same carpet. I washed my face and flaked out on the bed, ostensibly to read some of the notes I'd printed out at Rachel's, but really to fall asleep. Man, I was so tired. I don't think I've ever been that tired. I needed to sleep for a week just to catch up on the hours I'd missed in one night.

I woke up in the early afternoon, sunlight coming in through the narrow window, and rolled onto my back to stare at the boring white ceiling. Jack lay asleep beside me, and I propped myself on one side to look at him for a little while.

He was handsome, no doubt about that, with his big dark eyes and cutting bone structure and dark, shaggy hair. Maybe, back when we first met, when I'd been so scared and alone, yeah, I might have fancied him a little bit.

I tried to imagine life with Jack as my boyfriend. Would he come round for dinner at my parents' house? I couldn't picture it. Would he look after Tammy when I was away? I didn't think he really understood the relationship I had with my cat. Would he pick me up from Angel's when I'd had too much to drink and put me to bed without nagging me about my hangover in the morning? Okay, so Luke had a tendency to do that.

But while Luke was a handsome bastard who was trying not to let anyone know he was a good guy, I suspected Jack was a handsome bastard who had to try hard to be a good guy.

I dragged my eyes away and concentrated on the problem at hand. We had to talk to someone at BBC&H about Sarah Wilde, but if we just walked in like we had last time it'd never work. They'd know us by now. Probably they knew us before – after all, wouldn't they be interested in the case? Probably it was that snotty receptionist who took the appointment. She called the cops as soon as we went out. Cow.

An idea started to form in my head, and I lay there letting it wobble around on baby steps inside my head for a while before turning my head and catching a whiff of myself.

Eurch. Shower time.

I was beginning to lack toiletries and clean clothes in a major way. I did what I could with what I had on hand, which basically meant sossing my clothes about in the bathtub while I washed my hair and letting them dry over the shower rail. The rest I made up for with an overabundance of eyeliner and the high-heeled boots I'd got at Gatwick.

Then I settled down on the bed, got out my shiny new phone, and got to work.

It took me about twenty minutes to find what I wanted, by which time Jack was opening his eyes. He rolled to face me.

'Checking your horoscope?' he yawned.

'Absolutely. Pisces, today you will overcome great obstacles with an ingenious idea.'

Jack blinked at me.

'I've been working,' I said.

He looked me over. 'What kind of work?' he asked, his eyes lingering on my boots.

I bashed him with my phone. 'BBC&H has a website,' I said.

'That's nice.'

'And the website has pictures of all the partners, junior partners and reception staff,' I said. 'It's so regularly updated that there's even an obit of Sir Theo in there.'

'Great,' Jack said. 'Why the hell are you telling me this?'

'Because I figured out how to find out about Sarah Wilde,' I said. 'She was one of Sir Theodore's clients, right, but one of the trainees was on the case, too. She's a junior partner now. A Maura Lanley. I figure if we catch up with her we can try and get her to talk.'

'How?'

'Well, we could buy her dinner,' I suggested. 'Or I could introduce her to my associate, Mr SIG-Sauer.'

'Either way is good.' Jack yawned. 'What's the time?'

'A little after five.'

'Bloody hell!' He leapt to his feet. 'I'm gonna take a shower.' He went into the bathroom, kicking the door shut as he pulled off his shirt.

Five seconds later he pushed the door back open. 'Did I forget and book the laundry room?'

'Can you think of a better way to get clean clothes?'

'Buy new ones.'

'On whose account?'

'Well, maybe Maura Lanley's, if any of her stuff fits you.' He winked, and closed the door again.

It's a sign of my mental state that my overriding objection to that idea wasn't the morality of it, but the fact that barely anyone else's clothes fit you when you're five foot ten and have the bustline of a Barbie doll.

'Just put anything on,' I said irritably to Jack when he emerged from the shower, 'we have to go.'

He pulled on jeans and a sweater and we left, phones on silent and gun at the ready.

'So how exactly are we going to do this? Do you think she'll be at the office?'

'Doubtful, at this time of night on a Saturday. I looked for an address for her – there's one in Grays.' Jack frowned. 'Thurrock. About half-an-hour by train.'

Jack was silent a bit, then he said, 'What if she has a flatmate?'

'Then we shoot her,' I said. 'I'm joking. I don't know. We ... We get her to come outside. Or something. I don't know yet.'

'I can see you put a lot of thought into this,' Jack said.

'Do you have a better idea?'

He said nothing, and I made a face at him.

Despite it being the weekend, the train was as busy as a weekday rush-hour. We transferred at West Ham and I found myself pressed up against Jack in the crush inside the carriage. He didn't seem to mind a bit, but it bothered the hell out of me.

Maybe I could go see Luke again ...

No. If I went back now I'd never leave.

No one came round to check our tickets, which was just as well because they'd run out when we left the District Line. Not that I cared. If they wanted to fine me then they could go ahead and try. As far as I knew, Alice M. Robinson had been dead thirty years.

I was nearly dozing off by the time the train pulled up in Grays, and Jack had to nudge me into wakefulness. Outside, the air was cool and I could smell the sea. Took me a while to remember where we were, on the banks of the Thames Estuary.

We followed the road out of town to a new development

of yuppie flats with a buzzer system that threw me until I saw the tradesmen's buzzer, which seemed to me a shocking waste of a security system. We went up to the second floor and knocked on her door. Panic suddenly seized me that I'd looked up the wrong Maura Lanley – how many could there be?

'What if this isn't the right one?' I asked.

'One hell of a time to have second thoughts,' Jack said. 'Get your notebook out and try to look friendly.'

I was more than happy to oblige. Having got this far, I was terrified. I was Thelma and Louise both rolled in together. Only without Brad Pitt. It was not okay, it was definitely not okay.

Maura, for it was indeed she, answered the door, and from the slightly crumpled-looking suit she wore I'd guess she had in fact been at the office. Boy, sucks to be her. Around her neck was a lanyard holding a work ID for BBC&H. In the harsh light from the bulb over our heads, she looked pale and pasty. But then, I bet I did, too.

'Hello,' Jack smiled at her. 'Are you the householder?'

She shook her head at us. 'Are you Jehovah's Witnesses?'

'No, no, nothing like that.'

'I'm not buying anything.'

'We're not selling. This is just a quick door-to-door survey of houses in the area. It'll only take a few seconds.'

She looked us over warily, then gave a brief nod. 'I'm cooking something,' she said, 'so it'll have to be quick.'

'It will be,' Jack said. 'Are you the householder?'

'Yes.'

'Do you live alone?'

'Yes.'

'Are you alone now?'

Panic flared in her eyes, but it was too late. I pulled the SIG from my bag and levelled it at her. 'We're not going to hurt you,' I said, 'we just need to ask you a few things.'

'Do door-to-door surveys usually include guns?' Maura asked weakly.

'This one does. Let us in and close the door and don't touch anything.'

'But I really do have something cooking –'

I rolled my eyes and handed the gun to Jack. He looked more confident with it anyway. 'I'll go and switch it off,' I said, and went into the little kitchen while Jack followed Maura slowly into the living room. There was pasta bubbling on the stove and I took it off the heat, switched the power off, and got a bottle of Coke and some glasses out of the cupboard.

'I hope you don't mind,' I said, 'but I'm so damn thirsty.'

I poured out a drink for each of us, with Jack looking on, incredulous, then I looked around for something to immobilise Maura with.

'Sit down.' Jack motioned her to a wire-framed chair and she sat, looking terrified. 'The flex,' he added to me, and I saw an extension cable winding across the floor to a computer stand. I unplugged the lot and tied her wrists to one side of the chair, remembering when Jack had tied me up so many weeks ago in France. And now we were doing the same to someone else. Isn't co-operation a lovely thing?

'What do you want?' Maura asked nervously. 'I don't have any money in the house.'

'Damn.' I clicked my fingers. 'And being on the run is so expensive. Could you please tell me your PIN number? If you're lying I may have to kill you.'

She gave me the four-digit code and I wrote it down on my hand. Then I got her wallet and put it in my bag. Then I sat down beside Jack on the sofa and smiled at her.

'We're not going to hurt you. Really. I'm sorry we even

have to have the gun, but you wouldn't take us seriously otherwise. We just want to ask you a few questions.'

'About what?'

'Sarah Wilde.'

She looked blank. 'I don't know any Sarah Wilde,' she whispered.

'Think. You worked on a case with her and Sir Theodore Chesshyre –'

Her eyes widened. 'You're the one who killed him!'

'I did not! I didn't bloody kill him. I'm so sick of people saying I killed him. I did not kill anybody,' I ranted.

'Well, not this year,' Jack added, and Maura sniffed back some tears.

'Look,' I said, 'we just need to know some stuff about Sarah Wilde because we think she might lead us to the real killer. You worked on a case with her and Sir Theodore about ten years ago, when you were a trainee. Do you remember?'

Maura looked like she was trying very hard to do so. 'I – there was some woman who used a fake name,' she said. 'It might have been that ...'

'Yes,' I pounced. 'It's a fake name. What was her real name?'

'I wasn't allowed to know. Sir Theodore knew it ...'

'But now he's dead. What was the case?'

'She'd been injured and she wanted the costs of her surgery repaid.'

My mind whirled. 'Repaid by who?'

'I don't know. She got someone to loan her the money. Then she couldn't pay it back. I think. I can't remember. I just sort of worked on a few files for Sir Theo. I didn't have a lot of access.' Maura trembled.

'Okay,' I said to her. 'It's all right. We're not going to shoot you.' I looked at Jack. 'I do not like this.'

'I don't either,' Maura whispered, and I smiled.

'Look, I'm really sorry. I – we – don't want to frighten you. We just need to know. Can you remember who paid for the surgery?'

She shook her head. 'I know it was in America.'

'America's a big place,' Jack sighed.

'The surgeon had a double-barrelled name,' Maura volunteered. 'David-John or something.'

I frowned. 'Was that his first name, or his surname?'

'His surname. I think. He had, like, three first names all in a row. Michael David-John, or Paul David-John. Something like that. I can't remember. I'm sorry.'

I nodded automatically. 'Do you know where in America?'

'No.' There were tears falling down her face now.

'A surgeon called Something David-John in America,' I said. 'Not a lot to go on.'

'I'm sorry,' Maura sobbed, 'I just can't remember ...'

'Do you know what kind of injury it was?'

She shook her head. 'Something to do with her back ...? I don't know. It was all fixed, whatever it was.'

'The surgery was successful?'

'Yes.'

'What did she look like?' Jack asked.

'Oh.' Maura closed her eyes. 'Well, I only met her the once, and she had big sunglasses and a hat on, so ...'

'Was she short or tall? White, black? Green?' Jack asked tersely.

'White. And sort of, well, average in height, I guess. She was walking with a stick, but I suppose that was because she was still recovering.'

'Was she English, or American?'

'English. Sort of a, well, accentless, I suppose. Home Counties or something. Not anything you'd notice. Um,' Maura looked like she was desperately trying to think of something else to tell us before we got bored and shot her. But there was nothing else to come. We couldn't think of much else to ask her. She didn't know anyone else who'd worked on the case with Sir Theodore, and with it being so long ago, she couldn't remember any more useful details.

She was useless.

'So, good pick,' Jack said, standing up, still holding the gun.

'What? I didn't see you doing any better.'

'Yeah, and now she's seen us …'

'I won't tell anyone,' Maura trembled.

'No,' Jack said, and flashed her a Johnny Depp smile. 'Of course you won't.' And he smacked her smartly on the back of the head with the butt of my SIG. She slumped forwards in her chair, Jack stepped back and handed me the gun.

'Was that necessary?'

'We need to be well away by the time she wakes up.'

He started towards the door.

'What, you're going to just leave her there?'

Jack stared at me. 'We tied her up and threatened her with a gun,' he said. 'Plus, I really don't think one more charge is going to make all that much difference.'

'Meaning, even if we do get off for murder, we'll both still go to jail?'

We stared at each other.

It was never-ending. I'd never be clear. I'd go to jail. Whatever I did, I was screwed. Oh God, oh God.

Oh, God.

Why did he have to say that?

Bastard.

I started untying Maura's knots and dragged her through into her bedroom. I laid her on the bed and pulled the covers over her, telling myself that maybe she might wake up and think it was a dream. Or even if she wasn't fooled, she might let us off for being nice.

Jack was standing sullenly by the door. He didn't offer to help. We walked in silence back through Grays to the station, got on the next train back to London and went to bed. In the morning we might have to talk to each other, but for now, silence was the only way of co-existing.

Chapter Thirteen

'Holder of full UK driving licence for all categories of vehicles,' Luke said, digging the spade into the pile, 'including HGV and motorcycles.' He gripped the shaft of the spade's handle with his left hand and lifted it carefully.

'Experienced parachutist,' he turned, 'diver,' he walked to the wheelbarrow, 'and skier.'

With a splat, the manure hit the barrow.

'Holder of the Queen's Medal for Shooting Excellence,' Luke said, going back into the stable. Awkwardly, using the wrong hand, he dug the spade in again.

'Holder of Commercial Pilot Licence,' carefully lift the spade, 'with over fifteen-hundred hours' flying time.' Turn. 'Specialises in fighter jets,' walk out into the sunlight, 'especially Tornado,' splat, 'and helicopters,' he rested the spade on the ground and leaned on it, 'especially Chinook.'

He stared at the far row of stable doors. 'Fluent speaker of four modern languages and two ancient. Eton prefect. Bloodline going back to William the Conqueror. And here I am, shovelling shit with one hand.'

It was probably his grandmother's idea of a joke. Offer him a place to stay, install him not in one of the terrifyingly grand rooms in her terrifyingly grand house, but in the shabby Head Lad's flat, and get him to shovel manure out of the stables while the horses were being exercised.

It wasn't as if he couldn't ride a damn horse. He'd learned to do that almost before he learned to walk. He'd be more than useful in the saddle.

'I'm quite sure someone who wears a sling shouldn't be riding a horse,' she'd said calmly when he tracked her down in one of her many, many reception rooms.

'But shovelling manure is okay?'

'Beggars can't be choosers, Luke,' she said, and sailed out.

He got out his phone and checked for messages. It was beginning to be a compulsion. 'Definition of madness,' he muttered. 'Repeating the same thing and expecting a different outcome. Also,' he put the phone away, 'talking to yourself.'

Maura will have called the police by now, I thought, as soon as I woke up. God, we're going to be in so much trouble. There'll be men with assault rifles waiting outside the hotel for us. Harrington will have handcuffs at the ready. That's if they don't shoot us down, Butch & Sundance style.

I got up and showered and dressed in the bathroom. Jack was awake when I came back out and I said, without looking at him, 'I'm going out for breakfast.'

'I'll come with.'

'No,' I said, a little more sharply than I'd intended. Jack frowned, and I said, 'I'm really hungry. I'll meet you there.'

I escaped before he could even ask me where.

For some reason I couldn't even be in the same room as him. What had suddenly changed? Why had he said that about those charges? I mean, I'd sort of thought of it before, but he didn't have to say it. We were never going to get out. Never, ever. And it was all his fault.

I closed my eyes. His fault for reminding me. Not mine for being complicit in all the things we'd done. It was his fault. After all, he'd been the one who wanted to rob the cabbie, and he'd stolen that cop's wallet in America, and he was the one who'd hit Maura.

It was all Jack's fault.

I told myself that over and over again, but I was a rotten liar.

I stomped out to the nearest café, but I was too angry

to eat. Shopping, I thought. Shopping will cheer me up. Last night, Jack had stopped at a cash point and maxed out all of Maura's cards. I had plenty of cash. For, you know, essentials.

I headed for the nearest high street.

But shopping didn't cheer me up. In fact, every item I bought seemed to have a siren attached, blaring *Stolen money! Stolen money!* around the whole shop. I saw the most adorable little leather jacket that was well within my budget, but I couldn't make myself buy it. I'd hate myself that little bit more every time I wore it. Taking a bit of money from Jack's dim cousin was one thing – I didn't like it, but we were desperate and she barely seemed to have noticed anyway – but robbing someone at gunpoint felt horribly grubby. Like a stain on my soul I couldn't scrub away.

I restricted myself to essentials, and stomped back to the café for some sustenance. There'd been a rack of papers on the wall and I might as well catch up with what was happening in the rest of the world.

But Jack was sitting there, dark eyes watchful, as I walked in. I ignored him and got myself a coffee and my own table, on the other side of the room. I didn't see if he saw me, but I had my best Pissed-off Independent Woman expression on anyway. It wasn't an act.

I got out my phone and started a search for surgeons called David-John. Hours and hours (or so it seemed) later, I found a New York practice where one of the doctors had that name. He even did orthopaedic surgery. Triumphantly, I stood up to order myself a congratulatory beverage.

And nearly walked into a cup of coffee. And a muffin. Held by Jack.

A blueberry muffin.

I *love* blueberry muffins.

I avoided his gaze, but my stomach rumbled loudly. I tried

to remember when I'd last eaten properly, and realised that it was about two days ago. Airport food didn't count.

'Here,' Jack said, and held the food out to me. The snake with the apple.

'I'm not hungry,' I lied.

'Yes, you are.'

'Don't tell me what I am.'

'You're making a scene, is what you are. Do you want the food?'

Hell, yes. 'No.'

'Liar,' he said, but sauntered away back to his own table with the food, leaving me standing there looking like an idiot and feeling like a fool.

I went back online and set up a new webmail address in the name of psychohellbitch. No telling if the address I'd used to contact Luke had been compromised. Then I sent a message to NYgayartboy, went and got my own coffee (no muffin, because I knew Jack was watching), and waited for a reply.

It came instantly.

'Baby, where are you? Harvey said you're on the run ... How bloody exciting. Don't suppose you want to hide out at my place? I've never had a fugitive here. Not for want of trying, though ...'

Delighted, I replied in the affirmative. 'I'm just about to book a flight. What's your phone number again? I'll call when we land.'

'We? Please tell me the divine Luke is with you.'

'No. Someone else. Swear to me on your paintbrushes that you will tell NO ONE. Especially not Harvey.'

'Like I ever tell Harvey anything anyway. See you later, darling,' and he added a phone number. I started checking flights.

Then a shadow fell over me, and it was Jack peering at my phone.

'I can get us there for about half that,' he said.

'Get us where?'

'New York.'

'You found him, too?'

'Wasn't hard.'

'You book the flights. I'll get us somewhere to stay.'

He hit the chair opposite me. 'Let me guess. Harvey's brother this time?'

How did he *know*?

'You don't have to come,' I said.

'Someone's got to keep you out of trouble.'

So we collected our things from the hotel and went to Heathrow, and covered ourselves in fake tan and headscarves and baseball caps, and got on another plane, and watched more movies, and ate more plastic food.

I was getting really sick of this.

International espionage always sounds way sexier than it is. You never get endless scenes of James Bond lurking around in airports, buying rubbish magazines and trying to avoid people hawking credit cards. Jason Bourne doesn't have to eat crappy airline food. Jack Bauer never gets cramp from those rubbish plastic seats.

We landed in New York with no problems, got in a taxi and found ourselves in lower Manhattan, the curvy streets of the Village, after dark, cross-dressing hookers whooping at us.

'So where does your friend live?' Jack asked, and I blinked tiredly and looked around.

'Apartment 6a, Lincoln House.'

'What street?'

'Corner of Seventh and Fourth.'

'Which one of those is the street and which one the avenue?'

'Um, I –'

'Can't you call him?'

My battery was flat. 'My God, do you ever stop asking questions?' I marched up to the nearest transvestite hooker and smiled. 'Hi.'

He looked me over. He was wearing a PVC micro-mini that tastefully revealed the posing pouch matching his stockings. He wore a giant Afro wig and platform heels about a foot high. 'Hi, honey.'

'Do you know where Lincoln House is?'

'It'll cost ya.'

'I only have sterling.'

'Say what?'

'Sterling. English money.' I took a fiver out of my pocket to show him.

'Oh, my Gawd, that is so pretty! Girls, look at this pretty little money. How much is this worth?'

I opened my mouth to tell him, then thought better and said, 'About twenty dollars.'

'Lincoln House is right over there, honey.'

I smiled again. 'Thank you.'

Jack was watching me in amazement.

'So, seriously,' he said, 'is there anything you consider to be weird?'

I shrugged. 'Welsh people are pretty scary.'

'My grandfather was Welsh.'

'Liar,' I said, because Maria had told me where each of her grandparents hailed from, and they were all considerably more exotic climes than Wales.

Lincoln House was about four storeys high, sheltered by leafy trees. I dragged myself and my bag up the stoop and leaned on the buzzer.

'Y'ello?'

'It's me. Can I come in?'

'Did you bring anyone gorgeous?'

I wrinkled my nose at Jack. 'Yes,' I said, 'but he's a bit of a bastard.'

'Don't, you're getting me all excited.'

The door came open.

'Thank you,' I said, and we trooped in. The apartment was on the top floor, and there were no lifts. I remembered Xander complaining about it when he took over the lease. It was on the tip of my tongue to ask why he hadn't taken a different apartment, but then I knew that most Manhattan apartments were like shoeboxes with cockroaches for carpets.

I knocked on the door and when it opened, fell inside, caught by a warm, tall, handsome man wearing a t-shirt tight enough to show off his well-developed chest. I was enveloped by strong arms and a cloud of menthol cigarette smoke.

'Sophie, baby,' he cried. 'You look like hell.'

'Cheers. And don't call me Sophie. I'm Alice.'

'Sure you are.' He looked over Jack, and his square jaw dropped open. 'Oh, honey.'

'You have got to be kidding,' was Jack's only comment.

'Honey, he's divine!'

'Honey, he's fucking Harvey,' Jack snapped.

I opened my mouth to ask how he knew what Harvey looked like, then shut it. Being married to the daughter of one of the Seventies' most celebrated couples is a bit of a headache for an undercover operative. You tend to get snapped by paparazzi.

'God, how incestuous.'

'He's not Harvey,' I said patiently. 'He's Harvey's brother. Xander, this is –'

Jack threw up his hands. 'First his daughter and then his brother? Jesus fucking Christ, Sophie, what are you trying to do? I didn't think you would actually contact Harvey's brother!'

'Isn't it *fun* being a fugitive?' Xander asked with a festive wave of his cigarette.

Jack narrowed his eyes at me.

'Okay, you know what? That's it. I have had enough. You are a bloody liability,' he stormed.

'Liability? I don't see you getting us anywhere to stay.'

'What's wrong with a hotel?'

'We can't afford a bloody hotel! She'll have cancelled the credit card by now and –'

'Whose credit card?' Xander asked.

'You know, you're not the only person who knows someone in America,' Jack said. 'I know bloody millions of people. I damn well live here!'

'Well, if you have so many friends, you go and bloody stay with them!'

'You know what? That's the best suggestion you've ever made,' Jack said, and picked up his bag and walked down the stairs.

Xander leaned against his doorjamb, smiling at me. 'You are the most entertaining woman I have ever met,' he said. 'Drink?'

'God, yes.'

Xander had a new blender that crushed ice and he mixed me a strawberry-and-cream margarita. It lasted two minutes, gave me brain-freeze, and loosened my tongue.

'He's a bastard,' I moaned, curled on Xander's sofa, wrapped up in a pink fluffy blanket. He takes his sexuality quite seriously, does Xander Harvard. He's an artist, and after he got falsely accused of the murder of a rich client last year, he's become a very rich artist. Hence the new apartment. His last one was basically a warehouse, in which he was, legally speaking, squatting. He now does mostly nudes of very fit men.

Damn, I wish I could paint.

'He's seriously cute, though.' Xander sighed, handing me another drink, complete with cocktail umbrella and straw. 'Are you shagging him?'

'No. I'm shagging Luke.'

Xander put his head on one side. 'Uh-huh. And it's been how long since you shagged him?'

'A week,' I moaned.

'But I thought you'd been on the run for –'

'I sneaked back to see him.'

'Nearly three weeks now,' Xander finished. 'Harvey asked if I knew anything when he called.'

'Great,' I said gloomily. 'What'd you tell him?'

'The truth, I'd heard nothing.'

'Have you spoken to him since then?' Xander shook his head. 'Don't. He's not happy with me.'

'Why, what have you done? Apart from ...' He waved his hand.

'I went to visit Rachel.'

He frowned. 'Did you put her in any danger?'

'No! You think I'd do that?'

'I know you wouldn't, sweetie.' He patted my shoulder reassuringly. 'He'll come round, once he's calmed down.'

'Hmph,' I said.

'Listen, Harvey's at a complete loss on this. I don't think he knows you and this Jack guy,' here he gave a happy little sigh, 'are working together.'

'If you tell anyone, I'll turn you into a eunuch.'

'I believe you. I remember the mess you made of my last apartment.'

'Cleared your name, didn't I?'

Xander put his arm around me and held me close as I sucked up the last of my drink. 'You did,' he said, 'and I've pledged to love you forever for it.'

'And you won't tell Harvey I'm here?'

'I won't tell a soul. I even cancelled a sitting with a truly beautiful Polynesian boy tomorrow, just for you.'

'You needn't have gone that far,' I smiled.

'Wasn't your type, darling.'

'Still, beauty is always cheering.'

'What about me? *Time* magazine called me the hottest young artist on the scene today.'

'Really? Wow. Well done you. But you're not my type either, Xander. Besides, you remind me too much of Harvey.'

'Possibly because we were once the same egg.'

'It'd be like cheating on Angel.'

'But I am cute, right?'

I looked up at him. Kind hazel eyes, shiny brown hair, a very chiselled jaw. An all-American dreamboat.

'You're adorable,' I told him, 'and if I wasn't so madly in love with Luke I'd definitely fancy you.'

'You say the nicest things.'

'Actually, generally I say the nastiest things,' I reminded him. I snuggled closer and yawned.

'You tired, baby?'

I nodded sleepily. 'I've been up since about five a.m., local time.'

Xander looked at his expensive and, to me, unreadable watch, and whistled. 'Right. Bed time.'

He hauled me to my feet and took me across the room to one of the doors on the far side. There was a low, futon-like, unmade bed, strewn with clothes and books and magazines. Xander is a boy after my own heart: he's incapable of anything resembling tidiness.

'Isn't this your room?'

He shrugged. 'It's the only room. I have my studio set up in the other one, so ...'

'Where will you sleep?'

'I'm okay on the sofa.'

I put my arms around him and hugged him tight. 'What would I do without you?'

Xander laughed. 'You managed pretty well for the last twenty-some years of your life. You only met me in September.'

'I love you, Xander.'

'You're drunk, Sophie.'

'What? No, I'm not. I only had two drinks ...'

'I make a strong margarita. And you sound like you've hardly eaten in days. Go to sleep.'

He tried to push me towards the bed, but I clung to him. The last few days had been pretty bloody depressing, and I was lonely, and quite frankly the only other person likely to hold me in his arms was Jack and he'd almost certainly make a move on me.

Xander wasn't Luke. He didn't feel like Luke and he didn't smell like Luke, but he was big and strong and kind, and he promised to hold me until I fell asleep.

The phone woke him, and his heart clutched. Groping in the dark for the flashing, bleeping device, Luke wondered if he'd live long enough to see Sophie return home safe, or if she'd have given him a heart attack long before then.

He peered blearily at the screen. Not Sophie. Evelyn.

'What?' he said. The Head Lad's flat was quiet and dark, which had to mean it was really the middle of the night. People woke up early in a stable-yard.

'Just wondered if you'd heard the latest on your girlfriend,' she said with the sort of crisp efficiency one only got from automatons who had no idea it was three a.m.

'Don't tell me, she shot JFK.'

'If they could pin it on her, they would.'

'It was twenty years before she was born.'

'The mood Harrington's in, I doubt that matters. No. Does the name Maura Lanley mean anything to you?'

Luke fell back against the pillows and let his eyes drift shut. 'No.'

'Works for BBC&H. Kidnapped and robbed at gunpoint yesterday.'

'And?' Luke said, although he'd pretty much figured out where this was going.

'There's not much doubt who it was. Jack de Valera and your Sophie.'

As if she was a possession. 'She's not *my* Sophie,' Luke said, and wondered why he'd bothered.

'Yes, she is. And she's in a lot of trouble.'

'I know that. Why are you calling me at three a.m. to tell me this?' And on a phone 5 were almost certainly monitoring.

Evelyn seemed surprised. 'I thought you'd like to know.'

'At three a.m.'

'I've only just found out,' she said. 'Apparently nobody thought it was worth mentioning to me.' Which meant it was no longer a news bulletin. 5 were probably all over it already. 'Luke, this is serious. I can't even begin to calculate the charges against Sophie.'

'Did they hurt this Mary woman?'

'Maura,' Evelyn corrected, and Luke was pleased to hear a little annoyance in her voice. 'Knocked her out. Back of the head. Needed stitches.'

Great. So that was murder, unlawful imprisonment, assault, and theft. 'What did they take?'

'Money. And she had a gun, so that makes it armed robbery.'

'Wonderful. Anything else?'

'I'm not sure you're taking this seriously, Luke.'

'My girlfriend has been accused of murder, armed robbery, assault, and unlawful imprisonment.'

'Not just accused, Luke. She actually did those things.'

'She didn't kill anyone,' he said firmly.

Evelyn was silent a moment, then she said, 'Actually, technically –'

'Apart from when she was on Her Majesty's official business and had been authorised to use extreme force. Killing in self-defence isn't the same as murder.'

'But it's hardly going to convince a judge she's harmless, is it? Two confirmed kills. It's on her record.'

'They were both –' Luke began, then stopped. What was the point? He had more than that on his own record. And unlike Sophie's panicked, inaccurate shots, fired in defence not just of her own life but those of innocents, of colleagues, even of himself – unlike Sophie, he'd killed cleanly and coldly. He'd shot unarmed men before they could become armed. He'd taken lives in the dead of night, anonymously. It was his job.

'It's three a.m.,' he said eventually. 'I'm not having this argument with you, Evelyn.'

'But,' she began, and he ended the call.

He lay in the darkness, on a narrow and uncomfortable bed, thinking of Sophie and the first time she'd fired a gun. Faced with an armed criminal, a vicious murderer. She hadn't gone in alone, but her two colleagues had already been shot down. Wounded, frightened, armed with a gun she had no idea how to use, she'd fired blindly. He'd seen the body. Any fool could tell it wasn't a deliberate hit.

He'd gone to her afterwards, slipped into her bed and made her smile, made her laugh, praised her bravery and cleverness. He'd made love to her and she'd fallen asleep in his arms for the first time, soft and warm and trusting.

She'd cried in her sleep, kicked and thrashed and gasped,

'No,' over and over, and Luke had remained silent. Stroked her hair, calmed her, and never said a word about it.

The second time had been even worse. She'd woken, tear-streaked and miserable from her nightmare, and whispered, 'I thought I was losing my soul.'

People like Sophie didn't kill cleanly and coldly. They didn't take lives anonymously, in the dead of night.

People like Luke did.

He went to sleep, and dreamed of shooting dead every person who was chasing his girlfriend.

So I spent another night in the arms of another man who wasn't my boyfriend. If Luke ever found out he'd go mental.

If I ever saw Luke again. In my present sorry state I wasn't counting on it.

The scent of coffee woke me, and in the background I could hear the low babble of a radio. My back ached and my stomach growled and I stumbled out of bed, pulled my clothes on and made an expedition to the living room.

Xander was sitting at what might, under all the mess, be the kitchen table, reading a paper. 'Morning,' he said, and glanced at his watch. 'I mean, afternoon.'

'Mergh,' I said. 'Bathroom?'

He pointed, I gathered my things and locked myself in for a nice long, hot shower. The rest of Xander's flat – sorry, apartment – was in a horrible state, but his bathroom was presentable and I borrowed a clean towel from the warm rail, wrapping myself up and feeling more human. Clean clothes, make-up and toothpaste added to the illusion of normality, and when I emerged about half-an-hour later, the coffee smell was even richer and more yummy.

There was a bakery bag of deliciousness on the coffee table, and Xander sat there looking pleased with himself.

'You got me breakfast?'

'Dialled for it myself.' He opened the bag and handed me a cupcake smothered in fat icing. 'I know how much you like them.'

The cupcake lasted about ten seconds. It was followed by a doughnut (custard cream with chocolate icing and sprinkles: for the terminally indecisive) and a bran muffin that had been warming in the oven, spread with butter. Xander had ordered coffee from the deli, as well as making a big pot to back it up.

Sometimes I wondered why I didn't just cut my losses and become a fag hag.

Replete, I flopped on the sofa and Xander handed me my phone. 'Luke called.'

I stared in horror. 'You didn't answer?'

'No. I'm not stupid, sweetie. I looked at the display.'

The voicemail icon was flashing, and after a comic couple of minutes trying to figure out how to retrieve it, I eventually listened to the message.

'Hi, it's me. (pause) I haven't heard from you in a couple of days so I'm just calling to see how you are. (pause) Apparently you made a big splash in London on Saturday night. They added kidnapping and robbery to your rap sheet. (pause) Armed robbery. (pause) Anyway. I hope you're okay. (pause) Give me a call, stop me imagining you in a ditch with your brains blown out. (pause) I'll try the other phone you called me on. Probably you got this one blown up. (pause) Bye.'

Harold Pinter couldn't have put more pauses in there.

'What's he want?' Xander asked.

'Just checking I haven't got myself blown up.'

'Angel told me about the car you totalled.'

It's good to know I'm providing my friends with gossip.

I scrunched up my nose. 'Angel has a big mouth for someone who knows so many secrets.'

'Honey, it was an exploding car. These things tend to make the news.'

'With my name attached?'

Xander just laughed. 'A car gets blown up, and it's either going to be Al Qaeda or Sophie Green.'

'Thanks for that.'

I took my coffee and the remains of the bakery bag into Xander's studio – the largest room in the apartment with big windows and massive floodlights – and called Luke's number.

'I'm not exploded,' I said when he picked up.

'That's nice. Where have you been for three days?'

'Not London. Well, I mean I was there, but now I'm not.'

'Where are you?'

'Somewhere else.'

'Why didn't you call me?'

'I – I had things to do.' I ran my hand over my face, feeling horribly tired. Not for the first time, and not for the last, I wanted to crawl back into bed. Preferably Luke's bed. 'I have to find Sarah Wilde.'

'I thought she didn't exist?'

'She does. We found someone who remembered her.'

'Who?'

I might as well tell him. He'd probably found out from the source anyway.

'Someone from BBC&H.'

'The one you kidnapped?'

'We did not kidnap her! We didn't. She was in her own home, and we were very nice, and we –'

'Stole her wallet.'

'It's expensive, being on the run.'

'Yeah. You know, I could lend you some money ...'

'I'm still not telling you where I am.'

'Sophie. Please promise me you won't do something like this again. Armed robbery, for Christ's sake!'

'It wasn't armed robbery,' I began, but he cut me off.

'You threatened her with a gun and took her wallet. How would you describe it?'

'Desperation!' All right, clearly I was more tired and frustrated than I'd realised. I was starting to shout. 'Look, we just needed answers and she wasn't going to give them to us without a little bit of ... coercion, and I might add that hitting her over the head wasn't my idea. I didn't intend to hurt her. I still didn't hurt her,' I corrected. 'Look, I just took money. Credit cards. They're all covered by insurance.'

'It's still illegal. Look, Sophie ...'

He sounded tired. He sounded worried. A wave of affection swept over me.

'I can take care of myself,' I said. 'Don't worry about me.'

'Sophie, this isn't like playground games where the worst that can happen is you might get a detention. These might be minor crimes but they can still get you for them. Al Capone was done for tax evasion. Dick Turpin was done for stealing a sheep.'

'It was a horse, actually,' I said, the affection ebbing a bit.

'I'm just asking you to be careful. Not do anything that might draw attention to yourself. Anything ... stupid.'

My nostrils flared. All right, so sometimes I do things that are irrational and, er, maybe a bit hasty, but I'm not stupid. The aptitude tests I did when I applied for the job with Sir Theo actually proved that. But being tall and big-busted and blonde kind of moulds a girl. It's easy to put on the Dumb Blonde mask, and a whole lot harder to take it off.

What I'm saying is ... I'm kind of sensitive about the whole 'stupid' issue.

'I'm not being stupid,' I said evenly, my temperature rising. I stared at the picture opposite, a multicoloured canvas that seemed to depict three naked men dancing. I squinted closer. At least, I thought they were dancing.

'These people are dangerous, Soph.'

'I know they're bloody dangerous,' I yelled. 'They blew up your car and tried to kill Jack.' I tried to calm myself. 'Although maybe whoever it was had a point there.'

'What do you mean? What's he done?'

'Nothing, he's just – he's really, really annoying, and sometimes I think ...'

Sometimes I think I can't trust him. Sometimes I think he's the only person I can trust. And sometimes I think he's the biggest threat to me right now.

'Anyway, it doesn't matter. He's stormed off in a huff. I'm on my own again.'

'What?' Luke said, and there was something behind the incredulity in his voice that gave me pause. 'Oh, come on, Sophie, he's only been back with you – can't have been more than ... what, four days? Three?'

I gazed at the naked men, an awful suspicion stealing over me. 'How,' I said, 'do you know how long it's been?'

He hesitated a fraction too long. 'Oh, what you said when you called me,' he said, but I was already shaking my head.

'You're supposed to be a spy, Luke,' I said. 'You can lie better than that.'

'What – why would – what do I even have to lie about?'

'I don't know. Why don't you tell me?'

Silence.

'How did you know how long it's been since Jack and I teamed up again? And why did you sound so ... put out, when I said he'd gone again? Why are you so keen for me to be with him?'

Even as I said the words, my insides turned to ice.

Are you breaking up with me?

The words rose inside my mind but I couldn't form them.

'I just,' Luke paused again, 'I just don't think you should be alone right now. I don't think … look, this is a big thing and it's frightening and dangerous and you shouldn't be in it alone.'

I stared at the naked men, eyes wide and dry with horror.

'I just don't think you can do it alone,' Luke said, and I registered the pain in his voice, but it was nothing compared to the pain inside me. Or the anger. The sudden, angry blonde, I-don't-need-you, don't-call-me-stupid, vicious anger that the fear had only temporarily suppressed.

'You know what, Luke Sharpe?' I said. 'I was taking care of myself all by me onesie for a long time before you, or Jack, or anyone else came along to help me. And the way I see it, my life might have been boring but it was safe, and no one ever tried to kill me. So I think from here on out I'll take care of myself, thanks. I'm actually pretty good at it.'

'Sophie –'

'Screw you,' I said, and jabbed at the screen to end the call. This wasn't nearly satisfying enough, so I went over to a cupboard and punched it.

That was better.

I love Luke. I really, really do. I love the way he looks and smells and tastes, but I also love the way he cares and thinks and laughs and cries and holds me and loves me. I love him because I know him, although sometimes he can really, really piss me off.

I didn't know why he wanted to send Jack out to help me, or even if he had. Maybe I was putting two and two together and getting purple. Wouldn't be the first time.

But something wasn't right, and the very best of it that I could make out was that Luke thought I was incompetent.

The worst was that he wanted to break up with me, and thought pushing me together with Jack might soften the blow. I wondered if I should tell him that Jack had kissed me.

That I could easily have had sex with him that night. I wondered if I should pretend I actually had.

Then I caught myself, and sagged against the wall.

What if he was simply looking out for me?

I'd alienated my boyfriend, and two of my best allies. Well, that's some nice going, Sophie.

I sniffed and tilted my head back so the tears gathering under my lids wouldn't spill out and mess up my mascara, then I shook myself and went back out into the living room, where at least I still had one friend left.

'Your friend Jack,' Xander held up a section of the *New York Times*, the biggest fattest paper in all existence, trees get ready to be scared, 'was spotted in London yesterday.'

I snatched the paper, almost tearing it. There was a tiny filler article about him – apparently the Chesshyre and Shepherd story was still under wraps, and Jack was just wanted 'for questioning in connection with' Maura's kidnapping – and a long-range shot of someone who could have been him, leaving a café. I scoured the picture, but couldn't see myself in it. So if Luke knew I'd been involved in it, the Service knew about it – but the police didn't. Or at least they weren't letting on that they did.

Then I read, 'British police are checking the credit card stolen by de Valera and hope to trace his whereabouts soon.'

Oh crap. Jack couldn't have been stupid enough to use Maura's card to book the flights, could he? I thought he'd used cash from her account. Goddamn it, why did I let him do the booking?

I ran my hand over my face. If Harrington found our flights charged to Maura's card, he'd have our IDs in seconds flat. Hell, even if Jack hadn't used the credit card, they'd probably figure we were in New York just by talking to Maura.

They'd probably be staking out David-John's practice right now.

I was only half-a-step ahead now.

Dilemma. I needed to see the doctor. I needed to warn Jack about the doctor.

Or did I? Did I need to warn the selfish, moody bastard? Did he deserve it? He could be working for the FBI or the CIA or the NSA or MI5 or CID or the bloody RSPCA for all I knew.

Instincts, Sophie. If you can't trust anyone else, trust your instincts.

Yeah, because they'd been doing so well for me lately.

I ran my hands through my wet hair and blew out a sigh.

'Between you and me, sweetie, that cut doesn't do very much for your face shape,' Xander said, and I gave him a look that has floored lesser men. 'Well, it doesn't,' he defended weakly.

'It's a disguise,' I said wearily. 'Look. Xander. I need to get an appointment with a top orthopaedic surgeon.'

He looked confused. 'You have a back problem? Uh, is this really the time –'

'He's a lead,' I said.

'Oh. Oh. A lead. Right. Is he a suspect?'

'Nope. But he has treated one.'

'Who is he?'

'Leonard David-John. Lexington Avenue.'

'Lexington?' Xander whistled. 'Whereabouts?'

'Uh,' I grabbed my bag and consulted my notes. 'Between seventy-first and -second.'

'Damn expensive. When do you want this appointment?'

'Um, today?'

Xander looked at me like I was insane. 'Are you nuts? It'll take months to get an appointment.'

'What if it was an emergency?'

'An orthopaedic emergency?'

'Fine. I'll kidnap him, too.'

Xander sighed. 'Okay, all right,' he said. 'Do you have a phone number?'

I grinned childishly and handed over the number. Xander dialled, waited, and made a face at me. 'After this we're even.'

I smiled a bit more. He might be gay, but I could still get him to do whatever I wanted.

'Hi,' he said, and he was using the actor's trick of smiling as he spoke. 'Who am I speaking to? Sherlindria?' He made a dreadful face at me. 'That is the *prettiest* name. Where did that name come from? Uh-huh … Uh-huh … Well, that is the most fascinating story,' he mimed a gigantic yawn. 'What was that, honey? Well, yes, as a matter of fact, there is something you could do for me.'

Oh, please.

'I am trying to track down an old, old friend of mine, I've known him since I was a little boy, and the last I heard, he was earning godzillions as a doctor. His name? Lenny. Leonard. Leonard David-John, I always thought that sounded like he was three people … He does? Well, that is fabulous. Now, I know there's a huge long waiting list at places like yours, but do you think – oh, no, is he? Well, that is so disappointing.'

'What, what?' I mimed furiously.

'Well, I guess he works hard enough to deserve a vacation.'

Dammit.

'Where?' I mouthed.

'You know, we once went on vacation together, we went to the Grand Canyon … But then I suppose little trips like that are below Lenny now, huh? What sort of place does a top orthopaedic surgeon go to on holiday?'

Please be Barbados, please be Barbados.

'New England? Oh, that is just sooo Lenny. Whereabouts? Vermont? There was this little town – Maine? Oh, I see, yes, that would be funny. Uh-huh? Oh, yes, of course! I'd forgotten she lived there. How incredibly dense of me. You can see why it was him who became the doctor, not me. Well, then I shall give her a call ... You are a doll, Sherlindria. What? Oh, yes, you tell him Luke Sharpe called. No, you have a nice day.'

He put the phone down. 'I need to call the police. Whoever named that child Sherlindria is guilty of child abuse.'

'Her name's probably Sharon.'

'Yeah. So, what did you think?' He struck a pose.

'You missed your calling.'

'Didn't I just? Momma always said they should put me on the stage.'

'Probably the stagecoach,' I said, but I was genuinely pleased with him. 'So? Whereabouts in Maine is he?'

'Not far from Old Town. Sherlindria thought that was hilarious, because she thought there should be a New Town ...'

'Hilarious,' I said dryly.

'Precisely. He's staying with his sister, whose name is Belinda Marple, and she lives in a little town called East Penobscot off the river of the same name.' Xander fluttered his long eyelashes at me. 'You can thank me later.'

I jumped up and threw my arms around him. 'Anything!'

'Can I borrow Luke for an hour?'

My stomach clenched and I'm fairly sure the pain showed on my face, but Xander couldn't see it.

You're on your own now, Sophie. Time to pick yourself up and dust yourself off, because no one else is going to do it.

I straightened up and said as cutely as I could, 'You're welcome to try.'

It would be cold in Maine, Xander told me, and took me out shopping accordingly. I still had a bit of cash left over from Maura Lanley's wallet, but not nearly enough to buy the beautiful things I coveted in Barney's and Bloomies. Xander lent me the money for a beautiful and very smart jacket that was lined and warm, and we rooted out gloves, scarf and hat to match, just in case it turned really cold. I got some expensive walking boots (how much fun it is going shopping with a gay man, and how much more fun when he's paying!), thick socks, some sweaters and shirts with giant checks in the flannel.

'Can you remotely afford all this?' I asked as the clerk sorted it into Big Brown Bags.

'Sure I can. You'd be amazed how much people pay me to be painted in the nude.'

'Oh, you're that painter,' the salesgirl said. 'I could have sworn I read you were gay.'

'You're gay?' I said in mock horror. 'Xander, how could you never tell me such a thing?'

The salesgirl looked horrified. I covered my sniggers and went to look at luggage. I wasn't sure my bag would hold all this stuff.

So Xander bought me a very smart leather wheely bag, and we went back to his apartment to pack everything into it and have a snack from the deli on the corner, and book a flight for that evening to take me to Bangor International. You know, it's amazing how much going on the run can broaden a girl's horizons.

I always thought Bangor was in Wales.

'I'd come with you, darling,' Xander said as he kissed me goodbye at the cab door, 'but I'm sketching the most divine Latvian boy tomorrow. Doesn't speak a word of English, but he is so damn hot.'

'Is he paying you?'

'Yes,' Xander winked, 'but he doesn't know how, yet.'

I thanked him profusely, and settled back in the cab for the long ride to LaGuardia airport.

And then the loneliness hit me, as if someone had balled it up into one big, cold lump of emotion and thrown it at my chest. I'd thrown Luke's help back in his face, I'd angered Jack so much he'd left me – twice – and even Harvey hated me. Harvey, who I didn't think was capable of hating anyone.

I landed at Bangor International late at night and simply booked into an airport hotel. I could look into transport in the morning. Right now it was late and I was completely frozen, not to mention permanently tired, and still neither Jack nor Luke had called me. I sent a text to Xander to say I'd arrived, and he replied, so I knew my phone was definitely working.

Twice in the night, I reached for my phone and even got as far as dialling, ready to sob down the phone to Luke that I needed him, and twice I stopped myself. Crying down the phone wouldn't be the way to persuade him either that I was capable of taking care of myself, or that I was the sort of girlfriend he wanted to hang onto.

Alone and depressed, I pulled on extra socks and a sweater and crawled under the covers to spend most of the night lying awake, listening to aircraft land and hating everything about my life.

Chapter Fourteen

'Where exactly are you?' Evelyn said.

'Provence. Nice this time of year.'

She made an exasperated sound. 'I am trying to help you. The least you could do is be honest with me and tell me where you're hiding.'

'Why should it matter? I've found somewhere Harrington can't spy on me, that's all that matters.'

A man in a hospital gown shuffled past, puffing furiously on a cigarette. Luke breathed in longingly. He had one hand holding the phone to his ear and the other caught up in that bloody sling, or he'd have lit up and joined in with all the other smokers hanging around the hospital entrance.

'I wouldn't be so sure of that. Word is he's got people out looking for you.'

'Then he's not doing a very good job of it. Any idiot could find out when my follow-up appointment at the hospital is and wait for me there.'

Evelyn was silent a moment. 'How is it?' she asked. 'Your shoulder?'

'Fine.' In fact it wasn't fine, it hurt like hell every minute of the day and the surgeon had spent twenty minutes yelling at him for ever taking the sling off. She told him in no uncertain terms that he ought to have been in bed for a week and that if he didn't swear on his own life to rest properly, she'd have him re-admitted, sedated, and quite possibly handcuffed to the bed.

Luke didn't think it was a good idea to tell her he'd been shovelling manure for a couple of days, albeit one-handed.

He took a deep breath and swallowed what was left of his pride. 'Listen, could you do me a favour?'

She was silent again. Eventually she said, 'I don't know, Luke. I'm not exactly flavour of the month around here at the moment. Sheila's pretty mad at me for even speaking to you.'

'Oh, please, she loves that you're speaking to me. She can pump you for information afterwards. No, look, I just need a bit of info.'

'Well ... I don't know, Luke.'

'Please? Just a few little snippets.' Luke shook himself mentally and reminded himself that before he became a chain-smoking depressive with a fugitive girlfriend, he used to be a very charming man with an incredibly high success rate when it came to women.

'Look, if Sheila finds out I've been helping you with anything, she'll have my job.'

'Then there's no need for her to find out, is there? It's hardly anything anyway. Stuff you could do on your lunch break.'

'Then why can't you do it?'

Because I've called the Home Office twenty times today and they're not talking to me any more. Bloody Sheila.

'Because I'm *persona non grata* with the security services right now, and word's starting to get around.'

Another smoker passed, and Luke inhaled deeply.

'Just a couple of phone calls, and maybe we can meet for a drink later to discuss it?' he said, putting as much persuasion into his voice as possible.

'I thought you were in hiding,' Evelyn said, clearly torn.

'Well, then we'll have to find a really dark bar.'

Silence. He waited. And eventually Evelyn said, 'All right, what do you need me to do?'

Luke smiled.

I woke late and wondered where the hell I was. I took another shower in another hotel bathroom, just like all the other showers in all the other hotel bathrooms, and considered turning myself in, just so I might have some solidarity in my life. For the first time I started to feel really wretched. I started to think I was fighting a totally unwinnable battle. How the hell was I going to achieve anything? What had I ever achieved? I wasn't going to be able to outrun MI5 forever, and sooner or later Sarah Wilde, or whoever the hell was chasing me, would catch up.

And then I'd be dead.

And it would be over.

For one obscenely long moment I thought about it. How much would I be missed? Would my parents mourn because they had to, or because they wanted to? Would Luke be glad to be free of such an irritating, clingy, changeable, argumentative girlfriend?

Would the world be better off without me?

For about ten minutes I sat on the bed, ugly short hair dripping down my back, staring at a crack on the wall and trying to summon the energy to get up and get dressed and stop feeling so bloody sorry for myself.

It didn't come. But I still dragged myself up, still put on my clothes, still brushed my hair and checked the contents of my bag and made myself go downstairs. Pasted on a smile for the man who held a door open for me. Dredged up a bit of acting talent, and acted like I wasn't someone whose life had been flushed down the toilet so hard it was already halfway along the sewer.

At reception they told me that a bus was the best way to get to East Penobscot, so I put all my important things in my shoulder bag, removed all personal traces of myself from my room, and got on a bus.

East Penobscot was a small town – I guess in England we'd call it a village. Two main streets criss-crossing each other, lined with pretty whiteboard New England houses, a few smaller streets trickling off here and there, people walking about, a banner across the street announcing a local theatre production of *Death of a Salesman*. The sky was clear and cold and big and blue, and I was glad Xander had bought me some warmer clothes. If you look on a globe then Maine is further south than England – it hits the mark somewhere around the middle of France. About where Cécile's farm is. And yet April in France is pleasantly warm. April in Maine feels like winter in England. I suppose that's the Gulf Stream for you.

I went into a small diner-type restaurant and used the last of the cash Xander had given me to buy lunch and ask the waitress if she knew the whereabouts of one Belinda Marple.

'She was a friend of my father's,' I smiled, inflecting a somewhat softer version of the accent I'd used in Hartford, in an attempt to make myself less conspicuous, 'and I'd really like to try and find her. All I know is that she lived in this little town – my father used to tell me about it all the time.'

The waitress softened at this. 'Were they friends for long?'

'Oh, yes, for years. Until my father moved back home. He died,' I added suddenly, feeling I was losing sympathy. 'He died last year and I'm trying to get in touch with all of his old friends but it's not easy ... '

The waitress nodded sympathetically. 'My father died two years ago,' she said, 'and do you know what he said before he died? "I wish I'd kept in touch with all my old friends."'

They sounded like pretty crappy last words to me, but I nodded and sniffed and said, 'My father said the same thing.'

Thank God for small town gossips. The waitress – who told me to call her Louisa-May, my dear – not only knew who Leonard David-John's sister was, but where she lived, how long she'd been married, what her husband had died of, where he was buried, how often Leonard came to see her, what his New York apartment had cost (you could buy Scotland for the same amount), who his clients were, and what he'd had for breakfast.

In my village, if you walked into a teashop and asked for directions to someone's house, they'd stare at you until you went away. Community spirit is not big where I come from, which is kind of sad, really.

I thanked her, paid my bill and left her a tip, and sauntered down Main Street, enjoying what felt like winter sunshine. The air was cold and clean and felt good filling my lungs, especially after the thick congestion of New York City. I was used to living in a pretty place, but this town really was good to look at. Like a jigsaw puzzle I used to have as a kid of a street filled with pumpkins.

Don't think about home, don't, don't ...

I turned down Mason Street and looked for number 166, as I had been advised. In a street of tall, pretty New England houses set well back from the road, it was another tall, pretty New England house, set well back from the road. It was all very Crucible-ish. I half-expected to see women in Puritan bonnets carrying milk pails down the street.

I straightened out my clothes, ran a hand through my hair, and put on my best hopeful smile.

The lady who answered the door was probably not a huge amount older than my parents, but boy did she look it. You know how some people will be forty-five forever, and some people have already been forty-five forever? Well, Belinda Marple was probably born in her sixties. She had the look of someone who was never, ever young. Her grey hair was neat, her carpet slippers were dainty, her glasses were on a delicate chain around her neck.

She smiled at me like the sort of little old lady who has 'burgle me' written across her face.

'Mrs Marple?' Immediately I had the Miss Marple theme

tune in my head. Dammit. 'Hi. My name is Alice Robinson. I was looking for Dr David-John – he was an old friend of my father's, and I was hoping –'

But she was shaking her head.

'Oh dear,' she said, 'I'm afraid you've missed him. He goes out fishing, you see, whenever he can. He loves the peace and quiet after the bustle of the city. He really won't be back until quite late. Oh, but now what am I thinking? Won't you come in and have some tea?'

English manners aren't dead, I thought, feeling very kindly towards this sweet lady, they've just relocated. New English manners, so to speak. An update.

'No, thank you,' I said. 'I don't want to impose on you. Would he be in tomorrow?'

'Well, he might. What will it be, Wednesday? He might. I tell you what, dear, why don't I get him to call you when he's home?'

I gave her a card from my hotel and thanked her and walked away, wondering what would have happened if someone had turned up and asked the same of my grandmother. She'd probably not have even opened the door unless she was expecting someone. One does not last very long in certain parts of Sheffield if one simply opens the door to any passer-by and invites them in for tea. I could have had a gun in my bag.

Matter of fact, I do have a gun in my bag.

I went for a walk around town, appreciating it from all angles, and when I arrived back at my hotel near the airport it was getting dark. I'd have had something to eat somewhere in East Penobscot, but I really didn't think there was enough cash in my wallet for that.

I could fleece someone for money, but I'd get caught. You need to practice at that sort of thing. Dammit, where was Jack when I needed him?

I wandered disconsolately down to the hotel bar and sat on a sofa by myself. A waitress came over but I shook my head. 'Nothing for me, thanks.'

Wonder what they'll make of all this back at Stansted Airport? Will my boring book-selling job still be there for me? The amount of security checks they go through at the airport, just so you can have an airside pass ... They'd never let me back in with something like this on my record.

If I got back at all.

No. Bad Sophie. Bad brain for thinking that. It will all be okay, and fine, and I'll get home and Luke will make up with me and my boss will forgive me and possibly offer me a rise for all the emotional hardship I've suffered (yeah right) and everything will be rosy.

I paused to briefly consider the delicious irony of what had got me into this whole mess in the first place. Trying to get back into the world of espionage, because I'd been feeling bored and unfulfilled again. Well, scratch that. The British Secret Service can do very well without me, I'm sure. I've had about all the excitement I can stand for one lifetime.

Bookselling was beginning to look really, really attractive.

There was a group of people at the next table to me, talking and laughing, all in suits, businesspeople waiting for the next flight in the morning. Their table was festooned with drinks, some full, some spilled, all alcoholic. I sat and listened to their loud, self-important chatter for a while and consoled myself that at least I hadn't sold my soul to big business.

Then they all got up, gradually and loudly, and wandered off either in the direction of their rooms or the toilets, and one of the women left her bag behind.

The good girl in me nearly jumped up and cried, 'Did someone leave this here? Should I hand it in?'

But the bad girl kicked her in the head, stamped on her neck and quietly picked up the handbag, and walked out.

With someone else's handbag.

Just walked up to my room, got my coat and scarf, emptied the contents of her bag into mine, then went and caught the bus into town.

Christ. I'm a Grade A thief.

Go me!

There only appeared to be one bar in town, but it advertised food, so I went in, feeling very bad-ass, and ordered a pizza and beer. I don't know what got into me. I don't even really like beer. But I sat there, feeling moody, while the bar filled up and gradually emptied, and I got steadily drunker on beer that was too cold to taste of anything.

When you go into an English pub, people glance around to see if you're a local, and if you're not, they go back to their pints and their depressed talk of football and rain. In America, if you walk into a bar, people look at you. Waitresses offer you food. There are no horse brasses on the walls, but flags from local football and baseball teams, moose heads, signed baseball cards, old-fashioned adverts for beer and cigarettes.

God, I wanted to go home.

Somebody walked over to the juke box and selected Dire Straits' *Brothers In Arms* album. I love this album, and the first gigantic chords of *Money For Nothing* cheered me up no end. But then we got into *Your Latest Trick*, and the bluesy saxophone lulled me into misery again. The bar quietened down, I ordered another beer and considered asking for a bourbon chaser. In my head I felt like a Noir detective, sitting in a trashy diner, smoking away ...

Wait, no smoking in Maine. Damn.

Anyway, there I was, a gravelly Noo Yoik accent narrating my misery. *The weather outside was cold, as cold as my heart. Inside I was too frozen to care. The cops were on my tail and they weren't the worst thing. Wilde was after me, and sooner or later she'd catch up. She was a femme fatale if ever there was one. Everyone who met the dame bought it. De Valera had betrayed me and I was all on my own with a case that refused to be solved.*

I took an imaginary drag on my imaginary cigarette. *Far away across the ocean, the man I loved was sitting watching late-night movies on TV with his good friends Jack, Jose and Jim. He'd started smoking again, depression and failure heaping up on his shoulders. He was clutching at straws as much as I was. I didn't even know if he cared for me any more, or if he'd turned traitor and was even now handing me over to the cops.*

The bar was a dive, full of people like myself, too wretched to care who was walking in the door. Could be salvation, could be damnation.

A blast of cold air announced another lowlife looking to drown his misery in liquor and blues music. I didn't look up. It wasn't like I wanted to get noticed in this place.

But someone did notice me, sauntered over and stood blocking the dismal light until I mumbled, 'I'm not interested.'

'Can I at least buy you a drink?'

'No. Thanks.' I stared into the half-inch of cold beer in my glass.

Undeterred, he took a seat beside me and signalled to the bartender. 'I'll have a Bud, and whatever the lady wants.'

I ignored him.

'So how did a girl like you end up in a place like this?'

I looked up. 'Seriously, has that line –'

And suddenly the world crashed into blinding Technicolor. 'Jack?'

He flicked back his hair. Two days of stubble graced his

jaw, his eyes were dark and mean, and he reeked of cigarette smoke. He looked like he should be the guy with the black-and-white narration, not me.

'I guess we think alike.'

'I guess we do,' I said, still dazed. 'What are you doing here?'

'Same as you, I expect. Belinda Marple?'

I nodded. Jack took out a packet of cigarettes and lit up. The bartender swooped and shook his head.

'No smoking.'

'You're kidding?'

He nodded. 'It's a public place.'

'Jesus.' Jack picked up his bottle and stood up. 'You coming with?'

I looked at the half-inch of beer in my glass, then at Jack. 'Sure.'

Jack threw some notes down on the bar and I followed him through the door. Outside it was freezing cold, the kind of cold you can taste, and I gasped and swore as I shoved my hands into my jacket pockets.

'New clothes?' Jack enquired.

'Uh-huh.' I was too cold to think. 'Where?'

He pointed to a car. 'My hotel is just ...'

I nodded and stumbled after him. Jack stopped at a late-night liquor store and bought a bottle of JD. I suppose I should have been worried about that, but all I could think was that they almost had the same initials.

His hotel was a small, family-run, farmhouse type place, a B&B I guess, right out on the edge of East Penobscot, miles from anywhere. Certainly it was miles from any phone signal. It overlooked the river. It was white-boarded and pretty and Jack's room was in an annexe on the side.

He flicked on a small MP3 player and Sheryl Crow came on. *The Globe Sessions*. Music to drown yourself to.

'Bourbon, please,' I said, and held out my hands. I actually hate bourbon, but I was freezing cold and had a definite feeling I'd need something alcoholic if I was going to get through this. Jack might still hate me. The jury was still out on how I felt about him.

There were no glasses, so we used the little plastic cups from the bathroom. Big measures. Hot, burning bourbon. I shuddered like Buffy drinking tequila.

'You been okay?' Jack asked.

I nodded. 'You?'

'Never better.'

I looked away and drained my cup. This was a stupid idea. I ought to go back to my hotel, get some sleep and try to figure out my next move.

'I should go,' I said, and Jack looked surprised. A little hurt.

'No. Look, I'm sorry, all right? I blew up at you the other day.'

'Again,' I said pointedly.

'I'm feeling a lot of stress right now.'

'Ditto.'

'We really ought to work together on this. I mean, two heads are better than one and all that.'

I nodded. 'Just don't get mad at me any more, okay?'

'Well, don't give me a reason to get mad at you any more, okay?'

I took in a deep breath and let it out slowly. 'Right. Okay. Have you found out anything else useful?'

Jack settled down on the floor with his back to the bed. 'About as much as you have, from the sounds of it. I went to see David-John today but he wasn't home.'

'Me, too.'

'Maybe we should go see him together.'

'Sure.'

Oh, this was a disaster. How were we supposed to work together like this?

'Sit,' Jack said. 'Have another drink.'

I sat. I drank. I wondered how I was going to get back to my hotel since I didn't expect there'd be any buses and I was certainly over the limit for driving Jack's car.

Jack poured me a third drink, and I was drunk and miserable enough to drink it. And after that, I was drunk enough to suggest we play Truth or Dare.

He raised his eyebrows at me. 'Are we twelve-year-old girls on a sleepover?'

'No, we're people who don't know very much about each other but need to be able to get on.'

He ran his eyes over me speculatively. 'Strip Truth or Dare. If you don't want to answer, you take some clothes off.'

I considered this. In my semi-inebriated state, it seemed like a decent prospect. I mean, what kind of secrets did I have from Jack?

I nodded.

I therefore blame myself entirely for the sequence of events that followed this ridiculous decision.

'Is my sister really gay?' Jack asked.

I nodded. That was easy. 'Yep. I've seen them kissing.'

'Is it that Australian girl who is living with her?'

'That's two questions,' I said. 'It's my turn.'

He shrugged and took a swig of his bourbon. He lit up a cigarette. In the low light, he looked like Johnny Depp in *Once Upon A Time In Mexico*. Before the eye thing, obviously.

'Who's the last girl you slept with?'

Jack took a deep drag of his cigarette and blew a cloud of smoke in my direction. 'Uh, Michelle Santorio. She's now doing time for grand theft auto.'

'Did you know she was a criminal when you slept with her?'

'How do you think I caught her?'

Yipes.

I reached over and took a cigarette from the box, and held out my hand for the lighter. Jack looked surprised.

'I didn't know you smoked.'

'I don't.' I lit up and breathed in deeply. It was about the third cigarette I'd ever smoked, and it felt *good*. To fill my lungs with pungent, acrid smoke, breathe it in deep and blow it out, to smell the air and know I'd changed it. To suck the nicotine into my veins. It felt good.

'Why did you become a spy?'

I took another drag. At this rate the fag would last about another thirty seconds.

The real answer was that it was an unsolved mystery. Well – my own motivations were a bit murky, but I'd still never had an answer from Luke about why he hired me in the first place. 'Because you're hot,' was what he usually told me. I figured Jack could stand to live in the same suspense I was on the matter.

'Because I didn't want to spend the rest of my life checking baggage. And I really fancied Luke.'

I poured more bourbon into my cup and thought about my next question.

'Why did you become a bounty hunter?'

Okay, so not very original, but pertinent nonetheless. But Jack's reply was succinct.

'Money.'

'Seriously? Not through any deep-rooted desire to do good?'

'Is that why you became a spy?'

'Is that my next question?'

'Sure, why not.' Jack drank some more.

I thought about it. The God-honest truth was that I'd been bored, and frightened. Bored of my life, of the mundanity, the repetition, of the knowledge that while nothing about my life was bad, nothing would ever get that much better. I watched my friends, people I went to school with, graduate and progress in their careers and get married and start families, and while I knew I didn't want that, I wanted … something. I wanted more.

And I was frightened. That one day I'd wake up and I'd be forty, or sixty, or eighty, and I'd still have done nothing with my life. That the days which merged into weeks would become months that merged into years and I wouldn't be able to remember any of them.

I was a spy for less than a year, and I crammed more into that time than the rest of my life combined.

'Sure,' I said to Jack. 'I wanted to make a difference.'

I just didn't tell him who I wanted to make the difference to.

I shook myself. Jack was watching me through an untidy fringe of black hair.

'Did you ever kill anyone?' I asked.

He dropped his eyes. He drank some more. He sucked on his cigarette.

And then he pulled his sweater off.

It took me a few seconds to realise what he meant, then it clicked.

'You don't want to tell me?'

He shook his head.

'Wuss.'

'My prerogative.' He looked me over, and I wished I hadn't taken off my coat and scarf and shoes. 'Do you love your boyfriend?'

Easy. 'Of course I do.'

'Would you –'

'Hey, my turn.'

Jack ignored that. 'If he was guilty of something, would you turn him in?'

At that I stalled. It was on the tip of my tongue to say that of course I wouldn't, because I did love him, but how did that stand in the light of my pronouncement that I wanted to do good in the world?

'Guilty of what?' I asked cautiously.

Jack shrugged. 'Killing someone.'

'He kills people professionally. I mean – it's part of his job, sometimes –'

'I mean not professionally. Out of hate, or revenge, or maybe on your behalf.'

I opened my mouth, and closed it again. Because I knew Luke would be capable of that, just as I was.

I carefully put down my cup of bourbon, handed Jack my cigarette, and pulled my sweater off.

He nodded in a self-satisfied sort of way.

'Show me your tattoos,' I said, reasoning that he had to have at least one.

'That's not a question.' He handed me back my cigarette.

'Okay, will you show me your tattoos?'

'No.'

'That's not fair –'

'But it's true.'

'Aha,' I said, waving my fag at him, 'but if you take off any more clothes then you will be showing me. So that'll be a lie.'

Master of drunken logic, that's me.

Jack looked pretty pissed off at that, but he stood up, unfastened his jeans, and pulled them down to show me a small heart on his hip with the name Amie scrolled across it.

'Who –'

He narrowed his eyes at me and fastened up his jeans. 'Who's the last guy you cheated on and why?'

I tried to look offended. 'I have never cheated on anyone!'

'Never?'

'No.' Matter of fact, I'd only had one other proper boyfriend before Luke, and had the chance come to cheat on him, I'd have done the kind thing and put him out of his misery first. He just really wasn't worth stringing along.

And as for Luke ... well, hell. What was that thing Paul Newman said about not going out for hamburgers when you've got steak at home?

That is to say, assuming you've still got the steak at home.

No. It's just a blip, Sophie girl. He'll still be there when you get home. He has to be. Get your head in order and call him.

Call him in the morning.

Jack looked bored by this information. I wrinkled my nose, drained my drink, and asked the inevitable, 'Who's Amie?'

Jack wordlessly took off his shirt and leaned back against the bed. Hah, if he thought being bare-chested was going to distract me he could think again.

'Have you ever had a sexual experience with a woman?'

Men.

'Yes,' I said, and the cigarette fell from his lips and nearly burned a hole in the carpet before he scooped it back up again.

'You're kidding?'

'Well,' I poured more bourbon, 'I kissed my best friend.'

He looked relieved. 'That doesn't count.'

'Twice.'

'For a bet?'

'Passing on a message.' From Harvey, as I said. Before he and Angel got together. 'Have you ever had a sexual experience with a man?'

Jack went very still. Seriously, he didn't think I'd ask? Looking down at his feet, his gaze fell on his socks.

'They don't count,' I said.

'Of course they do.'

'Nuh-uh. Socks are not clothes. They're accessories.'

'Well, I say they count.'

'Well, I say they don't. Answer me or take your trousers off.'

Jack looked like he might have shot me, but I was the one with the gun. Moodily, he stood up, removed his jeans and threw them at me. Underneath he was wearing those stretchy boxer-brief things. I found my eyes lingering helplessly on his crotch, and made myself drag them away.

So Jack had got frisky with another bloke? Interesting. Very interesting.

'How many people have you really killed?' Jack asked me, settling back down on the floor, looking very fine in his underwear.

'Two.'

'Did they deserve it?'

I stared at him. 'One of them was responsible for killing a hundred-and-forty-three people,' I said, 'and the other one –'

'Yes?'

The other one ran over Tammy.

He'd murdered several people just to keep them quiet. He tried to kill me several times. He blew up Docherty's Vanquish, which ought to come with a death penalty.

He tried to kill my cat.

And now he was dead, and felt nothing. People rotting in jail could feel remorse for what they'd done. They could be pounded into shivering wrecks of humanity by guilt. Dead people were absolved.

I realised I'd been silent for a long time when Jack reached over, uncrossed my arms, and lifted up my t-shirt.

'No answer,' he said, 'no top.'

'No, I was thinking –'

'Nope,' said Jack, and pulled my t-shirt off. His knuckles grazed my breasts as he did, his eyes steady and dark on mine.

Whose bloody idea was this?

'Do you –' I asked, and my voice came out very shaky. 'Do you think I'm innocent?'

Jack was still kneeling beside me. 'Of what?' he asked quietly.

'Sir Theodore?'

There was a very long silence. Jack put his thumb under the waistband of his boxers.

Cold dread ran through me.

I grabbed my t-shirt from him, snatched at my sweater and started scrambling to my feet.

'Wait,' Jack tried to pull me back down, 'no, Sophie, wait, I didn't mean –'

'Let go of me.'

He had his fingers hooked around my belt loops. I smacked and clawed at his hands, shoved at his face, and eventually lashed out with my foot, connected with something soft and kicked him onto the floor.

'Fuck,' Jack gasped, eyes watering.

'Fuck off,' I replied, shoving my feet into my unlaced boots, grabbing my coat and scarf and bag, and wrenching the door open. Outside it was deadly quiet, very black and so cold my breath clouded in front of my face. Shivering immediately, I pulled on my coat and tried not to trip over my laces as I stumbled across the path to the road, stopped and tucked in my laces so I wouldn't fall and break my neck, and started running.

But I'm crap at running, I wasn't wearing the right shoes or the right bra, it was so cold it felt like my lungs were burning, and I was far too drunk to race about on an icy road in the middle of the night, somewhere totally unknown.

Flakes of snow started to fall.

I slowed to a fast indignant walk and started muttering prayers that I was going in the right direction. And then I heard footsteps pounding after me and knew it was Jack. I changed my prayers to wishing he'd fall and break his neck. Or at least catch hypothermia.

But evidently God wasn't listening, or maybe I'm too much of a sinner, because Jack caught up with me, wearing jeans and an unfastened shirt, his breath making hard, white clouds in the air.

'Go away,' I said, not stopping.

'No. Sophie, look, I didn't mean – I mean, I … I don't think you're guilty. I mean I trust you. As much as you trust me.'

'So not much, then.'

'You don't believe me?'

'No, Jack, quite frankly I don't.'

'So why have you been –'

'Using you to help further my own cause? Figure it out,' I snapped, glad it was so completely dark he couldn't see my eyes shining.

Jack stopped. 'You were using me?'

I nodded and carried on walking.

'The whole time?' He grabbed my arm and spun me round. 'The whole damn time? I don't believe you.'

I don't know what made me do it. I was pretty drunk, I've never been good with spirits, and I was angry and cold and homesick and horribly depressed. I bunched up my fist inside my scarf and slammed it into his face. Jack reeled back, lost his balance on the ice and slammed onto the dark, dirty road.

I reached into my bag, pulled out my gun, and aimed it shakily at him.

'If you come after me,' I said, and it would have sounded a hell of a lot better if my teeth hadn't been chattering like falsies in a bad comedy sketch, 'I'll fucking shoot you. Savvy?'

Jack stared at me, and I flicked the safety off, concentrating on the gun, quite terrified I just might shoot him.

For a long second neither of us moved. Snow melted on Jack's exposed skin and frosted his hair. My hands began to ache in the cold.

Then, one hand to his face, he raised the other in surrender. I backed away a few steps, subtly flicked the safety back on, and walked away.

It was about two miles back to my hotel, and the air was below freezing. By the time I got there, my toes were lumps of ice, my hands throbbed, tears were frozen to my face and I felt like I'd never be human again.

Luke opened his eyes to see an antique dressing table, a painted screen and a window twelve-feet high, draped with fine muslin.

This was interesting, since it corresponded to precisely none of the bedrooms he'd slept in during his entire life.

Groggily, he raised himself on his elbows, or at least tried to. His right arm was still bound up in the stupid sodding sling. He levered himself upright and looked around the room.

He recognised the wallpaper, because it was the same hand-painted stuff his Great-Aunt Matilda had in the bedroom where he used to sleep whenever he visited her as a child. But he didn't recognise the furniture, which mostly looked antique, or the pargetted ceiling, or the foot-wide floorboards, or the silken quilt sliding down to his waist.

He began to get a bad feeling.

He wore a t-shirt and underwear. Also not good,

although better than nothing. A quick glance around the room revealed no hint of where his trousers might be. His head pounded. Usually, his morning recall was a hell of a lot better than this. He felt as if someone had drugged him.

Oh hell. Had someone drugged him?

… and then put him to bed in a room so luxurious it made the Ritz look like a Travelodge?

He frowned and looked around again. There was no TV, no kettle, and only one door out of the room. It failed to bear fire-safety information. He wasn't in a hotel. He was in someone's bedroom.

Luke ran his hand through his hair and figured he might as well work out whose bedroom he was in. He stepped out of the bed, his bare feet hitting a soft, undoubtedly expensive rug, and crossed to the door.

A living room every bit as luxurious as the bedroom greeted him. More huge floorboards. More draping and swagging at the windows. A mixture of antique and designer furniture. A photograph on the wall, glossy and enlarged. An older couple and two girls in their twenties. Dark-haired. Good-looking.

One of them was Evelyn.

Chapter Fifteen

I called the airport from my mobile in the early morning as I stuffed things into my bag, and gave them the number of the credit card I'd stolen from the drunk woman in the bar in payment for a flight to Bradley International airport in Connecticut. My hands felt like Edward Scissorhands' and they ached, everything ached, from the cold. I piled on another sweater and a flannel shirt, extra socks and a pair of tights under my jeans, added gloves and hat, the lot. I was so cold. I'd never be warm again.

I felt hunted the whole time: waiting for the taxi, checking in, defrosting myself with strong coffee. I didn't feel remotely safe until I was through security, and even then it was as if everyone was watching me. I practised my fake signature and bought a lot of Euros, just to confuse whoever tried to trace the credit card. And then I got on the plane, checked the faces of everyone around me, and finally let myself relax. I'd been awake all night. I didn't feel remotely drunk any more. I was exhausted, but my mind was too nervous to sleep.

Jack didn't trust me. He was only working with me to keep tabs on me. Matter of fact, he could have been lying the whole time about everything, Irene, Maria, everything. How the hell would I know? He could have been working for Harvey.

Harvey, who still hated me.

I felt like I was in a car chase, or on a runaway train. Sooner or later someone would catch me, but how soon? And did I want them to?

Recollection hit Luke like a train. Evelyn, her hands and her mouth and her sweet-scented skin. Her warm, slim body against his. Her husky laugh.

'I think you've had a little too much to drink,' she'd purred, and Luke's head pounded in agreement.

Steadying himself, he ran a hand over his face. He desperately needed a shave and his mouth felt like it was lined with old carpet, but more importantly *he'd just woken up in his secretary's bed*.

He staggered through a pair of tall double doors into a kitchen that seemed to be mostly made of chrome, wincing at the brightness, and stuck his head directly under the tap. Cold water flushed his face, filled his mouth, and he stood up, reeling.

Sophie is going to kill me. She's going to actually dismember me.

Loathing himself, he made it back into the living room and collapsed on the immaculate sofa. Maybe he should call Harrington and confess to the murders himself. MI5 would be a picnic compared to what Sophie would do if she found out he'd cheated on her.

His eyes roamed the beautiful apartment. Evelyn clearly wasn't shy about accepting family money – she sure as hell couldn't furnish a place like this on her salary. The high ceilings, tall windows overlooking a beautifully maintained garden square, two bedrooms –

Wait. Two bedrooms? He counted doors. The room he'd just come out of, the kitchen, and two more. He opened one to find an expensive-looking bathroom.

He opened the other to find a huge bed, massive wardrobe, and exquisite chaise longue. At least, he assumed it was exquisite. He couldn't see any of it for the piles of clothes and cosmetics heaped upon every surface.

Relief shot through him. This was Evelyn's room. He could even smell her perfume here, and there had been none when he woke up. None on his clothes. And come to think of it, he was still wearing something, which he wouldn't be if he'd been having rampant sex with Evelyn all night.

Luke laughed out loud, which made his shoulder throb, which made him laugh even more. He wasn't sure he was even capable of rampant sex at the moment. He could barely feed himself, thanks to shovelling manure for days.

He went back into the room where he'd woken up, and from the door he could see behind the painted screen to a chair where the remainder of his clothes had been placed. Relieved beyond measure, he went through his pockets for painkillers and his phone, and called Evelyn.

It went straight to message service. 'Evelyn, it's Luke. Listen, thanks for putting me up last night. Appreciate it. Give me a call back if you can.'

He went in search of coffee, spent about half-an-hour trying to get her ridiculously complicated coffee maker to just give him some of the damn stuff, and a further ten minutes searching for a cup to drink it out of.

His phone rang, and Evelyn's name flashed up.

'And how are you feeling this morning?' she asked, her tone a little acidic.

'Like hell,' he replied. 'How much did I drink last night?'

'More than you should have, given the painkillers I found in your pocket.'

He winced. 'Right. Yes. Sorry. Didn't do anything embarrassing, did I?'

'Repeated loudly how much you loved your girlfriend,' Evelyn said, 'but we were in the cab by that point so no one else heard you. Except the driver, and I don't think he was Service so we should be safe.' She paused, while Luke mentally beat himself up. 'Look, you really ought to be gone by the time I get back. And try to be discreet. I don't think

I'm under any surveillance but it was rather a risk bringing you back home last night anyway.'

'So why did you?'

Evelyn paused. Then she said, 'You wouldn't tell me where you were staying and you were in no state to be left alone. Why on Earth do you live so far away?'

She said it as if Essex was Outer Mongolia. To a city girl like Evelyn, it probably was.

'I moved there when I started at SO17. It's convenient for the airport,' he said, which was a direct lie. It was convenient for Sophie.

'Look, do you remember what I told you last night? The information about this Sarah Wilde woman?'

He closed his eyes. Good job he only had one hand free or he'd be using the other to punch himself in the face. 'No.'

'No, I didn't think you would. There's a USB stick in my laptop bag. Take it, for God's sake don't leave it there. I don't want to be in the same trouble you are.'

He found it, and plugged it into the laptop. 'Evelyn, I can't express my gratitude enough.'

Another pause. 'Yes, well,' she said. 'I'm sure we can come up with a way.'

Landing in Connecticut not long after dawn, I shoved away memories of being there with Jack, and took a taxi to Irene Shepherd's house. On the way, my phone rang, and the display showed Jack's number.

I cancelled the call.

Then, feeling horribly low, I called up Luke's number, but I couldn't bring myself to ring it. What if he was still angry with me? What if I was still angry with him? Could we even have a conversation these days without erupting into arguments?

I sent him a text. 'Had Wilde been to Hartford before?'

The reply came back a few minutes later. 'Two years ago in June.' That was all. Another bare text.

'Where did she stay?'

No reply. The cab pulled up at Shepherd's house and I paid the driver with the dollars I'd got in exchange for my Euros when I landed at Bradley Airport. Smart, yes? I'd got changed into heels and a skirt, but I still felt really cold. I was shivering all the time.

I pressed the buzzer at the gate and when Consuela Sanchez's voice answered, tried to remember how we'd got in before.

'Alice Robinson,' I said eventually. 'I was here last week. Department of ...' Oh hell, what had I said?

She buzzed open the gate, and I walked in. She was waiting at the door for me.

'Your friend is not with you?'

'Er, no. No. We're making, uh, independent enquiries. Okay, Mrs Sanchez –'

'Ms Sanchez,' she said threateningly, and gestured to the sofa in the living room like it was an electric chair.

'Ms Sanchez. I do beg your pardon. I need to know if you ever met a woman by the name of Sarah Wilde.'

Her forehead wrinkled and she sat down opposite me. 'Sarah Wilde? I don't remember ...'

'It would have been a while ago. A couple of years. June, in fact, two years ago. She came to Hartford to see Judge Shepherd.'

Consuela shook her head, still frowning. 'What did she look like?'

Damned if I knew. 'She was about your height, white, English accent.'

'English? Oh no, wait. There was someone. I remember, she came on a really hot day and ordered drinks from me. Like I was a servant or something.'

I can't understand how she made that mistake. Possibly the apron and the sensible shoes and the fact that she answered the door for her mistress?

'Do you remember what she looked like?'

'She had sunglasses and a, uh …' she mimed a big brim around her head, 'a hat. Like she was going to a wedding or something.'

'And she didn't take them off?'

'Not that I saw.'

'Do you know what she wanted?'

'No, but Ms Shepherd was not too happy to see her. Told me if she came by again, to not let her in.'

Interesting.

'Did she leave an address or a phone number?'

'Not so I know.'

'Did Judge Shepherd have an address book or an appointment book?'

'They have it at the police station.'

Bugger.

'Did she only come that one time?'

'Yes.'

'Do you have any security camera footage of her?'

'No. Ms Shepherd only keep the tapes for six months. And the police have them anyway.'

Of course they did.

'Right,' I said, standing, too weary to think of anything else to say, 'well, if you think of anything else, then give me a call.' I took a sheet of paper from my notebook and wrote down my mobile number. 'Anything at all you can think of to do with this woman.'

'Why she so important to you?'

'She's just a lead,' I snapped, and went towards the front door. Sanchez saw me out, and I stood outside the gates, trying to think where I should go next.

My phone buzzed with a message just as I was deciding to go into town and look for a tourist information site, if there was one. It was Luke.

'Twain House Hotel.'

I could look up the details on my phone. I sent a swift, non-committal thanks, and found a bench on which to sit while I figured out where to go.

The Twain House Hotel was a big, modern building with an underground car park that looked to me like the sort of place where someone dodgy like Sarah Wilde could have struck a few deals. Or whatever it was she did.

Damn, I wish I knew who she was.

I booked a room, delayed asking about Wilde until I had recovered some brain cells, and lugged my bag up to a characterless, modern room. Taking a bath would have been a swell idea, except that I was likely to fall asleep in it. So I splashed some water on my face, hung a Do Not Disturb sign on the door, and curled up in bed, wearing as many clothes as I could, an extra blanket over the duvet, still feeling cold.

Luke leaned back against Evelyn's sofa and looked at his phone for a moment. Sophie hadn't called him. Hadn't added any endearments to her text. Hadn't given any indication she wanted anything more from him than information.

You'd never drown if someone pushed you in. He'd always thought that about Sophie, too, always known right from the start that she was a fighter. You could shoot her and drown her and collapse buildings on her head, and she'd survive. Sometimes he wondered if she was secretly a cartoon character. If he hit her round the head with a frying pan, she wouldn't collapse, she'd just see tweety birds.

But now ... had it all finally become too much for her? Was she ... was she drowning?

The urge to go to her, to metaphorically swim out and rescue her from the tidal wave, was absolutely overwhelming. Without being able to stop himself, he reached for Evelyn's laptop.

He'd Googled for Sophie's name, of course he had. But there was still nothing. 5 were still flattening the story. He'd checked Jack's name a fair few times too, because 5 seemed less interested in him and the CIA weren't quite as good at keeping quiet, but he'd got nothing useful. The Americans hadn't found the tabloid sob story from Maura Lanley about her Kidnapping Ordeal. 'I was robbed at gunpoint! I thought I was going to die!'

Gunpoint.

Exactly where was she getting her firearms from?

He thought back, carefully. The gun safe in her flat had been empty when he'd last checked. Her SIG hadn't been found at the crime scene.

She'd taken it with her. She was travelling with it.

How was she travelling with it? Driving to France was one thing, but getting on a plane? It was hardly the sort of thing she could hide in her handbag.

He got out his phone and scrolled through the contacts to D. Dialled.

'What can I do for you?' Docherty asked.

'You can tell me how the hell Sophie has kept her gun with her,' Luke said.

The horrible, shrill bleep of my phone woke me, and I wished I'd been bright enough to turn it off while I slept. But I rolled over, picked it up and frowned at the display. I didn't recognise the number.

''Lo?'

'Ms Robinson?'

An unfamiliar voice. Male, American, gravelly, a smoker's voice.

'Yes?'

'You came to Judge Shepherd's house this morning.'

'Who is this?'

'I'm her gardener. Name of Tommy Canolti. You were asking about a visitor the judge had, an English woman?'

'Sarah Wilde.'

'Yeah. I remember her. Can you come up to the house and we'll talk about it?'

I peered at my watch.

'It's eleven-thirty at night.'

'Is it so late? Oh. Well. I guess maybe you could come in the morning. Are you staying in town?'

'Yes –'

'I could come to your hotel –'

'No,' I panicked, 'it's okay. I'll come to the house. Shall we say, ten tomorrow? Okay. Good. See you then. Bye.'

I switched off my phone, feeling a little shaky, but definitely wide awake. That guy had freaked me out. Coming to my hotel? Meeting up so late at night? Like that wasn't suspicious.

Dammit. Why had I given the maid my number? What if the damn CIA had got hold of it?

I was too tired for this.

I drummed my fingers on the bedside table for a bit. Then I picked up the room phone and called Reception and asked them not to put any calls through, and to tell anyone who asked for me that I wasn't there.

I tried to sleep, but it didn't come easily. Frustrated, still cold, I gave up on sleep and ran a hot bath. In the middle of the night. Definitely cracking up here.

I was just getting dressed again when the phone rang.

Jesus. You give a receptionist one simple instruction …

I snatched up the phone. 'It's the middle of the bloody night.'

'Ms Robinson, I'm sorry, I know you didn't want to be disturbed, but a man just came to Reception, he wanted to see you and when I told him he couldn't go up, he showed me a CIA badge and just walked straight to the elevator.'

God bloody dammit! 'You didn't try to stop him?'

'He was *CIA*,' she said, as if this was the same as Dark Lord of the Sith.

I put the phone down and glanced at the window. Far too high to escape from. If I left the room now he'd probably see me.

Crap. Only one option left then.

I got dressed as quickly as I could, threw everything into my bag, and took a seat at the back of the room, one foot resting on the chair, arm across my knee, holding my gun steady. I had my thumb on the safety catch and my finger on the trigger. The room was dark and silent.

About thirty seconds later, someone knocked at the door. Then they knocked again.

'Ms Robinson? Open up. This is the CIA.'

I stayed right where I was.

'Ms Robinson?'

There was a clicky noise, I saw the light on the electric lock go green, and the handle turned.

A large shape blocked the doorway. 'Ms Robinson, my name is Agent Harvard of the – *Sophie*?'

I was so shaken my finger squeezed the trigger and it was a damn good job I had the safety catch on, or I might have shot one of my best friends. Well. Erstwhile best friends, at any rate.

'Harvey?'

He pushed the door shut and switched the light on.

'You're Alice Robinson?'

I bit my lip.

'Jesus. I thought –'

'Why are you here?'

Harvey chucked his gun on the bed in a gesture of goodwill and I hesitated about doing the same. He's saved my life in the past. And I've saved his. But that was before I turned up on his professional radar in the 'enemy' capacity, and, oh yes, before I endangered his daughter.

I kept my gun in my hand, but out of friendship I lowered it a bit.

'Don't trust me?'

'Don't really trust anyone right now. And I'm not sure I can honestly believe you don't have another gun about your person.'

Harvey inclined his head in a little nod. He's a good-looking bloke, taller than Luke and broader, too. He makes tiny little Angel look like a child sometimes. He's almost identical to Xander, only without the little scar Xander has across his eyebrow. The same glossy light brown hair, kind hazel eyes and square jaw that had greeted me in New York.

'Why did you tell Consuela Sanchez you were called Alice Robinson?'

'You really think I'd give my real name?'

'You're in a lot of trouble.'

'Yep.' And not just with the CIA.

He stayed standing, looking down at me.

'You gonna arrest me?' I asked.

He looked surprised. 'Why would I arrest you?'

'Um, I'm part of the whole case you're investigating? And, um. Well, I know I'm not your favourite person right now.'

Harvey scrubbed his hands over his face. He sat down on the bed. 'Yeah,' he said. 'About that.'

I winced, but when he took his hands from his face he didn't look like he wanted an apology.

'I'm really sorry about that,' he said.

Wait. What?

'Rachel chewed me out for it. And I mean, that girl can get ... *angry*. I don't know how the hell she ended up such a firebrand. Her mother was fairly normal. But she just went insane on me and told me if I went after you I'd be betraying a friend.'

'Rachel did?' I said, shocked.

'Yeah. And you don't want to know what she said to her grandmother. I have never seen Teresa Cortes so lost for words in my life. Rachel threatened to run away, and you know Rachel. She could be on another continent before you even realised her passport was missing.'

'She's a very smart girl,' I croaked.

'I know she is. I didn't know she was so ... loyal. She's decided you're her friend, Sophie, and nothing you can do can ever be wrong in her eyes.'

I stared at him, utterly flummoxed.

'So I guess the only threat I have to make to you from now on is not to do anything to disappoint her. Like get shot or arrested for murder.'

'I'm working on it,' I said faintly.

Harvey gave me a bit of a smile. 'Why are you sniffing around Irene Shepherd?'

I sighed. 'Do you have several hours?'

'Nutshell version please.'

'She ... has something to do with a lead I'm chasing up.'

'That lead wouldn't be a Tommy Canolti, would it?'

My fingers tightened around the butt of my gun.

'You're after Canolti, too?'

'Yeah.' Harvey sighed. He looked tired.

'Who is he?'

'He is someone wanted for numerous crimes. Not really connected to anything I'm doing – or wasn't, until I got a report he'd been sniffing around Shepherd's house. You wanna know how I knew he'd been there?'

'Why do I have the feeling this isn't going to be a happy ending?'

'He left a phone number with the housekeeper. And you know who else left a number with the housekeeper?'

I tried out a meek expression. It wasn't a good look for me.

'And do you want to know how I know she had both your numbers?'

'Surprise me,' I said heavily.

'She was found clutching them in her hand.'

I scrunched up my face. I knew what was coming.

'And just to accessorise the pieces of paper, she also had a bullet in her back.'

'Dead?'

'Yep.'

Shit. Bugger, bollocks and arse, in that order.

'So ... you figured it had to be either me or him who killed her ...'

'Canolti skipped town. I ran a search on Alice Robinson and found you right here.'

'I didn't kill her,' I said pre-emptively, and Harvey gave me a little smile. Then the smile faded.

'Did you kill Sir Theodore Chesshyre?'

'No.'

'Just checking.'

'I suppose you have to.'

'I suppose I do.' Harvey ran a hand across his face. He looked exhausted.

'So,' I said, 'why are you on this case? The Irene Shepherd case.'

'How do you know I am?'

I rolled my eyes. 'Don't you get all CIA on me. I know you are. It's not your bag, is all.'

'Not my bag?' Harvey looked amused.

'I watched *Austin Powers* on the flight from ... somewhere.' There'd been so many flights I just couldn't remember any more.

'Look, I wouldn't be, if it weren't for you.'

I raised my eyebrows.

'Supreme Court Judge gets shot, well, that raises a few alarms. Shot by a foreign national, that raises a few more. Especially when we find out said foreign national has a sister in the British Service. Then we hear this case is connected to the death of an MI5 officer, and that the major suspect for that is another British Service agent named Sophie Green.'

'*Former* British Service agent,' I stressed.

Harvey gave a ghost of a smile, then went on, 'Truth be told, Sophie, I volunteered for this. I didn't really think it was you, I thought ...'

What, Harvey? You thought what? But his face had gone blank again.

'Everyone's gunning for you. I just figured if I got here first I could at least ask questions before shooting.'

'Are you going to?' I asked. 'Shoot me?'

'Did you kill Shepherd?' I shook my head. 'Chesshyre?' Another shake. 'Then no, I'm not gonna shoot you.'

'So ...what happens now?' I ventured.

Harvey groaned and flopped back on the bed. 'I don't even know any more. Jesus, Sophie, don't you ever get tired of all this?'

What a question.

'Can you keep a secret?'

He raised his eyebrows.

'I'm so tired of this I – I was actually considering going home and turning myself in.'

He sat up straight and looked right at me. I looked right back. I had my gun in my lap and a weight in my head that made my brain ache and my eyes sting. I was tired, still pretty cold, depressed and rather frightened.

'I've been on the run for weeks,' I said. 'And I'm no closer to figuring this out than I was before. In fact I'm more confused than ever, because all I've been able to find out is that my main lead doesn't actually exist. She's a bloody ghost. And I've got no help from –' I stopped suddenly, remembering that Harvey was trying to find Jack.

I could drop him right in it, right now. I could tell Harvey where Jack was – or used to be. I knew his alias. I knew his leads and I knew how his mind worked. Well, sort of. I could probably figure out where he was going next.

Probably here. Right where Harvey was.

'From who?' Harvey asked.

'I, er – from anyone. You, even. Do you know who killed Irene Shepherd?'

He shrugged. 'There's a suspect …'

'Right, the guy you think is a secret assassin. Has he killed anyone else?'

'Not so far. Although I could probably pin Consuela Sanchez on him.'

'Do you know what kind of gun it was? What kind of bullet?'

'Nah. Only found her a couple hours ago. I mean, I'll know probably by tomorrow, but …'

I nodded. Of course, it was perfectly feasible that Jack actually had killed Sanchez. Just as it was possible he'd killed Shepherd.

He wouldn't tell me how many people he'd killed.

I opened my mouth, about to say that Jack de Valera was in East Penobscot, Maine, and did he want directions, when something hit the back of my head. I think it was my conscience.

I looked at Harvey's kind, tired face, and saw the same fierce intelligence that burned behind his daughter's eyes.

Harvey had just apologised to me for something that was my fault, all to appease the beliefs of a nine-year-old girl. A girl who thought I was her friend. A girl who valued loyalty.

If I told her I'd turned Jack in, she'd never forgive me.

'Will I be needing to get out of town?' I said instead.

'Yeah. I called Alice Robinson's name in, so she's a suspect now. Jesus, Sophie, I didn't think it'd be you. I thought I'd found another suspect.'

I closed my eyes. So, basically, I was screwed. No more plane travel.

'Can't you tell them it was a mistake? That it was actually Alison Robinson, or Robins, or you couldn't find anyone by that name, or you made it up, or ...'

Harvey's gaze was steady, the blank look I was so used to getting from Luke when he was Not Allowed To Talk About It.

'Right.'

'Sorry,' he said.

'Yeah.' I stood up. My gun was still in my hand. 'Going to arrest me?'

Harvey gave me a long look, and his eyes narrowed slightly. 'When I arrived at the scene,' he said, as if reading out a report, 'the window was open and the hotel room empty. Although I searched the vicinity, the suspect had escaped.'

I exhaled in relief. 'I need to get out of town. Without giving anyone my name.'

'No flying.'

'Nope.'

'If it helps, I won't tell MI5.'

'Cheers.'

'You want a ride?'

'Depends where you're going.'

'Can you afford to be picky?'

I guessed not.

'How's the train system in America?' I asked.

Ten a.m. and his head was pounding like an executioner's drum. Luke leaned back against the spiked railings opposite Thames House and asked himself if he was about to do something really, really stupid.

Yes, he answered back. Really, *really* stupid.

He considered the situation from all angles. Sophie was tired, desperate, and beyond caring if she revealed her location to him. She'd sent a text last night asking him about a man who didn't, officially, exist. There was no record anywhere of Irene Shepherd having a regular gardener, although when he'd looked up Tommy Canolti he'd found a man with fingers in lots of pies, all of them unsavoury. Could be the killer. Could be an accomplice. Either way, he was after Sophie.

Then there was this Sarah Wilde woman. He still doubted she even existed, but he couldn't deny that someone was using her name to travel around. Sophie was convinced a woman was after her. He'd had nightmares last night about Alexa Martin and had even called the Home Office again to see if they were absolutely, a hundred-percent sure she was still in jail. They wouldn't even speak to him.

He'd talked to Maria about her brother, but she hadn't heard from him at all for days. 'He can take care of himself, Luke. And he'll take care of Sophie.'

He hadn't told her Jack and Sophie had gone their separate ways. No need to worry her any more.

So, he recapped to himself. The woman you love has been accused of pretty much every crime bar arson in a naval dockyard. She may even be guilty of them. MI5 are after her but they don't seem to know where she is or what her alias is. At least one killer, possibly two, are also after her, and they definitely do know where she is. If you go after her you will be followed, even if you use a fake passport because the bastard things were issued by MI6 in the first place. Docherty, good though he is, simply can't get you a replacement in time to get you out there.

There wasn't any time to lose. Someone needed to get to Sophie before the killer did. Someone with greater resources and a vested interest in getting her back in the country, and in one piece.

Docherty might be able to retrieve her, but she'd still be a wanted criminal. He didn't trust Harvey not to turn her over to the American authorities. Maria, much like himself, was under lockdown while her brother was a wanted criminal. Jack had proved a dud. There was only one person Luke could trust to get Sophie back alive, and he really, really hated the bastard.

He stared up at the grand portico of Thames House and dialled a number with fingers that felt like lead.

'Harrington,' he said. 'Let's make a deal.'

Chapter Sixteen

Harvey very kindly called up somebody (rail enquiries, CIA personal travel planner, who knows?) and found out that the next train from Hartford going anywhere near Maine wasn't leaving for about another seven hours. If I hadn't had hypothermia before, I'd get it waiting for that.

'Okay,' he said, 'and I'm only doing this because you set me up with my wife, but how about I drive you to Springfield and you get the next train from there?'

I threw my arms around him. 'When will that be?'

He made another call.

'Eight-thirty a.m. I can get you there by then.'

What an adorable, wonderful man. Had I been less tired and confused, I might have suspected an ulterior motive from him. But by that point, he could have driven me direct to Langley and shackled me in irons, and I wouldn't have minded so long as I got a nice warm blanket and people stopped aiming guns at me.

I dozed off in his warm, fast car, and he woke me less than an hour later. I still had ages to wait, but it was a much faster trip than waiting for the train.

'Have I told you lately that I love you?' I said as I got out of the car, pulling my bag into the cold morning air.

He grinned. 'No, but you can tell me when this is all over.'

I liked his use of 'when' as opposed to 'if'.

I bit my lip. 'Um, and Harvey? You couldn't lend me a few bucks, could you?'

Harvey covered his face and started laughing, but he handed me a few notes, and I pledged to adore him for all eternity.

I hugged him close, knowing this little interlude of

friendship was over. As soon as he drove away, he'd be Agent Harvard again, and I'd be a fugitive. 'You're a good friend, Harvey.'

'I know.'

'Give my love to Angel and Rachel.'

'I will.'

'And to Luke.'

He hesitated. 'Okay, but not in the same way.'

I smiled. 'And remember, you didn't see me.'

'Interesting train of thought. Take care, Sophie.'

'It's Alice. No, it's not. It's, uh ...'

He kissed my cheek. 'I'll call you if I hear anything.'

'Ditto.'

He got back in the car, and I walked into the station, and we both knew the other was lying. Harvey was a good friend. He wasn't an idiot.

I made it with time to spare, changed trains with no problem, and as lunchtime approached found myself on a train travelling through Vermont, which was beautiful.

My stomach rumbled, and I realised I'd eaten nothing since that pizza on Tuesday night. It was now Thursday afternoon. Alighting in Portland, Maine, I had a couple of hours before catching my bus, so I found a fast-food restaurant, dug out one of the paperbacks I'd bought on the trip, and tried to stay awake.

Traffic was bad, and it was dark when I alighted in Bangor. Too tired to think about getting to East Penobscot by bus or train or taxi or foot or even sodding wing, I called Information, got a taxi service and told the driver to take me to the nearest hotel. He did, and I checked in as Ms Sara Lee Gateau. You can tell where my mind was. I just had enough about me to switch my phone off before I crashed out and fell fast asleep.

I couldn't bear the thought of any more travelling. This

was the last place I'd be going. If anyone wants me, I'll be in Maine, and I will not be sodding leaving until they clear me of all charges, bung me in an oubliette, or shoot me.

Right now, it's only the last one that's looking likely.

Luke woke for the second time in the immaculate spare bedroom of Evelyn's flat. This time recollection didn't hit him like a train, but reversed over him several times.

Harrington had invited him in, but instead of going to his office and discussing what information Luke had to share, like a civilised person would, he took him to a windowless room and got a big guy with far too many muscles to beat seven kinds of hell out of him.

'Where is she?' Thump. 'What's her alias?' Kick. 'How is she moving around?' Bit of light dismemberment.

All right, it was possible he'd hallucinated the last one. He'd fought back, but it had been a while since he'd been in a knockdown, dirty fight, and he was pretty sure he hadn't damaged so much as the pride of the big man. There wasn't a part of him that didn't ache or throb or pound with pain.

The door opened and Evelyn came in, carrying a glass of water and a bottle of pills. 'Good morning, sunshine,' she said.

'What's good about it?' His voice was a groan.

'Well, you're alive. Although I've honestly no idea how. Or why. What did you do to Harrington?'

Luke raised an arm and pressed it over his eyes. It hurt to move. It hurt not to.

'Offered to turn Queen's Evidence.'

Evelyn said nothing. Luke moved his arm and peeked at her.

'Did you say Queen's Evidence?'

He nodded. That hurt, too.

Evelyn sat down a little heavily on the chair by the bed.

It was the first time he'd seen her do anything without perfect catlike grace. 'In return for what? As far as I know you haven't been accused of anything, although I'm going to level a charge of Acute Stupidity at you.'

'For bringing Sophie back safe. There's a killer after her.'

'Besides Harrington you mean? Did you tell him where she is?'

He shook his head. 'Don't strike bargains with violent thugs.'

'Well, that's one thing.' She reached into her pocket and took out his secret phone, the one he used for calling Sophie. 'And at least he didn't get his hands on this.'

'Thanks for looking after it.'

'You might have asked, instead of shoving the damn thing through the letterbox. And no, before you ask, she hasn't called.' Evelyn studied him. 'I think you should see a doctor.'

She'd been saying that since she had found him lying bleeding in her doorway last night. Maybe they'd just figured he was shagging his secretary and dumped him there as the most obvious place.

'Yeah, maybe.' He was so damn tired.

'Although what you'll tell them is anyone's guess.'

'Ran into a door.' He considered the many ways in which he ached. 'A revolving one. Does Sheila know?'

'She's said nothing to me. I'm in two minds whether to tell her. She could throw the book at him for this.'

'She's got no authority over him.'

'Well, the Home Secretary has, and if she tells –'

'The Home Secretary has bigger things to worry about than this,' Luke said. 'Leave it.'

Evelyn looked troubled, but she nodded, and stood up.

'Anything I can get you?'

He shook his head. 'You've done enough.'

She stood looking at him for a long moment.

'And don't tell me I look like hell. I can't possibly look worse than I feel.'

'Luke ...'

Her pretty forehead wrinkled. Her perfect teeth bit into her perfect lip.

'The other night, when I brought you back here and you asked me why?'

'Yes,' he said cautiously. 'I wouldn't tell you where I was staying and was in no state to be left alone. If I recall correctly which, believe it or not, I'm usually quite good at doing.'

'Yes. Um. Well, there was something else, too.'

He closed his eyes. If she revealed to him now that she was a spy for Harrington, or that she was really the killer who'd framed Sophie, he wasn't sure he had the energy to do any more than cry.

Then a pair of soft, perfect lips touched his, and Luke's eyes flew open.

Evelyn was kissing him, leaning over the bed with her hand resting ever so lightly on his shoulder. She tasted like oranges, like sweetness and uncorrupted, uncomplicated passion.

Just for a second, he let himself enjoy it. Then guilt slammed him in the chest and he pushed her away.

'No,' he said, and Evelyn looked down at him with huge sadness in her beautiful eyes.

Then she nodded, and straightened up, her face blank.

'Evelyn,' he said, feeling wretched.

'No, I'm sorry.' She began backing away. 'I shouldn't have done that. I just thought ... I wondered ... but it's nothing. Just an impulse. You're in love with Sophie and that's ... that's fine.'

She reached the door and bumped into it.

'Just call me if you need anything.'

321

The door shut behind her with indecent speed.

'Fantastic,' Luke said out loud. He levered himself upright against the pillows and picked up his pair of phones. Nothing from Sophie. Three missed calls on the other one. He scrolled through: Evelyn, Evelyn, Lucie. He frowned. Lucie? His contact at the Home Office. There was a message from her, too.

'Luke,' her voice sounded hushed and furtive, 'I'm not supposed to be calling you, but listen. It's just been released here. That woman you were asking about? Alexa Martin? She escaped. She's not in prison any more. I don't know how she did it but ... all hell's broken loose. No one can find her. It's a massive disaster. Look, you can't tell anyone this, all right, if it's leaked I'll be for the chop, but ... well, you sounded rather desperate before so ...'

He didn't hear the rest. The phone fell from his hand.

Alexa Martin had escaped.

Alexa Martin, who'd turned against the British government for her own financial ends.

Alexa Martin, who'd killed his old boss.

Alexa Martin, who'd been instrumental in crashing a plane that had killed nearly a hundred-and-fifty people.

Alexa Martin, who'd been brought down by Sophie.

She'd escaped.

Before he knew it he was across the room, yanking the door open. Evelyn looked up, startled, and her gaze darted down. Luke realised he was wearing boxers and nothing else.

'Clothes,' he muttered, turning around.

'You shouldn't be out of bed,' Evelyn gasped.

'Don't care. Have to leave.' The room dipped and swayed around him. 'I have to call Sophie.'

He lurched back to the bed, Evelyn twittering around behind him, and scooped up his phone on the second try.

'Luke, what are you doing?'

He dialled Sophie with trembling fingers. It didn't connect. He tried again. Still nothing.

'Luke, you're frightening me.'

'Well good, because I'm fucking terrified. That woman – Jesus, Evelyn, that woman … she's a psychopath and she's out there and she's after Sophie.'

'Who is?' Evelyn said, her eyes huge as she watched him career around the room in search of his clothes.

'Alexa Martin.' He closed his eyes, horror overwhelming him. 'If she finds Sophie, she'll kill her.'

My dreams were fragmented and disturbing, dreams of Luke turning on me, working for Harrington, then Harrington working for Luke. Luke with a gorgeous, feline secretary, snogging madly on an expensive desk, ripping off each other's clothes and shagging enthusiastically as I watched, appalled, from the doorway.

Then a hand touched my shoulder and it was Jack, bleeding and burnt, and he fell to the ground and I kissed him, and then he was no longer hurt but naked, and so was I, and he made love to me on the bed in Irene Shepherd's house, and he was sensual and skilled and I found myself crying, crying hard in the dream, and Jack faded away.

I was alone, in the dark and the cold. It was really cold and I was hungry, alone, lost, in the woods, wolves howling, guns banging, getting closer. Then a shot echoed too close to me and I saw Harvey advancing with a smoking gun, shaking his head pityingly and sneering at me, 'You didn't really think I'd let you go, did you? I know right where you are. You've led me to Jack,' and there was Jack lying dead at my feet.

'You killed him,' Maria said, looking ghostly, 'you killed my brother with your lying and incompetence. You were never a spy, just a pathetic excuse for law-enforcement, thinking you were so tough, but you never did anything without help. My help, his help,' she pointed to Luke, who was leaning against a tree, his arm around Angel's shoulders, looking smug. 'All our help. Bailing you out, rescuing you, working for you, taking your stupid orders while you got us shot and crashed your car and cost everyone time and money and blood. Look at all the blood you've spilt,' she said, and like a ghoulish parade they all turned pale and started bleeding, Luke from his head where he'd been hurt in September, Maria's stomach where she was shot on my first mission, Harvey's head – no, Xander's head, where a stray bullet had grazed him. Docherty, bleeding from the two shots I'd fired at him. A hundred-and-forty-three dead people I hadn't been able to save because I didn't stop Alexa Martin before she sabotaged that plane.

I tried to back away, but my feet were stuck, and I realised someone was holding onto them, someone was holding me down, and pinning my arms behind my back, and then a gun was being brandished in my face and I realised it was mine, and the person aiming it was Sarah Wilde in her big hat and sunglasses and all I wanted to know was who she was and I was screaming, 'Who are you, who are you?'

And then there was a bang, and I woke up.

I was drenched in sweat and shaking. I felt sick. Tangled up in sheets, I thudded to the floor and made it to the bathroom but not the toilet before I was horribly sick all over the floor. Heaving and sobbing, I huddled in a ball, half-wrapped in a bed-sheet, wishing that shot had been real.

The hotel offered room service and I called for water and fruit, not feeling able to consume much more. I was so damn hungry though, and when my stomach didn't immediately repel the fruit I called for eggs and waffles and grilled tomatoes, all the ingredients of an English breakfast I could think of, wishing I wasn't vegetarian so I could have some sausages or bacon.

In fact, sod it.

'I'll have sausages and bacon as well,' I said. 'Lots of bacon.' Then, remembering the way my mum used to cook bacon for me when I was little, 'And don't overcook it: I hate crispy bacon.'

I ate all of it, all those bits of dead pig, and it felt good.

I cleaned up the bathroom, then dragged my revolting carcass into the shower and steamed myself clean, scalding my skin to get rid of the sweat and dirt, and scrubbed at my teeth and tongue until the taste of vomit was well gone.

I got dressed, packed my bag and went down to the lobby. As I walked past the Reception area, a phone trilled and one of the uniformed girls called out, 'Mrs Wachowski? Delta Airlines called back,' and an elderly lady got up from a chair and went over to the desk, leaving her bag behind.

Her bag, which fitted so easily into mine.

I checked out the contents as I sat in the back of a taxi heading to East Penobscot and found a wallet stuffed with cash, a credit card and, God bless her, a cash card with the PIN number Sellotaped to it. There was also a packet of Cheroot cigars and lighter.

When I got out of the cab I lit up and inhaled. The cigar tasted worse than a cigarette, but it felt so damn cool that I didn't care.

Check me out. Eating pigs, robbing old ladies, smoking cigars. I'm Sophie, and I'm *bad*.

I was still hungry, so I went back to my little diner where Louisa-May looked delighted to see me and got me a huge pizza and fries and a beer, and when I asked her if my friend Dr David-John was around, she said that he always helped his sister collecting for the Goodwill on Fridays but they should be home about twelve.

I thanked her, paid with the money I'd taken from the old lady, and walked out into the cold, clear sunshine. It was quiet in town, there weren't many people about. Which was odd for a Friday.

I left the old lady's bag in a bus shelter, telling the people there that I'd found it dumped by an ATM, and walked away.

And then I got to the bridge over the river, and looked down at the clear water, and wanted to throw myself in. What the hell was I doing? Eating an animal I hadn't touched for years? Smoking? Stealing from an old woman so I could buy beer and pizza? What the hell was wrong with me? What had I become?

The answer to that was too scary to contemplate. I chucked all the cigars in the river, and would have thrown the money in too, but I knew I'd need it. Instead I sent up a rather rusty prayer for forgiveness, reminded myself that I had saved the lives of dozens of pigs and cows and chickens, and would carry on saving them, and looked long and hard at the little scar on my arm that had ended up giving me septicaemia. No more smoking. No more meat. No more robbing anyone. Hadn't I decided I wasn't travelling any more? I'd stay in Maine until the money ran out.

Matter of fact, I'd stay in East Penobscot. I had a friend in Louisa-May, and a lead in Dr David-John, and the place was pretty and wholesome and hopefully not too expensive. Maybe I'd settle down here. Get a job. Rent a place. Find a new identity.

Die in a foreign country, alone and hunted.

Oh, for Christ's sake, I had to snap out of this. I felt black and blue all over. I hauled out my phone and when I switched it on, found several missed calls on it. Jack. Jack. Luke. Harvey. Jack. Luke.

Boy, you know, having three gorgeous men call me up so often is actually really heartening. Even if only one of them is actually talking to me.

There was only one message, and it was from Luke, and the signal was so bad I could barely make anything out.

'... phie, this is ... ant. Al ... ve only just found out ... can't fucking believe ... must be this Sar ... I'll ... need to – I don't know ... the cops, call ... safe. It's not ... God's sake, call me. I'll –' Then a series of beeps.

Gobbledegook. All I'd heard was anger in his voice. I wasn't in a hurry to find out why.

I called Harvey back first, since he was least likely to yell at me. 'How's it going?'

'You sound brighter.'

I shrugged, looking up at the clear blue sky. You know, today wasn't so cold. It might even have felt slightly spring-like, were it not for the scent of a bonfire hanging in the air.

'I'm feeling a bit better.'

'I tried calling you last night.'

'Yeah. I turned the phone off so I could get some sleep. I was so tired.'

'Did you get where you wanted to go?'

'Eventually.'

'Where are you?'

'Now, that would be telling.'

Harvey laughed. 'Angel says Luke's been trying to figure it out ever since you left.'

'Yeah. He keeps asking me.'

'Why won't you tell him? Don't you trust him?'

Good question.

'Of course I do,' I said, because not trusting Luke would

be a dreadful thing and I didn't want to dwell on it. 'I just don't want anyone to follow him.'

'He said you came back a couple weeks ago.'

Surely it had been months.

Felt like longer.

'Yeah. That was stupid of me.'

'Just a bit,' Harvey agreed. 'I told them when I got to the hotel, you were gone. Climbed out of the window. Probably left the state. No reason why they shouldn't believe me. It's not like they were there to measure the height of the window.'

'Thanks, Harvey.' Although it does make me look guilty. Why is it that I keep getting accused of crimes I didn't commit, and getting away with the ones I am committing? How is that fair? Especially since the crimes I am guilty of are only being caused by the ones I didn't do.

Or something.

'You owe me. Lying to the federal government is not something I want on my record.'

'Hey, can't we chalk this one up with introducing you to your wife?'

'I think that one's full up.'

'How about convincing her not to call the wedding off?'

'Hmm.'

'Telling her you loved her?'

'Hmmm.'

'Saving your worthless arse?'

'Hmmmm.'

'Harvey, did you turn into a hummingbird?'

He laughed. 'Sometimes feels like it.'

'I hear ya. Anyway. I should go. I have someone to see. Crimes to clear. Very busy girl.'

'Take care.'

'You, too.'

I checked my watch. Nearly midday. Dr David-John and his sister should be back by now. Feeling somewhat cleansed, I took in a deep breath of smoky air and headed for Belinda Marple's home.

Why was it so smoky? Mason Street was thick with it. It was as if –

Oh no! Oh God! Oh *hell!*

I knew before I got there that the police barrier across the road was protecting the burned-out shell of number 166. I knew it had burned down while I'd been robbing old ladies and smoking and sending myself to hell. And I knew Belinda Marple and Leonard David-John had been trapped inside. And had burned to death.

I knew, but it was still a shock to have it confirmed by the policeman guarding the barrier.

'Fire started slow,' he said, 'probably in the kitchen. Half of the house was burning by the time anyone noticed. No fire alarm. Wood-framed house. No one could get in. It was too dangerous. Those poor folks must have just suffocated.'

'Burned to death,' I said. 'Like a witch trial.'

'Ayuh,' he said, which seemed to be Mainer for 'yes'.

'Horrible way to die,' I said, shuddering.

'Ayuh.'

I backed away, and went back to the river, walked down to the bank over the rushing water, and sat and looked at it for a while. So it was not only Sir Theodore and Irene Shepherd who'd been killed by Sarah Wilde, but the security guard at Sir Theodore's office block, Consuela Sanchez, Dr David-John and Belinda Marple.

If indeed it had been her who killed them. For all I knew it could have been Tommy Canolti. Or Docherty. Or Jack. Or even sodding Harvey. I just didn't know.

My hands shaking, I got out my phone and called Luke.

I needed reassurance. I needed familiarity. I needed to hear the voice of someone who didn't want me dead.

Voicemail. God bloody dammit.

I only had one lead left. One more person who could help me figure this out. And if he wouldn't talk to me, then I had nothing.

Which was a bugger, because last I'd seen him he'd been flat on his back with a bleeding face and my gun aimed at his head.

Bugger.

JFK airport. Luke stumbled down the jet-bridge, ignoring the concerned queries of the cabin crew, and leaned against the wall, trying to turn his phone on.

Nothing. The battery was dead.

In his haste to get on a flight, any flight, to America, he'd brought no luggage. No phone charger.

He stumbled on through the airport to make his connection, desperation pounding inside him.

I got back to my hotel, paranoid about being watched. It wasn't going to be good news when Louisa-May told everyone I'd been asking after the good doctor. And once Mrs W's bag was found, and traced to the hotel, things could get really sticky. Probably it might be wise to keep out of East Penobscot for now.

I sat in my room for a while, thinking. So someone had killed Consuela on Wednesday night and Dr David-John this morning. Was it coincidence that I'd been to see them both? Or simply that whoever was killing them was interested in them for the same reason I was: that they knew something?

I couldn't believe I hadn't talked to Dr David-John. He probably knew a lot about Sarah Wilde. He must have known her real name. Where she was from. A medical record that could help me trace her. Doctor-patient confidentiality wasn't important: the SIG would have seen to that.

But now I was at a loss. And full of suspects: Tommy Canolti, Sarah Wilde, even Jack.

I needed to talk to him, and I needed to make sure I knew what I was talking about.

And I needed something else, too.

I changed my clothes, gathered my wits (what few I had left) and went down to Reception. 'Is there a mall around here that sells electrical goods?'

There was, and I was directed to the correct bus stop. Half-an-hour later I found myself in a big bland mall and wandered around until I found what I was looking for. It wasn't the tiny, wireless sort of device I was used to, but it would get the job done.

And no, it wasn't anything to with sex. I was buying a miniature digital audio recorder. Don't be filthy.

This sort of specialist device required specialist clothing, so I went to Abercrombie & Fitch and got myself a pair of combats with lots of pockets. The digital recorder fitted neatly into the top one. Perfect.

I experimented with it on the way back to the hotel, turning up the volume and seeing what I could pick up. It wasn't perfect, so recording anything more than a few feet away might be interesting, but I could just about make things out. I'd just have to stay close to Jack.

By the time I got back to the hotel it was getting dark. I rehearsed my speech to Jack as I walked along the corridor to my room. Sorry I lashed out at him, I was drunk and hurt and acting stupid. I was highly stressed. We should work together – I couldn't get it done by myself. Yeah. Be helpless and flirty.

God, I'm so crap at being helpless. And flirty works so much better with blonde hair.

I was just looking for my key when I heard it. A footfall. There was someone inside my room.

My heartbeat speeded up. I fumbled in my bag for the gun and my hand alighted on the digital recorder.

I stopped.

There was always the possibility, in this sort of situation, that I might end up shooting someone. And they might end up dying. And I might end up getting blamed. And so far, with the two other people I've done for, there was someone else there to confirm it was self-defence and that the deceased was guilty and confessed and, most importantly, that I shot them because they were trying to kill me. But right here and right now, there was no one. If I shot whoever was in that room, it'd be another mark on my rap sheet. And I really didn't need that.

I pressed the Record switch, dropped it into my pocket and flicked the safety catch off my gun. Then I slid the card into the door lock and pushed the door open with my foot, gun raised like in the movies. Possibly not the wisest move because I had absolutely no defence if I was picked up for carrying concealed, but then I didn't plan on getting picked up. By anyone.

If it was a cop in there I was buggered.

But it wasn't a cop – at least, if it was, the American police system was in trouble. It was a guy in sweatpants and a hoodie. He had a greasy, stubbly face, small dark eyes and dirty black hair. There was a gun tucked in his pocket. He looked at my SIG with interest.

'Nice piece.'

'Thanks. Who the hell are you?'

'Tommy Canolti. I believe we spoke on the phone.' Oh yeah, I recognised his voice now. One of those hard, Italian gangster sort of voices. Maybe he wasn't with the Mob, but he wished he was.

I narrowed my eyes at him. 'You're not Irene Shepherd's gardener.'

'Well, no, maybe not.' His hand strayed down to his gun, and I shook my head at him. 'Hands on your head.'

He did as he was told, leering, 'I like strong women.'

'What do you want?'

'You wanted to know about Samantha Wilde?'

'Sarah. Sarah Wilde.'

'Yeah. Whatever. I know about her.'

Yeah, sure, buddy. You know so much you can't even remember her name. 'What do you know about her?'

'A lot of things.' He looked at me slyly. 'For the right price.'

I stared incredulously. 'I have a gun aimed at your head and you're asking for a bribe? Listen, mate, without wanting to sound like Victoria Beckham, do you even know who I am?'

'I know you're wanted for the murders of five people.'

'Five?' Oh God, oh God.

'Forgot how many you've killed?'

'Just how many I'm accused of. I know there's probably not much room in that greasy head of yours for thought, but try this one and see if it'll fit. Me, gun. Me, dangerous. You, scumbag who I don't care about. How about instead of paying you for information, I just don't shoot you?'

'I don't think so well with a gun aimed at me.'

'Do you think any better when you're bleeding?'

He looked as if he was thinking about this.

'Okay,' he said eventually, and lowered one hand.

'Hey!'

'I got a phone number. It's in my pocket,' he explained patiently.

'You've also got a gun. That's in your pocket.'

'I could just be pleased to see you.'

I was not amused.

'You wanna get the piece of paper?' Canolti offered, and I'm afraid I actually shuddered. 'Okay. Look. Just one hand. Nice and slow.'

I kept my gun trained on that hand, but what I then failed to notice was his other hand, dropping down slowly on the other side and grabbing his gun.

And firing at me.

Chapter Seventeen

Hartford. A TV in the airport bar was showing local news. Police had named Sophie Green as the principal suspect in the double murder at Judge Shepherd's house. A photo of Sophie on the screen, a terrible file photo she'd always hated.

'Police warn that the suspect is armed and extremely dangerous. Do not approach. Please call our special hotline with any information.'

They'd named her. They'd actually finally gone public. She was stuck now, stranded. Her face was everywhere. Anyone could turn her in at any moment.

Luke stared up at the number and found himself considering calling the hotline, so they might put out the news about Alexa Martin, so Sophie might see it. Assuming she was still local. Which she probably wasn't. And he'd have contravened the Official Secrets Act. So he'd be in even more trouble. If that was possible.

He ran on, towards the taxi rank.

I ducked just in time. Something hot burned my arm, there was a crash and I realised the bullet had smashed into the wall behind me. Canolti took advantage of my shock to shove past me, yank open the door and race out.

I hauled myself to my feet and scrambled after him. I could hear shrieks coming from the left, so I ran that way, down the stairs, just catching a glimpse of him vanishing around the turn of the stairs. I fired off a shot and more people screamed and got in my way, milling around my feet like stupid chickens.

'Get out of my way!' I yelled, and then added as an afterthought, 'Police!'

I tripped and fell flat on my face at the bottom of the stairs, and accidentally shot out a chunk of wood from the Reception desk. More people screamed. It was getting tiresome now.

There was another clanging shot, and I curled myself into a ball. A few inches away, the carpet smoked as a slug buried itself in the tiles underneath.

I picked myself up again and raced after Canolti. I still wasn't sure who he was or what the hell he had to do with anything, but I knew innocent people didn't fire guns and run away.

Usually.

Outside, there were cars everywhere and people milling about in the dusky darkness, and I just had time to see Canolti grab a taxi driver and shove him to the ground, before someone cannoned into me.

'Sophie?'

I struggled to get past him, then my name pierced my consciousness. I looked up. 'Jack?'

'Are you okay?' He touched my arm, and it stung. I was surprised to see blood there.

'I'm – get out of the way.' Canolti was tearing out of the car park in the taxi.

'Why is Tommy Canolti firing at you?'

'I don't know. Do you have a car?' I asked urgently.

Jack gestured to a big, ugly, American car parked at the kerb and I bounced into the passenger seat.

No. Bugger. This was America. It was the driving seat.

'Gimme the keys,' I said, holding my hand out. 'Give me the goddamned keys!'

Jack gave me the keys, and just had time to throw himself into the back seat as I squealed away from the kerb.

'What the hell is going on?' he demanded as I made a

hard left and very nearly drove into a Jeep coming out of a parking space. 'Sophie?'

'Not sure yet.'

'Why are you chasing Canolti?'

'He shot at me.'

'He got you. Your arm is bleeding.'

I glanced down at it. Yeuch, that was a mess.

'Yeah,' I said absently, coming to the exit of the car park, onto a busy, four-lane road. Traffic streamed past, oblivious to me. I needed to turn left, straight across the traffic. It was never going to happen.

So I rammed my fist onto the steering wheel, surprising myself with a very, very loud blast of the horn, and shoved my foot to the floor.

The car shot forwards, distorted sights and sounds flew by me, something smashed into the back of the car and spun me in the wrong direction. Jack was yelling in the background and I remembered my brother telling me that if I ever spun a car, to turn the wheel in the opposite direction to make a bit of friction and stop the wheels skidding.

Other cars were screaming to a halt and crashing into each other, there were horns going off all over, and I thought, hell, I'll have lost him now. The car bounced off a cab, I rammed it into reverse and swore repeatedly at the stupid American automatic gearbox before I got the damn thing to go forwards again, and we ricocheted into the far lane.

Better.

'What the hell are you doing?' Jack howled. 'You nearly got us both killed.'

'Aren't you wearing your seatbelt?' I craned to see how far ahead Canolti's taxi was. Too far. Crap. The traffic moved so goddamned slowly. The longer we hung around here, the more likely it'd be that the police would turn up, and that was the last thing I needed.

Oh well. In for a penny and all that.

I swung the wheel to the right and we bounced up onto the sidewalk. Just like *Grand Theft Auto*. I was king of the road here. Or queen. Or whatever.

'Jesus, Sophie,' Jack moaned from the back seat.

'Can you think of a better way to catch him? And anyway,' I twisted round to look at him, 'how do you know Canolti?'

Jack had his hands over his face, but when he saw me looking at him he yelped, 'Pedestrian!'

I swung my eyes back to the road – or the sidewalk, as the case was. A startled woman was throwing herself into the hedge. Whoops. Nearly got her there.

'Jesus fucking Christ.' Jack was actually genuflecting.

'I'm not that bad a driver,' I reassured him.

'You're on the goddamned *sidewalk*.'

'I only failed my test twice.'

'Do I dare ask what for?'

'Um, well the first time I accidentally got onto the motorway –'

'*How?*'

'And then the second time I ran a red ...'

'Oh God.'

'He won't help you,' I said grimly, spying the taxi on the inside lane. And then I wondered, now that I had him, what did I do with him?

He was turning. Bugger. The bastard was turning.

He swung out left across the central reservation and bounced down a smaller road, veering into the left lane to overtake an MPV.

'Are you holding onto something?' I asked Jack.

'My sanity.'

'Try the seat,' I advised, and hammered the horn again before barging through two lanes of traffic, hitting three other cars on the way. The car shunted and groaned – but then that might have been me – and we made it through with only the loss of the back bumper. I swore at the gearbox again and took off after Canolti, switching lanes like he did. You know, overtaking is a hell of a lot easier on the wrong side of the road. You can see what's coming really easily. And they even sometimes get out of your way.

'Are you armed?' I asked Jack, who nodded.

'You?'

'Six left. There's a spare in my bag,' I chucked it back at him, 'if you could get it out for me.'

He did, and in between swerving pointlessly large penis-extensions masquerading as vehicles, I tucked the magazine into one of my pockets. I guess there's a reason they call them combats, huh?

'How did you find me?' I asked.

'I didn't. I found Canolti.'

'I – what?'

'Remember I said I went to see Irene Shepherd about a guy she'd posted bail on?'

There was a clunk in my head. The penny dropping.

'Canolti is your skip?'

'Yep. Shame I don't have the pickup papers on me. He's worth five grand to me.'

'Nice.'

'Why are you chasing him?'

'I don't like people who shoot at me.'

'Is your arm all right?'

I glanced back down. There was blood dripping onto the seat. 'It's just a scratch.'

'Why was he shooting at you?'

'I, er – shit, where'd he go?' If we were in *Grand Theft Auto* there'd be a giant pink arrow to tell me. But life does not come with big pink arrows. And there sure as hell aren't any Reload Game options.

'Right, down there,' Jack pointed, and between some buildings I saw the taxi careering away. I made another violent turn, managing to cross both lanes of both roads, before righting myself and speeding after him.

'Don't suppose you'd be able to shoot out his tyres?' I asked.

'I don't suppose so either. You were saying?'

'He turned up in my hotel room. Said he knew something about Sarah Wilde.'

'He just turned up?'

'Well, probably it had something to do with me standing him up on Thursday.'

'Come again?'

I explained briefly about going to see Consuela Sanchez, Canolti's phone call, and Sanchez's death. I omitted the part about Harvey. I'm not a complete idiot.

'You think he killed her?'

'I don't know. He could have.'

'She did post bail on him –'

I glanced at him in the rear-view mirror. 'I meant Sanchez. You think he killed Shepherd, too?'

Jack shrugged. 'I don't know. He could have.'

My head was swirling and my arm was starting to hurt quite a lot. Despite what they say about women and multi-tasking, I've never been very good at concentrating on two things at once. Well, I mean, I'm excellent at eating while watching TV or reading a book, and I can sing and drive at the same time, which I count as a major achievement, but as for thinking hard about a tangly murder case in which I play a large part, chasing after someone who appears to be (much as I hate to say it) a much better driver than me, and trying to figure out if I trust the armed man sitting behind me, well, that was all a bit beyond my exhausted and never very clever brain.

Canolti was heading out of town, taking as many turns as

he could. I glanced at the petrol gauge on Jack's hire car and was relieved to see it was mostly full.

'He's heading out towards East Penobscot,' Jack said.

'Oh, did you hear about Dr David-John?'

'Yep. Burned extra crispy.'

I winced at his insensitivity. 'And his sister, too. She was really nice.'

'You talked to him?'

'No, just her. I never got around to him. Don't suppose I will now.'

Jack was silent a bit. Then he said, 'Sophie, do you think it's a coincidence that Canolti was in Hartford when you were in Hartford, and in Bangor when you're in Bangor?'

'I don't believe in coincidences,' I said, screaming around a corner and saying goodbye to the exhaust pipe.

'No. You think he followed you?'

'Maybe he followed you. How did you even know he was here?'

'I saw him,' Jack said. 'In a diner in town. That was a total coincidence. I followed him to your hotel. Wondered what the hell he was doing here.'

'How did he find me?' I said.

'I don't – Sophie, Mack truck, *Mack truck* –'

I swerved back onto the right side of the road away from the unfeasibly large lorry. I don't know, it's just unnatural to me. People should drive on the left. It makes sense that way.

But when the truck had rumbled off and my vision of the road was clear, it was – well, clear. There was nothing there.

'He's switched his lights off.'

'No, he's gone off-road.'

'In that old banger?' Suddenly, I longed for Ted, my darling, old, battered Defender. Off-road, he could not be beaten. I hoped Luke was taking good care of him. Well, better than I did with his car, anyway.

I sighed and swung the wheel off to the right. We were in open country now, the wide Penobscot river stretching away a few metres from where we rattled along over a rutted field. There were cows standing and lying around and I could see Canolti's taxi wobbling around between them, obviously hoping to get them in my way. It was working: the cows were getting up and jogging around, looking menacing.

'There wouldn't be any angry bulls around, would there?' Jack asked with a hint of apprehension.

'No. Bull'll be in a separate field, away from the herd.'

'Farm girl.'

Far from it. Ugh, think of all the mud. I live in arable country anyway. But, doesn't everyone know you keep bulls away from the –

'When you say a separate field,' Jack said, and pointed over my shoulder to a fence. A fence that Canolti was now approaching at high speed.

'Never gonna happen,' I said, 'you've got to have a stronger car than –'

There was a huge, tearing crash. Goddamn. He made it.

'Makes it easier for us.' I shrugged, and followed.

And then I slammed my foot on the brake.

'What?' Jack said.

'Found the bull.'

'Well, they can't be that dangerous, can they?'

'You want to get out there and test the theory?'

Jack was silent. I was silent. We stared at the scene playing out in the headlights of the hire car. The bull ambled towards Canolti. Canolti didn't stop. The bull ran away. Canolti revved faster. Then he suddenly swerved, away from a tree. He spun on the mud, and then ended up facing us.

'Uh-oh,' Jack said.

'What?'

'You know bulls don't like red?'

'Actually, that's a myth. It's the flapping of the cape that angers them.'

'Whilst cars running towards them make them so calm, right?'

Canolti was revving hard, facing off, like a knight on a tilting field. Revving too hard – he was splattering mud all over. He'd get stuck. I'd seen it happen with my parents' car in the mud at the end of their drive. This is why my car is so useful. I'm always pulling them out of the –

'He doesn't like that,' Jack said, and I could see the bull pawing the ground like in a bull ring.

'He really doesn't like that,' I said, watching white clouds of air snort from his flared nostrils.

Canolti released the brake. The bull charged.

'I can't look,' I said, but my eyes refused to close, and I watched as the bull charged the car, which was horribly close to the sloping bank of the river. Canolti swerved away from the bull. Towards the water.

The bull hit the car, head down, with huge force, and the car was rammed sideways, much like some of the cars I'd hit earlier in the chase. Only none of them were on mud, nor so close to a river. The taxi hit a rock and started tumbling, twirling over, and the bull, still running, lost his footing.

'Oh no,' I gasped, and Jack flicked his eyes at me. 'The bull. He's going to go in –'

I put my hand on the door, and Jack yanked my arm back. 'Are you nuts? You can't catch a bloody bull. It'd kill you. Even if Canolti doesn't.'

Canolti's car slapped into another rock and flipped up in the air. It flew a few feet, rolling gracefully through the darkness, lights twirling prettily, and then it hit the water with a splash.

The bull followed.

'No,' I said, and got out of the car before Jack could stop me. I raced over the mud to the riverbank, Jack yelling behind me, and skidded to a halt on the rocks. I could see a dark shape that was probably the bull, bobbing away downstream. Maybe it was still alive. Probably it wouldn't be for long.

Of the car there was already no sign. The lights had gone out, there was no more disturbance on the foamy surface of the river than there had been before.

Jack ran up behind me. 'I think he's gone.'

'I think he is, too.'

'We need to get out of here.'

I looked up at him. 'Yeah. We do.'

The first electrical store the taxi driver took him to didn't sell phone chargers. The second one did, but didn't have the one he needed. The third was in darkness.

'It's pretty late, buddy,' said the driver.

'I don't care. I have to get this phone charged.'

'Can't you use a payphone?'

'Could if I knew the number, which I don't because she keeps changing it, and it's stuck on this stupid bloody goddamned phone.' A sensible government officer would have memorised such an important number, but what with the bullet wound in his shoulder, what felt like half-a-dozen broken bones, and the fact that his girlfriend was probably about to die, he wasn't feeling very sensible right now.

'Maybe you should back it up. My wife has this thing she uses to sync hers with the computer –'

Luke actually snarled at him.

'Or we could try Wal-Mart,' said the driver, and pulled away a little too fast.

We crossed the river and drove the few miles to the little B&B Jack had been staying in before. Where I'd got drunk and he'd got naked and I'd stopped trusting him.

Did I trust him now?

I truly didn't know.

He unlocked the door and I followed him in, blinking in the sudden light as he flicked on a lamp by the bed. He chucked the car keys on the Shaker table, kicked off his shoes and ran his hands through his hair.

'You okay?'

I shrugged. 'Yeah, I'm ... I'm all right.'

'Let me see that arm.'

He walked over, lifted my arm, and I winced. It was actually really starting to hurt now.

'Can you take this off,' he said, touching the sleeve of my hoodie, 'and I'll go and get some bandages and stuff.'

'Where from?'

'Landlady. Be right back,' he said, and left the room.

I peeled off my slightly wrecked top. No; not slightly wrecked, totally. The sleeve was ripped where the bullet had sliced through, and there was blood all over. I took it into the little bathroom and started trying to rinse it in water, but I wasn't getting very far. I squeezed it out and hung it over the shower rail. Probably beyond help, but right now the only warm clothing I had.

I looked at the gash on my arm. It wasn't very neat: the skin was torn and my whole arm ached, like when I had a measles jab and the stuff went into a muscle and sort of paralysed it and I couldn't use my arm for a week.

I dabbed at the blood with some toilet roll and went back into the bedroom. It was bright and cosy in here, with pine furniture and a bright quilt and watercolours of Maine scenes on the walls. A far cry from my dull hotel room.

I took out the tape recorder from my pocket and rewound it a bit. 'We need to get out of here,' Jack's voice said, and mine added, 'Yeah. We do.'

Well, at least it had worked in a technical sense. Canolti

hadn't told me anything useful. In fact, he'd been the opposite of useful: shooting me and then buggering off and drowning before I could figure out what the hell he had to do with any of this.

Wearily, I got my phone out and tried to call Luke again. No signal. Fabulous.

Jack came in just as I was checking my gun and clicking the safety back on.

'Still gonna shoot me?'

'Maybe later,' I said, as he took my good arm and pulled me to my feet, led me into the bathroom and sat me down on the edge of the bath.

'Think that's ruined,' he said, nodding at my bloody, wet hoodie.

'You think?'

He wetted a towel and started dabbing at the blood that was starting to dry on my arm. He was silent – everything was silent. I heard my own breathing and asked, 'What did she say?'

He didn't look up. 'Who?'

'Your landlady. Didn't she ask why you wanted the bandages and disinfectant and stuff?'

'I told her I tripped and cut my arm while I was out hiking,' he said, with a slight smile.

'She didn't want to see?'

'Thankfully, no.'

He finished cleaning the blood away, chucked the towel on the floor, and dabbed disinfectant on the wound. I flinched at the sting, but made myself watch. The layers of white skin, pink muscle, red blood. The world's most obscene layer cake.

'She told me to get a tetanus shot,' Jack said.

'Had one last year,' I replied. He nodded and started opening packets of sticking plasters.

'Uh, I think it's a little bit worse than that,' I said, but Jack gave me a look and started taping the plasters over the cut to hold it shut.

'Clever,' I conceded.

'You must be an old hand at this sort of thing,' Jack said, and touched the criss-crossed lines on my chest, visible above the scoop neck of my scruffy A&F tank top.

'I didn't actually fix them up. There was a doctor, and drugs.'

'Always helpful.'

'The doctor, or the drugs?'

'Depends on the situation.'

He was quiet a while longer, taping some gauze over the cut and starting to wind a bandage around it. He kept his eyes on his work, not looking up at me.

I reached out with my free hand and touched the big purplish bruise that spread around his right eye and across his nose.

'Did I do that?'

He nodded.

'Does it hurt?'

He nodded.

'I'm sorry.'

'You are freakishly strong for a girl.'

I gave him a little smile. Luke said the same quite often. 'So I'm told.'

Jack finished tying the bandage and stood up to clear away the debris he'd left. I went back into the bedroom, rubbed my arms because I was cold, and then winced, because my right arm bloody hurt.

'Don't suppose you got any painkillers?' I asked.

'She was fresh out.'

I searched his MP3 player, hit play, and the wonderfully familiar, gloriously comforting opening chords of *Fall At Your Feet* came on.

Jack emerged from the bathroom, drying his hands.

'You've got Crowded House!' I exclaimed. He shrugged. 'I've got lots of stuff, so what?'

'They're the greatest band in the history of the world!'

He raised an eyebrow.

'I maybe have lost some blood,' I conceded.

He nodded. 'You should take it easy. You want a drink?'

'Nooo.'

A small smile. 'I meant like water or Coke?'

'Oh. Water. Please.'

I sat down on the bed and listened to Neil Finn and the boys play my favourite song in the whole world. Luke's a fan, too. He saw them live before they broke up, and still has the tour t-shirt.

Jack brought me a glass of water and I sipped at it politely while I tried to figure out what I should be doing. Probably, going back to my hotel after the spectacle I'd made would not be a good idea. But all my stuff was there. I mean, I had the essentials: gun, passport (much good it'd do me, thank you very much, Harvey), money, bullets – but some clean clothes would be nice.

Jack stood leaning against the door. Smart guy: he knew I wasn't going anywhere.

'Sophie,' he said, and I looked up. God, that eye did look painful. I get strong when I'm drunk. It's like spinach for Popeye. Only I tend to fall over more often. 'When I first started out bounty hunting they sent me after this guy who ran a gay club. I forget what offence it was – something to do with drugs. I had to go undercover to get to him. He took a shine to me. He thought the handcuffs were for play.'

I blinked at him. What the hell was he going on about?

'Amie was a girl I met in Paris. She was a model and a student and she was the most beautiful woman I've ever, ever seen. And she broke my heart.'

Hold on a sec.

'Once I shot a guy but he survived. I was fucking terrified I'd killed him.'

'You never killed anyone?'

'No. Not one. Unless you count Canolti.'

'I don't.'

'Me neither.'

Shirt, sweater, jeans ...

'Do you think I'm guilty?'

He blew out a sigh, and shook back his hair from his face.

'After that car ride, I'm starting to think there's nothing you're not capable of.'

I checked I had my gun close.

'But I don't think you killed Chesshyre.'

I closed my eyes.

'Or Sanchez. Or David-John and his sister. Or that security man. You're one of the good guys.'

'Damn right I am.' I opened my eyes. 'And you? Are you one of the good guys?'

Jack walked the few steps to the bed and knelt down in front of me. 'Right now I'm as good as you are,' he said.

I wasn't holding out much hope, then.

'I –' I began, and then I jumped a mile when something banged on the door. Jack's eyes met mine, he pressed his finger to his lips, and from under the drape of his shirt took a pistol with a silencer attached. He held it behind his back as he opened the door.

I sucked in a sharp breath, too shocked to scream.

Canolti stood there, white and dripping, stark, dark blood on his face. He raised a hand with a big knife –

– and then there was a muffled phut, and Canolti fell backwards into the darkness as Jack stood with his gun still raised.

'Be right back,' Jack said, and walked out of the room, shutting the door.

I sat there, frozen, and grabbed my gun for comfort. I stopped the music and listened, terrified, for any more noise. Goddammit. I know Canolti was an evil bastard who'd tried to kill us, but we really could have used some answers from him.

But when, several long minutes later, the door opened again, I had my gun aimed right at it. I guess I'd have shot Canolti, too.

'Don't shoot me,' Jack said, 'I'm in a bad enough state as it is.'

He shut the door and locked it, drew the curtains over the windows, picked up the Jack Daniels bottle and drank straight from it. Beneath his tan his skin was bloodless. He gripped the bottle so hard his knuckles were white. I thought he'd break it. He shook a little with each breath, his teeth rattling against the glass as he gulped neat bourbon.

He looked at me.

'You ever watch *Butch Cassidy* –'

'*& the Sundance Kid*,' I finished. I knew what was coming. 'When Butch shoots that Bolivian guy on the mountainside?'

The bottle rattled against the table as he set it down, his hand blurring a little.

'They really do fall in slow motion,' he said.

'What did you –'

'In the river,' Jack said.

'Again.'

'Dead this time.'

'Sure?'

'Bullet in the head.'

'Ah.'

He was still standing. His eyes were rooted on a patch of wall somewhere to my right. Out of nowhere, I heard Luke's voice in my head. *I just don't think you can do it alone.*

'Jack –'

He turned to me and grabbed me. 'Jesus fucking Christ, Sophie ...'

I stroked his hair. 'It's okay. He's a certified bad guy. Even the courts agreed on that.'

Jack had his eyes squeezed shut. I was frightened for him.

'It's okay,' I said again, uselessly, and kissed his forehead for reassurance. But Jack touched my face, eyes opening, kissed my mouth and held me tight with hands that trembled.

And I kissed him back.

Jack's skin was cold, icy where I touched it. I shoved away his shirt, trying to warm him. Touched too much of his skin. I trembled too, and felt tears start, and kissed him to make them stop. Everything else was falling apart, the world was getting smaller and colder and darker – I'd lost Luke, I'd lost my freedom, I'd nearly lost my life. I didn't know how much longer we had.

It could all end tomorrow, and the only thing I had left in the world was this man, solid in my arms, needing me, wanting me. And I was tired. Of being alone, of needing someone to hold me and tell me it was all right, someone to be with me.

'It's all right,' I told him, kissing him again and again. 'It's okay. Jack, it's okay.'

But it was not okay. I didn't stop at just kissing Jack. Not this time. I took off his clothes and crawled under the duvet and made love to him, and in the end of course it wasn't about him at all. It was about me, weak, lusty me, evil, hurtful me, stupid, selfish me.

Chapter Eighteen

The hotel had a bar. And the bar had a plug point. Luke plugged in, switched on, and swore repeatedly at the phone until it found a signal.

The barman, who looked as if he was going to ask Luke not to plug his phone in, quickly turned and went back to the counter.

The phone beeped at him. He dialled again. More beeping.

'Just bloody connect,' he begged it.

More bleeping.

He swore inventively, then forced his brain to do what it should have done days ago and memorise the number, and lurched over to the bar.

The look the barman gave him was one of pure terror. Luke didn't think he was scowling that fearsomely, but then on the other hand he did resemble the walking dead right now.

'Do you have a payphone?' he asked, and the guy pointed down a corridor. 'Change for ten dollars?'

He was handed a pile of quarters with far greater speed than was possible for accurate counting.

He dialled her number on the payphone. Waited. Heard a series of beeps.

Oh God, she's going to die. Alexa Martin will find her and kill her and I'll be sitting here being useless because her damn bloody phone is switched off.

He stumbled back to his seat and pressed the heels of his hands against his eyes, which wasn't a wise thing to do since less than forty-eight hours ago some bastard had punched him there, hard. But it was better than crying in public. Probably.

'Excuse me, sir?'

He looked up. A young waitress with a tight body was standing there holding a tray, on which was a bottle of Jack Daniels and a couple of glasses. She set them down on the table.

'I didn't order anything.'

'It's a gift, sir. From the guy over there.' She pointed to the far side of the bar. Luke's head and neck and back and everything hurt too much to turn. He was too tired. Sophie was going to die. He couldn't do anything.

Who the hell was sending him bottles of Jack? Who knew he was here? Well, Harrington, probably, or whichever goon he'd sent after Luke now.

He wasn't sure he could take any more of this.

'What does he look like?'

'He's really cute,' the waitress said, smiling, then blushed and cleared her throat, hugging her tray against her body. 'Maybe six-one or two, brown hair, nice eyes, great smile. He's in really good shape.' She leaned closer. 'I think you should go for it.'

'What?' said Luke.

'He's smiling. He's totally into you.' She straightened up and winked at him.

'Oh, fantastic.' Now he had some guy coming onto him. He turned to tell this new suitor he was barking up the wrong tree, and those nice eyes and great smile beamed back at him from five feet away.

Luke groaned and poured out a shot. 'Well, fuck.'

'Thanks, but you're really not my type.' Harvey poured bourbon into his one of the glasses. 'Despite what she thinks.'

'I mean, do I look gay?'

'You look like shit,' Harvey said bluntly. He slid into the booth opposite Luke.

'I'm hearing that once a day now.'

'What happened to you?'

'Inter-departmental co-operation.'

'In English?'

'Harrington beat the shit out of me for information.'

'Robert Harrington?' Luke nodded. Harvey whistled. 'You give it to him?'

Luke gave him a look.

'Okay, all right, just checking. Listen, I spoke to her this morning.'

Luke's head jerked up, which introduced him to a new specific kind of pain. 'You did what?' She hadn't returned his calls, any of them, but she'd speak to Harvey? Was their relationship really in that much trouble?

'Yeah. Saw her a couple of days ago, too. She's doing okay. Well, I mean she's tired, but –'

'Where is she?'

Harvey's eyes narrowed the tiniest fraction. 'I can't tell you that.'

'You bloody well can. I don't care what rules or orders or whatever you're disobeying, but I have to know where she is. I have to warn her.'

'Warn her what?'

He felt like crying. 'Alexa Martin. She's out, Harvey. She got out of jail.'

Harvey stared, the most shocked Luke had ever seen him. 'But – how? She's a psychopath!'

'I know. And she hates Sophie. Think about it. Who else is as likely to be behind all this?'

Harvey frowned, tilting his head. 'I don't know, I mean … are you sure?'

'That she's out? Yes. They're trying to keep it quiet. Don't want to panic the populace. I mean, she did kill –'

'A hundred-and-forty-three people. I remember.'

'And maybe more now. And Sophie has to know. I have to warn her. So I need you to tell me,' Luke leaned forward, 'where she is.'

Harvey gave him a long, considering look. Then he said, 'I can't do that.'

'Tell me or I will shoot you in the head, right here in front of everybody.'

'I can't tell you because I don't know.'

'But you saw her –'

'Two days ago. I saw her onto a train. Going north.'

'North? North where? We're in bloody Connecticut, where the hell else is north of here?'

Harvey looked down at his bourbon. He drank some. 'Luke,' he said, 'I am not saying this as a CIA officer. And I'm not saying it to you as an MI6 officer. I'm saying it to you as a friend who thinks you really need some advice.'

'I don't need relationship advice from someone whose job involves getting shot at five thousand miles away from his pregnant wife.'

'It's better than getting shot at in close proximity to my pregnant wife,' Harvey said calmly. 'Did you fly here under your own name?'

Luke shrugged and nodded. 'The Service know all my aliases anyway.'

'Right. And you'll have been under surveillance, yes?'

'Since she disappeared, more or less, yes.' He'd stopped even looking for them now.

'So it's not unreasonable to suspect someone's followed you?'

'Well, you did, right?'

'We've had tabs on you since you got on the plane.'

Of course they had. 'I expect half the people in this bar are MI5.'

'Right. And they're going to continue to follow you. And if you lead them to Sophie, what do you think they'll do?'

Luke stared at him, too tired to think. 'They'll arrest her and bring her home –'

'Will they? The people who beat the shit out of you? Luke, I've heard about this guy. He's a pitbull. He thinks Sophie is a traitor. He finds her, he'll rip her apart.'

'He can't –'

'Can't? Like he "can't" beat up a fellow officer?'

'Funny story there,' Luke said. 'Not entirely sure if I am a fellow officer right now.'

Harvey stared at him. 'Jesus, Luke.'

Luke drained his glass.

'Look, I know you're tired. I know you're worried.'

'Exhausted and terrified is more like it.'

'I was trying to spare your British pride. Listen, what are those books Sophie's always reading? The fantasy ones.'

Luke looked up, frowning at this non-sequitur. 'Terry Pratchett?'

'Yeah. She was telling me once how they introduced her to the concept that personal isn't the same thing as important. You have to think with your head on this one.'

He stared at the table. Sheila had told him the same thing, what felt like decades ago. Sophie herself had refused to give him her location.

Harvey drained his glass. 'Look, if our situations were reversed, if it was me going after Angel, what would you tell me?' He held up a hand pre-emptively. 'Barring the question of what Angel would be doing on the run in the first place. Would you let me run after her? Or would you tell me to use my goddamned brain and back off?'

There wasn't anything Luke could think of say to that.

In the last, slow hours of morning I got no sleep. I lay awake for hours, Jack asleep in my arms, his breathing soft and even. He was calm at last. Comforted at last.

But in comforting him, I'd destroyed myself. Too shocked to cry, too numb to feel pain, I lay awake in the moonlight, cradling my lover.

My *lover*.

Everything else had fallen away from me at some time during the night, and I could see with horrible, exacting clarity exactly what the situation was. Luke and I had fought. We hadn't broken up, we'd *fought*. We'd fought because he'd sent Jack after me. Not, as my confused and frightened psyche had decided, because he wanted to break up with me, but because he was concerned about me.

Appalled, I stared at the ceiling. Why now? Why couldn't I have realised this before I slept with Jack? Why had it taken this, this … *stupidity*, to jolt my brain out of its terror and confusion and see clearly? Why now, when it was far too late?

Luke was still in contact. Still texting me. Still sending voicemails. He didn't hate me, didn't want to be free of me.

But he had threatened me, and he didn't even know it. I was in trouble, so much trouble, and not just from the deranged killer who seemed to be stalking me. From Jack, who I'd considered a threat to my life, to my freedom – but never to my relationship.

And Luke had sent him to me.

I wondered what Luke was doing now, if he was sitting at home worrying about me. If he was up all night searching through files for information about this Sarah Wilde. If he was still trying to call me, while I'd run away to my remote hideaway where he couldn't reach me. If he knew, if he'd find out what I'd been doing. And if I wanted him to.

Jack shifted in my arms, his unshaven cheek rough against my neck. He felt good in my arms. But he didn't feel right.

What the hell had I done?

He saw the dawn in with the last of the bourbon. The TV

burbled away, showing programmes he didn't recognise, adverts for products he'd never heard of, news reports on stories he really didn't care about.

He flicked from channel to channel, trying to find something, anything, that actually had any meaning. A bulletin about an escaped British prisoner. A car chase in which said prisoner was gunned down and killed. A report about two fugitives being taken into custody.

But there was nothing. He lit another cigarette and peered at the clock. The first flight out was in a few hours. He could get on it, as Harvey had told him to, or he could get in a car or on a train and go north and utterly fail to have any idea where Sophie might be. Or he could stay here in this hotel room and drink himself to death.

He flicked from channel to channel. He picked up his phone and dialled Sophie's number. Nothing.

He changed channels again.

I guess I must have dozed a little: my body was exhausted, even if my mind refused to shut down. What woke me was the shots nearby.

Jack jerked suddenly awake, clutching at me. A kind of clammy nausea gripped my insides, the shock of memory hitting me as if one of those shots had been aimed at me.

'What the hell was that?' Jack hissed.

I shook myself. Focus, Sophie. Gunshots are more important than the shoddy state of your conscience.

And then there was another one. Definitely a gunshot.

'Shit,' Jack said, and scrambled out of bed. He pulled on his jeans first, tucked his gun under the waistband and shrugged into a t-shirt. 'Stay there,' he said, and left the room, barefoot.

I stayed there. For about ten seconds. Then I threw the covers back, wincing when my arm reminded me I'd been damn well shot, and pulled on my own clothes. I checked my gun, tucked it in my waistband, and checked the recorder in my pocket.

It was cold outside, still really freezing cold, and pre-dawn dark. There was just enough light from the stars and moon that I saw the door of the main house standing open. Jack was nowhere outside, so I guessed he had to be inside. Where the gunshots had come from.

The air was cold, but so was I. Frightened, in a deep ball down inside somewhere, but externally I suddenly felt bulletproof. Reckless. Last night had been the single most stupid thing I'd ever done in my entire life. Whatever waited for me inside the house couldn't be worse.

I crept up the steps to the porch. Two of them creaked and I shushed them, my heart pounding. Evidently it hadn't heard about being bulletproof. Probably it was nothing, uh, someone cleaning a gun like in *Gone With The Wind* or something. Yes. Except that wasn't really anyone cleaning a gun, and besides, who cleans a gun in the early hours of the morning?

I got to the front door. The house was dark, but if I listened really, really hard, I could hear someone moving about inside.

Here goes.

I flicked the safety off, held my gun high and walked inside as quietly as I could. My ankle clicked loudly and I froze in agonised silence for what felt like about ten minutes before I yanked together enough courage to move again.

I was in the hallway. To my right was a dining room, to my left a cosy living room. Ahead of me were stairs and a corridor leading to a kitchen. All of it was very, very dark, the sort of total dark you only get in the country.

A shadow moved in front of the kitchen window. My trigger finger suddenly felt very stiff.

It'll be Jack, I told myself. Just Jack.

Just Jack. How *Will & Grace*. See, funny, think funny things. You told Jack it was all okay, and you can't lie to him, not now. It will have to be okay.

For him, at any rate.

The shadow bent down to something on the floor, and as my eyes adjusted a little I could see that it was a person. A man. The shadow was Jack and the thing on the floor was a man. A dead man. Jack had a gun in his hand and the floor was covered in a dark pool of liquid

I took a step back, and as I did my eyes flickered up to the landing. And there behind the beautifully turned spindles of the wooden railings, was a body in a pale wrapping. A woman, blood staining her nightgown. She sprawled down the stairs, unmoving, unnatural. Dead.

'Jack,' I croaked hoarsely, and he looked up, and opened his mouth to say something.

And then the world exploded.

Well, not so much the world, but the kitchen. There was a bang and a massive fireball, and I stood paralysed. Jack had been flung across the kitchen and now I couldn't see him. Tremors shook the building.

And then I found my feet, and raced forward, into the furnace of the kitchen. Everything was burning. Everything was made out of wood or fabric, and it was all turning to smoke and dust. I couldn't breathe. My eyes burned viciously. It was all so bright and so, so goddamned hot. It was like hell in there. The fire was deafening, crackling so loud I couldn't tell if I was imagining the bangs of gas tanks and oil reservoirs exploding. And I could see something behind the flaming, crackling wreck of the kitchen table, something that might have been Jack. But I couldn't tell.

'Jack,' I yelled, but the fire was too loud and I couldn't even hear myself. 'Jack!'

I took another step forward, but the air was choking and I fell back. I raced back into the living room where the flames were just starting to break through, stared wildly around and ripped a throw off the back of the sofa. I slung it over my shoulders like a shawl, pulling a fold over my nose and mouth, and ventured back into the furnace.

The furnace. Of course. Someone must have shot a gas tank or something. That would account for the explosion.

I took a few cautious steps further forward than I'd been before. Christ, it was so hot. Sweat was trickling down my face. I could see Jack, and I was sure it was him and I knew he was still alive. He was blackened and still, but I couldn't leave him.

And then something creaked and cracked above me, and I looked up and saw a hole in the ceiling. I saw it, moved, and seconds later a beam smashed down onto the floor where I'd been standing. Flames blossomed from it and when I ventured closer, my blanket caught fire and I shoved it to the ground, hopping back hastily before it toasted me, too.

Wall cupboards started falling down. The walls were disintegrating. I looked back at the hall and saw the fire spreading. If I didn't get out now, I'd never get out. I wasn't bulletproof at all.

'I'm sorry, Jack,' I choked, and stumbled out of the kitchen. As I ran through the hall, dodging the bannister spindles which were tumbling one by one, flaming like a cheerleader's batons, I heard more loud bangs, and figured it was more things exploding in the house, until I glanced through the front door to the porch and saw a figure outlined there by the flames, a silhouette with a gun. Firing at me.

I ducked and darted into the dining room, which was a bad choice because most of the furniture there was made of wood. Suddenly, I realised what it must be like for those hedgehogs who curl up in bonfire pyres and then can't get out when they've been lit. I grabbed a chair by the bit that wasn't flaming and started smashing it at the far window. Then I hurled myself through it, and found to my surprise that the house was built on a hill, and this was the bit that sloped downwards. I fell six or seven feet before I landed, and my ankle gave a loud crack as it took the full weight of my five feet and ten inches of well-padded frame.

I rolled down the hill and lay at the bottom, a safe distance from the burning monstrosity of the house, panting and sobbing without even realising it. I could hardly breathe. My lungs felt full of ash, dry and hot and about to turn themselves inside out with coughing.

I hauled myself onto my back. Sweet merciful crap, my ankle hurt. I couldn't move it much. There was no question of standing on it.

And then it got worse.

Just as I was trying to figure out how far away my gun was and where it might have ended up after that tumble down the hill, I heard footsteps running down the slope. I looked up.

It was a woman, dressed in black. Her hair was dark, tied back and clinging to her neck with sweat and grime. She had a weapon belt on and a gun in her hand.

Her hand.

She had her index finger on the trigger and her middle finger curled around the barrel. Except that it wasn't her middle finger, it was simply her other finger. Where the last two should have been there was nothing. The outside of her hand was just *not there*.

'I don't know why you're staring,' she said, and I dragged my eyes up to her face. 'You did it.'

The funny thing was, despite all my denials, despite all the reasons why it couldn't have been possible, I wasn't surprised. It felt as if I'd always known, that the knowledge had always been there inside me, and it was only now that it was emerging.

'Alexa,' I said. 'Fancy seeing you here. How was prison?'

'Revolting,' she said, 'but sadly you'll never find out. I've been torn between letting them catch you and killing you myself, but you really are a bugger, Miss Green. You just won't be caught. Run, rabbit, run, rabbit, run run run …' she sang, miming running with the fingers of her free – and whole – hand. In her voice the nursery rhyme sounded sinister, distorted. As well it might. The woman was bloody insane.

'How did you get out?' The last I'd heard she'd been sentenced to about a million life sentences. People who committed crimes like Alexa had didn't get parole.

She shrugged. 'Bribery. Blackmail. Drugs. Distraction. It's not hard when you're an evil genius and the authorities are all incompetent and easily corrupted.'

'You're Sarah Wilde,' I said.

'Yep. I look damn good for someone who had a broken back five years ago, don't you think?'

'Did you ever get your money?'

Her nostrils flared. 'You've been digging. But of course, that's just what you do. You find out the truth. And you stop the bad guys.'

'While you kill the good guys.'

'Oh, come on. Irene Shepherd tried to blackmail me. Well, she didn't try, so much as succeed. She knew, you see, what I'd hidden from everyone else.'

'That you weren't really crippled in a wheelchair?'

'Exactly. Hard to start a new life when everyone knows about your old one. It's expensive to run for Supreme Court Judge, you know. She was going for Chief Justice next year.'

'But why Jack? What's he done to you?'

She shrugged again. 'Right place, right time. Could have been anyone.'

I squeezed my eyes shut. Oh, Jack.

'Sir Theodore?'

'Failed to get me my money. Imagine my absolute glee when I found out you were visiting him. You! Two birds with one stone. Just couldn't resist.' She put her head on one side, as if considering who else she might have murdered. 'And of course, he knew my secret, too. The security guard got in my way. Couldn't take the risk. The maid ...' she shrugged. 'Could have figured it out –'

Could have? Christ.

'So I got Canolti to help me out. Christ, he was an arse. What sort of idiot leaves his phone number with a woman he's been sent to kill? Thanks for taking care of him, by the way.'

'It was Jack,' I said, my voice breaking ever so slightly on his name. 'He shot Canolti.'

'Well, what do I care?'

'Why the doctor and his sister?'

Alexa shrugged. 'The sister was collateral damage. I knew you'd go running to the good doctor for answers. And he was a good doctor. Look how much I can move.' She kicked out at my ankle and white-hot pain shot through me. 'More than you can, anyway. Hey, Sophie?'

'Yes?' I was trying hard to concentrate on breathing. It wasn't easy. I shifted my eyes to the glorious wreck of the house up on the hill. Keep breathing. Survive. Someone has to.

'You wanna know what I'm going to do after I've killed you?' She looked excited. Her face was still pretty, but rather older than it should have been, and the light in her eyes was just pure insanity. 'I'm going to get on a plane, find your boyfriend and tie him to a bed and fuck his brains out. And then I'm going to blow his brains out. 'Cos he's been pissing me off as well.'

I bit my lip so hard I tasted blood.

'Any last words?' Alexa asked, the barrel of her gun gaping at me. I saw my death approaching.

Fuck it.

'Yeah,' I said. 'When you're back in the slammer getting raped by a three-hundred pound woman who smells like a French toilet and calls you her bitch, remember that I was the one who got to shag Luke. Not you. He'd shoot himself in the head before he'd ever –'

She pulled the trigger.

I sucked in my last breath.

And then I let it out, because the gun clicked and did nothing else.

'Fuck.' Alexa sighed, and transferred the gun to her other hand to empty the cartridge and get another one from her belt.

And then something extraordinary happened.

'Hey,' someone called from higher up the hill, and her head snapped round, and at first I thought it was the smoke in my eyes or the pain in my ankle or the delirium of knowing I was going to die, but I thought I saw Jack up there.

'Duck,' he yelled, and threw something at her. Something burning. She yelped and danced away, and I gritted my teeth and rolled to my left, and felt something hard under me.

My gun.

Oh, *frabjous* day.

I could have said something smart about changing my last words, or hearing hers, or saying hello to the people she'd murdered, but instead I just lifted my little SIG, aimed, and pulled the trigger.

The first shot hit her leg. Told you I'm a bad aim. But it felled her, and I hauled myself incredibly painfully to my knees and aimed a shot at her heart. Bad target. Not sure she had one.

The third bullet hit her between the eyes. I knew she had a brain.

She fell back and I edged closer, checking the mad psychotic creature for signs of life. But people only survive being shot between the eyes in superhero movies. Alexa's eyes stared up at me, blank with death but somehow ... surprised.

'Bitch,' I said, and slapped her face.

Something came tumbling down the hill, and I realised as it got closer that it was Jack. He fell against me, and I threw my arms around him, desperately relieved. Jack didn't deserve to die. He'd saved my life. I was the weak, stupid traitor here.

'I thought you were dead,' I said.

'Not quite.'

'I couldn't get to you. How did you get out?'

'Back door,' he said, and I groaned. 'You okay?'

'Uh, mostly. You?'

'Not so much.'

I realised he was breathing very shallowly and that there was something wet pressing against my shirt. I held Jack away, laid him down on the grass, and looked him over. His clothes were torn and burnt and underneath I could see charred and bleeding bits of skin. I started to feel slightly nauseous.

This was not good.

Ambulance, I thought, he needs an ambulance. My phone was in my bag in the room. The room which couldn't have escaped the fire.

'Your phone,' I said, and he shook his head.

'Lost it,' he said. Attempted a smile. 'No signal anyway.'

No. There hadn't been. Despair swamped me.

'Sophie.' He suddenly gripped my wrist, and I was utterly terrified that this was it. When he breathed in I heard a rattling sound. But then he said, 'Do you love him?'

'What? Who?'

'Your boyfriend. Your Luke. You love him?'

Pain stabbed at me. 'Of course I do,' I said, and tried to pretend that it was the smoke that was making my eyes water.

'Don't … fuck it up.'

I half-choked on a laugh. 'Bit late for that.'

''m sorry.'

'No. No, it wasn't your fault.'

He nodded. Scraped in another breath. 'It was,' he said, and his fingers slipped around mine. 'I always … wanted you.' His lips stretched in a painful smile. 'I didn't think you'd ever …'

I gulped in smoky air. I didn't think I'd ever, either.

'Sophie?'

'Yes?'

His hand came up to touch my hair, my awful smoky ashy hair. 'You're a mess.'

Another half-laugh. 'You, too. You know,' I looked around into the deep dark night, 'someone's going to see this fire and pretty soon a fire engine and ambulance and everyone, they're all going to arrive and they're going to laugh so hard at the state we're in.'

Jack shook his head.

'Or not. Maybe not. They'll take you off to hospital, 'cos I think you need some treatment.'

He shook his head.

'Now, that's just delusional, Jack. I mean, you're going to be okay, but …'

He was still shaking his head. He looked up at me, and he smiled, and that smile absolutely terrified me. It was so calm and serene. He was no longer shaking.

He reached down and pulled up his t-shirt, peeling it away from his stomach, and I gagged as I suddenly realised what that second explosion in the kitchen had been. Jack's gun. The heat had exploded it, and the consequences weren't pretty. A few hours ago I'd had first-hand knowledge of the smooth, firm flesh of his stomach, and now in its place was a bloody mess of gut and bone and horrible little ribbons of skin.

'Oh God.' I sucked in some smoky air. 'Jack, hold on, there'll be someone, I'll, I'll go and get help or something, you're going to be all right ...'

But Jack put his hand against my face and shook his head. His eyes were glistening. 'Don't be so damn stupid, Sophie,' he said, and his voice broke through the fake little smile he gave me. 'I'm dying.'

Chapter Nineteen

At somewhere around ten or eleven in the morning, Luke stopped checking his phone for messages. He'd made it to JFK, and the horror of the flight from Connecticut was beginning to fade.

The panic, the sheer mind-numbing panic that he was doing the wrong thing, that he was abandoning her, that Alexa would find her and kill her and –

He'd tried to dull the fear with alcohol, but the cabin crew had taken against him, decided he was a drunk, and refused to serve him anything but coffee. So now he was in that dreadful twilight between drunk and hungover, and there were still hours to go before his flight back to London.

If he checked the news on his phone one more time, the battery would die again.

He sat in a coffee shop, watching the news on the TV screen on the wall, desperately trying to convince himself he was doing the right thing.

As it turned out, both Jack and I were right. Someone had seen the fire and called the emergency services, and it wasn't long before fire engines and ambulances and police cars screamed up to the farmhouse. But it was long enough. Jack died in my arms in the early hours of the morning, and by the time anyone found us, it was just me left alive, gulping and sobbing snottily, still holding Jack's body, both of us covered in a thick black film of dirt and sweat and ash and blood. A few feet away, Alexa's corpse cooled gently in the cold morning air.

Out of the policemen and firemen and paramedics and men in suits walking around with police radios and mobile phones and openly holstered guns, came a man in a grey suit. I thought I recognised him, and when he scowled at me I knew who it was.

'Fires, gunshots, corpses. I hear the news and somehow I know it's going to have Sophie Green in the middle of it.'

'Harrington,' I guessed. He scowled harder.

'Put that dead body down.'

I looked down at Jack's face. I'd closed his eyes but there was no way I could convince myself he was asleep. He lolled in my arms, still and cold.

'Ma'am?' said a more gentle voice, and I looked round to see a man standing next to a gurney. It held a body bag.

'Be gentle with him,' I said, but it came out as a sob.

Harrington scowled at me some more. He dragged me roughly to my feet and I let out a cry as Jack's body flopped ungracefully on the ground.

'He's already dead, it won't hurt him,' Harrington said, and I'd have punched him if someone else hadn't already got hold of my hands and held them firm. I felt the cold metal of a handcuff slip around one wrist and saw a woman in a plain dark suit snapping the other cuff to herself.

'Sunita Sakib,' she introduced herself as I wavered on my useless ankle. 'It's all right. It's all over now.'

'Oho,' said Harrington. 'For you, Green, it's just beginning.'

'Sir,' Sunita said, 'shouldn't we take her to a hospital?'

'She'll live,' Harrington said. 'Four fresh bodies, Green. Big trouble.'

But I wasn't very afraid. I was shaking and trembling, but that was because it was cold and my body was in shock.

When Harrington had parked the car outside a motel and heckled me into a room, still chained to the female agent, he pushed me down on the bed and barked, 'Sit,' like I was a dog.

Prize bitch. Ha.

'Well then,' he said, and I reached for my pocket. 'Oh, no, you bloody don't.' He whipped out a pistol. A revolver. How quaint.

'Could you get it for me?' I asked Sunita. 'This pocket here.'

'Erm, I think this is a no-smoking room,' she began.

Given that about eighty percent of me was covered in ashes, I thought that was kind of funny.

'It's not cigarettes. It's a recording,' I said, and she produced the little machine from my thigh pocket. 'Alexa Martin. She confessed to everything.'

You know, doing this job – whatever job it is I do now – has taught me a few things. Like, if I was going to shoot someone, I wouldn't confess a bloody thing to them. I wouldn't say anything at all. I'd just shoot them. And I wouldn't get anyone else to do my dirty work, lazy though I am. They just get in the way.

We listened to the recording, which wasn't very clear and had got slightly corrupted by the smoke, but it had recorded enough to make Harrington go purple. I'd been afraid that my fall down the hill might have damaged it, but it played out okay.

It put Harrington in a foul mood, which I quite enjoyed. He looked like he wanted to do me violence, but the presence of Sunita was keeping him in check.

After about the third replaying of the tape, though, I was starting to get bored. The adrenaline rush of surviving was wearing off and I was starting to get to the 'Oh God, I nearly died' bit. I think I was very nearly at the 'Oh God, Jack died' bit, when the door slammed open and Harrington jumped to his feet, hand on his gun.

'I thought I said no one –' he started, and then stopped as he realised who it was.

Harvey raised his eyebrows. 'Thanks for telling me my number one suspect is dead,' he said. 'But then you know, you're not too good with the information at all. Sophie,' he looked at me. 'You don't look too good.'

I stared at him for a bit, trying to get the strength to stand up, and then I did it, and rushed over and threw my arms around him. But unfortunately by then my wrists were cuffed to each other, so I nearly strangled him before I got it right.

'Hey, Sophie,' Harvey said, patting my back, 'I'm going to need those lungs back.'

'Sorry.' I disentangled myself, and as I was lifting my arm back over his shoulder Harvey grabbed it and stared at the outside of my wrist.

'You got caught in the fire, huh?'

I looked at my arm. There was an ugly reddish patch there, bubbled and blistered and peeling away. You know, I thought something hurt, but I just couldn't figure out what. Harvey looked over the revolting bandage on my other arm, my bare foot where I'd taken my shoe off because it hurt so much, my greasy black skin and sore, blinky eyes.

'And you didn't get medical treatment for her because …?'

'More important things to do,' Harrington said in clipped tones. 'Mr Harvard, I will be happy to fully liaise with you in the morning, but –'

'You know what?' Harvey gave a big fake smile. 'It already is morning. And Sophie,' he still had hold of my arm, which was just as well because I was having trouble staying upright, 'is the number-one witness in my case. A federal case. And she's been shot, and burnt, and she can't stand upright. Frankly, she's got so many holes in her she's starting to look like a pincushion. And you don't think she needs medical treatment?'

'She's not –'

'You didn't even know Alexa Martin was out,' Harvey said, and I'm afraid I laughed. Harrington shut up. Harvey smiled. 'I'll bring her back later,' he added, and put his arm around my shoulders. 'Come on, Sophie.' To Harrington he added, 'And I want that recording.'

'I'll have a copy made –' Harrington began, and Harvey bared his teeth.

'You're on my turf now, buddy. I get the original and you can have the copy.'

'Sakib,' Harrington said. 'Go with them. She's still to be cuffed to you.'

'Sir.' She nodded, and linked my wrist to hers again, giving me an apologetic smile.

Harvey led me out to his car and didn't even laugh too much at my hopping. 'Where are we going?' I croaked.

'Hospital. I still owe you one.'

'Really?'

'Well, not really. But what's a favour between friends, huh?'

Sometimes, I really, really love Harvey.

Luke woke from a disturbed sleep to find that, improbably, his entire body hurt even more than it had before. He strongly suspected the kid behind him had been kicking his seat.

'I hate cattle class,' he grumbled.

'Sir?'

He glanced up. The cabin crew on this flight were less suspicious than on the last one, and kept offering him alcohol. This one had a tray of miniature bottles of wine.

'Are you people trying to keep me drunk?' he groused.

'Sir? There are non-alcoholic drinks if you'd prefer.'

He accepted one and tried to wake himself up. Only a few hours until they landed, and then he could go back to the hatred of his boss, the inappropriate admiration of his secretary, the disdain of his grandmother and the aching, terrifying fear of his own paranoia.

Beside him, a guy in a suit was watching cartoons. Luke found a set of headphones in the seat pocket, plugged them in and flicked through the channels. Cartoon. Cartoon. Ancient episode of *Friends*. Really dodgy-looking romantic comedy. News.

News.

'... leaving the vice-president in charge. Now, we've been reporting all week about the events unfolding in a small town in Maine, but the story seems to have come to an epic conclusion just this morning,' said an overly made-up American anchorwoman. Luke was about to turn off, until he saw pictures of Sophie and Jack flash up on the screen. His heart stuttered.

'That's right, Sara. Reports reached us this morning of a showdown in the town of East Penobscot worthy of a movie,' said the alarmingly white-toothed anchorman. 'Take a look at this.'

The picture changed to that of a reporter in a bright red suit, standing a few hundred yards from a burned-out building, crawling with emergency services. The air around her was thick with smoke.

'Thank you, Scott. Yes, here I am in East Penobscot, and you can see that the events unfolding here have been pretty dramatic. Following a double case of grand theft auto last night, comes a case of arson and several murders. As yet the police have refused to comment, but more than one body has been removed from the site.'

Luke stopped breathing.

'The CIA are involved in this case, which we can confirm is linked to the murder of Judge Shepherd in Connecticut a few weeks ago. Now the main suspect in that case, Jack de Valera, has been seen in the company of a British woman, Sophie Green, who is suspected of murdering a British Intelligence officer.'

Again, Sophie and Jack's pictures appeared, flashing up in the corner of the screen. 'It's believed the two of them teamed up on this crime spree, which has seen multiple murders and at least one instance of armed robbery.'

'And have the suspects been caught, Karen?' asked Sara.

'Are they amongst the dead?' asked Scott.

Luke leaned forward so far his nose touched the screen.

'It's impossible to say at this stage, Scott. The police haven't released any information about the identity of the bodies, but it is known that only one person was found here alive, and has been taken into custody. Right at this moment we don't know if it's Mr de Valera or Ms Green.'

'So one of them is alive, and one is dead?' said Sara.

'That's right, Sara,' said Karen, and beamed at the camera.

'All right, thanks for that, Karen, and now let's move on to our next story,' said Scott. 'Have you ever wondered how that groundhog always knows when it's spring? Well, here to explain some more to us ...'

'No,' Luke yelled, and every single head on the plane turned to face him. Grabbing the nearest member of staff, he gibbered, 'How current is this? The news? When's the next update?'

She said something he couldn't hear. Ripping off his headphones, he demanded, 'Again?'

'I'm afraid it won't be until after we land, sir. That's a pre-recorded programme. But it is as current as we can make it. We receive it just before we take off so the news is as fresh as possible.'

She beamed at him.

'No, you don't understand. I need to know more.'

'I'm afraid you'll have to wait, sir,' she said, her smile slipping.

'Can you get the pilot to find out? Radio down?'

'No, I'm afraid we can't do that, sir.' Her smile had flattened into a grim line now.

Luke got out his phone and switched it on.

'Sir, I'm going to have to ask you to switch that off.'

'No.'

'Sir, airline regulations prohibit –'

'I don't care.'

'Please give me that phone.'

'No.'

She snatched it from his hand, and Luke lunged after it, shoving her back against the opposite seat.

The nearby passengers gasped.

The stewardess righted herself, glared at Luke, and said, 'I'll have the police waiting for you when we land.'

Luke opened his mouth to tell her to go ahead, but if he had to go through the whole being-arrested thing he'd never get to find out anything about Sophie. He had no ID on him to prove he was an intelligence officer. Nothing to keep him from being shoved into the system while the woman he loved lay rotting in a Maine mortuary.

He raised his one free hand. 'All right. Fine. I'm sorry. I'm going through a little bit of stress right now. I've been shot, I've been beaten up, and there's a strong possibility my girlfriend's dead. Now, can I have my phone back?'

The vindictive bitch glowered at him. 'No,' she said.

The cabin crew all glared at him as he got off the plane. Luke didn't care. He switched on his phone but the bastard battery had gone dead again. None of the TVs he passed in the terminal were showing the news. It wasn't shown on any of the papers. Sophie was the most important thing in the world, and the world didn't care.

He made it to the car, fell inside, and fumbled for the

phone charger plugged into the dash. Waited the agonising interval for it to find a signal. Dialled Sophie again.

Nothing.

Harvey. Nothing.

His fists slammed against the steering wheel, again and again, the car rocking with his frustration. Tears burned his eyes. Spilled over his cheeks. Sophie. Oh God, Sophie.

She lay soft and warm in his arms, the two of them listening to the music drifting up from the ballroom. The band was playing something slushy, and as the faint sounds drifted up he found himself straining to hear the words. Romantic, melodramatic words, which nonetheless fit his mood perfectly.

'Reckon Angel and Harvey have taken their eyes off each other yet?' Sophie asked drowsily.

'Probably not. Has she been making googly eyes at him all day?'

'Yes, but I figure if you can't make googly eyes at your husband on your wedding day, when can you?'

'Never,' Luke said. 'You ever go googly-eyed on me, I'm leaving you.'

She punched his shoulder. 'Liar.'

He smiled and stroked his hand down her back. Her skin was hot, damp with sweat, her body draped luxuriously over his. He quite literally couldn't remember ever being so happy. He barely wanted to move, in case he broke the spell and the perfection ended.

Sophie wriggled a little closer, her lips brushing his jaw. She didn't seem to mind he was about twelve hours past a five o'clock shadow.

'Did you miss me?' she asked. 'While you were out in Saudi?'

'Stop fishing for compliments. You know I did.'

'I missed you,' she said quietly. 'I mean, really missed you. I was frightened you'd ...'

'I'd what?'

'Forget me,' she mumbled, her head buried against his neck.

'Sophie, believe me, you'll be burned into my memory until the day I die,' he said. 'I love you, in case you hadn't noticed.'

At that her head came up, her eyes bright with surprise. 'Then you have stayed me in a happy hour, for I was about to protest I love you,' she said.

He stared incredulously. 'You're quoting Shakespeare at a time like this?'

'He says it better than I could.' She cupped his jaw in one hand and kissed him softly, tenderly. 'I love you, Luke. I really do.'

'You see,' he murmured, 'I think you said it pretty well.'

The shrill tone of his phone woke Luke, and as his head shot up his neck snapped in protest. Reality crashed into place around him. He wasn't lying in bed with Sophie telling him she loved him. He was sitting in an airport car park, aching in a million places, and Sophie was – was –

She was lost in America, and she might never come back.

Swearing, he picked up the phone and peered groggily at the display. 'Evelyn?'

'Hello, Luke. I was just wondering if you were quite finished with my car? Only I'd quite like it back.'

He stared at the dashboard. Yes. Evelyn's BMW. He had a nasty feeling he might have stolen it.

'Your passport says you're back in the country.'

Luke stared some more, this time at the car park outside the window. It seemed to be daylight. The clock on the dash said it was just after seven. He remembered putting his head down on the steering wheel and weeping, but he hadn't realised he'd cried himself to sleep. Humiliating.

'Luke? Are you there? Only Sheila would quite like to see you. Damage limitation, she says.'

'Damage limitation?'

'Yes. Apparently 5 had no idea about this whole Alexa Martin débâcle. Quite humiliating for them. The whole Service is in trouble.'

'Right,' Luke said vaguely.

'And now your Sophie has blackmailed her way into freedom – although by now I'm sure the Home Office has claimed it as their idea ...'

She was still talking, but Luke wasn't listening.

Sophie blackmailed her way into freedom.

Sophie is alive.

'She – she did what?'

'Told the Foreign Secretary you were one of her best officers and that now there was no conflict of interest, she'd quite like you back. So then –'

Sophie said that? When did she ever speak to the –?

Understanding dawned. The world was too full of powerful women.

'No, not Sheila,' he said, with what he thought under the circumstances was heroic patience. 'Sophie.'

'Oh. Yes, apparently she's managed to convince Harrington that she could sell her side of the story to the papers. Made out she's best friends with Penny Grayson – you know, she writes for *The Times* now – and turns out they were both bridesmaids at Angel Winter's wedding. Personally, given what you've told me of Harrington, I think she's mad, but I suppose by now there are enough people who know the Home Office has screwed up over Alexa Martin that Harrington hasn't much choice in the matter. After all, when you take away all the crimes we had pinned on her that Alexa confessed to, there's just a bit of petty larceny, and I'm sure we can talk that Lanley woman around about the armed robbery. Your friend James Harvard has even managed to pull some strings to get her off the rest of the charges in America – well, what's a charge of Grand Theft Auto between friends? Luke? Are you still listening?'

His head fell against the back of the seat. He felt giddy, mad, dizzy. He wanted to laugh.

'Is she all right?' he asked.

'Sophie? A bit banged up, I think, but she'll live.' Evelyn paused. 'Hasn't anyone told you any of this? Did you even know she was back in the country?'

Luke shook his head, then when the silence stretched on, managed, 'No.'

'Ah,' said Evelyn. 'I think perhaps you'd better come in.'

He ended the call, and on the display were several missed calls and messages from Harvey, who apologised for being on a plane to Langley when Luke called. Sophie was alive and Jack was dead. Harvey was about to make a phone-call to Maria about her brother unless Luke fancied doing it for him. Sophie was being taken into custody. Sophie had somehow managed to wangle her own freedom. Sophie was being sent home to her parents' house, which was information Harvey had had to flirt out of someone called Sunita and he hoped Luke wouldn't tell his wife about that.

Luke's finger hovered over the 'return call' button, then he dismissed it. There was something else he needed to do first.

He dialled, waited, and when the furious voice answered, he smiled.

'Harrington,' he said. 'Old boy. Hear the case is all wrapped up.'

Harrington let out a stream of invective that rather impressed Luke.

'Precisely,' he agreed. 'Now, just to clear up a few things. Do you want to tell my boss you beat the shit out of me, or shall I do it?'

By the time I'd gone over the repeatable parts of the story with my parents and my brother, and my mum had phoned everyone she'd ever met and my brother had texted everyone he'd ever met, I was exhausted. I hadn't wanted to talk about it in the first place, and after going through the minutiae of it with Harrington yelling and swearing at me, the sympathy and horror of my family was too much to bear.

'Have you contacted Luke?' Mum asked me about seventeen times a minute. 'You should call him.'

I scrunched my eyes shut. I had absolutely no idea what to say to Luke; and anyway, I didn't even know what phone number he was using these days.

And even if I did, the thought that MI6 would almost certainly be listening in at this stage made me want to weep. A tearful reunion was one thing. A tearful reunion listened to by half the Service was quite another.

After Mum had offered me every sort of foodstuff in the house, plied me with wine and hugged me about a million times, I excused myself for a lie down, escaping to my old bedroom with Tammy clutched in my arms like a teddy bear.

For once, my contrary little cat didn't protest, but let me hold her and stroke her and sob into her fur.

I must have fallen asleep, because it was getting dark when the doorbell awoke me. I blinked at the curtains and the lamp, at once familiar and unfamiliar, and tugged at my pyjamas. No, not pyjamas. They'd given me scrubs to wear in the hospital in Maine and I'd never got around to changing them for proper clothes.

I sat up, wondering if I had anything wearable in the wardrobe here, trying to calculate how many hours it had been since I last took a shower or changed my clothes, and my mother opened the bedroom door.

'There's someone to see you,' she said, picking up Tammy as she made a bid for freedom. Cat sympathy only lasts so long.

'Who?'

'You'd better come down,' Mum said, and didn't move until I'd limped past her and hopped down the stairs. My ankle wasn't broken, only sprained, but it had stiffened up something terrible while I slept, and felt like someone had taken a sledgehammer to it.

'Oh,' I said when I got to the front door.

'Hey,' said Luke, standing there in the late afternoon gloom, looking tired and dishevelled and strong and, above all, *right there*.

'Hey.'

Conversation thus exhausted, we stood in silence for a bit. I wondered if he could tell, if I looked different in a fundamental way, if all my misdeeds were written across my face in scarlet letters.

'How about if I go and put Tammy in her box,' suggested my mother, 'and you can take her home?'

I nodded, still avoiding eye contact with Luke.

'Do you have a car?' I asked, gesturing to the splint on my foot.

'Brought yours.'

I nodded. More silence. This was excruciating.

My mother handed me Tammy's travelling box, complete with grumpy cat, hugged me about a million more times and told me to call her soon. Tomorrow. Tonight. The second we got in. For heaven's sake, I only live around the corner.

We got into the car. My car. My lovely Ted. I fell against the cold vinyl seat, stroked the battered plastic dash, breathed in the faint scent of wet dog that seemed to have pervaded from the previous owners.

Tammy miaowed, and I focused my attention on her, not on the man sitting less than a foot away, lean and handsome and silent.

Nobody said a word until Luke parked the car outside my flat and came around to take Tammy's box from me.

'I can manage,' I said, and started to get down from the car, only to realise I'd left my crutches in my parents' living room.

'No, you can't,' Luke said. He slid his shoulder under my arm and tugged me from the car, leaving Tammy's box on the seat. I was so shocked at the thrill of contact that I couldn't think of a word to say.

Luke's arm went around my back and I leaned on him, my body against his, feeling the heat of him through his clothes. And every part of me went, *Yes. This one. This is right.*

He helped me round the corner, into the little courtyard outside my flat, and then opened the door and I was home.

For a long moment we stood in the darkened vestibule, and I willed him to say something. To put his arms around me. To kiss me. To tell me he'd missed me and he loved me. To tell me that despite the horrors of the last month, I was still the same person, still the girl he fell in love with. To not know, to not care, about the things I'd done.

'I'll get Tammy,' he said, and walked out.

A sob tore itself from my throat, as if a giant hand had punched me in the stomach and forced all the breath from me. Another sob. Another. My hand covered my mouth and I half-limped, half-fell across the room and onto the sofa where I doubled over, grief and pain wrecking me. I couldn't breathe.

I hadn't cried when I found Sir Theodore's body, when this all began. I hadn't cried nearly as much in the last month as I might have. But I cried now, now that it was all over; great, huge, ugly sobs that shook my whole body. Whatever had been keeping me going – adrenaline, hope, blind stupidity – fell away and I couldn't hold myself together any more.

I'd ruined everything.

I didn't notice Luke coming back in. Didn't hear if he closed the door, didn't see if he let Tammy out of her box, just curled there on the sofa in the darkness, weeping so hard I thought my body would shatter into pieces. Those silent, racking sobs, so violent they had a life of their own.

Then a light came on, and Luke said, '*Sophie*,' and then he was there, arms around me, pulling me against his body, stroking my hair. He rocked me gently, murmuring things I couldn't hear above my own violent weeping.

Eventually what he was saying penetrated my ears. 'It's all over now. I've got you. Sophie, talk to me.'

I raised my face to his. I must have looked like hell, but Luke gave me a gentle smile and kissed my forehead.

'I read the transcripts,' he said. '5 sent them over. No one should have to go through what you did.'

'It's all my fault,' I hiccuped.

'Don't be ridiculous,' Luke said with such authority I stared up at him, startled. 'None of this could possibly be construed as your fault.'

I pressed my face against his shoulder. His shirt was wet through where I'd sobbed and snotted all over it. 'You don't know,' I said, voice wobbly. 'The things I've done.'

'Of course I know,' Luke said, but he didn't sound like he wanted to kill me so he probably didn't. 'And I don't care. I just don't care what you've done.'

You would if you knew, I thought bleakly.

'None of it changes who you are. I've seen your charge sheet. It's just theft, Sophie. It's just things. Money. Most of it's covered by insurance.'

I shook my head, wanting to tell him I was guilty of so much more, wanting it and not wanting it at the same time.

'There's nothing on that list you can't come back from,' Luke said.

I stayed silent.

'I know you, Sophie Anne Green. I know you're brave and loyal and honest, and if you steal someone's credit card it's not out of malice or greed. I know you'll do what you have to in order to survive.'

The awful desolation of the last few days howled through me, like a great wind scouring out everything inside me and leaving me hollow. Surviving? Was that what I'd been doing with Jack?

The worst part was that I thought it might.

'I thought I was going to die,' I said, my voice cracked. His arms tightened. 'I thought I'd never see you again, and I was desperate, and ... oh Luke, I did awful things.'

'I've done some pretty awful things, too,' he said. 'But look. You didn't murder anyone. You didn't hurt anyone. Everything else can be fixed.'

Including us? I thought. Can we be fixed?

'I wish you'd never sent Jack to me,' I whispered, and Luke murmured appalled apologies into my hair.

I shifted my grip on him to sit up properly and tell him how much I loved him, but Luke flinched, agony in his eyes as I gripped his right shoulder. He covered it fast, but I hadn't missed it.

'What is it?' I said. I took in the bruises on his face, much more apparent in the light. 'What happened to you?'

'Nothing,' Luke said, swatting away my hands as I tried to pull open his shirt to see. 'Fell down some stairs.'

I gave him a disbelieving look. Luke had the grace and balance of a cat.

'I'm only graceful and elegant ninety-nine percent of the time,' he said irritably.

'Let me see.'

'Sophie –'

His right arm was decidedly more sluggish than the left. I

hadn't noticed it before in all my self-absorption, but it had been his left arm doing all the work. For a right-hander like Luke, this was unusual.

I gripped his left wrist and grappled one-handed with his shirt buttons. Luke fought back, struggling against me, and then he slumped and said, 'All right, fine,' and let me unfasten his shirt.

His right shoulder was all the colours of the rainbow, purple and blue and yellow with bruises. There were more marks on his ribs, his stomach, his chest, but it was the shoulder that looked really ugly. A puncture wound was partly healed in the middle of all that bruising.

I looked up at his face in shock, and saw now that we were in the light and I wasn't being horribly self-absorbed, that he was sporting a terrific black eye, and that the shadows on his jaw weren't from stubble so much as bruises.

'Fell down some stairs?' I demanded.

'Some large stairs. With fists.'

'And landed on a bullet?'

'You think you're the only one running around getting shot at?' he said mulishly.

'What happened?'

'Well, I got shot,' he said, as if it was obvious.

I'd have shoved him in the shoulder for that, if it didn't look as though I might rupture something.

'But – when? And how, why? And why isn't it covered up? Did you even see a doctor? There should be a dressing on this, you should be wearing a sling –'

'The sling annoyed the hell out of me,' Luke said.

'Oh, come *on*. Do you have any idea how dangerous this could be? I mean, the bullet could have chipped a bone, could have torn an artery, that's your main axillary artery right there in the shoulder, if that's damaged you could lose the use of your arm, and all the nerve damage ...'

He stared at me.

'You have to be *careful*,' I stressed, because he could have been killed or maimed; my beautiful precious Luke. He was too important to lose.

'Since when did you learn about axillary arteries?' he said, looking at me as if I'd grown a second head.

'Since I spent a lot of time in the hospital last year,' I said. Also since I watched several episodes of *Scrubs* and *Grey's Anatomy* on the flight home. But I didn't mention that.

I laid my head on his good shoulder and carefully put my arms around him. He held onto me, stroked my hair, kissed my temple. And suddenly a great wave of emotion swept over me, even stronger than the grief that had nearly drowned me. I loved this man, this beautiful, contrary, brilliant, stubborn, angry, gentle man. Loved him fiercely, desperately. Loved him too much to let anything come between us. To contemplate losing him, losing what we had.

A man like this, a love like this, was far too rare to throw away in a fit of conscience.

'You have to be careful,' I repeated, 'because I love you.'

Luke pressed his cheek against my forehead. 'Pot, have you met Kettle? You're both black.'

'Hey, I was on the run. I had MI5 after me. And a psychopathic killer. I think I did pretty well, considering.'

'A sprained ankle, a second-degree burn and a gunshot wound to the arm,' Luke said. 'That's doing well?'

'It's really just a graze,' I said. 'And how do you know about the gunshot wound?' Currently, it was covered by the sleeve of my top.

'I'm in military intelligence,' Luke said, slowly and deliberately for the benefit of his idiot girlfriend. 'Occasionally we read reports about stuff. Where do you think I've been all day?'

'You could have come to see me instead of reading about me,' I said, a tad sulkily.

'That's what I said,' Luke replied, and the weariness in his voice tugged at my heart.

We sat together like that for a while, curled together on the sofa. On the floor, Tammy prowled about, hunting for dust bunnies and finding none. I wondered if my mother had been in and tidied up. The place did look suspiciously clean.

Luke stroked my cheek with one gentle finger. 'You have to be careful, too,' he said. He took my hand, stared for a moment at the ring there, and kissed my fingers softly.

'Well, I will be from now on. No more murder or armed robbery. Promise.'

'I mean it, Soph. I've been in hell this past month. I didn't know where you were or if you were safe, I had no idea if that Jack guy was going to turn out to be a maniac and try to kill you or shag you –'

I winced, and Luke saw it. 'Sorry,' he said. 'I really am sorry about Jack. But – and I don't care how this sounds – you have no idea how glad I was to hear he was dead.'

'Luke!'

'Because all I knew was that only one person was left alive in that place, and I ...'

He broke off suddenly, and gripped me very tight. Against my hair he muttered, 'I was so frightened it wasn't you. I thought you might be dead, I thought ... Sophie, I can't lose you.'

I tilted my head up. Luke's eyes were damp. His lip trembled. I reached up and cupped his cheek, the fine line of his jaw against my palm, my thumb stroking his magnificent cheekbone. Gently, because he'd been hurt.

'You won't lose me,' I said, and vowed there and then that he'd never know what had happened between me and Jack. That it, like stealing credit cards and leaving hotels without paying, was stupid and reckless and the product of a month's insanity that nearly destroyed me. That it, like everything else heaped upon my soul right now, was in the past, and could only have consequences if I let it.

'I love you,' Luke said, and my heart squeezed. 'I love you so much.'

I kissed him then, touched my lips to his and licked into his mouth. Breathed in his scent, tasted him. Captured the feel of him against my skin. All these sensations, all these memories I'd been trying so hard to keep alive, came flooding back and I lost myself in the tide.

'God, I've missed you,' Luke said, and I kissed him again. 'Even if you are insane,' he went on between kisses, 'and reckless,' another kiss, 'and you've taken ten years off my life in the last three days alone.'

'Don't forget how your family hates me,' I added.

'Weirdly, they seem to be coming round.'

I stared at him. 'I get accused of murder and *then* they decide they like me?'

'I didn't say they were sane.' He nuzzled my neck. 'I think my grandmother even expects us to get married.'

'Well, that's a stupid idea. Your grandmother is mad,' I told him, and he stilled for a second. I cursed myself. 'Sorry, I didn't mean –'

'No, you're right. It would be ridiculous to marry you just to keep tabs on you. Besides,' he kissed my ear, 'it's not as though I've got to get you up the aisle to get you into bed.'

'Am I that easy?' I said lightly.

'You've never put up a lot of resistance to me.'

'Yes, but who could?' I said, and regretted it when Luke grinned wickedly.

His hands were creeping up under my top, and somehow I'd ended up straddling him, my whole body pressed against him. His shirt was unfastened, and through the thin cotton of my top I could feel the heat of him burning through. Every hormone I had surged into life and I arched against him, in what turned out to be exactly the wrong spot. Luke winced.

'We should probably stop,' I said reluctantly.

'Absolutely not.'

'I mean, it can't be a good idea. You're ...' I waved at his violently discoloured shoulder, 'and I'm ...' I waved at my bandaged wrist.

My attempt to put some distance between us was immediately curtailed by Luke's hand on my waist.

'Don't care,' he said, beginning to kiss my neck in a manner that was extremely distracting.

'It's just that, well, right now ... I mean, physically ... *can* you?'

He sat back, regarded me with strident disbelief. 'Sophie, I have a black eye and bruised ribs and a gunshot wound and there's barely half-an-inch of me that doesn't ache, but *that* really hurt.'

'I'm actually trying to be considerate here, Mr Axillary Artery.'

'Well, don't be.' He pulled me back against him. 'Think of it as kissing me better, but in a really big way.'

'You are so incorrigible,' I said.

'That's me.' He tugged at my top. 'You're looking at a desperate man here.'

'Well, maybe I'm not in the mood,' I said, just to mess with him. I was so in the mood I couldn't think of anything else. 'Maybe I just need time.'

Luke's face fell. It was actually pretty comical.

'Okay, I think that's enough time,' I said, and he actually thumped my shoulder.

'You are in so much trouble,' he said, wrestling me down onto the sofa, and I laughed with pure giddy happiness.

'Must be a Tuesday.'

About the Author

Kate Johnson is a prolific writer of romantic and paranormal fiction. She is a self-confessed fan of Terry Pratchett, whose fantasy fiction has inspired her to write her own books. Kate worked in an airport and a laboratory before escaping to write fiction full time. She is a member of the Romantic Novelists' Association and has previously published short stories in the UK and romantic mysteries in the US. She's a previous winner of the WisRWA's Silver Quill and Passionate Ink's Passionate Plume award.

Kate's UK debut, *The UnTied Kingdom*, is shortlisted for the 2012 RoNA Contemporary Romantic Novel Category Award.

For more information visit: www.katejohnson.co.uk

More Choc Lit

from Kate Johnson:

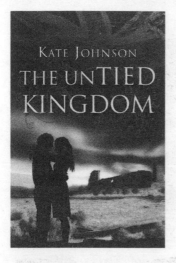

The UnTied Kingdom

Shortlisted for the 2012 RoNA Contemporary Romantic Novel Category Award

The portal to an alternate world was the start of all her troubles – or was it?

When Eve Carpenter lands with a splash in the Thames, it's not the London or England she's used to. No one has a telephone or knows what a computer is. England's a third-world country and Princess Di is still alive. But worst of all, everyone thinks Eve's a spy.

Including Major Harker who has his own problems. His sworn enemy is looking for a promotion. The General wants him to undertake some ridiculous mission to capture a computer, which Harker vaguely envisions running wild somewhere in Yorkshire. Turns out the best person to help him is Eve.

She claims to be a popstar. Harker doesn't know what a popstar is, although he suspects it's a fancy foreign word for 'spy'. Eve knows all about computers, and electricity. Eve is dangerous. There's every possibility she's mad.

And Harker is falling in love with her.

Visit www.choc-lit.com for more details including the first two chapters and reviews, or simply scan barcode using your mobile phone QR reader.

More from Choc Lit

If you loved Kate's story, you'll enjoy the rest of our selection:

Visit www.choc-lit.com for more details
including the first two chapters and reviews

Introducing Choc Lit

We're an independent publisher creating
a delicious selection of fiction.
Where heroes are like chocolate – irresistible!
Quality stories with a romance at the heart.

Choc Lit novels are selected by genuine readers like yourself.
We only publish stories our Choc Lit Tasting Panel want to
see in print. Our reviews and awards speak for themselves.

Come and support our authors and join them in our
Author's Corner, read their interviews and see their latest
events, reviews and gossip.

Visit: www.choc-lit.com for more details.

Available in paperback and as ebooks from most stores.

We'd also love to hear how you enjoyed *Run Rabbit
Run*. Just visit www.choc-lit.com and give your feedback.
Describe Luke in terms of chocolate and you could win a
Choc Lit novel in our Flavour of the Month competition.

Follow us on twitter: www.twitter.com/
ChocLituk, or simply scan barcode using
your mobile phone QR reader.